CEMETERY
Secrets

CEMETERY
Secrets

*Sherry Long &
Kathryn O'Hara*

Xulon Press

Xulon Press
2301 Lucien Way #415
Maitland, FL 32751
407.339.4217
www.xulonpress.com

Printed in the United States of America.

ISBN-13: 978-1-54566-245-8

Dedication

To Warren A. Gorbet, a proud Force Recon Marine, a leader in the timber industry, and a man of honor, integrity, wisdom and generosity who accepted as his personal calling the stewardship of the land and its natural resources. He stood proud amongst others showing his gratitude for God's gift of this earth and for life. His pride and dignity of his Indian culture, his love of family and his pursuit of excellence in all things were quiet and powerful inspirations to many.

January-23-1936---June-8-2013

CHAPTER 1

My father is the wisest, wittiest and smartest person I know. In his presence, I feel safe. His firm hand and gentle spirit guided me into adulthood. Reaching back through the mists of my childhood, I am unable to remember a time he seemed weak or ineffectual. The intensity of his listening and his quiet response to my questions and concerns was a bulwark of calm for me. His deep voice and slow smile reassure me. His personal fortitude and robust love for life anchor me. Now I struggle with my guilt. Had I left him alone too long? Had I taken his verve and strength so lightly, I had overlooked the encroaching health crisis?

I felt the tears burning hot in my eyes, and inhaling deeply, I rolled down my car window in order to smell the fresh mountain air. I had driven four hours from the Bay area to my hometown of Greenville, California. With trembling knees, I stepped out of my car and crossed the small parking lot and pushed through the front doors of the modest and unpretentious hospital.

Just inside the foyer, I hesitated and then was met by a thin woman with grey hair and a gap between her front teeth. She had nervous eyes darting here and there with the gestures of a frightened bird. I had never seen her before, but she moved forward and greeted me.

"Camille?" she asked.

I nodded my head. "Yes," I answered.

"Please, right this way," she instructed.

"How is he doing?" I asked.

"He's anxious to see you my dear," was her only response.

It was obvious she was avoiding my direct question. I began to chew on the inside of my cheek with a familiar tension. Without even a hint as to my father's present condition, she escorted me down the hallway to room number four. Pausing by the door, she turned to face me. With a gentle smile, she gestured through the doorway with a raised hand, but the fact that she avoided eye contact with me, instantly turned up my internal thermostat. That alone made me want to back up and run away from the heartache awaiting me just past the doorway where I stood.

"You can go on in. Your father is expecting you."

After an awkward pause, she turned and my eyes followed her thin figure as she slowly moved down the hallway leaving me alone with my frantic thoughts. Panic set in and I could feel my heart pounding and I broke out in a nervous sweat. A surge of nausea swirled in my stomach. Was I too late? Is he even coherent enough to talk to me?

I stepped into the room and eyed the single bed under the lone window. The room was not very large, but I felt a vast distance as I forced my legs to move. I approached his bed, groping for the chair alongside the wall and dragging it behind me. I carefully sat down staring over at the oxygen-drizzling nubs that had slipped out of his nose. I reached over to properly adjust them back into his nostrils. I felt a stab of pain in my chest and reminded myself to breathe. I gazed down at the still figure in the bed, which instantly filled my eyes with stinging tears. My father was resting quietly, a pulse beating lightly in his temple, visible under the skin. His hair was slicked back in a way that was foreign to me. Normally, it was parted on the side with each strand allowed to travel its own path in a tangled mess of natural waves. I reached over and stroked his brow, his skin the color of old ivory was cool to my touch. He looked plasticized which horrified me. He wasn't dead yet, so why did he look like a wax figure in a museum?

The heat of the day had broken, and I shivered with a sudden chill. I took in another deep breath, inhaling the dry air of his hospital room. The sharp tang of alcohol in my nostrils cleared my head. I leaned forward and gently kissed the side of his cheek. I caught the faint scent of his Old Spice cologne which transports me back to my youth and a much healthier father.

I shivered at the sight of the needles puncturing his frail skin. There were two IV's in his right arm and what looked to be one failed attempt in his left. His large hands rested peacefully on his blanket with an occasional twitch of involuntary movement. I gently touched the back of his hand, resting mine on top of his.

His eyes opened the instant I touched him. He gazed at me, his eyes filling with tears that spilled down his waxen cheeks. As he studied me for a moment, I could sense his hesitation and uncertainty, so I gently squeezed his hands in mine. But when his face twisted in pain, I immediately let go.

"My chest hurts. The pain is radiating up through my shoulders and pulsing into my skull," he said. He shook his head as if to dislodge the ache, but I could tell by his wincing expression that it brought him no relief.

"Dad, please take it easy. You've had a heart attack and you need to calm yourself," I pleaded in a soft tone. The word terminal still sizzled in my ear. That phone call everyone dreads usually comes out of the blue when you least expect it. Mine came ten minutes before a job interview giving me no false hope for his survival.

I rubbed the tiny vein just below the surface of his skin in his wrist, but even the least amount of pressure seemed to cause him discomfort. I just held his hand. I was wrestling with myself to find the right words to say, yet I am amazed at his ability to describe his symptoms in explicit detail. I knew his clear communication was a part of his strength.

"The darkness in my right eye is spreading and my vision is blurred," he muttered. "I'm drifting Camille, but I must hold tight, despite the pain. Despite the reality of what is inevitable."

I watched in horror as he struggled to breathe and could feel my fear building with each shallow breath. I could almost taste the air, dry and sterile. His chest heaved erratically and awareness crept over me in a slow, rolling tide. He was slipping away and there was nothing I could do to stop it.

"Dad," I repeated. "Please take it easy. You're only making things worse by struggling."

"My daughter, beloved and only child. I am facing death now and need to tell you something. The time has finally come. You need to know the truth," he sighed. Taking in a deep breath, the rattle in his chest sounded hoarse. "The cemetery has secrets, Child," he carefully whispered his words. "You must hear me."

"Dad please, whatever you are trying to say can wait," I begged. "Settle down. Don't exert yourself. You will be ok, I promise you. We can talk about everything tomorrow when you are feeling better." His face pinched in pain. I felt this weird mix of fear and disappointment welling up inside of me. I feared the worst that his time here on earth was limited to mere hours or maybe even minutes. I was disappointed in myself for not saying all the right words to lift his spirits. My responsibility is to help him, not hurt him with my inadequate ramblings. But all the right words seemed to get strangled before they are born. My father knows exactly what's happening and nothing I say can shield him from the ugly sting of reality. Playing dumb is a poor substitute for facing the truth, especially when he can see right through my facade.

"Have you not heard me Child? There is something you must know now," he spoke more clearly, weakly lifting himself up on his elbows, his hands grasping for the bed railings.

"Dad I don't understand. I'm so sorry. I'm trying to grasp the meaning of what you are trying to say."

Through the haze of his pain, I could see the tears swell inside his lids and hear the tremor in his voice. I wanted badly to comfort him, but I was powerless to move.

"Dad you must rest," I reminded him. "You are in the hospital. I love you and I am here with you and I won't leave. But please, take it easy and conserve your energy. You're weak and this is only making things worse."

Then in slow motion he released his grip on the rails, dropping his head back down to his pillow. His lips began to quiver. "I can no longer hide inside my terrible lie. I've been imprisoned by this great burden for much too long. I must set myself free before death claims the old and my new journey begins," he said in a low whisper, followed by a raspy cough.

"Okay dad I'm listening. Go on," I coaxed. If whatever he wanted to tell me was that important, then I needed to let him speak openly.

My eyes fixed briefly on the sweat beading on his forehead. He sucked in a deep breath, his eyelids fluttered. His body shuddered and his next breath sounded hoarse coming from deep in his throat. Then a gurgling sound escaped his mouth. I closed my eyes and fought back my tears, pleading with the universe to spare my father's life. But when his jaw dropped open and one last gasping breath escaped, I knew it was the breath of departure.

"No stay with me dad," I demanded. "Fight dad. Please fight this."

His head rolled to the side and his eyes stared out in a death gaze. Peace spread its' soothing wings over him. The only sound was my own murmured cries. For a few long seconds I felt numb, insulated from the reality of what had just taken place.

"Dad no," I heard myself scream. "Don't leave me." Suddenly I felt like a little girl again. That little girl hidden deep inside the well-educated and independent adult woman. I wanted my father back, healthy and full of life. I wanted to indulge in another one

5

of our heart to heart talks which always resulted in moods lifted and spirits soaring.

My stomach clenched and churned as I fought desperately to deny what my eyes were telling me. Crushed by fate's heavy weight, I fell across his lifeless body and let the dam burst over my lids. Everything inside of me collapsed into a heap of numbness. Then up from the gut came an explosion of sound. I erupted into uncontrollable wails. I didn't care how loud I was or who heard my weeping. I've traveled this brutal road in the past so I was no stranger to this kind of pain. I have survived tragedy twice before in my twenty eight years and now the cruel hand of fate has come to claim what little is left of my emotional reserve.

For a long time, I lay beside my father with the pain of his loss burning throughout my body. I waited for that numb feeling to return, but it never came.

Death is unbearable and shows no mercy. That thought burned hot in my conscience. The devastation is real, but only time and distance makes it possible to fully understand what death means in terms of human tragedy. We all know our days are numbered. For some of us sooner than others. I wished I had never learned to count.

CHAPTER 2

I do know without a doubt that life after grief is possible. My heart continues to beat, despite pain like liquid fire within my chest. A different day; the same torment. No matter how hard I try, I can't escape the misery. It calls to me like an old friend in a voice hoarse from years of screaming over the noise of everyday life. I have learned to function even though loss is a part of my identity.

A heart can beat inside one's chest, even though the breath of life is just a physical response to that life. I, Camille Morning Star Cameron can attest to the intense heartache that is my constant companion. I hold the triple crown of emotional agony within my very soul.

It is seven thirty in the morning. I stand in front of the mirror in my bedroom in the midst of one of my darkest hours. My image shimmers in its' reflection. I am not sure if it is the mirror or the tears in my eyes. The slight wave in the cheval glass catches my reflection unevenly, and I shift slightly to get a clearer view of myself. I remember the sharp feeling of annoyance caused by the flaw in the antique mirror in my teenage years, finding the slight shift irritating. Now as an adult, I wonder how I could have been so shallow as to be annoyed by something so insignificant. In the midst of my current pain, I realize the ease with which I have slipped back into my youthful and immature mindset.

The young woman in the mirror gazes back at me and I see my dark, straight hair, cut in layers and resting on my shoulders. My olive skin, a gift from my father, had a faint tan and my dark brown eyes have shadows smudged under them from the lack of sleep. I forced myself to smile, and the tears rose in my eyes again. My lovely straight teeth were provided by expensive orthodontic care that my father paid for by repairing his old backhoe and waiting on the purchase of the new tractor he badly needed. The first few months of braces, whenever I smiled at him, he would say, "Oh hey, there's my tractor in your mouth." Or, "Smile big, Camille, I want a better look at my shiny new tractor." With a hearty laugh, he would then give me a hug which let me know my welfare was much more important than the best new tractor that money could buy.

Would I ever be able to think of anything without a memory of him and a stab of grief? Probably not for a long time.

I tugged on a lightweight, black shawl, smoothing my trembling hands down my dark skirt. Taking in a deep, shaky breath, I tried to ready myself for the tumultuous emotions of attending my father's funeral. But reality had already crystallized in my mind, so the intensity of my sadness once again descended upon me like a hawk soaring ever closer, darkening the sky for the kill. My efforts to escape its clutches are in vain.

Nervously, I smoothed my skirt once again and picked up my purse. I stepped out into the hallway of my childhood home and moved through the kitchen with a slowness that was foreign to my usual bounce; the sorrow I felt in my heart causing me to move as though through a fog. I proceeded to walk out onto the deck and slowly, painfully, descended the stairs to the gravel parking area below. I started my car and drove carefully down the incline, taking a left on the highway and making my way into Greenville. A short five minute drive to the north side of town and another forty second walk placed me inside Souder's Funeral Home before anyone else arrived.

With an understanding smile tugging the corners of his lips upward, Mr. Souder's, the town undertaker for years, greeted me at the front door. "Good morning Camille," he said in a kindly tone.

I couldn't speak. I responded with a nod of my head.

"Come on in. You have plenty of time to spend with your father alone before we get started."

I stepped over the threshold. The door creaked and closed with a click behind me. He led and I followed, fighting a racing heart and a strong urge to just turn around and run the other way. This is the first time since my father's passing that we will meet face to face.

As he ushered me through a dim hallway, I straightened my shoulders and inhaled deeply the sharp scent of carnations and willed myself strength. Beyond the formal foyer is a spacious room that seats one hundred and fifty occupants. The walking space along the wooden walls allows for at least fifty more people to stand during the crowded service. The room is immaculate, paneled in rough cut lumber, a nod to Greenville's timber history. Filled with the many colors of floral bouquets, the severity of the room is softened by the sight and fragrance of the blooms, but the air holds the grieving energy of the bereaved before me.

Mr. Souder's stopped just shy of my father's casket and turned around to address me again. "Camille, I know there is little I can say at this moment to comfort your grieving heart, but I do want you to know that this entire community mourns the loss of your father along with you. You must know that your father impacted everyone's life in such a positive way. Such a loving and generous man, he gave and did not expect anything in return," he spoke to me from the heart, in a low whisper. "If there is anything you need, just ring that bell over there by the door."

I nodded. "Thank you." To my surprise, instead of leaving me alone with my father, I watched him close his eyes and move his head from side to side. I could tell that he had more to say to me. There was definitely more on his mind he needed to unload.

"I can't begin to find the words to tell you just how much we will all miss your father Camille. Like I said, you are not alone in this. There's not one person in this town that doesn't owe your father a debt of gratitude in some fashion. I, for one, would have never gotten this business up and running if it hadn't been for your father. He put in all the plumbing and a new roof on when I couldn't get the loan I needed. Didn't charge me one red cent either. That's the kind of man he was. Your father was a caring leader in this community and will be deeply missed." He swallowed deep and his lips fell silent for a few seconds. "What a waste," he said dismissively.

His words rested heavily on me. I knew what he said was true, but I also knew those amazing characteristics were something I would never see or hear again in the present tense. "Thank you," I said again. "I so appreciate your kind words. He had a way about him that didn't just make people smile, he made them happy. Every thought of him opens a space in my heart that longs to hear his nurturing voice just one more time telling me how much he loves me. His words were always compelling and spiritually profound and within them was always a powerful lesson in hope and healing. The older I get, the more I realize just how fortunate I was to have such wisdom to walk beside me through my life. I can't even pretend to understand the sage intelligence of this remarkable man who saw the human race; their ideals, faults and imperfections as part of a disorderly yet wonderful fellowship," I explained in more detail than I had intended.

"I agree totally. His perspective, as he often told me, was to meet everyone on their own level and I think it was his firm belief in God and the principles of the Ten Commandments that led and strengthened him," he speculated.

I had no intentions of talking all churchy right now. That was the only area where my father and I didn't see eye to eye. I could feel my emotions beginning to swirl around me. I tried to establish some inner mental balance which was hard to do since his eyes were still attached to mine. I could tell he was waiting for a response. This entire day I knew there would be conversations to have and questions to answer, even during the storms of my grief. I wanted to be the courageous little girl my father proclaimed me to be and I wanted to honor his memory with dignity and respect. I had high expectations for myself and my decorum for the day, but the tightness in my shoulders and in my stomach, coupled with the heartache I've carried since the day I got the call alerting me to my father's massive heart attack, I was unsure how to proceed without his calm presence in my life. "I wish I could be more like him. Then maybe I wouldn't dread this day as much as I am. Maybe I wouldn't question God's reasons for taking him from me," I said, unsmiling.

"Don't try to figure it all out now Camille. Just take one day at a time. After all, there is no how-to manual to follow on how to handle yourself when fate throws you a curveball that hits you smack dab in the middle of your chest."

"I suppose you're right," I agreed, but in my heart, I knew the truth. I was still a slave to the raw, open wounds of my former heartaches. "Maybe I should settle for just one hour at a time," I declared.

"Sometimes that is best," he said, nodding his head. With an easy smile, he turned his short, chubby frame around to leave. I stared at the back of his balding head as he departed out a narrow walkway which led to his office.

Finally alone, I stepped slowly over to my father's coffin. I was able to smile down at his beloved face and I laid my palm on his icy cheek. It was a gesture he frequently shared with me during my growing years. The feel of his work roughened palm and the sense of his quiet strength soothed many an anxious moment for me. Fighting the rising lump in my throat, I could feel the hot tears slipping down my cheeks as I contemplate the future without receiving that loving, reassurance again.

"Oh my goodness, gracious! Is that really you?" came a cheery voice from behind me.

Turning to see who had interrupted my much needed private time with my father, I tried to hide my irritation as our eyes met. A woman I did not recognize was smiling broadly at me. "Excuse me," is all I could manage to say.

"Just look at you!" she said in a much too joyous tone for this solemn occasion. "Here you are all grown up and as pretty as a poppy in May. It's so wonderful to see you again Camille." She obviously knew me far better than I knew her.

I was puzzled by the identity of this cheerful brunette dressed in a black skirt and matching jacket. I felt a clutch in my stomach and I knew my voice would be hoarse. I just stared in mute silence.

"No worries my dear," she said, with a casual wave of her hand. "I don't expect you to remember me."

"I'm sorry. I've been away."

"I know. Ten or so years now, right?"

"Actually a little more than twelve years."

"I heard you were pursuing a good education. A doctor of some sort?" she asked.

"I've been seeking to complete a PHD in Clinical Psychology," I answered purely out of politeness.

"And did you succeed?"

"Yes," I answered, finding it hard to repress my sudden impatience. I felt that answering her questions was giving her tacit permission to invade my privacy and personal space. I breathed deeply to control my emotions and suddenly felt a swirl of nausea coiling up from deep within myself. It was the scent emanating from this lady as she leaned closer and enveloped me in a bear hug. The fragrance was staggeringly overpowering and bordered between one of Nordstrom's best sellers and Avon's discontinued scents, but I managed with a hard swallow to keep what little food there was in my stomach in place.

She patted me on the back like I was a stray dog and then backed away, releasing me from her unwelcome embrace. "You know, Greenville is but a tiny dot on the California map. But to generations of people who have lived here, it is a diamond in the rough, a gem of prime value to treasure because of acres of plentiful trees, its' mineral rich soil and vast pasturelands available for future generations of loggers, farmers and ranchers," she explained in detail.

I stood speechless. Was this really the time and place for a history and geography lesson?

"You know this is a town that welcomes the return of its' straying youth," she went on to say.

"I really don't think my situation fits into that category. It was important to my father that I get my education," I pointed out rather sternly, feeling the need to correct her.

"Oh I didn't mean anything by that comment. I knew your father was big on education."

I needed to guide the conversation back to when, where and how she knew me. "So exactly how did we meet?" I asked point blank. "I'm afraid I still can't place you."

"That's okay. Completely understandable since we only met a few times when you were about knee high to a tadpole," she said, her use of the phrase dating her. Her voice was cheerful and much too enthusiastic for me, standing so near my father's casket.

Unsure of what to say, I stared at her waiting for her next comment. I could not recall her and was somewhat taken aback by her familiar and friendly mien.

She smiled wide, exposing a white set of false teeth and held out her right hand. "I'm Susie Gardner. I owned the bowling alley out in Oakey Flats many moons ago. You know, the old Cottonwood Club," she confirmed as if I hung out there on a regular basis as a child.

Again, I found myself involuntarily squinting as I examined every inch of her attractive face, well, nice looking considering her age, but I still couldn't find her in my memory bank. "I'm sorry, I still can't place you," I said in an apologetic tone.

"I knew your mama," she emphasized which surprised me considering the wide margin of differences there were between the two women. "God rest her soul. Such a shame," she added as if I didn't already know. "So young. Too young to die such an agonizing death. My second cousin's wife died of pancreatic cancer. Not a pleasant thing to witness. It had to be so hard on you, having lost that little boyfriend of yours a couple of years earlier. They never did find him, did they?" she asked, seamlessly moving the conversation forward without even inhaling between subject changes.

"No," is all I could say on the subject. I was here because of the present tragedy in my life, I did not want to be reminded of two others. The loss of my mother and Eli were still deep, open wounds within my heart. I could feel my tension begin to rise, but I was determined to remain cordial, despite the fact that this woman was creating an irritating sensation just beneath my skin.

"Well anyway, I came back to Greenville for your father's funeral. And," she drew out the word, lowering her voice, "to tell you something," she added as if only she was privy to some big secret.

Her tone was so mysterious and I could feel a little spark irritation at her timing. "Oh, did you know my father well?" I asked, not really caring other than wanting her to re-define knowing. Well, I suppose if truth be told, maybe because of her sudden change in demeanor, my mind responded with more than a flicker of curiosity.

"Not as well as I wanted," she confirmed, dropping her chin to her chest as if she still grieved a lost love. "I was rather sweet on him, you could say. For a good number of years I did my best to win his affection, but unfortunately for me, the feelings were never mutual," she confided, her gray eyes fixed on me in a focused gaze. Her disappointment even after all these years was palpable.

Disturbed by the direction of her thoughts, I was confused and felt a prickle of annoyance at the idea of a romantic involvement between the two of them. It was silly to entertain such a ridiculous notion. Even in my wildest dreams, I could not imagine my father being attracted to this blowsy woman.

"Your father did quite a bit of repair work on the bowling alley. Actually, that's how we met," she informed me, her voice suddenly cheerful.

My thoughts spun around in dizzy circles with the notion of what could have been possible. My cheeks warmed at the realization of what her scheming intentions were back then. All I could think was thank God, luck, chance or anyone else out there pulling strings for small favors. This woman couldn't hold a candle to my mother's innocence and natural beauty. Although attractive in a coarse fashion, she definitely went too bold with her makeup. With exaggerated lash extensions, heavy eyeshadow and bright plum lipstick, she looked like she had taken a dozen wrong turns in life. Her blouse was low cut exposing her sun damaged decollate. Her feet were wrapped tightly in high heeled sandals and her skirt barely skimmed her wrinkled knees. She lowered her voice again, "I've kept quiet all these years about something, but I made up my mind that I would make things right," she confessed, staring at me with eyes alive with a mysterious quality.

I could feel the tug of curiosity in my gut, coupled with a subconscious warning to proceed with caution. "Oh really," I replied as calmly as possible to avoid the appearance that every breath I took depended on her revelations. No need to sound overly anxious. "So what is all this secrecy about?" I asked, still feeling the need for caution.

Her head tilted toward my father's coffin. "Forgive me my dear friend, but this can't hurt you now," she said as if he could hear her every word. Then her intense gaze caught my attention again. "One day when your father was putting a new roof on my house,

I caught him crying. I've seen a lot, but I'd never seen a man cry that hard. He told me a pretty disturbing story, but after a couple of minutes, I made the mistake of asking a question, then suddenly he clammed up. He wouldn't talk any more about it and wouldn't answer any of my questions. I just wanted to help him, but I could only presume the reason was guilt on his part after telling me the truth. I had already picked up the gist of what he wanted to say, but clearly there was much more he needed to get off of his chest," she said dropping her head for an instant and glaring down at her thumbs hugging tightly at the joints. "I really cared and I wanted him to know he could talk to me about anything," she went on to say staring at me intently. "Despite my prodding, he refused to speak any further about the subject. But I had already heard enough to suspect that your father knew something about Elisha's disappearance," she ended.

Her words hung over me like a dark cloud, heavy with the weight of misery and grief.

My eyes widened as a sudden anger rose within my chest. I could feel fire burning in my veins and with the surge of powerful protective emotions, I could hear my voice quiver. "That's utterly ridiculous. If my father knew anything about Eli, he would have told the authorities. And he certainly wouldn't have let Eli's mother suffer all these years never knowing what happened to her son." Now the anger began to bubble just under my breastbone and I wanted to strike out at this viper, her poisonous words and her truly terrible timing.

"Look honey, I didn't come here to upset you more than you already are. I had to get this off my chest. It's been a burden to bear for way too many years. I've done what I vowed to do and now I must go. I'll leave you alone with your father. It's up to him to tell you the rest," she said in a flat tone, her eyes guarded.

"Are you for real," I snapped back in a sharp tone, not even trying to suppress my rising hostility toward her. Although this wasn't my usual behavior, right now I felt my self-control slipping. "In case you didn't know, the dead don't talk," I blurted, adding rudeness to the unsettled energy around us. Also, I wasn't ready to let her go just yet. She had more explaining to do because her speculations about my father were unbecoming of his honorable and trustworthy nature. "How can you make such ridiculous accusations about my father when he's not able to defend himself? And you claim to be such a close friend of his," I said, with a hard, mocking edge to my voice. "Shame on you!" I snapped, my body quivered with a tremulous motion.

The color seemed to drain from her face. Her jaw tightened, "Your father was a good, honest man. He had his reasons for doing what he did. I have no doubt that at the time, it was his only recourse. And I know in my heart he will find a way to put this matter to rest," she firmly stated, adding more confusion to my mind.

How could she accuse him of keeping a terrible secret for many years and call him a good man in the next breath? "Really?" I asked, raising my eyebrows. I was dazed at the absurdity of what she had said. My anger simmered just below the surface and robbed me of any words. I gave a bewildered look and shook my head in utter disgust.

"Confessions never come without consequences Camille. I didn't expect you to receive this information with joy, but I had hoped you would be open minded about it," she said. Then she turned her head away from my confused and disapproving gaze as if seeking the words to clarify. Apparently, she wasn't successful because she just moved her body completely around and began a slow walk toward the front door, leaving a dark curtain of hostility between us in her wake.

My muscles felt rigid and the heat in my cheeks revealed my resentment toward this woman. I took in a deep breath and tried to compose my voice. "Is that all you have to say?" I called after her sarcastically. "Surely there's more you want to share with me.

If my father was such a devious hypocrite as you claim, then he must have committed a few more crimes against humanity, right?" I probed, the words tormenting me as they came out of my mouth.

Susie stopped just shy of the door and turning slowly, she met my angry stare. Her expression was pained and her voice was low. "That's all I have to say on the matter," she confirmed. Again, she turned her head away from my hostile glare and placed her hand on the door handle, but hesitated for a moment as if something of importance had come to her mind. As far as I could tell, she must have thought better of it, because with a slight shake of her head, she slipped out the door.

All I could think is that I had been visited by a madwoman. In the last slipstream of our conversation, she confirmed that age doesn't guarantee intelligence or wisdom. Neither does faded physical beauty layered with heavy makeup and scent. My father was a hard-working, single father who managed to fill both parenting shoes after the death of my mother. He didn't have a deceitful spirit or any meanness in him. What would make a woman talk unkind and act so rude as to speak so carelessly to me at this sensitive time? After a moment's contemplation of the untrue things she had said, I presumed she was a bitter, lonely and probably much rejected woman.

I turned back and looked down at my father again. I felt a cascade of emotions wash over me as I mourned with the primal grief of a lost child. "You are and always will remain a good man to me," I promised him in a soft whisper.

I reached down and gently placed my fingertips over his lifeless lips that would never again tell me how much he loved me. At that very moment, even though the finality of his death has descended upon me like a heavy cloud, I am reminded of his final words. During his last few moments of consciousness, his mumbled words were mysterious and added to my confusion over Susie Gardner's words just moments ago. And as a small flicker of realization began to glow in my mind, I believed she was right about one thing and only one thing. He actually was speaking to me from beyond the spirit world. How well he knew me, this good and loving father of mine. In his passing he left me a mission that would give me a purpose beyond my sorrow and loss. He knew I would follow the untidy strands of his last words to completion. Even as my tears well in my eyes, I know my deep love and respect for this wonderful man will lead me to unravel this mystery.

More determined than ever I hear myself repeat the words out loud. "What are the Cemetery Secrets?"

CHAPTER 3

My father's service was elegant in its simplicity. Crowded to capacity with a few extended family members, lifelong friends, business associates and acquaintances. Basically the entire population of Greenville. I am grateful for the company of my fellow man, but I feel removed from the good people of my hometown. And in a moment of forgetfulness, I scan the crowd for my father's beloved face, hungry for his presence and thirsty for his voice of true assurance, telling me he'll always be with me. Deeply disappointed, I got neither. A wave of renewed understanding has reminded me again of the finality of his absence.

Through fresh tears, I try to focus on his service. A few prayers, a hymn, kind words spoken by several elders and memories shared by friends and family. An hour spent remembering him as a man of his word, a craftsman, always ready with a joke or honest wisdom. I valued each word, and tucked them into the little box of treasured memories I keep deep within my heart.

And as we journey to the cemetery below my childhood home, I see dozens of vehicles, dusty pickups, older cars and newer model SUV's. All with headlights on in a respectful and sedate caravan to my father's final resting place.

When I finally parked in a long line behind the chain of vehicles, I got out and molded in with the crowd of people that filled the green spaces of the cemetery. I found a seat in the middle of the front row of chairs and stared straight ahead at the box that held my parents.

My father lies in a work of his own creation, my mother's urn nestled in his arms. Chosen many years ago, the urn is glazed in purple and white, my mother's favorite colors. I gaze upon their final and eternal embrace and I feel the tears begin again.

"My papa owes your papa two hundred dollars," a small voice behind me proclaimed.

I spun around in my chair.

A little girl with flaming red hair, maybe six or seven, dressed in a bright pink dress smothered in ruffles sat in a chair in the next row with a serious expression on her face.

"Honey, not now," a woman of small stature seated next to her scolded. A pained look tightened her face. I guessed them to be mother and daughter. The resemblance between the two was striking, with the auburn hair, dark blue eyes and a spatter of freckles over both of their noses.

"But I brought money. Papa always told me you must pay all your bills. I want to pay off papa's bill."

"I'm sorry Miss Cameron. My daughter doesn't understand this isn't the time or place to talk of such matters," she apologized.

I shook my head and forced the corner of my lips upward into a generous smile. "It's okay. Really it's rather refreshing to see such kindheartedness and honesty in a child."

"Here," the little girl said as she thrust her right hand toward me. "This is my first payment."

I held out my hand and she dropped some coins into my curled palm. All the while I'm thinking how are earth does she even know about payments at her young age?

"Your papa helped my papa to build my playhouse. It's the big-gest one I have ever seen. My papa didn't have enough money for the wood and paint. I will make another payment next month. My papa is buried over there," she said. She pointed a finger toward the narrow road that cut the cemetery in half.

"I'm sorry for your loss."

"Don't be sorry. My papa is with Jesus. He was a carpenter too. Now they can build playhouses for all the little kids like me who are in heaven. My papa told me not to be sad. He had a lot of pain. Now he has no pain."

"Okay Lexi. That's enough. We must let Miss Cameron say her good-byes to her papa," her mother said in a soft tone.

Lexi's face fell. She looked scolded.

I gave her the best smile I could muster. "Thank you," I said, which made her cheeks twitch. Seemingly untroubled, she continued to grind on a piece of gum between her teeth and stare at me.

I spun back around just as my father's coffin was closed and lowered into the arms of the earth he cared for. The little girl's words about carpentry work reminded me of what an expert craftsman my father was. I recall how he skillfully constructed his coffin with his own hands.

My father built many of the newer homes in the North Valley Road area and hated to let any leftover materials go to waste. He would bring home lumber and other construction scraps from jobs and stow them neatly in his large workshop behind our house. Whenever he was involved in a project, he would jokingly 'shop his personal hardware store.' He was somewhat of a Boy Scout. "Be prepared," was his motto and his collections of salvage were a testament to his thrift and his personal commitment to the concept of reducing, reusing and recycling long before those were trendy buzzwords.

One by one, the elders drop a handful of dirt on his pine box. Distressed and feeling surreal, I stand and take a few shaky steps to the edge of his grave and bending down, pick up a handful of the crumbly dirt. Holding my hand high over my parent's coffin, I drop the dirt and hear the clatter of small pebbles falling into eternity. I inhale deeply to control my emotions, the scent of the sage smudge and mountain air filling me with a degree of calm and control. The wind sighs through the pines at the edge of the cemetery and although the sun is shining warmly, I shiver with an internal chill. The bond of child to parent is a primal one and I feel its loss deeply, aching to the core of my being as I somberly return to my seat.

My father's maternal cousin, Dugan Aguilar, steps forward from the crowd and carefully prepares to honor my father by speaking the Maidu resting prayer and blessing. Dark skinned and lean with black hair and deep, serious eyes with the erect posture of the warrior he was as a US Marine, he slowly raises his hands to the sky gesturing toward the heavens. "I light a bundle of white sage," he said. "I hold it in each direction as I say these words; North represents winter and the positive. South represents summer and the negative, to keep everything in balance. East represents spring and the beginning of life. West represents fall and the passing of life."

Next, Dugan circled the sage in his hands and pointed to all the four corners and began to speak again. "May the evil spirits follow the smoke up and away. The Maidu believe in the fifth direction, where your father's spirit will go to rest," he said, making direct eye contact with me. "It will be either Mt. Lassen or Homer Lake, whichever he feels most comfortable," he added. Nodding respectfully, he stepped back and resumed his position in the crowd with a quiet dignity.

I watch as men of our extended family and friends begin to fill the grave, using shovels they brought from their own homes. I remain in my seat, the chill within me holding me in place. Staying with those who have passed on until the grave is completely covered is an important part of the burial process for the Maidu and has been adopted by the local folks. I want to pay this very last respect to my father. The grave is filled and raked smooth; family and friends begin to place flower arrangements carefully on the mound. In my mind, I thought it looked like a massive floral tribute, fit for the shrine of a king.

I huffed out a short breath as I could almost hear my father's rolling laughter. Yes, he would have a long and loud laugh at that. Although he was jokingly called the Sultan of the Cemetery, he was a gracious and humble man. He had been the caretaker of our town cemetery for many years, giving careful and respectful service to all those who passed before him. He loved his time caring for the cemetery and would wink at me and say, "Somebody has to do it Camille. And you know, people are just dying to get in here." His oft repeated joke caused many eye rolls in my youth. Now he has joined the others he had faithfully cared for during his life.

I am recalling some of my father's worldly advice. "Go make your own way in this world. Life is what you make of it. What you reap, you will sow. And, never ever forget to thank our Heavenly Father for your many blessings."

But that's it; how can I make my way in a world with a life that has been filled with pain and sorrow? I struggle to make some sense of how this so-called Heavenly Father who supposedly made us in His own image and loves us as a father loves his child, would cause me so much pain? But then, as always, when I feel the need to lash out at someone or something, I recall through the mists of time, my mother's words during her last weeks of life. "Even when your heart is full of pain, remember that God is a God of love. Even when you are in the midst of your darkest hour, He is with you," she said in a weak whisper.

At that young age, I felt lost. I couldn't feel or see this God, so how can I believe in His existence or feel His comfort? I remember smiling weakly at my mothers' beloved face and clutching her hand. "Through it all, good, bad or indifferent, you still have your memories. No one or nothing can take away your memories," she reminded me. I am hopeful that I can find my good memories and create a little happiness. At this time in my life, that possibility is my only link to remaining sane.

Awash in memories, and unable to move from my seat, I review my life, the memories sharp within me despite the sepia tone of the past. I face the darker shades of my life over and over, which only renews the suffering within me. My life until now has been a bittersweet story of life, death with an abundance of love in between. I carry deep within me an enormous appreciation for the remarkable upbringing my parents gave me, their only child. Together they captured the true meaning of parenting. Because of their dedication and deep love for me, I know I must embrace the legacy my parents have both left behind for me. One of love, kindness and understanding in man's less than perfect human nature. When I feel trapped by my disappointments, I recall one of my father's life lessons. "Camille, there will come a time when our faith is put to the test. Just remember these words when your time comes," he instructed. "It is man who freely makes his own mistakes, not the other way around. God doesn't want puppets on a string, so He has granted us the gift of choice. Only he who sees through the eyes of a loving God, can truly understand that and live a life to its' fullest."

So in a world full of unspeakable pain and suffering, how could a Supreme Being; this God my parents loved so deeply, presumably full of love and hope really exist? His transparency is much too lucid for me to absorb and maintain as a solid basis for any religious convictions. To me, He is just a nice, old man with white hair and a beard whose legend has passed down through history with grandiose ideals of mythical proportions.

Slowly, I wrap the tapestry of my memories that my parents have bequeathed me by their own words and actions, and rise on shaky legs to leave.

CHAPTER 4

The gentle breeze wafted through my hair and I closed my burning eyes to just feel the soft caress on my face for a moment. Troubled thoughts still tumbled over in my mind as I stood there with my head lifted toward the sun. Like an elastic force, I could feel my inner tension clench my jaw tight. "So what am I supposed to do now?" I asked beneath a frustrated breath. I didn't even know for sure who I was addressing with my question and that caused my panic to swell. But after a moment of deep consideration, I knew there was no point in denying exactly who I was speaking to. I was calling out for advice from the mysterious Almighty whom my parents trusted with every fiber in their soul. Despite the coldness and hardness of my heart, their integrity and love of God remained with me.

With that thought alone, I could feel the bitter pill of reality stick in my throat as my doubts of His existence intensified. But despite the fact that His existence was yet to be determined and my discomfort in reaching out to a God I cannot hear, see, smell or touch, and of Whom I have no trust, my questions continued to roll off my tongue as if I was well practiced at this thing called prayer. To my dismay, instead of an exchange of tender words, I lashed out at Him in a furious rage of anger. "So tell me, am I obliged to stand here and engage in friendly conversation with any and everyone who wants to ask a thousand questions about me that is really none of their business, or say a thousand kind words about my father that I've already heard a thousand times before? I'm not a curiosity quencher. A drenching spray of questions will not lessen the heavy burden I carry, nor will it help to heal what is broken. So why do I, the one left behind, the one who is broken and bleeding, have to fill the needs of others? Why must I be the one appeasing inquisitive minds, especially when my emotions are already pulled in every direction? Why is it left to me to comfort them?"

But then, as if this tiny voice in the back of my head was speaking to me ever so softly, I am reminded that I'm not the only one hurting here. There are other broken hearts beside my own. Some of these people knew my father long before I filled his life with tears and laughter. I owed it to my father to stand tall and brave and listen with an open and understanding heart to all the words expressed in honor of a man who was truly loved and respected by this entire community. My failure to be more compassionate and understanding of their needs suddenly became evident. This self-absorbed attitude of mine is wearing me out. More troubling, I ask myself. "Was that my common sense kicking in or a gentle tap on the back of my head from Someone far more loving and faithful than me?

"I am so sorry for your loss, honey," came a raspy voice just inches from my right shoulder.

Flinching, I lifted my head to face a voice I knew well. A voice kind and tender, but annoying in persistent determination to peel off the scab in one's mind in order to reveal the unknown secrets we store for our own personal survival. I force my face into a gracious smile in an attempt to cover my raw emotions and my poor attempts at self-control.

"I know this is a terrible thing that has happened to you, my dear, but there is always the prospect of marriage and lots of little babies one day to fill your void. Life does go on, you know," she said, poking holes in what little there was left in my emotional reserve.

Agnes Morrow, a smile creasing her worn face. A woman of medium height and a heavily weighted body, she wore a brilliantly colored muumuu of bright greens, purple and yellows that hung on her stout body like a 1950's bark cloth drape and broke over her backside like a bustle. Odd that I could overlook her insensitive words and focus on the violent display of color in her clothing. Her nut brown face, seamed with age, years of gossip and general busyness in the affairs of others, was enhanced by a perpetual smile, gaps of missing teeth showing with every word and causing a slight lisp. Mutely, I stood quietly, absorbing the wild eruption of bizarre color combinations in her dress as her words washed over me.

"It is so good for you to be home here in Greenville. A person needs to be around friends and family at a time like this, don't you think? How long do you plan to stay?" she asked, and I found myself admiring her skill of speech while inhaling. "You know, the city life just isn't the same as being here in your hometown. Folks here knew your dad and care about you. Why, you'll see lots of them this afternoon at the wake."

She continued on in her good hearted but unwelcomed gush of advice, her voice becoming just a harsh buzz in my ears. I briefly closed my eyes. I tensed up just thinking about how I was going to respond to such generic rubbish. I wondered if she had memorized her little speech long before she trapped me into this one way conversation. I could feel myself beginning to sway.

"Agnes! Shame on you! That is the last thing this poor girl needs to hear today, of all days. Give her a moment and let the questions rest. In fact, why don't you head on over to the reception; it is at the high school gym. It will be crowded and you'll want to find a seat. Now give Camille a hug and we will catch up with you later," Carolyn Young spoke firmly from behind me. I felt her arm around my back, the warmth of her hand a small touch of comfort.

With a wide smile that highlighted her missing molars and with a complete lack of embarrassment, Agnes nodded vigorously and concurred. "You're right, Carolyn! At Cal Thompson's funeral last month, the food ran out. And that is just not right; it is important to feed everyone who shows up to pay their respects, don't you think?" she asked, still not giving either of us an opportunity to respond. "I'll get on over there now. Do you want me to save you a place?" she asked under a whispered breath as if someone might be eavesdropping and beat her over there to secure the last available seat.

"No, no thank you, Agnes. I'm sure I'll find one. You go on, though," I quickly responded.

Carolyn and I watched her silently as she maneuvered herself with a surprising grace, given her bulk, through the headstones. With the vibrant colors of her dress swinging around her she made her way to her ancient Ford Fairlane that she had been driving since the 1970s. Agnes had been, and still was I supposed, the town gossip. Not really harmful or hateful, but always full of news, eager to share it and relentlessly curious about the affairs of others. As teenagers, my friends and I had dubbed her the 'Greenville Town Crier,' for her penchant for unwittingly disclosing information to our parents and/or other adults that we teens would have rather kept private, such as where we actually were on Friday night, and not where we told our parents we would be.

I pulled my gaze off of Agnes and landed my eyes on the sweet woman standing next to me. Carolyn is Eli Young's mother and one of my late mother's best friends from their youth. The loss of her son, coupled with the grief of the unknown cause of his disappearance left her with no closure or comfort and affected her marriage as well. The loss of my mother was another blow to her heart. Always a faithful member of Greenville's small Christian church, Carolyn clung to her faith with a fierce determination. Eli's father, unable to cope with the loss of his only son, fell into a deep despair that ended when he took his own life. It was no secret to anyone over the years, that Carolyn's belief in her Lord was her source of strength and life and the tenuous, yet powerful thread that held her to this life. Sometimes though, her conversations drifted between this world and the next.

Turning back to me, Carolyn said, "I know she can be somewhat annoying, but she really does mean well. As difficult as it is, just try to work your way through her commentaries with a simple smile." She paused for a few seconds with squinted eyes and her lips pressed tight into a thin line. "You gotta love her. She has the innocence and kindness of a child. Bless her heart, she never misses a social event, wedding, funeral or christening. And now that her husband has passed, those social activities are all that she has to give her a sense of purpose. She just wants to be helpful," Carolyn added as if that increased her kindness.

I mustered a weak grin. Finally my words sawed through the bars of silence. "A little too helpful, but harmless, I suppose," I agreed. After all, none of this was novel news to me.

Dressed in a black skirt and a soft gray silk blouse with the collar fastened by a large oval cameo, Elisha's mother stood face to face with me. The grief she had worn since the day of her son's disappearance still shone on her face. Softened by years, her sadness had become a glow that made her countenance take on the appearance of old ivory. Her salt and pepper hair hung in the same pageboy cut I remembered from my childhood and her clear blue eyes held the pain of past years in their depths. Always a small woman, she seemed to have shrunken. And when I clasped her hand, it felt as though I were holding a bird's claw, thin and bony. Even in my own emotional storm over losing my father, I could feel a thread of empathy for her. For what sadness could be greater than to have your twelve year old son pedal off on his bike on a Saturday morning, never to be seen again? My pain runs deep, but in time subsides to a dull ache. Carolyn carries the burden of unease that accompanies an unclosed tragedy for a lifetime.

"It's good to see you, Mrs. Young. Thank you for being here," I said, reverting to the respectful address of my childhood.

"Oh please, Camille, call me Carolyn. We are both adults now. You were always such a respectful young girl. Your mother would have been so proud of you and the beautiful and accomplished young woman you have grown into."

"Carolyn it is, then" I responded. She never was one for formalities. Maybe that's why I could relate to her so easily as a child.

"I am so sorry I didn't make it to your college graduation, but I thank you for the invitation. I am afraid I don't venture much further than the post office or the grocery store these days." She hesitated, with pride rising in her eyes. "What an accomplishment, I must say and congratulations! I suppose I should call you Dr. Cameron?"

"Oh heavens no!" I told her. "We are both adults now, and you can call me Camille!"

We both laughed softly, together, finding a small ray of humor in our shared sorrow.

Carolyn's creased face flushed pink as she smiled up at me and tears gathered in her soft, blue eyes. Her ever present sadness swirled and twisted around both of us as she struggled to speak again. Almost as if I could read her mind, I knew what she was thinking. Her dreams of her son and his life, so cruelly taken from her had included me. Elisha and I had been such good childhood friends and Carolyn and my mother had been close friends as young women as well. I knew their hearts back then and I recognized that same hopeful gleam in her eyes right now, which made me wonder, does every young mother dream of her child marrying the mate of her choosing? As close as Eli and I were at our young ages, marriage had never entered our thoughts, but as an adult now, I could see and understand our mother's dreams a little better. My heart felt bruised by the emotions contained in this tiny and broken woman and I wanted to save her from any more conversation that would cause her pain.

Taking her hand again, I said, "We both share a heartache, and I hope that we don't make each other miserable with our gloomy thoughts and grief." I knew I could not bear my own pain and hers as well. I wanted to avoid that type of conversation with a fierce commitment that gripped my whole body. What is that old quote? Physician, heal thyself…I knew that despite my extensive education in the field of psychology, I was emotionally, completely unequipped to walk with Carolyn in her long standing sorrow and still stagger through my own life .

"Oh Camille, don't worry about that. You must keep faith, child. Faith fills your heart and gives you strength. I still have hope, Elisha will return to me, I know it. The Lord will provide and take care. Also, I believe in miracles and I know for certain that you did as well, once upon a time." She spoke softly but firmly. Her face glowed with a radiance that emanated from her inner being. "Remember Kitty Grey? We all thought her case was hopeless. Even Dr. Colby over in Quincy said there was no chance of survival. But you, you wouldn't take no for an answer. You nursed her back to health despite the odds against her coming thru all of her wounds. You were expecting a miracle and you received it!"

"Ummm, Kitty Grey was a cat, Carolyn. That hardly compares to losing your son almost 19 years ago. You cannot possibly compare the two and expect a miracle at this late date," I fumbled as my words could not keep up with my thoughts. The surprising speed with which she had leapt from cogent speech to crazy took me by surprise. Was it her age?

"Yes, Camille, I can and I do. That my dear, is called faith. My faith in the Lord is all that I have and it is what has kept me going all these years. It really is all that I need. It is all that any of us needs and to fall in love with the Lord is the greatest love affair there is. And you know, Eli's body was never found. To me, that means there is hope and he may just be lost and he may return to me. He will be found," she finished firmly.

Her unbreakable faith and strong belief almost had me convinced, but then my common sense and logic reasserted themselves and with a sigh, I realized that it wasn't only her husband who had lost his mind those many years ago. "Oh dear heavens," I breathed telling myself. "She is delusional."

Carolyn continued, "I can feel it deep within myself. God has given me this great hope. It is as real to me as you are, standing here now." Taking a deep breath, she seemed to return to this world of sanity, and straightening her shoulders, she said, "But we will talk of this further on another day. When you are ready and things have settled a bit, please come for a visit. We have so much to share."

My words got strangled before they were born, so I just nodded weakly and smiled at her faintly. How do I arrange social matters with someone who is out of touch with reality? With great kindness, I remind myself. A moment of awkward silence fell between us.

Sensing the awkwardness, Carolyn placed her frail hands on my shoulder and tugged me gently into a tight hug. I could feel a surprising strength in her bony frame. Patting me on the back, she hummed slightly in my ear. "Anytime my dear when you are ready to talk. We have so much to catch up on." Then dropping her hands, she turned away from me and without another word, walked away, weaving in and around the granite markers of remembrance.

How much more complicated could my life become? I wanted only to hide and grieve the multiple losses in my heart. I did not want to share that space with another. And I certainly didn't want to flirt with faith and all of the apparent craziness that it implied. Taking another deep breath, I resolved to keep my contact with Carolyn at a minimum. But as soon as I did, I recalled another element of her ridiculous notion. There are amazing and factual accounts of people surviving years of emotional bondage and sexual abuse and returning to their families. Her conviction could possibly be true. The key word being 'possible.'

But in the end, after careful consideration, I decided that it was virtually impossible for Eli to have survived whatever accident or occurrence that had taken place and removed him from our lives. It was just a ridiculous notion that a boy who had disappeared over 18 years previously could just reappear like a ghost from the past. "No," I said to myself. "No, no chance."

I gave my head a firm shake and walked down the gravel drive toward the kindly gentleman from Souder's Funeral home who held the black book with all the signatures and meaningful expressions of admiration for my father from those who attended his funeral. I clutched it with both hands. I knew the writings in this book would be a comfort at some point in the future. For now, it represented an unbearable finality to a life taken way too soon.

During the short drive to the high school gym, I found myself wondering if my maudlin emotional storms of many years were unhealthy and if I could change and become like one of these good folks. Could I find a place in the peace of this mountain town and actually receive the goodness and care of my fellow townspeople? For longer than I could remember, I eat but never have enough. I clothe myself, but I'm never warm. I scream at night, but no one hears my cries. I know my concerns about the past and my worries about the future cannot add one single minute to my life. I know the consequences of a brain overload. My studies in the past several years have led me to reach this inevitable conclusion. Stress smothers one's breath and slows an already struggling heart. Taking a deep breath, I resolved to show myself that I could be as strong and brave as my father by graciously receiving the friendship and offers of condolences of my hometown family and friends.

Later that night, physically exhausted and emotionally spent by the funeral and subsequent wake I fell into a deep, troubled slumber. As if I had been touched by the past, it was the first time in many years that I dreamed of Elisha Simon Young.

CHAPTER 5

My lids blinked open; the veils of sleep drifting in ribbons before my eyes. With a clouded brain and not fully awake, I widened my gaze and stared out in blank confusion as to why I was even awake at this late hour. I saw the silvery glow of moonlight spilling through the paned window and heard the oak tree outside the window rustle in a faint movement. I figured it must have been the brushing of the leaves against the panes that had wakened me. A coyote called in the distance, answered by others further away. A chorus of lonely wails breaking through the night. Lying in my bed, listening to the nighttime music of my childhood, I let myself relax with the hope of returning sleep.

But then, a slight movement across the room startled me out of my dreamy state. Nothing was distinguishable at first, but as I peered deeper into that corner, I saw a figure in the wavy mirror, seated on my grandmother's old rocking chair. My heart began to pound and the beat roared loudly in my ears. I was paralyzed with alarm, unable to move. Coalescing in the moonlight was the figure of a young boy who smiled at me. Then he rose, emerged from the mirror and slowly approached my bed. The light of the moon illuminated him as he drew closer and without a doubt, for the first time in many years I saw the face of Elisha Young.

Although I had imagined him many times over the years, I did not believe that I could see him as clearly as I could now. The wavy, sandy hair, creased from the wearing of his Little League ball cap which he clutched in his hand, a couple of stray curls hanging over his forehead, the freckles sprinkled over his nose and cheeks, his sturdy, lanky build. His skin was chalky and he glowed with a faint luminescence, his eyes a deep green as brilliant as emeralds shining bright and alive. He wore a wide stripe red and white T-shirt and the Toughskin jeans I remembered from my own childhood. A crazy question shot through my mind. Why is such an irrelevant fact about the jeans something I would consider at a moment like this?

The human mind is funny during a stressful moment; I fixated on the memory of those jeans. My mother purchased Toughskin jeans for me from the Sears catalog. Shopping in Indian Valley for clothing was an expensive proposition with limited choices, so most parents shopped either in Reno, 100 miles to the east, Chico, 85 miles to the southwest or used the catalog services of Sears. Toughskin jeans were worn by most of the valley kids in my childhood.

He gave me the gap toothed grin, his eyes crinkling at the corners, and asked in a whispery voice, "Have you found it yet?" Raising his eyebrows, he looked intently at me, a slight smile still resting on his lips. I had no answer for him and he questioned me again, "Did you look for it at all? It must be there."

Still unable to speak, I stared at him, our eyes locked on one another for an eerie, but silent moment. Finally, I opened my mouth and with all the strength I could muster, struggled to speak, but no words came out, just a weak soundless gasp.

Eli gave a slight shrug and lowered his head, his neck appearing to shrink. His voice gave me the shivers; as if it were a voice spoken from beyond. I was frozen in place, overwhelmed by the vision of my childhood friend, fearful of the unknown and of awakening in the dead of night. I wanted the sound of his voice, much missed thru the years, to be music to my ears and for the sight of his face to fill me with a joy and childlike excitement that I had not felt in a long time. I wanted to be transported to a time when I was young, all was well in life and I eagerly anticipated the adventures of each day. But as I gazed upon him, he began to waver and quiver in the moonlight, becoming slightly fainter with each passing moment.

Desperate to hold his presence with me, I found my tongue and my words rushed out. "Found what, Eli? What are you talking about?" Despite my longing to leap up and throw my arms around him, I could not move. Much to my dismay, he seemed to diminish and disappear, drifting outside. I forced my unwilling body from my bed, down the hall and out the door. I began to follow him, increasing my pace as we moved beyond the big porch, out onto the lawn and across the gravel. He moved faster, his upraised hand waving me on and we descended the big gravel drive and crossed over the highway to Hot Springs Road. I could feel the graveled surface under my feet and the damp, late night air chilled my cheeks. Panting, I increased my speed to catch him, just as I had when we were children. He smiled back at me, beckoning me into the stand of trees at the end of the road and disappeared into the thick growth. I slowed, breathing hard, feeling the lump in my throat arise and my vision blurred with tears.

"Wait! Wait up!" I called out to him. Shaken by his disappearance, I shook my head and struggled to open my eyes to search for movement in the trees ahead, but beheld the soft pink walls of my room instead. Gulping deeply for air, the pounding of my heart slowly subsided and my room emerged, the familiar objects bathed in the blush of moonlight. The rocker creaked faintly, polished to a sheen in the silvery glow and the empty mirror dimly reflected only the luminescence of the moon. Surrounded by the familiar childhood treasures and back in my own bed, I took a deep breath, followed by another and another.

"It was a dream," I told myself, "Just a dream." The realism of the dream remained with me, ebbing slightly as my heart calmed.

I savored for a moment, the return of his smile and the sight of his much loved figure.

My room comforted me; the familiar lavender quilt draped over my bed and the lace panels shimmering in the window panes. The shelves filled with books and sports memorabilia representing my years of softball and basketball. The middle shelf held my most prized trophy. It was a gift from Eli the summer I was 9 and he was 11. Most Valuable Player was inscribed on the bottom on a little brass plate, and topped by the still figure of a boy, crouched in batting stance awaiting an unseen pitch. Eli received it after his successful season playing for Greenville's Little League All Star team. Presenting it to me, I remember his words well like it was yesterday. "It makes it better to share it with you," he told me. Although I had not earned the trophy myself, I loved it because of what it represented; my friendship with Eli and that he sought to win the trophy for me.

My emotions swirled within me, a renewed sadness and grief at his disappearance, compounded by the emptiness created by the loss of my parents. The sadness and despair that were my constant companions, reared their ugly heads and tugged sharply at my heart. I felt a surge of anger at the thought of being left behind by those I loved and breathed deeply to control my emotions. Strangely enough, I also felt a tickle of excitement, or maybe it is hope? Eli had revealed something of importance to me and I was curious to learn what he had meant. My father had left me with a mystery as well, and I needed to uncover the secret he took to his grave.

With a big sigh and exhausted by the dream and my disjointed thoughts, I flopped back onto my bed and I reflected on what a week this had been. Losing my father, surrendering his body to its' last earthly home under the pine trees, being confronted with Mrs. Young's fanciful beliefs, awaiting her sons' return with open arms and a quiet spirit. The love and compassion of my friends and family. And now Eli himself, visiting me in that world between sleep and dreams, giving me the hint that there is something I need to find. Is it possible that the emotion I am feeling is hope? Hope that my life, will continue with a calling that will bring resolution to unanswered questions? Eli has touched my soul, filled with the hidden pain that began with his disappearance, and given it the gift of the soft and gentle glow of hope.

As my mind stilled and my body relaxed, I knew despite my grief, I would look forward to tomorrow. My mother's much loved voice drifted through my mind, speaking her favorite morning, saying; "This is the day the Lord has made. I will rejoice and be glad in it!" The familiar Scripture quote calmed me and I knew that I would awaken in the morning and seek to find the answers to some important questions. What are the cemetery secrets my father tried to share in his last gasping breath and what is it that Eli hopes I will find?

CHAPTER 6

My dream last night had a surprising effect on me in the early light of morning. As I watched the sun's warm fingers creep through the pine trees, I reflected on the previous week of shock and grief. I have felt my father's loss as a physical pain in my chest that added weight to my arms and legs and made even my head feel heavy upon my neck. This morning however, I noticed an easing of the physical pain I associate with loss. The tightness in my chest had relaxed during sleep and I am feeling refreshed for the first time in many days. Recalling the dream and Eli's words create a sense of hope and purpose in me and I want this to be a day of renewal.

In the way of the universe, my presence here in Greenville has been perfectly timed. My father's death has coincided with the completion of my studies. I no longer have the pressures of student teaching and graduate work. Two days prior to my father's unexpected death, I had been preparing for a summer of rest and desultory job seeking. But I am somewhat disoriented with the change of pace and I wonder if the constant rush of academic activity would have helped me cope with my emotions and grief. Since it is a moot question, I will choose to welcome the quieter life. However, as with all things in life, there are twin pillars of objectives to consider. Although being released from the pressures and commitments attached to getting a higher education is a welcoming thought, unfortunately, that places me in a sink or swim situation. I have no job or income which means my preferred attitude about taking the summer at a slow pace and blowing caution to the wind would bear a heavy consequence. Maybe I can hold off for at least another week or so before I once again pound the pavement.

Having experienced grief in the past, I know I will feel my father's loss keenly in the next months, but I am resolved, here in the rosy glow of morning that I will not allow bitterness or isolation to overcome me as I have in the past. I know that the quality of my life will reflect my inner thoughts and I want to grow through this grief into a better person. I want so badly to honor my father's memory and the life he lived and I know I must make some changes within myself to achieve that. If only grief came with an instruction manual. It makes much more sense to be skilled at managing grief, instead of stoking the embers of misery and agony, causing it to flare up with renewed intensity. But then I am reminded of one of my many heart to heart talks with my father.

"We are all going to die someday Camille," my father's words tug at my ears. "When my day comes, I don't want you to be sad, because I'll always be with you. Right here," he said, tapping his fingertips to his heart. "The death of my body will not be a final, severing event between father and daughter. Instead, look at it as just one step in a long, gradual process to bring us back together again."

I must remind myself that death doesn't necessarily mean goodbye. I'd like to think it just means I'll see you later. At least that's how my father explained it.

"I believe that there is a profound human connection that lasts well past death. The deep link with a loved one doesn't end at the grave. We are forever tied together through our memories, Camille. Don't ever forget that."

"I won't forget dad," I said, my voice sounding less than a whisper.

Padding out to the kitchen, feeling the wide pine flooring, smooth and soft, under my feet, I prepare the coffee beans for grinding. Still contemplating my determination to be at peace with my life and accept the things I cannot change, I find that the mindlessness of the task soothes me. I fill the carafe with water and pour it in the brewer. The machine burbles and puffs a little bit of sass with a small plume of steam. I deeply inhale the scent of fresh brewed coffee and reflect on the simple joys of life. I resolve again to keep my thoughts focused on gratitude and appreciation. I sternly admonish myself to make a concerted effort to look for small wonders throughout the day. This makes me smile; knowing full well that my emotions will be playing tennis before lunchtime and I will be rocked back and forth between despair and resolve. I know that I do not want to create self-defeating thoughts that result in a circle of more suffering and my main objective is to survive and possibly thrive in the upcoming seasons of my life.

I carried my coffee and a bowl of oatmeal out to the deck and sat at the little table that faces the cemetery down the slope in front of the house. I felt the sun on my tight muscles and I welcomed the warmth it brought to my body. I held my coffee in one of father's old mugs as I gazed down upon the tidy rows of remembrance in the sweep of grass. I reflected how proud he was of the grounds and the stewardship with which he embraced his responsibility for maintaining the cemetery. Faint wisps of moisture rose above some of the headstones and the remaining dew sparkled in patches of sunshine, like transient diamonds. A gift of the spirits, my father called those; the sprinkles of glittery drops on green grass. I focus on those lovely sparkles, glistening in the sunshine and feel the sadness in a lump arising in my throat as I recalled a conversation with my father about the dew drops in the morning sun.

"Lovely is the woman who wears drops of dew around her throat," he said one morning. I argued with the conviction of an irritable teenager, that it was not possible, literally, for a woman to wear dew. He laughed at me. "It's one of my metaphors for the earth," he explained with a smile. One thing I loved about my father; he never spoke with condescension to anyone, including me, even during my surly teenage years when he was probably tempted. Every word he spoke to me was a lifelong lesson on relationships and self-understanding.

"To steward such a beautiful gift as Mother Earth and to enjoy every precious little sight provided by the Great Spirit is a privilege, not a duty," he went on to say. "Trust me Camille. God doesn't make mistakes. Man is responsible for his own failures," he pointed out with kindness and understanding in his eyes.

Although I do not recall the entire conversation between us, I do remember rolling my eyes at his outdated notions of the world and its' Creator. The old fashioned ideas of a Supreme Being and its' beneficence certainly did not fit my young and questioning mind.

Now in the glow of the morning sun and the loveliness of the day emerging from the rosy dawn, I wondered if my father had it right. That the earth is a gift to us from Someone, all powerful and all good, and watching over us with loving care despite the miseries of our lives. What makes the difference? Is it our choices, actions or thoughts? Or do we live at the whim of this Supreme Being having no personal power of our own? And if this Supreme Being really was good, why do bad things happen to good people? Shrugging, I decided to eat. I would leave that pondering for another time.

Just as I took my last bite, and as the early morning sky had finished painting itself with a fresh coat of blue, I heard a faint noise off in the distance. I stood and walked to the south end of the porch and peered through the trees toward the distressing sound. I saw a young woman still dressed in her pajamas draped over an upright headstone. My heart dropped to my stomach when her mumbled cries turned into loud sobbing. I crept down the stairs and slowly followed her footsteps through dew, blanketed grass.

"I'm sorry to disturb you, but can I help you in any way?" I asked.

At first she said nothing. I thought maybe she didn't hear me, so I asked again. "Could I help you with something?"

The young woman with matted, brown hair let out a long sigh and turned her tear drenched face up toward me. "You can't help me. Nobody can help me," she declared.

"Maybe I could try."

"Unless you can raise the dead, there is nothing you can do."

"I'm sorry for your loss."

"I'm sorry too, because my poor husband will never see his son. He will never hear him say daddy I love you. He will never tell his son, good game young man." Then she fell back into deep guttural sobbing.

I inched closer to the trembling young woman, knelt down on one knee and wrapped my arms around her. There were no words passed between us as I held her tight. The stark realization that there really are people out here whose stories are just as heart wrenching as mine suddenly became more real to me.

"My guilt grows like a mold on my emotional reserve," she said which confused me.

"What do you mean?"

"Maybe God is not prone to bless people like me who are lazy in prayer and lacking in faith."

I felt the panic strike my brain. All I could think was that here I am questioning this same God she is referring to, so how am I supposed to help comfort her when I can't even help myself. My father danced with wisdom, but when I was younger, I couldn't hear the music. I've grown older and now my dance has begun. Maybe this is when my understanding finally cuts in. Thankfully, some of my father's wisest words bloomed in my mouth. "I know during times when your pain has risen to the marathon level of unbearable, it is hard to think in terms of patience and faith. Those two spiritual giants can seem like two beasts that don't follow the same master. But I assure you, they do. And, God does hear your prayers."

"I am but a puny person. Do you really think God sees this one grain of sand amongst billions of others on the shore?"

"Yes He does. The wisest man I ever knew once told me that in times of waiting, God builds our trust. Hope is the engine that takes us from where we are to where we want to be. Hope keeps you trying until a solution is found. The Bible is a Book of solutions. Maybe start there," I suggested. All the while I'm thinking how did I remember all this stuff my father tried to teach me?

"There is no solution to my problem. My husband is dead because of a war we shouldn't be fighting. I'm forced to raise our child all alone," she confirmed, rubbing the huge mound protruding from her midsection. "Every day I wake, I feel like I'm sticking my finger in a light socket. And, sometimes my mind is full of awful thoughts."

"What kind of thoughts?"

"Maybe we would both be better off if...." her words trailed off into silence. She began to shake and cry hysterically.

"Don't even think in those terms. No doubt we live in a broken world. Murders are on the rise, behavioral issues have worsened and sometimes our loved ones are taken too soon, but that doesn't give us the right to give up on life. The enemy is just pulling your vulnerable strings. We cannot change what has happened in our life, but we can control how we handle it. Everyone trusts in something that gives life meaning. Trust that God has given you a special gift. You carry that gift inside of you. That gift is also a part of your husband that will live on as long as you nurture and give your baby the chance to blossom and grow into the fine young man your husband would have wanted him to be. The ugliness of this world has taken your husband, but don't let those same evils take your son as well. You can do this. Take one day at a time in the knowing you are showing the greatest respect for the memory of your husband by bringing his child into this world and raising him just as your husband would have wanted you to."

The woman gasped as if my words had sucked the breath right out of her. "I guess I have been a little self-absorbed through all of this," she admitted.

"Understandably so. Just take one day at a time and try to push through the darkness to reach the light. With the passage of time the pain you hold in your heart will evolve into a dull annoyance. Focus now on what you do have. This special life growing within you will give you the courage to go on and build a new life. Not a life completely void of your husband, because a piece of him lives on through your son. You know, Heaven is full of prayers never asked. Prayer can be your steering wheel as well as your spare tire. Don't give up on yourself and don't give up on God," I advised through the very words my father taught me.

"Thank you."

"No, thank you. I just lost my father and I needed to hear these very words he once spoke to me," I enlightened her. "I needed a good dose of my father's medicine, because lately I have been swimming in a pity pool myself."

The young woman rose to her feet and gave me a long hug. "Thank you," she said and then turned away to retrace her steps toward wherever she came from. I watched her slowly amble off until she vanished into a thick forest of trees. I hoped in some small way the words of my father had satisfied the gnawing hunger of her heart.

I glanced down at the granite stone. "PFC Justine Robert Huber," I read the name out loud. "Thank you for serving. Our task is to help others. You have done that and paid the ultimate sacrifice. I hope in some small way my father's teachings have helped to lift your wife's spirits and give her reason to love and live again."

I shuffled off toward my house feeling better than I had in quite some time.

Later that same day as I washed dishes and tidied the kitchen, I could feel the compulsion of cleaning coming over me. I emptied the refrigerator and tossed old food. Scrubbing out the fridge took me back to my childhood as I recalled my mother cleaning it. I wondered as I wiped the shelves as she wiped the very same shelves, what she was thinking while doing so. With the memories of a child comes some distortion, as the memories are viewed through the naive eyes of innocence, but I remember my home as a clean and welcoming space. The fragrance of good food and fresh laundry, my mother busy with her tasks but with a moment for me if I needed her. My father was a tidy man, but the house lacked the attention to cleaning detail that a caring woman can bring to a home. In my absence, pursuing my education, the house had taken on a somewhat neglected air. Not mistreated, just lonely, maybe. My mind wandered as I performed the simple tasks of organizing the counter top. Thanks to the generosity and kindness of the neighbors and other Greenville friends, I had enough casseroles, cakes, and salads to last me rest of the summer. I piled several jars of homemade jams and jellies, gifts from loving hearts and hands, in a basket on the counter. Spraying one of the many windows with cleaner, I reflected on the view of the cemetery.

The cemetery, a gently sloping area, intersected by crisscross graveled roads and walking paths for access, has been part of the town since the 1870s. The American and California state flags fluttered in the breeze and Wolf Creek chattered along the western border, just out of sight behind a stand of fir and pine trees. During the spring months the exuberance of the water was a splashing hum in the background and the summer months brought a low burble. The creek wound around the cemetery and snaked its' way south through Indian Valley before its' final rush to join the waters of the Feather River. The cemetery originated in a time when headstones were a monument to the loved ones lost; there are a variety of shapes, sizes and colors, some mossy and stained with age and others newer, their lettering clear. The stones, carved of limestone, marble and local granite glow different hues in the sunshine. The wings of angels cast sharp shadows on the grass and crosses abound in every row.

My friends teased me about living above the cemetery. It was jokingly called the Bury Patch, but none of my friends treated it with physical disrespect. There was never any drinking, making out or littering on dark nights. In retrospect, that was probably due more to my father's vigilance than the respect of town teens for the deceased. Although cemeteries are stereotypically cast as dark, scary places, complete with wild rainstorms, lightning and frightening spirits, I had always found it to be just a part of my family's front lawn.

On complaining to father on one occasion about a classmates' teasing, he laughed, gave me a hug and said, "Hey Camille, people are dying to get in here, you know." Haha, Dad. And although he abused that witticism frequently, what I would give to hear that gentle pun one more time.

Looking to the north, I see Indian Head. The stately mountain soared over the town, dark green now in the summer, but autumn will bring a riot of color as the oak trees celebrate the fall season with their glorious red, orange and yellow hues.

Standing here, I find it easy and comforting to lose myself in another one of my father's favorite stories about this valley.

"Indian legend tells the story of an elder of the early native people who settled here in the valley. He was a great chief, leading and guiding with a firm hand and great care, keeping his people in peace. Upon reaching the age when an elder is finished with the walk in this world, he left his people to climb the mountain. He was never again seen, but the mountain took on the profile of his visage. If you look closely Camille, you can see his brow silhouetted against the summer sky and the prominence of his nose sloping down to the ridge of his lip. Legend has it that the old chief became the mountain, forever to watch over and care for his beloved people in the valley by night and he gazes up into the heavens during the day."

I am entranced by the beauty my eyes behold, and I gaze slowly across the valley floor. On the northern sweep of the valley, Greenville is nestled in the protective shadow of the old Chief. The fields of the valley below the mountain hold sloughs of water, rich with cattail reeds, green and yellow grasses and are dotted with herds of cattle. In the distance, I can see the faint lines of fencing throughout the pastures and the tracing of North Arm Road around the base of Indian Head. My hometown is a place of the country agricultural lifestyle and care for the land is evident.

I started to mop the wide pine plank flooring, inhaling the clean fragrance of lemon juice and olive oil, appreciating the sheen of the clean wood under my hands. This home, built by my father in the early years of my parents' marriage, is a testament to his skill. He didn't just build houses, he crafted homes. As I worked over the kitchen floor and into the living room, I realized that my father had put the same care into me. Recalling memories of his teaching, I realize that he put his personal touch into his parenting, his construction work and into his many long standing friendships. The keen awareness of his love and my loss brings fresh grief and my tears are mingled with the lemon oil on the soft flooring.

Finished with the first round of household chores, I stepped out onto the deck with the last cup of coffee. The sun had continued its' march across the sky and shone down brightly making me squint as I surveyed the cemetery. To ease my eyes, I lift them to Indian Head and consider if the ancient elder is watching over me today.

"Hey Camille! Sorry to bother you, but I got a couple questions for you," came a voice from below.

Peering over the railing, I squint to see Brian Wilson and little Jimmy Doyle below me, holding shovels and ready to put today's chores behind them.

My father had hired Brian, just out of high school many years ago as a grounds assistant. He was tall, well built and fit for his age, deeply tanned and wrinkled from his time in the outdoor elements. His thick graying hair was kept in place beneath a NY Yankees ball cap and his reading glasses were tucked into the front pocket of his plaid shirt. His speech was peppered with baseball metaphors and his team loyalty changed from season to season, giving him a wide selection of ball caps. Brian was a reliable and hard worker, his only vice being his love of cigarettes, a habit he refused to surrender. Always carrying the scent of the unabashed smoker, I recalled searching for him, in my youth, wherever he was working by following the odor of cigarette smoke.

Little Jimmy, small and delicate from a childhood kidney disease that very nearly took his life, was also wizened by the sun. He was painfully thin with receding hair and dark, sad eyes. He was a gentle soul who spent much of his time following Brian. My father had given him work to keep him occupied. His health was frail, but he was a determined soul who overcame his challenges with courage and he had a sweet and kind spirit that endeared him to everyone in town. Wearing dirty Carhartt work pants, it appeared that both men had been hard at work for some time.

"Good morning, gentleman," I smiled down on them. "Hey Jim, how are you? You're looking good today."

He gave me a wide grin and his eyes lit with pride, "Couldn't be better, Camille. I got me a clean bill of health my last trip down to UC Davis," his voice a high treble. "I'm doing real good."

"That's great news, Jimmy. I am glad to hear it," I told him. "I know you have been through a lot. You deserve a good spell."

Looking back at Brian, I said, "And you are not a bother, you are never a bother. You can ask me anything you want, but I may not have the answers!" I laughed quietly, remembering again, that I while I am alone, I am not on my own. "I have been meaning to talk to you guys, but you know how it is at a time like this. I feel like I am in a fog, moving in slow motion."

Brian gave a sympathetic nod of his head. "That's understand-able, Camille." Glancing at Little Jimmy, he continued, "We sure know what you're going through. Can't hurry the heart, girl. Gotta give it some time."

I felt a rush of affection for this rugged and work worn man. He had been a fixture for so many years, that I had not really appre-ciated his kind compassion to grieving families until I was on the receiving end of his thoughtfulness.

"Well, guys," I said. "What's up?"

"You remember China Boy, don't you?" he asked? "The old guy who had the take-out shop on Main Street."

"Oh sure, isn't he about 110 years old?" I asked. "How is he doing?"

"Well, he isn't doing anything now. He passed away right before your dad, Camille. I'm sorry, I thought you knew. Our elders and the older generation are passing on. In fact, I check the obituaries daily to make sure my name's not at the top of the list," he said with a twinkle in his eye and a hearty laugh.

Hearing my father's words coming from Brian makes me smile again and I know this rugged and gentle man will miss my father as much as I will.

"And I think he was only 70 or 75 at the most," he corrected me. "You kids can be so cruel in your youthful miscalculations," he admonished me. "Well, as the story goes, it appears that China Boy was walking from Oakey Flats into town sometime last month and was attacked by old man Balmer's nasty pit bull. Tore him up something terrible and he just never recovered. Some infection or something along those lines. Of course, old Balmer is so nasty himself, it's no surprise his dog tore into someone."

I shuddered at the thought of the sufferings of China Boy and then noticed the sheen of tears in Brian's eyes as he took off his ball cap, smoothed his hair and replaced the cap. These were the actions of a man trying to hide his emotions. I remained silent, remembering that Brian had never married and he had made use of China Boys' take-out several nights a week.

Jimmy spoke into the silence between us. "So, old China Boy didn't have much money. I think maybe he gave away too much free food," he observed in his high, thready voice. "We put out coffee cans for donations at the feed store and the gas stations. We just want to make sure he gets a good send off."

I nod in agreement. "That was a great idea. I will donate the plot and maybe the collections will cover some of the other expenses. I'll take care of the rest, somehow." I shake my head as the realization hits me that I am now performing the same duty my father did so many times. The care for the deceased is important, especially those who had little in the way of worldly goods, but were generous to the people of our town.

Little Jimmy roughly brushed his eyes and I felt a surge of pity for him. He had spent many hours with China Boy, sitting on a stool in the narrow space between the counter and wall in the tiny take-out shop. Chatting in his high voice with various customers about the weather, discussing the current high school sports season, insulting their pickup trucks or commenting on their menu selections and I knew he would miss the old man deeply.

China Boy was a small man who hitch hiked, arriving in town with a van of hippies over 45 years ago seeking quietude, as he told folks. Although he was an unobtrusive and private man, he had become a reliable and friendly part of the community. His kindly acceptance of the presence of little Jimmy in his shop and his gentle teasing and tutoring of the young Jim in basic chores had been a positive force in Little Jimmy's hard life. Tolerating little Jimmy's presence and verbal chatter with the customers was a great and unselfish kindness. The circle of life really isn't a Disney concept in a movie. It is community; a dignified life of honest work and now the death of an old man, mourned and cared for by one he mentored out of compassion. I determined that this would be a quiet and dignified affair, just like China Boy. And somehow and in some way, would bring comfort to both Jimmy and Brian.

"Well, this isn't spring training, Jimmy, and you can't stand here all day talking to pretty ladies even if she is your boss." Brian slapped little Jimmy on the back, causing him to stumble forward a step. "Don't want Lady Coach here to send us down to the minors, now, do we?"

We all laughed together and the guys turned toward the west side of the cemetery and I watched them as they ambled toward the stand of pines in that corner, listening to the low rumble of Brian's voice and the occasional piping reed of Jimmy's replies. I reflected on the thought that even grave diggers mourn and in their sorrow, turn to labor to ease their pain. And make dumb allusions to baseball metaphors, as well.

"Death and taxes, you can count on them both." I heard my father's voice in my ears. The talk of covering China Boys final expenses made me realize that I would need to venture into father's office in the very near future. After spending so many years as a starving student, I knew I could manage somehow with whatever means were available, but I needed to have all the facts first. I wanted to be sure I could cover China Boys' final expenses, and I really needed to be sure I could at least continue to pay Brian and Little Jimmy.

CHAPTER
7

I stepped back into the tidy kitchen; clean and fresh after my morning labors. Knowing that I needed to go into my father's study and begin the laborious process of sorting his papers and personal items that I had chosen to delay far longer than I should have. I rummaged among the bags of Black Rifle coffee beans in the cupboard opting for Red, White and Brew, my preferred blend. I proceeded to grind some to make a fresh pot of coffee. Fighting tears as I shook loose a filter for the basket, I recalled my father ordering the beans online. "Just because I know how you love that yuppie, overpriced coffee," he joked with me on a previous visit. "It comes in cans already ground and ready to go at the supermarket, you know. You don't have to spend extra money and all this time grinding those beans," he'd reminded me. A fathers love; it shows in the most unlikely and little ways. As a former US Marine, himself, he had quietly appreciated the veteran owned coffee business even as he teased me about the added expense and bother.

My sadness remained with me as I entered his study, a small bedroom he had converted to office space for cemetery and personal business. The wood paneled walls and the built in desk still held his presence as if our human spirits can energize our very surroundings. The window overlooked the driveway and I could see Indian Head in the distance and that brought me comfort. I knew someone was watching over me.

I looked at a picture of my parents on their wedding day which had been placed on his desk right after my mother's passing. The understanding that my father would never walk me down the aisle on my wedding day made me sad. The fact that I had no current boyfriend was immaterial; doesn't every girl dream of that white dress and that floating walk down the aisle, clutching the arm of the first man who ever loved her? The groom is just a blurry figure in the future, but a father; he is a loving figure, right here in the present. He may be complaining about overpriced coffee beans, but he is a figure of strength and love. I feel as if I am spinning without an axis and it is only a matter of time before I twirl dizzily out of control and crash. And the thought that my children, also blurry figures in the future, would emerge into a world without my father, without his strength, humor and goodness brought tears to my eyes once again.

I could hear my father's voice in my mind; his words of encouragement drifting along an eddy of memories. He had on more than one occasion told me to buck up and focus on the positives in my life. "Look for the silver lining in every cloud," he'd said to me. "There is always a silver lining, but you have to look for it!" Speaking firmly, but with a gentle smile on his lips.

Rubbing my burning eyes, I brought myself back to the present, in his office that still held a faint whiff of his aftershave, his mug with the sludge of days' old coffee in the bottom and his cell phone dropped on his desk as if he were just momentarily gone. Blearily I wondered, how will I proceed, especially if I could no longer see; my eyes puffy from crying and my head pounding from my incessant sobbing? I had not imagined my life like this, both parents gone before my 30th birthday. My grief is that of the orphaned. Then I remember his last gasping breath and the message he struggled so hard to give me and I know I will follow the thread of his last word given in his last breaths to its' completion. "Cemetery Secrets." Those few words echoing in my mind give me a sense of purpose. I feel the prick of curiosity, plucking at the threads of his final words to me. They were not voiced by chance. I am coming to understand that his intention was to gently nudge me into an avenue of inquiry that would carry my mind away from my grief and loss. He understood how my mind could take me to the dark place of sadness that was difficult for me to leave.

Taking a deep breath, I sat at his desk and rested my hands on its' scarred surface. Taking several more deep breaths, I calm myself. And as I blow my nose on a paper napkin, I remind myself that this is one of the last respects I can pay my father. I want to complete his business here on earth and follow through with any commitments he may have made. There is also the promise I made Brian and little Jimmy to cover the costs of China Boys services. I blow my hair out of my eyes with a weary puff of breath and I wondered how I could have been so foolish to make such a promise with no idea of the landscape of my financial future.

Seated in my father's chair, I wince at the familiar creak as it rocks back on its wheels. I leaned over and yanked on the top drawer. I began the task of sorting through the contents and methodically examining individual pieces of paper, every little item and each notebook creating loosely organized stacks of paper. My father had badly mangled the job of keeping his professional records and personal keepsakes separate. In the second drawer, I found last year's expense records, neatly collated by date and stapled, with a collection of programs from my high school athletics programs tucked underneath. The third drawer revealed articles from the Indian Valley Record newspaper which were clipped and tossed haphazardly in several different sections of the divided drawer, but each one featured my name for an athletic or school event. There were snapshots of me with my father and other family and friends sandwiched in between every sheaf of paper. The deep fourth drawer on the left side contained a collection of Christmas cards. Hidden beneath those cards, I found his maintenance records for the tractor along with my graduation announcement in the same folder. I ponder over my father's thought processes as I continue the excavation and sorting. I found his tax returns and my mother's scrapbooks in the same drawer.

Distracted by the sheer volume of paper and discouraged by the realization that this project would take much longer than I had anticipated, I tugged the scrapbooks onto my lap. My mother had kept mementos of my infancy and childhood. Little snippets of information neatly jotted in her beautiful penmanship. I hold the precious gift of her memories in my hands, reading and rereading her thoughts. She loved my smile and the way I laughed when she played peek-a-boo with me. The story of losing my first tooth and how the 'tooth fairy' sort of forgot to find the tooth the first night. That made me smile. Losing her at such a young age compelled me to create a somewhat fanciful picture of her as the perfect mother. It was warming to discover her humanity and somehow it made her more real for me. Colorful drawings and scrawled 'I love my mom' notes in my childish hand. Report cards from my elementary years showed I was a good student, but I never seemed to score the 'S' in deportment. Apparently I was a chatty little thing as noted by more than one teacher over the years. I cringed at the photo of my first formal school picture, my hair in a neat braids and a smile with gaps of missing teeth.

Tucked into the pages in various place were photos of Eli and I. I sucked in a deep breath and gathered them in my hands, examining each one carefully. Toddlers, Eli wearing a little shirt with Bert from Sesame Street, holding my hand. I was wearing a Strawberry Shortcake outfit, my disposable diaper peeking out from under my shirt. Sitting on the front porch, a little later, our two year age difference showing; we are both eating watermelon. Wearing a great deal of the reddish juices on his face, Eli's head is tipped back and he is laughing at something and I am laughing at him. Standing next to each other at the Little League field in Greenville behind the grade school. Eli in his Yankees uniform, filthy from his time behind the plate catching the game. His broad smile is directed at me as I stand at his side, proud of my friend. Our faces lit with joy, we are both clutching ice cream cones in our dirty hands, an after game treat. The last one was taken the summer he disappeared, we are both on our bikes poised to ride off into the sunset. Smiling widely, my grin shows my joy and delight in spending time with my friend. Eli's face showed the promise of what could become a killer smile as he entered his teenage years, his lanky legs and long arms supporting his bike. The thought of his loss flickered through my mind and I thought to myself, that other than his parents, I felt that I was deeply affected by his disappearance. Coupled with the death of my mother, I built a fortress around my heart and created a deep silence only my father could penetrate. I realized my gloominess was beginning to affect my breathing, so I quickly placed the photos back inside and closed the album.

I continued my search on the right side of the desk in the bottom drawer only because it was a much larger compartment than all the rest. I found my father's banking records under a stack of gardening catalogs and more pictures of my 4-H projects. He had well over $2000 in his checking account and $5000 in savings. Why he had secreted them under gardening catalogs and other detritus baffled me, but it made me smile. "A place for everything, and everything in its place, Camille," I heard him remind me.

"Okaaay then, Dad, now what?" I asked out loud. I knew I would be able to cover cemetery expenses for the near future, at least. It was a relief that I would now be able to pay Brian and little Jimmy as well. I then found his insurance, a burial policy for $10,000, payable to me as well another smaller policy that would pay dividends. Then I gasped loudly as I made a startling discovery. Bound in a dark brown folder was a life insurance policy for $250,000 and neatly typed into the line for beneficiary was my name.

Sitting in my father's study, holding the policy that gave me financial freedom for at least a few years and then some, I began to wonder why most people are worth more money dead than alive. How can a price be set on the value of a loved one? The incredible worth of a human being reduced to a dollar amount was staggering to me. I had only graduated my days as a starving student a few months before and now I was fatherless. But in his departure, he left behind reminders that he cared, ensuring that I could make decisions that were best for me rather than what was financially expedient. My tears dripped onto the pages as I once again felt his love and the warmth of his hand on my cheek. I would give back every dollar, every penny, if I could only have him with me, hug him once again and be able to roll my eyes at his old joke, "Folks are dying to get into my cemetery, Camille."

I promise myself, and in so doing promise my father, that I will cherish every relationship in my life in the future. I will treat each one as it were a precious commodity and give it the value each deserves. This softening of my heart somewhat alarms me, as I contemplate the pain I have suffered and a slight frisson of fear causes me to wonder if it is safe to embark on a path that nurtures relationships, since the ones most important to me ended in death and loss.

I will take one more baby step. I want to experience my life as my father did, sharing his journey with the Almighty One. So my last promise of course, would put a broad smile on my father's face and warm his caring heart. Even before the words come out of my mouth, I can almost picture what my eyes cannot see and hear his voice from beyond the great barrier that separates us. "For you dad, I promise to give your God a fighting chance to dwell in my world and in my heart. It won't be easy," I admitted. "But I will try," I added. "However, in return, you have to promise me one thing. You have to forgive me if I fail," I whispered, my voice trailing off into empty air. But deep down I know his love for me is stronger and more lasting than the sun hanging high in the sky. His love for me has no boundaries and all of my many failures combined cannot crack his impenetrable wall of love for me.

Sighing, I begin to stack the organized piles of paper back into the drawer. I cleared a small mountain of clutter from the top of the desk, discarding the nonessential and tucking the remainder into a semblance of order. Then, in a burst of manic energy, I gathered the trash into a large garbage bag, and carried it out to the dumpster. Returning to the office, I pulled down the curtains and threw them in the washing machine and washed the windows. I wiped down the walls of the small room and polished the desk chair. I swept the pine floor and mopped it, inhaling the lemony scent of hot water mixed with olive oil and lemon juice.

As I finished, I could feel exhaustion creeping over me, giving the familiar feeling of lethargy. I took a quick shower and went to bed early, only to ask myself the almighty, 'What If's'. "What if I had come home more often, then maybe my father's deteriorating health would have been detected in time? What if I had spent the summers here with him, instead of working jobs in the city? If I had spent more time with him, maybe his last words to me wouldn't have been about a secret between us. My guilty thoughts beat a discouraging refrain in my mind and once again, I am confronted by the decision I must make. Will I continue forward in my grief and pain or will I find a way to control my mindset and my wild emotions?

CHAPTER
8

I spent the long, hot days of summer, working, filling my time with the task of sorting through my parents belongings. Sifting through the possessions of loved ones, no longer in this world made me gloomy at times and I kept myself sane with long runs in the mornings. Keeping what I wanted and cherished, I held a big yard sale over the 4th of July weekend. There was a tug on my heart as I watched childhood memories of belongings, walk down the driveway, held in the arms of new owners. I knew that releasing the past in the form of belongings would help me in the opening and growth of my future. In between cemetery duties, I spent time cleaning the house, and two weeks painting the interior. I replaced rugs, curtains and added some different furniture to the deck. The freshening of my childhood home, coupled with creating a space that reflected my personal taste, was a healing and gratifying process and I began to allow myself to actually enjoy my projects.

I made weekly trips to Chico, seeing my father's attorney and completing the necessary tasks of tying up all the loose ends of his estate, shopping at Costco, buying supplies for the cemetery and having lunch with a couple of friends who lived in Chico. Back in Greenville, on my rounds of errands, I frequently found myself chatting with an old family friend or making time to have a glass of wine with a former classmate.

I was finding the administration of cemetery duties to be close to a full time job. With Brian's help, we replanted several flower beds and pruned trees. The roads needed a top dressing of fresh gravel and the brush along the creek had to be thinned to avoid fire danger.

"The grounds look better than old man Beevers' award winning garden in springtime," Brian had complimented.

"I second that notion. We have three acres of perfectly manicured landscaping with an explosion of colors that dazzles the eyes," I added.

"Compliments of Mother Nature," Brian muttered.

I had turned and faced him. "Maybe in part, but thanks to you and Little Jimmy, I believe this cemetery could be featured on the cover of Home and Garden."

Brian let out a hearty laugh. "I wouldn't go as far as making that dynamic claim. Maybe the forests surrounding this cemetery could be featured in Field and Stream."

I rolled my eyes. "If you say so. I can tell you this much. I'm beginning to understand why my father loved this place so much. It doesn't get any better than this."

He smiled in my direction. "Can't argue with truth."

Unlike his messy bookkeeping, my father had kept the cemetery neat and orderly, but the seasonal nature of mountain life created an endless cycle of tasks that had to be completed every year. I was grateful for Brian's presence and for his years of experience. He was a knowledgeable and wise caretaker, but he wanted nothing to do with the clerical side of the cemetery functions, so I was slowly learning how to manage the paperwork that accompanies all burials. Little Jimmy worked side by side with Brian on most days and always had a smile and friendly word for me.

There were several funerals with burials in the cemetery, three new headstones arrived and were set into place. I was learning to communicate with funeral directors and grieving families with gentleness. A group of genealogists, traveling through the state of California, spent a weekend touring the cemetery, photographing and taking rubbings from headstones. I answered many phone calls about plot purchases and the costs related to floral tributes for loved ones on their special days. I was finding the tasks to be time consuming, yet somehow soothing.

Performing the same duties as my father had for so many years brought a sense of dignity to me; I felt his spirit with me, calming and encouraging me. I was also beginning to have an inkling that death was a part of every ones' life, not just mine. And that grief accompanies the loss of every loved one; that pain was part of the process of loss and certainly not unique to me. I began to see a glimmer of life beyond my own storms of feeling and in private moments, I was somewhat embarrassed by my maudlin and self-pitying emotions. Each time I witnessed the love and pain of a grieving family, I felt anew my pain of loss was that of a heartbroken child and it was now time for me to be grown woman and to put grief into its' perspective as part of the life cycle. Having said all of that, I still had my bouts of weeping and moments of despair, but I began to perceive the possibility of brighter days ahead without plunging into the darkness of despair every time I think of my future without my father.

Although I was too busy to meet with Carolyn Young for the promised visit, she phoned several times and asked me to accompany her to church. Despite the softening of my heart and the promise to my father, I was not prepared to enjoy the vagaries of Christianity with its' unrealistic hope as evidenced by Carolyn. It's all a part of timing. And I didn't feel comfortable right yet to thrust myself full throttle into all that religious stuff. I successfully evaded her gentle invitations after the first handful, but, as fate would have it, I finally relinquished on her sixth request, due to the fact that this particular summons was performed in person the day prior when we bumped into one another face to face at the B&E Market on Main Street.

The church hour finally ended when the clock struck twelve. Once the Lord's Prayer was recited, we were all dismissed to go our own separate ways. Carolyn and I ventured past the pastor's receiving line after a few smiles and of course an invitation to come back next Sunday. I smiled sweetly, but gave no promises. I didn't know if I could sit through another hour and a half of his monotonous preaching. Pastor Davis certainly was a tireless voice for Christianity.

"Come on, I'll treat you to lunch," Carolyn prodded me.

"Oh, no. Lunch is on me," I insisted.

"Camille, I invited you first and it's not polite to argue with your elders," she said with her sweet, ingenuous smile. I accepted and decided to make the most of the opportunity by choosing to be gracious and grateful for her offers of friendship.

The short drive to the Coach House Cafe was filled with the inconsequential chit chat from two people comfortable with each other's presence. I found myself relaxing and enjoying her company. Once inside the cafe doors, the waitress dressed in blue jeans, boots and a plaid western shirt spoke up from behind the counter. "Seat yourself wherever your little heart desires." Carolyn and I advanced toward a table for four in the corner just below the window parallel to HWY 89.

The waitress approached our table and placed before each of us a glass of ice-water and thick menus with an eye-catching picture of Indian Head Mountain on the front. "Take your time," she said. "I'll be back to get your order." With that, she proceeded to greet four more people at the door and repeated the same instructions she gave us.

Carolyn and I ordered and smiled at one another as we waited for our meals. My BLT arrived and I ate with relish, not realizing until then just how hungry I was. We chatted between bites and even our silences had a comfortable feel that I found strangely enjoyable in my new found acceptance.

Finishing her Cobb salad, Carolyn patted her lips with the paper napkin, "So how did you like Brother Davis' sermon this morning?" she asked simply.

"Well, he's certainly not at a loss for words. But to tell you the truth, some of it didn't make much sense to me," I answered shrugging my shoulders.

"Oh really. What part was difficult for you to grasp?"

"You know the same old tendency to put Jesus in a category of limited use; Great Teacher, Prolific Prophet, Grand Story-Teller, Good Samaritan. Old beliefs highly over-rated. The fear of the Lord becomes transformational. Where is He during the difficult times in life?" I could feel my bitterness return with a sickening physicality and heard the ragged tone in my voice.

Her fragile face softened even more and she held my eyes in a direct gaze filled with kindness. "When you are in a storm that overwhelms you, don't run from the one who heals all wounds, run toward Him. Ask the Lord to show you who He really is," she said. "Believe, Belong, and be Blessed."

"I'm sorry Carolyn, but I don't see where that view point got me anywhere. That philosophy has worked well for you. But then you are the epitome of Christianity. Full of love and hope. I haven't experienced the blessings you refer to. I feel as though everyone I have ever loved has been taken away from me. Not literally, of course, I still have friends I care about, but my parents and even Eli." I swallowed hard to repress my tears, "I just don't see the point in turning to a God who does not listen to me or even notice me." The instant those words released from my mouth, I was reminded of the pep talk I gave the young widow at the cemetery. What sounded important and believable at the time has obviously faded from my convictions. I realize that I have reverted back to my usual way of being somewhat self-absorbed.

"Oh, my dear, sweet girl," she said with sadness ever present in her eyes. "It doesn't happen overnight. It takes time. You begin by believing God is real and not some archaic cultural artifact. God changes people. He changed me and changed my life," she explained, her face softening and a faint smile touching her lips.

"Whoa! Wait a minute here. What do you mean He changed you? What? From Nancy Nun to Mother Theresa?" I said in a mocking tone.

"You see what you want to see, my dear child. You hear the unsullied history that you want to hear. But looks can be deceiving. Maybe it's time I share something with you. I know only too well the anguish of a painful childhood. Sometimes the unthinkable can happen to the young and innocent. Sometimes children, through no fault of their own, are subjected to violence and shocking depravity that there are no words to describe it. I will spare you the ugly details, but believe me when I say, that for that very reason there is a hell here on earth.

Stunned by her revelation, I stumbled over my questions. "What? What are you talking about? Are you talking about yourself?"

"There were no service organizations such as Children's Protective Agency or Children's Home Society. However, there were neighbors with eyes and ears. A long story short, my sister and I were placed in a faith based orphanage for a while until we were adopted by a missionary and his wife. God does answer prayers Camille. If God can save me and my sister from the cruelties of a father who was nothing less than a monster, then God can mend your broken heart. My strong faith in the Lord has given me back my life. When I live by His commandments, I am rewarded. At times we all want to be in control, but the Almighty above us has more knowledge and wisdom than all of us put together. I chose to trust Him and let Him direct my life. I'm merely His child in motion. My salvation wasn't by chance, it was planned and crafted by His mighty hand. Within all of us is the ability to endure the ugliness in this world. You have to believe and trust in Him. Most important, you have to ask Him to help you," she explained.

I was speechless as my mind pondered over the implication of what she had endured as a child and matured into a woman of kindness with such a nurturing soul. I also wondered how on earth she could harbor this secret for so many years and never tell anyone. "I don't know what to say. I had no idea that you had such unspeakable hardships." I shook my head in confusion.

Carolyn laughed gently and I was touched by the way her smile reached into her eyes. "Don't put me on a pedestal Camille. None of us can live up to God's perfection. I didn't become who I am today without some suffering. Fear was my constant companion for many years. But fear is a common human emotion and we all have it at some time in our lives. I feared the monsters under my bed and the boogeyman in the bushes. Afraid that my father would get out of jail and make good on his threats to kill both my sister and I for telling the truth about his abusive behavior. Thankfully, God's plan for us is always bigger than what our fears dictate to us. So don't let your fears imprison you Camille. His perfect love will drive out your fear of loss and your fear of allowing yourself to love someone as much as you loved Eli, your mother and father. Choose to focus on life and on joy and gratitude, ask for His grace," she smiled at me again and I felt touched by the power of her words. Her authenticity and kindness made an impact on me that the morning's sermon had failed to do.

Dropping my head and looking down into my lap at my twisting fingers, I whispered, "I'll try Carolyn. That's all I can promise right now. I will try."

"Good enough," she said. A smile spread across her face that warmed my heart.

What an amazing woman. I am humbled and inspired by her perspective on life. I reflected on the history she had divulged in such a gentle and kindly way. I was touched by her inner strength, hidden under her benevolent exterior and I marveled in the knowledge I was learning from her. One blessing in my life that I readily admit to. If I try to be just half the woman she is then I know I can survive the ugliness and cruelties so prevalent in this world.

Tonight will be the first time in a very long time that I will put prayer to good use.

Summer winded its' way through the remainder of July and into August, the days long and hot and the evenings cool and breezy with mountain air. Every day was filled with tasks and I fell into bed every night, exhausted with a list of the next day's chores running through my head. I had been so busy that the days had passed in a blur and I had the sudden realization that I had not thought on my father's last words in several weeks. A passing thought here and there, but it didn't disrupt my sleep at night as it had before. Maybe the cemetery secrets didn't hold as significant importance as it once did. I knew I needed answers, but I felt a sense of peace and renewing confidence that I would weather the emotional storms of my grieving with grace and that the secrets would unfold before me as I moved forward.

CHAPTER
9

T he summer heat can reach triple digits in Indian Valley, and after sunset, the temperature could plummet 40 degrees or more, the rapid cooling due to the high mountain altitude and a welcome relief from the day's warmth. This made mornings a pleasantly cool time, with the heat returning with a blistering vengeance just before noon. Late August brought the careless winds that would fan forest fires, bringing the scent of smoke in its wake and the heat of the late afternoons could wilt the sturdiest of mountain dwellers. The evenings brought cooler, refreshing air and a reminder of the ending of summer.

I inhaled the clean air of dawn wafting through the open window as I ground some BRCC Freedom Fuel beans for my morning cup of motivation. I stepped out onto the deck with my first cup of coffee of the day. Seated in my favorite chair and savoring the fragrant coffee and the fresh morning air, I knew the day would be hot and I wanted to enjoy these first few moments of the quiet. The birds chirped in the tree below me and I heard the muted rustle of the creek behind the trees. Indian Head rested quietly to the north, his nightly watch over for the day. I heard the backhoe rumble to life and I knew that Brian had started a new task in one of the far corners of the cemetery. I had come to appreciate these quiet moments before the day unfolded with its' various tasks and I closed my eyes to the sun warming my face and just listened to the sounds of the cemetery around me. Although it was late summer, autumn was fast approaching and I had many projects that needed to be completed before the cold of winter.

Hearing the crunch of tires on gravel, I opened my eyes to see a late model Jeep Wrangler park in one of the gravel roads that crossed through the cemetery. After a moment, a tall man swung out of the driver's seat and began to pick his way through the rows of monuments and headstones. He held a cell phone in one hand and consulted it several times. Inspecting each headstone, he made his way through the section, occasionally holding up his phone and sometimes actually shaking the device. Watching his movement, I admired his lithe form and athletic build. As I thoughtfully sipped my coffee enjoying the crisp morning air, planning for the day, I occasionally checked on the stranger wandering through the cemetery sections. I wondered where Little Jimmy was. He generally appeared shortly after a visitor, offering his services as a guide or general answer man, but he was nowhere in sight this morning. The man walked along a row and then turned and retraced his steps, stopping at each headstone again. Squatting by one of the older monuments, he held his phone up over his head and waved it back and forth for a moment. "What on earth?" I asked out loud. Regretfully, I placed my cup on the rail and determined that I would offer my assistance.

Making my way down the slope and along the gravel path, I wondered who or what he was seeking. A genealogist, perhaps? Someone seeking a long lost relative? Maybe one of those creative types who occasionally stop by to obtain rubbings from headstones? As I neared the man, he straightened and looked my way giving a friendly wave. Coming closer, I was suddenly struck with his good looks, his fair hair a little wild in the morning breeze and his eyes a deep, emerald green, so clear that you could almost see through them. Dressed in jeans and a t-shirt with 'The Wake Imperial Stout' emblazoned on the front and wearing running shoes, he smiled and his eyes crinkled at the corners as he turned toward me.

"Good morning," I said. "I noticed your phone seems to be giving you a little trouble? Cell coverage in this area is sketchy and your mobile data probably won't work quite as well. My name is Camille and I am an interim caretaker here," I said, belatedly realizing at this close proximity to him, how very handsome he was.

Peering at his phone, he shrugged and slid it into his pocket. "Oh well," he said. "It was a long shot, anyway."

"Can I help you find something or someone?" I asked. "Nice shirt, by the way. Very appropriate for hunting through a cemetery."

He pulled his shirt away from his body, releasing a faint spicy woodsy scent, peering at the lettering. "Oh, huh," he said. "That was totally unintentional. Most of my t-shirts are freebies from local breweries. But you're right, it is completely appropriate for my mission." He smiled and shook his head.

Without clarifying his mission, he gestured toward the mountain and said, "You have some beautiful scenery here in your little town. Is there anything I should take in while I'm here? I am interested in the history of this area."

"Finding myself in the presence of such an attractive man who seemed to be unaware of his good looks, I was a little abashed at my appearance; fat baby boots with frayed jean shorts and a red tank top. I was fleetingly grateful I had run a brush through my tangled curls and pulled my hair into a messy bun before shrugging on one of my dad's old flannel work shirts in order to ward off the morning chill. Have I been away from the city so long that I cannot remember how to dress appropriately? I began to chatter to cover up my embarrassment. "That mountain to the north behind us is called Indian Head."

"Really! Catchy name. I'm sure there's a good story behind that name?" He raised his eyebrows as he looked down at me with his intense green eyes.

He looked interestedly at me which made me even more self-conscious, but I continued despite my insecurities. "The mythology of the local native people, the Maidu, tells the story of the first chief and how he led and cared for his tribe. He raised them and taught them the wise ways of the ancient elders. It is said there are a lot of similarities between these teachings and the Ten Commandments. The legend has it that when he approached the age beyond elder hood, he climbed the mountain, never to return. And the mountain took on his profile as a gift from the Great Spirit to his people. The story goes that he gazes up into the heavens during the day, but at night, he turns his eyes on the people down here in the valley and protects us from harm. A guardian angel archetype and most Indian mythology is found in storytelling. There is actually no written truth," I ended lamely and somewhat pedantically. As I spoke, I could hear my father's voice in my own words and I felt comforted in the thread that connected us still and I felt confident in my sharing.

"Hey, that is a great story," he said. "And I'd never underestimate the value of the Ten Commandments. They make a lot of sense."

I let a short laugh escape. "You sound like my father. He depended on God to answer many of life's questions."

Raising his eyebrows again, he asked "Is that a good thing or should I be concerned?"

"It's a compliment, I can assure you." I quickly changed the subject. I did not want to get involved in a spiritual conversation of any sort, since I was still testing the waters of my own faith. "So what can I do to help you? Are you looking for anyone or anything in particular? I have cemetery records dating back to the dark ages that might be helpful," I said, with a chuckle.

"That far back, huh?"

I looked at him with a smile. "Just a little humor."

We looked at each other for a moment and I felt my anxiety begin to arise. Scuffing my boot in the gravel, I waited for him to speak.

"Oh no, I don't want to bother you. I'm just looking around. My name is Kendall, by the way. Kendall Danielson." He stuck his hand out in greeting.

I grasped his hand which made me feel tingly all over. I quickly tugged my hand back after our handshake, hoping he didn't feel me quiver or see through my insecurities, but I could still feel the crackle of energy between us.

"I am in town for a few weeks and am just wandering around seeing the sights. My folks used to vacation at Lake Almanor years ago and had lots of stories about this area. This valley is beautiful; the scenery is just spectacular and folks are really nice here. So I am exploring the area for myself and I am really liking what I see," he said as he stared straight at me.

I felt my cheeks heating in response to the intensity of his gaze.

"And, I like to read old tombstones," he added. "There is always so much history to consider. Every cemetery is like a reflection of the local people and traditions. It's just interesting to me."

"Really," I said, but not quite convinced the story ended there. Why was he really here? A great looking guy, obviously not from this area, wearing a t-shirt that proclaims his love for beer and he enjoys prowling around cemeteries for historical interest. I felt a small prickle of suspicion. Something didn't quite add up to me. My eyes automatically squinted and the left side of my mouth pressed toward my ear. I quickly tried to unfold my frown.

Glancing at me, he shifted a little, turning his gaze over the rows of headstones. "Sorry," he said. "That must sound a little random." He shrugged.

I decided to ignore my suspicions. "Not really," I replied. "It is entertaining in a Twilight sort of way," referring to the book and movie series of a high school girl and her vampire consort. That made me laugh to myself, comparing his historical interest in cemeteries to the fatuous antics of immature vampire lovers. "But if you want to see more, there are a couple of other burial grounds in the valley that aren't in any directory or map."

"Oh that's great"' he enthused. "Could you give me directions to them? Or even better, maybe even show me?" His eyes widened slightly as he seemed to realize what he had said. "Oh that was awkward. I'm sure you're busy and I don't mean to treat you like a tour guide. Sorry about that!" He paused as if choosing his words carefully. "But, I'll buy you lunch and a beer. Or maybe multiple lunches and many beers if it takes us a while." He shrugged and smiled eagerly, as if he was hopeful that I would agree.

I didn't immediately answer. I was surprised at myself for actually considering his proposal. "Yeah, I guess I could find time to show you some of the local color."

"Ah good then," he said, "Thanks!" He rummaged in his back pocket for his phone and gave me his number. "Text me when you are free." He grinned at me, "Maybe this afternoon?"

Astonished, I really didn't know what to say, so I quickly turned my attention to my phone. Hesitating a moment, I entered his name as Kendall D and saved it. Then I reconsidered; maybe he was a rapist. Or a serial killer. Or quite possibly a white slaver who was looking for a Native American to merchandise as exotic to his foreign clients. My conscious mind wondered if I was crazy and/or foolish for agreeing to show him around Indian Valley. Yet, subconsciously, I felt comfortable with him, as though I had known him before. A feeling of familiarity that was reassuring. I shook my head to dispel the cloudbank of negative and miserable thoughts, determined to be open minded.

"And don't worry, I'm not a creepster," he continued, almost as if he had read my thoughts. He extracted a rumpled business card from his wallet and gave it to me. "You can call my office or whatever you need to do to check me out. You can never be too cautious, you know." He shrugged again and smiled.

Uncharacteristically throwing caution to the wind, I made my decision. "Well, how about tomorrow morning?" I asked him. "I can clear up my morning and show you at least one of the cemeteries."

"That sounds good to me," he said. "I'll meet you here in the morning. Eight or nine? What works best for you?"

"Let's meet up at eight," I returned. "It can get pretty hot later in the day."

"Great. Eight it is, then. And thank you. I'll just wander around here for a while if that's alright."

"Sure. Make yourself at home and there's always someone around if you have any questions," I told him.

We looked into each other's eyes for an electric moment, then he shrugged and smiled, made his way back through the headstones and followed the gravel path to the far fence. His athletic body and confidant, lithe movement made his progress graceful.

I felt the morning breeze on my face and I closed my eyes, the warmth of the sun on my eyelids. Oddly enough, though we had just met, I felt safe in his presence. I had become accustomed to the wild storms of my emotions and the constant struggle for control of them and to feel safe with someone was a somewhat unfamiliar sensation. The shrieks of blue jays began overhead and I opened my eyes to the realization that I had felt safe with my father, too. That was the familiar feeling I had experienced. Shaking my head, I hoped I was not losing my sense of self preservation and personal safety and I decided that I would pack my can of mace with me in the morning just in case his good looks had gotten in the way of my better judgement.

It was a long and busy day, answering questions for Brian, making arrangements for a monument replacement, making a run to the landfill and another one to the hardware store and mowing the grass around the house. I was physically exhausted but still alert. Later that evening after a solitary dinner of a banana and a glass of wine, as dusk deepened and cast long shadows over the cemetery I pulled out my laptop and fished the crumpled business card from deep in my pocket. It was time to verify my possible serial killer and find out who he really was and what he was doing here in California.

KENDALL J. DANIELSON, Associate, Georgetown, Maryland. Specializing in Real Estate, Water, Construction, Eminent Domain and Civil Litigation. ADVICE. DOCUMENTS. PREPARATION. LITIGATION. Law Firm of the Year: 2013 and 2015. Honored by Best Lawyers in America for Real Estate in 2014. Recognized by Super Lawyers of the New York Times.

I trawled through the website. Kendall appeared to be part of a small law firm, comprised of several attorneys, all of whom specialized in real estate in some way. Eminent domain, zoning and land use, construction and preservation. His was part of a highly specialized law firm. I clicked on his Biography and was relieved to see his photo matched the man I met this morning. His hair was neatly combed and he looked quite professional in a suit and tie, a much different appearance from the man in the cemetery earlier. His education followed by his professional accomplishments made me realize he was a hard-working and dedicated attorney. Or it was possible he inherited his business from wealthy and privileged parents, I thought cynically. What brings him to a small town in the Sierra Nevada Mountains, just to look through cemeteries? Surely there were cemeteries closer to Maryland. Unless his pilgrimage here was of a personal nature.

My busy day and my questions about him were tiring me, and I yawned as I closed my computer. Shuffling off to my bedroom, I remembered to pull my can of mace from the basket on the kitchen counter and tucked it in my backpack before I fell into my bed. I rolled my head back on my pillow, but my thoughts continued to twist and turn in my head. Realizing this nonsense could go on all night, I jumped out of bed and retrieved two Aleve tablets out of the medicine chest in the bathroom. I swallowed them with a few sips of water, knowing in less than fifteen minutes they would relax my tight muscles and dull the slight ache in my back. I quickly flopped back into bed. A short time later, after my meds began to ease my pain and quiet my mind, I finally drifted off to sleep.

CHAPTER 10

I was up early, before the sun touched the nose on the old Indian with her first golden finger, feeling refreshed and looking forward to the day. I was relieved that I had made the choice to have a field trip this morning. I was looking forward to a morning free of insurance considerations, plot payments and burial dates. As much as I wanted to honor my father, the day to day administration of a cemetery was an unaccustomed labor for me and I welcomed the break. Spending part of the day away from my childhood home and my memories was appealing to me.

I scrambled some eggs while the coffee brewed, filling the air with that rich tantalizing aroma peculiar to fresh coffee beans. This morning it was Spencer Smooth medium roast. I toasted an English muffin for a breakfast sandwich, laying a slice of Tillamook cheese over the hot eggs. I ate standing at the sink. Bad habit from my student days. I could almost hear my father's voice admonishing me. "Sit down Camille and take the time to appreciate your food or you'll get a belly ache." It is hard to do that with just one person, I told myself and besides, who needs extra dishes to wash?

I quickly tidied the kitchen and put the still warm pan in the sink before stepping out to the porch to savor my last cup of coffee. I leaned against the railing and stared out over the stillness and quiet of the early morning. A slight mist arose from the creek and drifted over the edges of the grass. The sun began to warm the grass, the glistening beads of dew that had settled during the night beginning to disappear. I breathed in the cool mountain air, the scent of the pine trees strong in my nostrils as I watched a gray squirrel scamper over the grass. The headstones and statues stood above the grass in mute testimony of a life well lived or unfulfilled hopes or a child departed too soon. My mind drifted over the surface of the stones, wondering about those resting beneath and those left behind.

The peace and quiet of the morning coupled with the lovely view, overseen by Indian Head to the north made me long for my father's presence. I missed his strength and kindness and that left a gaping space I couldn't even define, only experience. Taking another sip of coffee, I recalled the time of the past when there were three of us standing on this porch and I could feel the tightness in my chest at the memory. Simpler times, when all I needed to worry about was the availability of cookies with lunch, or if I would be allowed to bike along Wolf Creek with Eli to fish. Our treasure hunts for quartz crystals or the perfect pollywog meant hours of uninterrupted joy for two small town kids. Any new adventure or discovery, with the innocence and enthusiasm of unspoiled young-sters' led to more adventures and discoveries. Memories flooded through me like a crashing wave as a tear dropped onto my chest. I closed my eyes to the warming sun and again thought of my deter-mination to live life fully and wondered how I would ever begin to make that happen. As my spasm of grief subsided, I opened my eyes again and looking at the cemetery, I whispered to myself, "Camille, people are dying to get into here, so lighten up and don't be in such a rush to join them. You are going to have a lovely day and that is all there is to it!" Having given myself that pep talk, I finished my last sips of coffee.

I heard the pop of gravel under automobile tires as it came up over the hill and into the yard. Stopping below the house, the jeep shut off and I could hear the engine ticking under the hood. After a moment, Kendall stepped out, and stretching in the morning sunshine, arms raised over his head, he looked over the cemetery. He was wearing jeans and hikers, with a brown hooded sweatshirt that proclaimed 'Guinness. It's Good For You.' He stood on his toes, stretching his long legs, arms raised over his head. Completing his stretches, he turned my way.

Smiling up at me, he said, "There you are, good morning! Are you ready for this? I hope I am not taking you away from anything that was fun and exciting and should make me jealous? I do appreciate your guide service."

"Oh hey," I said, trying to act as nonchalant as possible but feeling the sudden thump of excitement in my heart. "Yeah, I am. Let me get my boots and I'll be right down. And no, there is nothing happening today that won't happen tomorrow. A cemetery is kind of like a big garden. There is always something else to do!"

"You sure your family won't mind?" he asked. "Like your husband or kids or anything?"

Ah, he was seeking information! I didn't enlighten him to the fact that I was an adult orphan and had no one to wait for me to come home. Brian would probably wonder in a few days where I was, Little Jimmy maybe somewhat sooner. The thought depressed me slightly. "Be just a minute," I answered and then ducked back into the kitchen.

I pulled on my boots and laced them tightly. I put a couple bottles of water into my backpack and tucked my phone in the front pocket. I added my wallet and a couple of granola bars. Thinking again, I pulled my phone back out and quickly texted Brian, telling him where I was headed and that I would be with a new friend. Grimly, I debated stepping out to get the car's license, but shook my head at my cynicism and sent the text. Brian was grudgingly learning technology and he complained about texting because he always had to put on his reading glasses to see them, but at least I knew he would get it and eventually read it. The thought of Brian triggered another surge of sadness, feeling parentless yet still surrounded by friends and long time, small town acquaintances. It was an emotion that opened a whole new window of feeling for me and I shook my head to clear it. Then, at the last minute, I removed the can of mace from my backpack and slid it into the front pocket of my shorts.

I clattered down the stairs, two at a time as usual, and found Kendall leaning patiently on the jeep. He smiled at my dance down the stairs and said, "Are you anxious to get started?"

I shrugged my shoulders. "Nah, just habit," I said. I shook my head and continued toward the jeep. "It will be about a 20 minute drive through Greenville and around the north side of the valley," I added. Climbing into Kendall's jeep, I appreciated that it was clean inside and comfortable. He rummaged in a brown leather satchel filled with maps, papers, charging cords, and other clutter and pulled out a gps and tossed the bag into the rear seat. As he turned back to buckle his seatbelt, I detected the spicy woodsy scent that was particular to him and immediately chastised myself for noticing that small detail. "Get a grip, Camille. This isn't high school prom night," I firmly admonished myself.

He held the GPS in his hand and said, "Let me introduce you to Ramona. I appreciate your help; I am not sure she knows how to find all cemeteries."

I watched as he skillfully entered the local towns, Greenville, Taylorsville and Crescent Mills. "Now Ramona may try to argue with me occasionally, but she is a good gal and we've shared some great adventures together."

I looked at him doubtfully, but he was serious, frowning slightly as he finished updating Ramona and then he set her gently in the console. "Alrighty, then."

He caught my look and with a slight smile, shrugged and said, "My mom named her."

I pinched my face into an understanding grin. "Mom's. Gotta love em," I muttered.

He smiled wide at me which made me wonder what he was thinking. I felt my heart flutter as his eyes turned away from me.

We crunched down the road and I was relieved to see Brian at the main gate. Impulsively I rolled down my window and waved at him. He peered at me over his reading glasses, phone clutched in his hand. Hopefully reading my text and noting the make, model and license number of the car as well as an accurate description of Kendall himself. A lot to ask, I knew, but at least one person would see me before I departed. He raised his hand in a brief wave and continued to stare as we swept out onto the highway and turned toward Greenville.

"Was that a friend? Or family?" Kendall inquired.

"Ah, still trying to dig my brain for more personal information," I thought to myself which felt flattering. I paused for another few seconds, unsure of how much I should reveal about myself. "Oh that's Brian. He is one of the caretakers here and kind of rides herd on me." I boldly lied with no regrets, feeling the can of mace in my pocket pressing against my thigh. "He's been working this cemetery for several decades and knows just about all there is to know. At least for that time period. If you have any questions, I'm sure he will be a great resource."

"Good to know," Kendall said happily.

We drove over the little bridge spanning Wolf Creek and followed Highway 89 slowly through Greenville, which took about one minute. We passed the Evergreen Market, the high school, a few homes and our hardware store, Better-Deal-Exchange, a couple of gas stations and two beauty salons. There were no traffic lights to stop us as I directed Kendall to turn right at Main Street. We passed through the outskirts of town and began threading around the north side of the valley.

"Lots of older homes and historic buildings in this town," Kendall observed as he drove carefully through town.

I nodded my head in agreement, waving toward the old elementary school, which is now the Senior Community Center. "My parents actually attended grammar school in that building," I commented which immediately turned his head in that direction.

"If only the walls could talk," he said, arching his head back my way. "A history lesson like none other," he added.

I met his stare and grinned. "Unlimited stories are more fascinating than any fiction you could find in a book I'm sure," I agreed.

"Can't argue that point," he said with a wide grin and a shake of his head. His attention went back to his driving and my eyes took in the scenery which never grew old or boring.

The road clung to the north side of the valley, winding east and snaking along the base of Indian Head with the fields and sloughs stretching out to the south of the road. Cattle dotted the pastures and most of the grass was the parched yellow and browns of late summer. We passed a hayfield with rows of baled hay, ready for pick up when the day warmed and the hay dried. Rolling down my window I inhaled deeply. "Can't get enough of this mountain air," I remarked; the scents and fragrance of my home valley were unique. A combination of grass, dust, livestock and the sharp odor of crushed weeds filtered by clear mountain air.

"Won't argue that point. I'd take this over the stink of a big city any day of the week," he said.

I turned my head to face him just long enough to give him a faint smile. For a brief instant, our eyes met and I realized, I really liked this guy. I liked everything about him; his generous smile and his hot looks, his careful and confident driving, but most of all, his easy conversation. The sense of ease was that of being in the company of an old friend.

I turned my eyes back to my open window and watched as we passed the old Indian mission on the left and continued on for a few more miles. Agriculture and timber were more than just a career in this valley. They were a way of life for most families, a long honored tradition. Love of the land and good stewardship were part of the people here. Whether it was a selective logging project and replanting in the surrounding mountains or the sowing of a new hayfield, people held the land in high regard and considered it a matter of personal integrity to care for their property. I was beginning to fall in love again with my home valley and I was a little disturbed by the thought. Would I be able to make a decent living here? Certainly, I could make a life here, but would I be able to eat or pay my bills once my inheritance ran dry? I would try. I was positive about that.

A few miles down the road, I realized my thoughts had taken me far away and I had been silently ignoring Kendall all this time. But it seemed that he had not noticed my mental wanderings and he drove with an easy skill and grace, smoothly taking the twists and turns of the road with little braking. I noticed his hands were strong, with long fingers and neatly clipped nails. He turned his head to eye the fields and then up at the mountain and back to the road. He appeared to be under the same Indian Valley spell as I was, made silent by the beauty and the pace of life, set in place by the cycles of nature, not those of man. I admired his profile and his tousled sandy hair, belatedly noticing the reddish highlights in the curls. He caught my eye and gave me a quick grin.

"Turn left into here," I told him. The narrow dirt track that led to the somewhat irregularly shaped parking area was almost hidden by a pine tree and large clumps of manzanita bushes. The jeep bumped over the rough patches and Kendall parked in the dappled shade of a stand of pines.

The wire fencing straggled around the cemetery, drooping in between posts and the gate creaked in protest when I pushed it open. "This is one of the original cemeteries of the valley. In fact one of the latest graves here is dated 1928," I told him, feeling somewhat proud of myself for remembering that tidbit of information. I only knew that because Eli and I had played the date game here one time when we were on an exploratory jaunt. The one who found the oldest grave marker would be rewarded with a seven day supply of Bazooka Bubble gum. I felt myself begin to smile at the memory.

"The voice of history is calling my name," Kendall's' voice broke into my reverie.

Many of the stones were embellished with delicate patterns of lichen. Some of the wooden crosses were tilted and pine needles carpeted the entire space. The needles crunched softly under our feet and released the salty odor of pine. It was a quiet and peaceful place, gathering its neglect around it like a well-worn cloak of dignity. A blue jay called out his alarm at our presence and a gray squirrel chattered and scolded us as he ran up and down an oak tree by the gate. There were two chipmunks deeper in the forest, come out to socialize that paid us no mind.

I stood by the gate, gesturing for Kendall to enter and he silently passed through and immediately began walking the outer perimeter of the cemetery. He then paced slowly from stone to stone, peering closely at the names and dates. I watched as he stooped to brush pine needles from a stone set flat on a raised bed of cement. He was intent to find something and referred to his phone, frowning a little and I could see his lips moving.

"Are you looking for a family or a name in particular?" I called out to him. "This is the original cemetery for Indian Valley and is the oldest local burying ground. Some of the families have died out and others have moved away. I don't think there are any living family members around here anymore, but I'm not really sure. Most of the stones are local granite. This cemetery has records somewhere, or maybe one of the town old timers can remember something, but you'd have to hunt it down. Or you can check the Greenville Library. They have a little local history section," I explained.

He didn't answer. He just gave me a smile that appeared to be appreciative and then stooped down and took a photo of a stone.

"There are no Indians in this cemetery, if you are looking into the history of Native Americans. They have their own resting place at the Indian Mission and some are buried in family plots around the valley. But none are here."

Turning his head toward me, he caught my eyes. "Amazing, isn't it? If only these stones could talk. I would sit here for hours listening to history unfold," he offered, then turned back to continue whatever it was he was doing. Using his boot, he cleared an area under one of the old lilac bushes and bent over to look closer, brushing away the dead leaves. Consulting his phone, he shook his head. "Funny how each generation followed with the same traditional names. The Mildred's and Myrtle's and Virgil's and William's in the early nineteen hundred's and the Kathy's, Susan's and the Danny's and Jimmy's in the mid nineteen hundreds. Creatures of habit we are," he added.

"Yeah, can't argue that point," I agreed. "If you are interested," I went on to say. "I can give you a little history about some of the early white inhabitants of the valley."

"Oh yeah, that would be awesome!" he enthused.

"Well, one of the earliest settlers in this area was a man from Pennsylvania by the name of Jobe Taylor. He came here in 1851 looking for Gold Lake," I continued. "When he arrived, there were so many Maidu living here, he decided to name this area Indian Valley. He posted a notice claiming much of the acreage for himself and there is a town across the valley he named Taylorsville, after himself, of course. He was quite enterprising. He grew wheat and barley crops and raised vegetables. He built the first barn in the valley, opened a store in Taylorsville which he also used as a hotel for travelers. He built a saw mill and harvested timber. He was the first white pioneer here."

There was no response from Kendall other than a quick thumbs up telling me he had taken in all in with appreciation.

"Guinness is good for you," I said quietly with a mental eye roll.

Continuing to look at the aged stones and graves, he moved with an easy grace and his athleticism was apparent as he squatted by the low markers, stood again and then moved on. The moments passed as I watched him moving to the far reaches of the sagging fence where he again stooped to brush a marker clean. He shook his head and stood with his phone in hand surveying the entire cemetery.

"So, the wooden crosses that have no name, who do they belong to?" he inquired. "There doesn't seem to be any names or dates."

"Not sure really," I told him. "These are all so old, no telling what their rhyme or reason for that was," I admitted. "What exactly are you looking to find?" I boldly asked again.

He wrinkled his brow, pursed his lips and shook his head. His hair lifted in the slight morning breeze giving him the look of a disappointed little boy with mussed hair. "Anything and everything about the history of this valley," he said, which still didn't answer my question.

However, that remark made me smile inwardly and I hoped that despite his odd silence here, his search, whatever it was for, would be successful. His vague response merely fed the intensity of my interest in his real reasons for coming here. I began to wonder what exactly he was hunting. His interest in history aside, he seemed to be searching for something in particular, but was loathe to share it.

He made his way back to the gate and as he passed, he grinned at me his eyes crinkling and said, "Yes, Guinness is good for you."

So he had been listening. Somewhat abashed, I pulled the gate closed, wincing at the scream of protest from the aged hinges. The squirrel on the oak tree shrilled a warning about returning to his territory.

Climbing back into the jeep, turning to me with another grin with his green eyes bright and rounded, he asked, "Is Jobe Taylor's hotel still open? Think I can get a room there?" he asked in a humorous tone.

I smiled and then let out a throaty giggle. "Oh no. It closed years ago." I stared at him, not quite sure if he was teasing me.

He gave me a goofy grin as he deciphered my expression. "Just kidding," he said and laughed out loud as he fastened his seat belt firmly.

At his nod, I said, "Good. Then I won't have to repeat that history lesson." As I directed him back onto the two lane road that skirted the valley, Ramona instructed us to turn left and proceed for 12 miles and we made our way south to Genesse. He gently tapped at Ramona a couple of times and turned her off.

We chatted companionably about history and college sports as we proceeded. We passed a few vehicles, dusty pickup trucks or 4 wheel drives and maybe a car or two.

"What's rush hour like here?" Kendall asked with a grin. "I bet you get backed up for hours, huh?"

"Right," I agreed with my brows pinched. "But that's only if you get caught behind a tractor or a herd of cows."

He smiled at me and I found myself once again with a pounding heart filled with admiration for his attractiveness.

We swept around the last curve and as we thumped over the bridge and followed the two lane into Taylorsville, we passed a light brown pickup with a blonde woman behind the wheel. I waved and she smiled and honked. "That's Krisi Gorbet. She lives in the middle of the valley in a three story house with a view to die for. She lost her husband recently and whenever she has errands, she drives his pickup. I think it makes her feel close to him again. It was a second marriage for both of them and they treasured each other."

"Do you know everyone around here?" he asked. "I know the population of the valley couldn't be that high, but you have waved at every person we've passed so far."

"Oh, I am sure there are some city slickers who are new to the area that I don't know. Or maybe some tourists. But yeah, I do know a lot of folks here. It can't be helped in a valley with three small towns crammed within that tiny perimeter and only one high school," I explained, keeping my eyes on his perfect facial profile.

"Makes sense," he muttered.

It was hard to tell, but he seemed to be satisfied with my answer. At least he didn't question me further on the matter.

Entering Taylorsville, we turned left and traveled up a much narrower two lane road toward Genesse Valley and the next cemetery. The road twisted and turned, shaded by the deep green of the tall trees. Reaching the small parking area and entering the creaky gate, it became a repeat of the first visit. Kendall searched each and every headstone, quietly checking his phone without speaking and I realized it must have stored information that he was consulting. I had learned my lesson, though, and I waited by the gate, sitting on a large rock and enjoying the peace and the warming of the day. My curiosity returned and I wondered idly what on earth he was seeking? Would he eventually share his mission with me? Despite the mystery, I was beginning to enjoy his company. I traced the outline of the can of mace against my thigh and planned the fastest way to remove it without spraying myself. As the morning passed, he continued his thorough search and I was glad I had taken the time to have that scrambled egg muffin earlier.

He interrupted my reverie by coming through the gate and pulling it closed behind him, the hinges shrieking in protest. His green eyes sought mine and I felt a little flutter in my stomach. I touched the can of mace to ground myself and hopping off of the rock, I asked, "A lovely place, isn't it? Did you find anything of interest?"

He shrugged and pulled off his sweatshirt and I again caught the spicy woodsy scent that had become familiar to me, but he didn't answer immediately. He popped the back hatch with the key, stowed his sweatshirt and pulled out a small ice chest. "Hungry?" he asked. "I have some subs and other stuff."

I was hungry, but I was a little annoyed that once again he hadn't answered my question. Was it because it was a private matter? Too private to share with a stranger? Or was he just a history buff seeking new names, dates and experiences. A real mystery man. Great, just what I don't need at this time of my life, I sternly reminded myself. Good thing this was a one time, morning jaunt. Green eyes and athletic body aside, I had no business indulging in an attraction for a man with long legs and wavy hair that refused to stay in place; an easy grin and a dry sense of humor with a sense of strength and calm about him. Mentally groaning, I sat down on the cemetery steps, anxious to eat lunch and suppress my feelings about this good looking man. Trading one appetite for another; there was a psychological term for that, but I couldn't recall it just now.

Kendall unwrapped a couple of turkey sub sandwiches and handed me one. Rummaging in the ice chest, he brought out a bag of chips and another one of apple slices.

"Want a beer?" he queried. "I have a couple of Sierra Nevada pale ales in here and they are cold."

Reluctantly, I accepted, envisioning this as the first step of my demise and eventual death at his hands, but the cold beer tasted good in the warm sunshine. Washing down the sandwich and crunching a few chips, we ate in silence appreciating the quiet warmth of a late summer morning. And I may as well die on a full stomach as on an empty one, right?

He ate quickly and neatly, occasionally licking mayonnaise from his long fingers as it squeezed from the end of his sandwich. He balled up the wrapper, tossing it into the ice chest and took a long sip of his beer.

"Ahhhh," he said. "There is nothing like a cold beer on a hot day," he proclaimed.

Nodding, I focused on my sandwich, trying to hold it together and keep the chips I had added under the bread inside. I wondered yet again, what he was seeking and how I would extract that information from him.

Hey," Kendall said. "I know we just met yesterday and I am not trying to be awkward or anything, but I hope we can be friends. I'm sure you had reservations about coming with me today to show me these cemeteries, but I'm glad you did. I enjoy your company. You are easy to be around. I'm staying up at Lake Almanor for the next several weeks, so I hope we can catch up again when it fits your schedule to see any more cemeteries Ramona and I may not be able to find on our own. And I intend to do a lot more exploring while I am here."

I tilted my head back a little, trying to keep the bite of sandwich in my mouth as I finished. Swallowing, I took a sip of beer and nodded. "Yeah, I can do that", I replied. "You seem like you are looking for something specific and can't find it. Or maybe you are looking for something specific and you don't know how to look for it? That just made me wonder a little bit." An uncomfortable silence filled the air. I felt uncertainty rise inside my chest and wondered briefly if I had been too nosey and had finally gone too far with my repetitive question.

He turned his head away from me and stared out over the field in front of the cemetery gates and nodded slowly. "Camille, it's complicated," he enlightened me with his tone tinged in a hint of sadness.

"That's okay. Maybe another time, but you'll find I am a good listener," I said, letting the subject go. At least I was pleased to see that I had pried the mystery door open just enough to feel confident to bring up the subject again sometime when the timing was perfect.

"Thanks." He appeared to be thinking and I gave him the quiet time he seemed to need.

I pulled more apple slices out of the ice chest then retrieved my backpack from the jeep and opened a bottle of water. The cold beer had tasted good, but 1:30 in the afternoon was a little early for me, especially since I had more work to do when I returned home. I finished drinking the water and poured the last bit of it over my face to cool me. The sun was high overhead and burning brightly and warmly on us.

Kendall brushed off his hands and stood up, stretching his long arms over his head and raising up on the balls of his feet. Then he swung over and touched the ground in a smooth motion. He gathered up the remains of our lunch and packed away the ice chest, stowing it in the back of the jeep again.

"Well, I guess I had better get back," I said. I've got some chores that need to get done. You can call or text me if you have any more questions."

A warm smile crossed his face which created a little shiver inside of me. "Could we meet again when you have the time?" he asked. There was a nervousness in his voice as if worried I would say no.

I was hoping he would ask, but I didn't want to appear too anxious. With my lips pressed tight, I paused for a few seconds and let my eyes dance around before I answered him. "Oh, I think I could find the time. There are two other cemeteries in the valley that might be of interest to you and several private family cemeteries I'm sure I could get permission to visit. Unfortunately, I'm sort of tied up for the next few days," I said. "Perhaps I can help you out after that."

He smiled. "Sounds good to me," he enthused. "I'll gladly take any time you have so just text me when you are free." He flashed a wider beaming smile at me which again spooked the butterflies in my stomach.

I gave him one of my casual grins, all the while trying hard to hide my excitement over the two of us getting together again.

The ride back to my home was quiet, but comfortable. We chatted idly about California history and the native people, the gold rush and agriculture.

"Thank you for your help today, Camille," he said as he pulled up the gravel road to my home and parked the car. "And if it is ok, I'd like to go through this cemetery once again, if you don't mind."

Nodding in agreement, I replied, "Of course, take as much time as you need." I unlatched my seat belt and opened the door. Turning back to him, I added, "I have some projects to do, but if you have any questions, you can come find me or Brian for help."

"Thanks again for everything," he said, his voice was gentle.

"My pleasure." I smiled at him as I jumped out of the jeep.

He exited the car and stood by it while I took the stairs two at a time. I could feel his eyes on me as I neared the top. I turned and saw that he was still gazing up at me. I gave him a wave and entered the kitchen. Feeling a ripple of relief at returning home alive and unravished, I pulled the can of mace out of my pocket and tossed it into the basket on the counter. Shrugging off my backpack, I finished the last bottle of water and tossed the empty one into the sink.

My little field trip was a welcome distraction, but now I really needed to finish clearing out the back bedroom and then there was some more paperwork that needed my attention before the end of the month. Sometimes being an adult and being solely responsible for an enterprise like the cemetery was an overwhelming job.

I opened the closet door and began to remove some smaller boxes. My mind once again returned to the tall stranger who was beginning to get under my skin in a way that seemed to add an unusual amount of brightness to an ordinarily dreary day. I was flattered by the attention he showed me. But the same old burning question ignited my curiosity. What on earth was he really seeking? I found myself wanting to help him in any way I could. But was it merely human kindness that spurred me on, or to find out why this beautiful creature made my heart thud erratically every time he looked at me? Deep down I knew the answer, but the rational part of my mind refused to accept it.

CHAPTER 11

The month was coming to a close with Labor Day quickly approaching. The rest of the week passed in a blur of late summer chores. Two local high school boys looking for odd jobs helped me clean all the gutters on the house and outbuildings and one even generously changed the oil in the snow blower in an early preparation for winter. Brian and Little Jimmy mowed and weeded, dealing with an irrigation crisis with the aplomb of experienced yard hands. Brian also insisted that the cemetery be perfect for the Labor Day weekend, which would bring a short memorial service to honor the veterans of Indian Valley. I was beginning to truly appreciate his presence and extremely thankful that I could keep both he and Little Jimmy on the payroll to complete the tasks that I was unable to do myself. The cemetery was not what you would call a booming business, thank goodness, but with the aid of my father's insurance policy, I was able to keep my head above water. I found the daily work soothed my spirits and gave me a connection to my father. If I could continue his work, somehow I would be able to move through my grief at his loss and I found I also wanted to carry on as long as I could as an act of respect for him.

With the busyness of my days keeping me occupied, I did not have much time to think of the tall stranger from back east. Well, maybe he did cross my mind a time or two. He came by once, asking for directions to the Quincy library, a town 25 miles away.

Although I knew Ramona could have easily directed him right up to the front door, I was flattered to think that possibly it was a legitimate excuse to just see me again. Or was that wishful thinking on my part? We had a quick chat, but I was on my way out the door for a trip to Chico and had very little time. Leaving me with the memory of his bright green eyes and slow grin, I forced myself to think of other things. Such as his mission. Stranger still was his search. Perhaps he had found what he was looking for and I would never see him again. So, his text on Thursday was a welcome surprise. He was hoping to meet up this weekend to find more local history and any other burial plots that he had missed.

The weekend would be a busy one, bustling with more activities than one person could manage in a day. In addition to being a holiday, it was one of Greenville's most celebrated events; Gold Digger Days. It was a moving way to honor the mining past of the valley. The entire weekend had a full schedule, with a parade, bazaar in the high school parking lot, live music and a carnival on the football field. Friday evening featured the Loggers Ballet. An entertaining event with men employed in the timber industry; big, burly and hairy men dressed in tutus, clumsily dancing to popular music. The men were all possessed of a large sense of humor to wear a tutu, dance in a public spectacle and they created an atmosphere of hilarity. Well supported by the locals, the proceeds were donated to the Indian Valley animal shelter. As always, Saturday would begin with a solemn and touching ceremony in the cemetery, conducted by the Indian Valley Veterans of Foreign Wars, honoring all the deceased veterans buried there. The street dance on Saturday night was always a fun and rambunctious event. Many valley folks who had left, like me, often returned just to celebrate this hometown extravaganza. It was an exciting small town gathering enjoyed by everyone.

I returned Kendall's text with an invitation to the spend Saturday browsing through the town, celebrating Greenville's history and culture. I knew I would have more time and possibly more of an inclination to take cemetery jaunts with him next week. Besides, I really wanted to participate in my hometown festivities. Kendall was happy to comply and we agreed to meet on Saturday morning.

I awoke just after daybreak. For a few glorious moments I lay in bed watching the suns' glow come through my window and brighten my world. I reluctantly rolled out of bed and stumbled over to my window. Peering out I could see the early sun spread across the grassy sweep of lawn and burnish the headstones outside. A heartwarming sight no matter what time of day, but it was especially lovely in the dawn's first glow.

I showered quickly and threw on a sleeveless red sundress with a white hoodie to ward off the chill of the crisp morning air. I twisted my hair into a ponytail and piled it on top of my head. I pulled on my Keen sandals and went to the kitchen to grind coffee beans and find some breakfast.

Kendall arrived just as the coffee finished burbling through the filter. I walked outside and peered over the rail. "Want a fresh cup of java?" I called down to him.

"Coffeeeeee," he growled up at me, "Yes, ma'am!" He climbed the stairs to the deck and stepped into the kitchen right behind me. Wearing dark blue cargo shorts, a red t-shirt emblazoned with Polygamy Pale Ale, and running shoes. The spicy, woodsy fragrance that accompanied him made me weak inside. But those green eyes smiling warmly at me made my knees feel like Jello.

I tried to play it cool and gave him one of my casual smiles. I couldn't resist commenting on his t-shirt. "Ah, that's interesting!"

"The back of the shirt is the best," he stated and proudly turned around to show me.

I read the printed slogan out loud. "Polygamy Pale Ale. Once you've had one you want another and another and another..." We both burst out laughing.

Turning serious again, he said, "Oh man, that coffee smells good. I haven't had a cup yet and I'm dying for a hit of caffeine"

"Cream or sugar?" I asked him. "I've chosen Freedom Blend for this morning. I thought it would be fitting for the day."

"Neither. Just hot and black. Then I can tell if it is a good roast or just expensive junk. But I do like your choice. I hope the taste lives up to the name," he replied with a silly grin.

"Withhold your judgment until you've finished a full cup," I cautioned. "I too have somewhat of an addiction to a good roast. My father grudgingly purchased Black Rifle Coffee beans for me on a regular basis. I've been exploring coffee since I left for college and I'm always trying new roasts. I couldn't rely on my father's ability to get good coffee, he liked the stuff that comes in cans and can be boiled over a campfire. So he had standing orders to just get the Black Rifle coffee beans online for me. That way I could count on a decent cup of java when I was here. I have like seven bags of beans to use up now. My Dad complained nonstop about my fancy, yuppie coffee, but he appreciated that the company is veteran owned. So he made sure I had plenty of it on hand." My smile faded and my stomach clutched at the sudden thought of my father and I turned away, looking out the window to hide my sorrow.

In the sudden silence, I could hear him inhale slowly.

"I lost my mom early this spring," he said softly. "I recognized the signs of grief without asking. I am so sorry for your loss."

He reached out and gently rested his hand on my back. Despite myself, I shivered but then relaxed under the warmth and latent strength of his palm. I was touched by his kindness and sniffed quickly, trying to control my emotions. I thought how perceptive he was and I was gratified that I did not have to explain myself to him. We stood quietly for a few moments, sharing the understanding that can be between the recently bereaved. Sometimes, words just aren't necessary. Finally, he dropped his hand as I turned back to him and I caught a glimpse of the can of mace, still resting in the basket where I had tossed it after our first meeting. Fleetingly, I considered how I could tuck it in my pocket and keep it covert even though he was standing right next to me. Thankfully, he didn't seem to notice and just gave me a slow smile that reached his green eyes. Then he simply took another sip of coffee.

"Come on. A cup of coffee tastes ten times better when you're relaxing in my outdoor living room with a view," I suggested. I felt a surge of pleasure just looking into his intense green eyes looking back at me.

"Sounds good to me. There's something about fresh mountain air that makes you feel good all over. The day feels special without effort," he added.

"Now there's some real meaning behind those words. I couldn't agree with you more," I said with a one sided grin.

I led him out onto the deck where we stood in the sun and drank our coffee, enjoying the freshness of the morning air with the promise of heat later in the day.

"Well, will you look at that? A hummingbird's heaven," he pointed out with his forefinger directed at mixture of begonias and fuchsia lining the south wall of a small tool shed beside the house.

"Party time down in the garden this morning," I joked.

"They make work look so easy." He gave me a crooked smile.

I nodded in silent agreement and gazed at the tiny birds seeking nourishment from a variety of flowers still in full bloom. Their tiny bodies hurtled to and fro, darting up and down, their wings barely visible with such rapid motion. Then my eyes drifted down through the wide open spaces of the cemetery. My front yard was bursting to life with a totally different kind of activity.

We both watched as the men and women of the American Legion gathered on the gravel path and prepared for their military salute. When it came to honoring our servicemen and our fallen soldiers who gave the ultimate sacrifice for our freedom, the community went to great lengths to honor their memory.

"You want to go down and see the ceremony first hand?" I asked.

"Sure. Lead the way," he said with a nod of his head.

Finishing our coffee, we left the cups on the little table by the door and went down to join the good folks of my hometown to honor the deceased. We meandered through the crowd of people, which had filled the lower portion of the cemetery, spilling over onto the gravel path. We found a good spot to stand with a bird's eye view of the formal commemoration.

The military ceremony was dignified and touching; the raising of the flags and the firearm salutes creating a spirit of respect and gratitude for those who had sacrificed for us. I felt the lump returning to my throat as I thought about my father. "I'm proud to say that my father served our country as a US Marine."

"I'm humbled by the fact that I'm an acquaintance of a beautiful young lady whose father served in our military," he spoke in a solemn tone without hesitation.

With blurred eyes, I dared not glance up at him because it was an emotional moment, so I just watched as the flag whipped and snapped in the morning breeze. The last notes of Taps drifted on the wind, then the whoops and shouts of the Boy Scouts in attendance rose up as they jumped on their bikes and rode down the hill to the pancake breakfast they had been promised at the Legion Hall. Surrounded by the chat and conversation of locals, I once again felt a surge of gratitude for my hometown.

My eyes surveyed the crowd. I noticed Brian and Little Jimmy standing just up the hill from where we were situated amongst the tall pines. Both men were bunched in with maybe two hundred other people scattered across the area. I turned to face Kendall. "Come on, I want you to meet someone," I coaxed him.

"Sure," he quickly returned with an easy smile.

With a wave of my hand and a last glance to confirm he was right behind me, we advanced in their direction. A little out of breath once I got there, I waited for Kendall to step up beside me.

"Brian and Little Jimmy, this is my friend, Kendall Danielson. He's here from back east on vacation. Exploring our beautiful countryside," I added.

"It's nice to meet you," Kendall said with an outstretched hand.

"Likewise, Mr. Danielson," Brian said extending a welcome handshake in his direction. "You've come to the right place if you like breathtaking views. Prepare to be astonished."

"I couldn't agree more," Kendall said with his eyes darting in my direction which warmed my cheeks. Then he quickly broke eye contact with me and turned his attention toward Little Jimmy and extended his hand out toward him.

"Yeah, yeah, nice to meet you too," Little Jimmy piped up and gave Kendall a hearty handshake as well.

"Both of these fine gentlemen are a good source of information about this cemetery and probably some pretty juicy gossip about this entire community."

I noticed Kendall's easy grace and friendliness with them both. "Good to hear. So which one of you is the authority on all the hot fishing holes in Wolf Creek and Lake Almanor?" he queried.

"Little Jim here is the go to man on that subject. He holds the present record on the largest trout caught at Lake Almanor," Brian said. "Any questions about this cemetery, I'm your man," he proudly boasted.

"I'll keep that in mind while I'm here," Kendall responded. "Grateful for any advice I can get," he added.

I appreciated that he was courteous to my friends and he seemed quite comfortable with the small town atmosphere. "Well guys, I guess we'll see you later. We had better get going if we want to take in most of the festivities," I explained.

"Best stay away from that dunking booth, young man," Brian advised. "Old man Dillon is still dead on with his aim. Pitched in the minor leagues for a few years you know," he added.

"Thanks for the warning! I'll keep that in mind," Kendall responded with a thumbs up.

Ambling back down the hill and on toward town, we chatted easily about the day ahead. I kept the conversation simple at first only asking about his plans for staying in the area. He said he had a few more weeks of leave and hoped to stay for the entire time. Finally, as we crossed the Wolf Creek Bridge, I was unable to restrain myself, so once again I asked the same question that so far he had not been able to speak openly about. "What is it exactly you are looking for? I might be able to help you better if I knew exactly what it is you are hunting."

We walked along in silence then, his brow furrowed in a little frown. "Honestly Camille, to tell you the truth, I don't know what I'm looking for," he finally admitted. "I've had a lot of stuff change in my life lately. My mom passed away and my dad is in an assisted living facility with advanced Alzheimer's. He said some things to me that have made me wonder about my childhood and I want to find some answers. I'm not even sure of the questions, though." He shrugged and turning down to look at me, he said, "So that's my story. Sorry I can't give you more. I'm not trying to be, hmmmmm...," he stopped speaking as if looking for the right word to describe his situation.

"Clandestine?" I prompted. "Covert? Secret op? Mission impossible?"

An easy smile creased his face. "Ah yeah. No, none of those," he reiterated. "Well, maybe it is a mission impossible. I think I will know it when I find it, but I can't say what it is in advance. And just in case you are wondering, I don't generally operate on such an open ended style. I usually have my stuff together and am organized and have a plan. This just kind of hit me out of nowhere and I am not sure from day to day what I am doing. But I am enjoying my time here."

Nodding at him, I said, "Okay, mystery man. Sorry, but on so few clues, I have nothing to offer in the way of advice. When you finally figure out what your primary reason for being here, then maybe I can offer you some help. Until then, we better get going before the traffic gets too thick and we get hemmed in between the overpass and the road. Meanwhile, remind me next time we have coffee to open the bag of Mission Impossible beans. Don't you think that would be appropriate?"

"By all means," he laughed lightly. "Lead the way," he added with a wave of his hand.

We continued along the dusty verge of the highway, hemmed in by the constant flow of vehicles and a white metal fence with light deflectors. "So, let's plan on this," I ruminated out loud.

"And what might that be?" he asked with interest.

"Explore, work up a good appetite and eat."

"Haven't been too successful with my exploration practices, but eating, I can wolf down with the best of em. It's a family thing. Come from a long line of gourmet cooks. The Danielson's do enjoy their food."

I rolled my eyes, but his play on words tickled my stomach.

We shared a few more laughs as we continued to walk. I was relieved to think that we seemed to be bridging the gap between us regarding why he had traveled this far to a place he had only heard about in passing conversation. At least I knew this much. His avoidance on the subject of why he was here wasn't really any clearer to him than it was to me.

Once we arrived, we were surrounded by the sights and sounds of small town festivities. Throughout the day, I introduced Kendall to many of my friends and some extended family members. We enjoyed the parade and the high school band concert following it. We browsed through the booths of local artisans and businesses and hit the Chamber of Commerce garage sale. The day passed companionably and we found ourselves at the 4-H truck, purchasing street tacos for an early dinner. Finding a patch of shady grass, we sat down to eat while listening to an acoustic guitar player set up across the street from us.

Opening a bottle of water and taking a deep drink, Kendall looked over at me as he replaced the cap. "So, tell me, Camille Cameron, a little about yourself. I know you live here in Greenville at a cemetery and yeah, people are dying to get in there. But, tell me about you."

I was unsure how to begin; after all I was trained to listen to people, not to talk first. Hesitantly, I stared down at my water bottle in order to avoid looking into his gorgeous eyes that tended to get me a bit rattled. "Well, there's not much to tell. My college years were spent in San Francisco, and I have just recently completed my PhD in Psychology. Of course, with the unexpected death of my father, I haven't had much of a chance to do any real serious job searching. Right now that is on hold," I said. "Indefinitely," I added mostly to myself.

"Understandable. These things take time," he said. His voice was calm. "Tell me about your childhood days growing up here in Greenville," he probed. "You know, back when you were barefoot and fancy free running these streets without a care in the world."

I huffed out a laugh. "I don't know if I was ever to the point that I didn't have a care in the world."

"You know what I mean. Back when a kid's mind wasn't bogged down with all the 'What If's' in life," he reiterated.

"Well, not much different than you I suppose. I had a normal but wonderful childhood. We weren't wealthy by any means, but I was rich in the sense that I was loved beyond measure. I couldn't have asked for better parents. Life was simple, full of fun and adventure, right up until my mother passed away when I was twelve." I paused to take in a deep breath. I turned my head away from his glare and pretended to listen to the soft music across the street. The slow tune mimicked my sudden melancholy mood.

"I'm sorry Camille. Experiencing the death of a parent at that age is incomprehensible," he said, his eyes looking just as tortured as how my heart felt at this moment.

Again there was a passage of silence between us until he broke through the uneasiness of the subject matter.

"All we can do is take one day at a time. There is no time limit on grief, Camille. Despite what the experts say, each and every one of us have our own way of dealing with pain. There is no one shoe that fits all. And don't let anyone tell you anything different," he said, his tone was gentle and kind.

His attentiveness loosened my usually reticent tongue and I found myself sharing funny stories of my grade school days and many of the crazy adventures during my high school years in Greenville. "I was a bit on the shy and awkward side, so I had no love life back then to speak of, but more friends than a girl could count," I told him. And then inexplicably to my surprise, I recounted the loss of my best friend. "My first heartbreak was at the age of ten. Besides my parents, Eli Young was the most important person in my life. He and I were inseparable. We did everything together. A friend like that comes along only once in a lifetime. But then he rode off on his bike one Saturday morning and was never seen again. I still miss him and wonder what ever happened to him."

Kendall listened without interruption, his green eyes on me and when I finally finished, his whole face was drained of color. "His poor family. I can't imagine enduring that kind of pain. There are some things that are worse than death and that definitely is at the top of the list."

"Oh, I am so sorry," I said. "I didn't mean to drag your spirits down with my unpleasant history. You probably wanted a short story and I gave you the unedited version."

His head shook from side to side. "On the contrary, I wanted to hear every word of it. I've always been one to listen with an open mind. One thing I've learned about life is that you can never say, well I've had the bomb drop on me so I shouldn't have to worry about it coming back for a second go-around. But as you well know, life is like a grenade and the pin can be pulled out at any time. Some of us are hit harder than others," he explained and paused to take in a deep breath. "But, I'm here to tell you, pretty lady, that I hope to bring some sunshine back into your life. That's if you'll give me a chance to take a shot at it. I'm hoping you enjoy my company as much as I enjoy yours. To tell you the truth, I haven't had the time to spend with any woman, much less one as beautiful as you and enjoy her company for a few years. Since law school, actually. My one and only long term girlfriend and I broke up and then I decided to focus on my career for a while," he said with a sigh, his long lashes fanning his serious eyes.

My face pinched in disbelief. "And you've been out of school for how long? And you don't have a girlfriend?" I asked, my interest intensified. With his good looks I would conservatively estimate that he had sifted through at least two dozen women before he took his bar exam.

"Five years since law school," he said matter-of-factly. "And I have lots of lady friends just none in particular. Actually, I am kind of old fashioned; I believe that the right woman will enter my life at a time God wants her to and I have always wanted to be free when that day comes. So in answer to your question, I don't date much. Maybe an occasional night out on the town for dinner and drinks with a crowd of friends, but I am not in a serious relationship right now," he said.

"Just on idle, huh?" I heard myself ask which warmed my cheeks.

He laughed. "Well, I suppose that's one way of putting it. But actually, I'd like to think of it as letting God do all the footwork while I stand back patiently and reap the benefits of His wisdom and knowledge. You can't go wrong with God at the steering wheel," he confirmed.

Astonished, I continued to stare at him. This man sounded so much like my father. Incredibly confident in the stringent principles by which he governed his lifestyle and obviously strong in his belief in God. I did not understand the call of the Great Creator in the lives of others, having never experienced that for myself. I appreciated the value of the Ten Commandments and its' teachings, but to personally own a relationship with God was confusing to me because I associated it with pain. This would require some thinking on my part. But his confidence and strength made me feel safe and I missed that feeling in the absence of my father.

Kendall smiled at me again and asked, "Tell me more about your friend, Eli. If you don't mind," he amended quickly.

Strangely enough, I didn't mind. Talking to him was as easy and spontaneous as breathing. However, keeping my mind on what I was saying instead of examining his playful smile without blushing was utterly frustrating. Still gazing into those green eyes, now darkened to the shade of the fresh verdure of spring oak leaves, I felt myself relax. Only seconds ticked by when I began to color a picture of my younger days to this man I barely knew, but intuitively realized that I wanted to know better. "My mother and Carolyn Young were such good friends. Much beyond the normal definition of friendship. For the longest time I thought they might be related somewhere down the line, but they never let on to that fact if they were. I would have to say the same applied to Eli and me. And even though Eli was 2 years older than me, we were almost inseparable. We had so much in common. We both loved to collect rocks, especially quartz crystals. I went to every one of his Little League games and as a child, I believed that my mother took me so I could watch Eli play. Funny how a little kid's mind works. But as I reached adulthood, I came to understand that she probably took me because then she and Carolyn and the other baseball moms could visit. I'm sure even if my mother didn't have an ulterior motive for taking me to the games, she would have at least dropped me off and picked me up later," I explained, knowing my mother's giving nature.

By the look in his widened eyes, he seemed to be waiting for me to say more. It wasn't hard to oblige him when it came to Eli.

"How I loved riding bikes along the creek with him and stopping to fish or to splash that cold water, smelling of the earth and mountain peaks, on our sweaty faces," I explained, pausing to take in a deep breath. "Without a doubt, those were the best years of my life."

I gradually ran out of steam, my words slowed and I drifted into silence, listening to the background music of the guitar being played across the street and the low chatter of conversations going on around us. I sat quiet for a moment longer and appreciated the time Kendall allowed me to do so. I reflected on my friend and how very much he had been a part of my childhood. "Eli's disappearance set my stumbling feet on the path to maturity before I was ready to start that journey," I pointed out. "Yet the journey was inevitable in the wake of his loss," I added in a low tone.

Kendall asked gently, "His disappearance has never been resolved?"

I shook my head. "No," I said grimly and paused. "Most of Plumas County joined forces in a tireless search for him. And that went on for a month or so, but they never found one trace of where he went or what happened to him. The whole town rallied around his parents but unfortunately, it was too much for his dad to handle. He committed suicide about three years later. His mom still lives in town, but I suspect she is not doing as well as she appears. I've talked with her and she is showing signs that this terrible, tragedy has taken a toll on her as well. She's a strong woman, but she cannot change what happened by believing her son is going to suddenly reappear out of nowhere. Inevitable I guess, when your child walks out the door one day and never returns," I said. I shook my head again to dispel the memories and the pain it caused to plumb the depths of my emotions.

The silence that hung in the air between us grew a bit awkward, so I quickly pushed the unpleasant ball into his court. "What about you? What skeletons are you hiding in your closet?" I asked, more than eager to dig into his little pocket of secrets.

He crumpled up his taco wrappers and tucked them neatly into a ball which he lofted into the air and watched as it swished into a nearby trash can. "And he scores!" he crowed proudly. "Danielson with a 3 pointer at the buzzer!" he bragged again and gave me a wink. Then he turned away and stared out across the street. He let out a long sigh, followed by another moment of serious silence.

I waited for him to gather his words.

"Well, I grew up near Washington DC. I played basketball and baseball in high school and was an Eagle Scout, so I can fix just about anything. I went to college in Helena, Montana and then law school at Gonzaga in Spokane, Washington. I'm an associate in a law firm that handles mostly real estate and land issues. I like golf and hiking, fishing and watching baseball. And I love finding a good microbrew. But here is a factoid about me that might surprise you!" he said with a touch of excitement in his voice. "I was actually born right here in Greenville." He smiled at my startled expression. "Yep, my parents used to vacation up at Lake Almanor almost every summer and they were here the summer I was born. I arrived a little early and surprised them, apparently. They didn't come back after I was born. Too busy, I suppose, but they always talked about Northern California and the Sierra Nevada mountains. My mother especially loved the lake and the little mountain towns. One of her favorite things to do was to browse in the small mom and pop stores for unusual and unique spoons. She had quite a collection by the time she passed on," he marveled.

"No way," I said, amazed at this bit of news. "Really? You were born here in Greenville?"

"Yep. That's how the story goes."

"So, is this your first visit since your birth?"

"Yes, again."

I felt my brows pinch and my eyes squint. "What brought you back after all these years?"

"Well, with my mother's death and my father's progressing' dementia, I wanted to find out more about this place. I knew it was special to them, but I didn't really understand the draw. I mean, they came here for years and now I know why. Who in their right mind wouldn't want to enjoy this small dose of heaven? It's so beautiful and peaceful. Before I was born this entire area was their summer playground. But for reasons unknown to me, after I was born apparently their annual trips just stopped. Too busy, too pre-occupied with me? Who knows why they quit coming. But since I have never been here myself as an adult, I decided I wanted to see what it was like. Maybe find some of my own history," he explained.

That was my ah ha moment. Now we are finally getting some-where. Perhaps that is the tie that binds his heart to this town.

He stood and held out a hand to me to help me up off of the grass. I sensed that he was holding something back, or maybe did not know how to say it. Doubt flickered through my mind and squeezed my heart as I wondered what his real motivation was and why he was reluctant to share the whole truth of his search of local cemeteries and the history of the surrounding area. Maybe his per-sonal history was as painful as my own and his reticence would be understandable in that case.

Despite my misgivings, we strolled the sidewalks in search of some good music and Kendall was intent on finding a local microbrew, 'possibly a craft beer from Sierra Nevada Brewing' he suggested. The evening ended companionably and by the time we reached the steps to my front door, I realized I wasn't quite ready to call it a night. We were standing under the shelter of the porch roof and I could clearly see the intensity of his emerald eyes demanding my full attention. A lump rose in my throat. I felt the blood flood my face, but finally I formed some words in my mouth. "Thank you for today. I can't remember when I have felt so at ease and separated from all my troubled thoughts."

"On the contrary. Thank you. This entire day has been a breath of fresh air and so out of the ordinary for me," he proclaimed with a gleam in his iridescent eyes. "It has been a day free from the mental and emotional stress attached to everyday life where I live. It exhausts me just to think of going back to that rat race," he added with a sudden sadness washing over his face. Then he let out a long sigh and grabbed my attention with his serious eyes. "Can we meet again?" he asked. "I have some other local history I want to verify and hoped that you would be available as my guide."

I knew he wasn't being totally honest with me. He didn't really need my help because our local library could answer any questions that Google couldn't. I tried hard to harness my uncontrolled enthusiasm over spending more time with him. And, despite the fact that I had a busy week ahead, I jumped at the chance to see him again. "I'll text you when I have a free day. Is that ok?" I asked in the best toned down voice I could muster.

"Sounds good to me," he returned. With a wave and one last grin, he turned around and walked toward his jeep. Once inside, his motor roared to life. He followed the driveway down to the highway. As he turned left to return to Lake Almanor, he honked his horn.

I smiled to myself as I waved back knowing he wouldn't see me in the deepening dusk, but I found the honk endearing for some silly reason. Stepping inside, I locked the door behind me and kicked off my sandals. After a long, hot shower, I stood in front of the sink brushing my teeth. As I ran a comb through my hair, I wondered yet again, what he was really searching for. I wasn't expecting to discover that he was involved in some meaningful world effort to save the blue whale or protect the wood beetles from extinction. It had to be something more personal, because I could see the suffering in his eyes and sense the depth of his sadness. Why wouldn't I recognize the awful curse of unanswered questions?

I staggered into my bedroom and plopped into bed with a heavy sigh. It made me tired to wonder so much.

CHAPTER
12

I was determined to clear out some of the clutter from the big barn behind the house. Brian and I had discussed the needs for the winter and he was hoping for a larger space to repair some of the bigger pieces of second-hand equipment that my father purchased from the Beeson family just months before he passed. Up until now, he had worked in the garage attached to the house, but I was hoping to keep my car there during the colder months of our mountain winter. Winters here can be brutal. Once the first blanket of snow falls, it can be a thirty minute chore just trying to scrape the windows clear enough to drive safely. As I stood on the deck in the crisp September morning air, I realized that today was a day that would be as good as any other to start that project.

My phone buzzed with an incoming text and I felt a slow warmth in my stomach as I saw it was from Kendall. Laughing at myself, I opened it to see that he was hoping to visit a cemetery or two today. Regretfully, I replied that I had to clean a barn today. His answering text made me smile and sent an electric current of excitement through me.

"Need help? I have a strong back."

Unwilling to surrender to the enjoyment of his company, I dithered for a few minutes trying to decide if I wanted his help and strong back involved. Dust and dirt didn't exactly mix well with a potential romantic afternoon with a handsome man who was now visiting my dreams more often than I cared to admit. I went back inside the kitchen and ground beans for a second pot of coffee while pondering his offer. I emptied the dishwasher, threw in a load of laundry and then decided, what the heck. I could use the help and company. Texting him back, I promised him peanut butter sandwiches for lunch.

Kendall arrived about an hour later, wearing a red t-shirt emblazoned with a draft horse and Heavy Horse Scotch Ale. In jeans and boots, he appeared ready for work. As I led him up the drive to the barn, I could faintly smell the woodsy, spicy scent that he exuded. I admonished myself to focus on the task at hand, and as I pulled open the big doors in the front, I was almost overcome by the sight of the full barn. Daunting to say the least, I considered closing the doors and finding another project not so time consuming for the day. Packed with the detritus of my father's full life, I was discouraged by the sheer amount of stuff.

I sought Kendall's eyes with mine. "Are you sure about this? I would understand completely if you turned and ran like a beat dog. This is daunting to say the least. So if you suddenly remember you have other plans for the day, I would understand completely," I told him sincerely.

"Oh, I think I'm up for it," he replied and gave me that silly grin again that made his dimples deepen.

"Hmm," I said and eyed him suspiciously. "In the event that you twist an ankle or hurt your back, you can't say I didn't warn you." I said.

"I'll keep that in mind," he replied with his same goofy grin.

I let my head swing back in place and switched on the overhead lights. "Okay. Maybe you start right over there by the work bench and I'll begin sorting through this pile of whatever right here by the door," I instructed, but even before the words left my mouth I was regretting that I had even come up with this hair-brained idea of spring cleaning in the middle of fall.

Kendall slid in the door beside me and took a long sweeping look around. "Hang in there Tadpole. We got this," he said.

"Speak for yourself, Wreck-it-Ralph," I answered. Our eyes met and we both busted up laughing.

Once we got started it didn't seem so daunting. We began picking our way through the clutter, stacked and packed along the walls and on the floor. After a good ten minutes, again I could feel the discouragement and depression weighing me down as I removed tarps that covered various pieces of equipment that had seen better days. I rummaged through piles of boxes, the air redolent with the smell of wood and engine oil and dust. Sighing, I stopped and shook my head. I was overwhelmed and I did not know where to begin next. Each side of the shop had built in work benches that my father had used for engine repair, wood-working and restoring old bicycles. Covered in parts, tools and various projects, each bench held memories of my father, almost as if he were to walk through the door and begin tinkering. As I picked up a level and T-square, I remembered how he built homes and did wood working for Jim Hatch Enterprises. Together, he and Jim had built and remodeled many homes in the valley.

With a laugh, Kendall picked up a small bicycle and held it over his head. "Was this yours?" he asked.

I did not recognize the bike, but I knew my father had collected bikes and fixed them for many of the kids in town who couldn't afford new ones. He would host a Boy Scout troop each spring for a small clinic and teach them the rudimentary skills of bike repair. He allowed the boys to tear apart bikes and to use his tools to reassemble them, and I was used to seeing bicycle parts and skeletons in the barn. I felt a pang of missing my father and I swallowed hard. "Nope. Not mine," I answered with a forced grin. "Are you sure you're up to this task? It's a bit overwhelming to say the least. I'm still feeling guilty I got you involved in this mess."

"As sure as sure can be. A little dirt never hurt anyone that I know of."

I shrugged my shoulders and shook my head. "Die hard Danielson," I spouted off with a shake of my head.

Kendall smiled wide and quickly took charge and organized a triage of the barn. Pulling down various tarps, he started dust swirling and motes drifted in the sunshine pouring in the open doors. He dragged them outside and shook them vigorously. Moving several boxes, he opened them and had me look through. Quickly assessing what to keep, what to donate and what to throw away, we worked as smoothly and efficiently as possible. His objectivity and energy began to infect me and I began to actually enjoy the sorting process. I was interrupted by childhood memories as one or the other of us unearthed an object that triggered my recall. Despite the distractions, we worked companionably as we cleared through years of clutter. Throughout the day, I swore several times, "Not me. I'm not going to put such a heavy burden on my children someday if I ever have any." But of course, in the back of my mind I knew that was a mushy promise. I know of many people who had difficulty managing the clutter of their lives and their homes mirrored that unfortunate characteristic. I was determined to be different. But would I really?

The day wore on and after two trips to the town dump, we took a break after mid- afternoon for lunch. I was dirty and disheveled from the dust and the dirt floor of the barn, but Kendall was fairly clean. We washed our hands at the kitchen sink and ate lunch sitting at the kitchen table. Peanut butter sandwiches with an orange each and some cookies that I had found in the freezer. Bounty left over from my father's funeral week. Kendall ate quickly and neatly, and demolished a half dozen cookies. Refueled with lunch, we headed back to the barn, still chatting about the amount of clutter we had cleared.

Making our way through the cleared space, I decided to attack the left side wall and Kendall stepped into the far back corner of the barn. Behind a small stack of lumber, there was an old pickup, draped in a large tarp, anchored with bungee cords. A seafoam green, 1951 Chevy truck, it was my father's pride and joy and he had parked in the barn many years ago after replacing it with a newer model.

"Well now, what have we here?" Kendall asked as he tugged the tarp halfway free from the bed of the truck. Curiosity was etched on his face as he leaned in the drivers' window and then opened the door. As the door creaked in the protest of long unoiled hinges, he turned to me and grinned widely. "This is one sweet ride!"

"That's my father's old truck. It gave him bragging rights beyond belief. Until he needed a new one, of course. He drove it everywhere when I was a kid. I put a lot of miles on, riding in the bed of that truck!" Through the mists of time, I recalled hearing the truck grumble up the hill in the evening, knowing that my father was home and dinner would soon be served.

"Do you mind if I look it over and check it out?" Kendall asked with excitement in his eyes and his tone definitely one pitch higher.

"Oh no, go right ahead. If you can get it started, you can take it for a ramble around the valley, if you want," I said which widened his eyes. I felt that the old girl deserved an interested man to check her out. Shaking my head and laughing at myself, I whispered under my breath. "Boys and their toys. Some men never change." I turned back to the box I was emptying.

Kendall pulled the tarp the rest of the way off the old truck, loosening the bungee cords gently and dropping them on the floor at his feet. "Wow, this baby is in great shape!" he exclaimed. "The paint hasn't faded much and the body is in pretty good condition too. Your dad must have taken really great care of it."

"No doubt about that," I agreed. "My father cared for all of his possessions with pride and the old truck had been one of his

116

favorites. I had loved to bounce along the valley roads, sitting on the bench seat next to him or hunkered in the back with our old dog; Happy Jack. Those were the good old days for sure," I added. Then a strange thought came to my mind. "Oddly though, I did not remember riding in it as much after the summer Eli disappeared.

Kendall ducked below for a moment behind the truck, reappearing as he tugged at the tailgate latch and pulled the remainder of the tarp out of the bed. "Hey, there's another bike in here," he called to me. "Is this one of yours?"

"No, I gave my last bike to a girl named Barbie Jackson before I left for college," I said. "I ended up buying another one after I hit the big city. Bikes were much more useful than a car and I could always bring it home for Dad to fix for me, if I needed."

"This bike here looks pretty well busted up, so what do you want to do with it?" he asked, peering at me over a bent handlebar he held before him.

I dropped the box of mismatched nails I was holding and joined him at the tailgate of the old truck. "I suppose if it's beyond repair then we'll just put it in the junk pile," I said. And as I looked at the bike, instantly I was thrust back into my worst nightmare. Submerged in pain, a soundless scream escaped beneath my breath. My heart sunk to my stomach and the blood pounding in my ears was deafening. I could feel the swirl of nausea churning deep in my stomach and the tightness in my chest threatened to drop me to my knees. The knot in my throat grew in size and constricted my breathing. I struggled to speak, but couldn't form the words. Then the screaming began, wails of grief and loss echoing in my head. Shaking, I put my hands over my ears and then over my face as I bent over in a paroxysm of pain that rocked me to the core. I could vaguely feel the cold cement floor on my knees and a wave of nausea rode over me and receded as my vision cleared.

I could feel his strong hands on my back, supporting my shoulders. "Camille, are you ok?" Kendall asked in a tone tinged in fear.

I groaned. "Just give me a minute," I managed to say. I took a few deep breaths and then lifted my head to see Kendall just inches in front of me. He stepped to the side, still with a firm hold on my shoulders.

"Are you sure you're ok?" he asked again. Our eyes met. I could see deep concern etched in his narrowed eyes.

I didn't answer. I was still trying to regain my normal breathing as I felt his arm slide down around my back.

"Come on, up we go. I got you," he said, but his words sounded faintly in my ears as though he were at a great distance.

Shaking my head to dispel all the pressure building inside, I breathed deeply again and again. "What did you say?" I asked him, my voice sounded strained in my own ears. My mind was still trying to absorb what my eyes beheld before me in the bed of the old pickup. The secrets of the past lying quietly under a dusty tarp in my father's barn. All the terrible stuff, all the horrific memories attached to that bike came flooding back with a vengeance.

"Are you ok?" he repeated gently, leaning into me. "You went white as a sheet and dropped to your knees like you were fainting. You're still shaking and cold and clammy to the touch," he said his voice still submerged in restless apprehension.

"I'm fine. Really."

"You're not fine. You're shivering. Here, take my sweatshirt," he said in a demanding tone, yet not offensive. He shrugged off his sweatshirt and wrapped me in it firmly, returning a little warmth to my cold and trembling body.

I closed my eyes and inhaled his spicy, woodsy scent and felt his strong arms around me and began to relax. I could feel his breath in my hair and his gentle hands rubbed my back in tiny circles. Lifting my head, I finally said," I can't believe this is happening?"

Leaning back to peer into my eyes, he spoke to me as if I was an injured child. "What Camille? What has happened?" he asked.

Taking another deep breath and exhaling slowly, I tried to calm myself. But my mind was spinning with questions I couldn't answer. Why would this bike, of all bikes, be in the bed of my father's truck, buried beneath a dusty tarp for all of these years? A logical reason for this, I was sure, but none of the awful thoughts that ran randomly through my mind made any sense. "This just can't be," I finally whispered. "It just can't be."

"What can't be?" he asked. Concern made his green eyes wide, absorbed with my sudden change in demeanor. He studied my every movement.

Swallowing hard, I forced out words that literally clawed at my heart. "That's Eli's bike. The one he was riding the day he disappeared." I let my lids' close for an instant and pressed my fingers into my burning eyes. My head was still spinning, so more than ever I was grateful for Kendall's strong arms around me. At this moment, I felt as if I had been thrust into the eye of a hurricane with my torn emotions whipping with such a force I could hardly breathe. I needed his strength and power of reasoning to keep my sanity intact.

"Are you sure, Camille?" his voice was hesitant.

"Yes, I'm sure. He painted it red and black himself. I watched him do it. It was a one of a kind, mountain bike with a homemade cushion for a seat that his mother had sewn for him. His dad bought it at a garage sale in Quincy. It was bright purple. Eli said it looked too girly, so he painted it," I rambled on mindlessly.

Looking over my shoulders at the bike, Kendall whistled. "Well, it is mangled now. Whatever happened to it was pretty forceful to cause this much damage. The handlebars are twisted sideways and the frame is completely bent."

"I can see that." I said and let out a deep sigh. "Oh dear God, please don't let my father be at fault for this!" The words left my mouth unbidden, blurted out in fear.

"What do you mean?" he asked. His voice was low, but his mouth fell open and his eyes bulged wide.

I squeezed my eyes shut and shook my head trying to formulate an accurate picture of what must have happened. "I thought my father was the wisest, kindest and bravest person that ever lived. He was my hero and could keep me safe. He would never lie to me or anyone for any reason. But this, I see the evidence that he was living a lie. A horrible, heartbreaking lie!" I blinked back my tears. "That must be what he was trying to tell me as he was dying. This is his cemetery secret. That he killed Eli and hid the evidence in his truck, back here in a dark corner under a tarp," I surmised. "I can hardly believe it!" I cried out. "All these years, the truth was right here hidden in the barn!" I was stunned by the discovery of the bike and the implications that discovery held.

Releasing my shoulders, Kendall tilted my chin up with his fingertip. Our eyes locked. "Camille, don't," he ordered in a gentle tone. "You cannot judge your father if you don't have all of the facts. Trust me, I have seen lots of cases where the discovery is completely changed when all of the facts are finally disclosed. I'll agree this looks bad, especially since there's definitely some damage to the fender of your father's truck as well. But keep in mind, you don't know if your father was actually driving the truck at the time it hit Eli. Assuming of course, that Eli was on the bike at the time of impact," he explained with the typical verbiage of a legal counselor.

For one blissful moment I found myself wanting to believe his every word. I conceded he may have a point. But then that knowing little voice in the back of my head quickly convinced me otherwise. I let out an exasperated gasp. "No one drove this truck but my father. No one," I reaffirmed my conviction in a defeated tone so low I could barely hear myself.

Then I recalled a few other facts that didn't seem important at the time, but now there was no denying that all of it in its' ugly content deserved a deeper consideration. I remembered that my father had stopped drinking around the time of Eli's disappearance. Shortly after, he pulled the old truck into the barn, deep into the back corner and purchased a newer truck. I suppressed my internal cringing at the mere thought those two facts represented.

Uncomfortable with my speculations and feeling self-conscious of his stare that hadn't wavered from my face, I turned away from him and stepped over to the passenger side of the truck. Immediately, I spotted the red scuff marks on the headlight and front fender which left no doubt in my mind that this is where Eli met his destiny, which only intensified my fears.

Kendall cautiously moved in beside me, placing one hand on my shoulder which drew my attention back toward him. Our eyes met and I glared at him briefly. He seemed to be measuring my expression. "Are you okay?" he gently asked with feeling.

"I'm fine," I answered, shaking my head. "I'm just a little shocked at what you have uncovered. Don't get me wrong, I wanted answers, but I wasn't expecting this," I admitted with narrowed eyes and a pinched brow. My voice was faint.

"Look, you don't have to subject yourself to this agony right now. Would you rather we just call it a day and finish this some other time?" he asked in a hesitant tone.

"No," I blurted before I could harness my harsh tone. "I'm not going to run from the truth, no matter how much it hurts. I have to see this through to the bitter end," I added even though the words ripped at my heart.

I tore loose from his intense stare and let my eyes wander back over to the truck. My head shook involuntarily. "I'm just thankful you are here with me. Thankful I didn't discover this on my own," I admitted as my eyes traveled back over to his. A gentle smile of understanding stretched his lips into a thin line. "Go ahead. Examine the damage for yourself and give me your thoughts," I urged him. I nudged him with my fingertips toward the truck.

He gave me a long, somber look with a grim downward twist to his mouth. "Are you sure?" he murmured.

"Yes, I'm sure," I answered before I had to chance to rethink my decision and run the other way. But all the while, my mind was racing. This can't be true. How could my father be so deceptive and go on to live a seemingly normal life?

A faint smile separated his lips, and he nodded. Then he turned from me and moved in for a closer view. I watched as his eyes zeroed in on the damaged area. His fingers flowed slowly over the red paint against the green body of the truck. I felt a sense of gloom and despair begin to enshroud me. Shaking my head again, I completed a circle of the truck, going again to the back to stare at the disfigured bike that lay in the bed like a wounded bird. I stood stiff and rigid, internally searching for answers. Like snapping on a light switch, Kendall's tender voice brought me back to reality.

"You cannot rule out the possibility of someone else driving this truck, Camille. You were only ten at the time and a lot may have happened back then that you weren't aware of," he pointed out. "Maybe someone used the truck without your father's permission or quite possibly, he may have loaned it to someone in desperate need. At this point, it is a mistake to rule out anything. Anything is possible and you need to step back and take a deep breath. Don't allow this to create hate for your father or disrespect his memory without evidence. Sometimes fathers do hard things for the people they love. So try to focus on the facts. Yes, someone drove this truck and judging by the damage to the front end, it somehow came into contact with Eli's bike. There is enough red paint on here to tell us that much. But we don't know who was driving the truck or who was riding the bike at the time of impact."

Again, his eyes moved back to the bike. For a long moment, he focused then turned his gaze back to me, his voice growing deeper and a little sharp. "It is really important that we do not get half-crazy with quick assumptions and very few facts to back them up," he added.

The sharpness of his voice drew my attention to the meaning of his words. I began to appreciate that this was a shared discovery, but I held deep reservations about my father's participation in this long hidden secret hiding under a dingy tarp in the dark corner of the barn. I was still shocked by my father's apparent complicity in the disappearance of my best friend. And even worse, how on earth could he keep this evidence from the authorities? Maybe this kind of information could have taken their investigation in a totally different direction and resulted in some answers to what actually happened instead of leaving his poor mother heartbroken and grieving for the rest of her life. How could he do this to all of us?

I let out a long sigh. Although Kendall's words made logical sense and had been for a few moments very persuasive, I pursed my lips skeptically. My heart cried out in anger and pain and I could feel the blood rush to my face. How dare Kendall speak words like these to me. He doesn't know how things were back then. He doesn't know how my father's mind worked. My father would never loan out his truck to anyone. He would take care of the task himself before just handing his truck over to someone else. I shook my head and said, "You don't understand. No one other than my father drove this truck. No one," I confirmed again. Then my eyes fell upon the wrinkled fender. "How could he do this?" My words came out in blatant disbelief.

"Camille," he snapped in a sharp tone which brought my eyes in his direction. His smile had faded and his forehead was creased. His intense stare made me feel uncomfortable. "Then think about this. If all you say is true, and your father allegedly is responsible for the death of Eli, it was most likely a terrible accident. I can guarantee you that your father paid the price for his silence if that's the way this whole situation played out. Can you imagine the pain and torment he experienced trying to keep the truth from your mother and from you? And from everyone else? It is like that movie Groundhog Day and every day he relived that hell of an experience. You should feel compassion for your father, Camille. Don't hate and condemn him," he said in what sounded more like a begging tone.

A brief moment of wordless communication passed between us. I turned my eyes away, embarrassed over my angry response. The wisdom and authority with which he spoke caused me to see the contrast between his words and my emotional reaction. Surely the reaction of a wounded child, not that of a grown woman. The sight of Eli's bike had opened an old wound and my broken heart had cried out with condemnation. How could I misjudge the many years of life I had shared with my father and my conviction that he was a good and honorable man? I made a quick choice to keep an open mind. And to my surprise, as my father had done so many years ago, I would also keep this discovery a secret as well. "You're right," I conceded. "My father was not the kind of man who would keep this kind of secret without a very good reason. There has to be more to this than meets my eyes. I know in my heart that he wouldn't hide it just to protect himself," I remarked as I grabbed his gentle eyes with mine. "I guess I got caught up in the emotions of the moment."

"Understandable Camille. You're only human and that's what we humans do; react to the situation. Sometimes our words have a will of their own."

"I suppose you're right." Looking up into his kind eyes, I blurted out, "Will you help me find the truth?"

He smiled at me and shrugged slightly and then pulled me in closer than we had ever been before. "Yes Camille, I will. That's why I have come here in the first place. To find the truth."

The residual of pain and confusion still played in my mind; otherwise I would have caught the full meaning of his words.

CHAPTER
13

T he week following our discovery in the barn was a whirlwind
of emotions for me. The tempest rocked me between grief,
anger, loss and pain. I struggled with the knowledge that my father
knew something about Eli Young's disappearance and I vacillated
between the disappointment and discontent that my father kept
a secret from me and concern that he felt alone with that secret.
Kendall's reminder that I was only ten at the time, and possibly
my father was protecting me was a thought that I struggled with as
well. I eventually resolved I would pursue what I could, and leave
the rest to gather dust in the past.

Sworn to silence, Kendall and I covered the truck back up with
the tarp and secured the bungee cords. We left Eli's bike exactly
where we found it. Now we too, had become a part of my father's
little secret.

Fortunately, I was kept busy with cemetery tasks that had to
be completed as fall deepened and the cleanup of the barn was
ongoing and tedious.

I had just finished my second cup of coffee and was contemplating one more. I was leaned against the railing overlooking the
cemetery when Brian popped out of nowhere.

"Hey there, Camille! I was just putting some finishing touches
on Brad Moseley's stone. Maybe when you get a minute you could
take a peek at it and tell me what you think. I reckon Sally will

approve. I even placed some of my mom's lilacs in the planter she requested."

"Oh, she's pretty easy going. Never been one to complain. I'm sure she'll be pleased."

"Little Jim and I worked till dark last night in the old wood shed. Stacked what little wood is left in the back and put some new hinges on the door. We managed to create a space for two of the small mowers during the bad weather months. Might have to board up that window for good. Gets broke nearly every year when winter settles in. I think we may have put a good sized dent in our fall chores."

"Sounds good!" I responded enthusiastically. "I wish I could say the same thing about the never ending paperwork and bill paying."

"Can't help you there little lady. Don't do well with numbers. That's why I'm the go to guy for maintenance of the cemetery, the house and all the outbuildings. The buck stops there," he confirmed, giving me a wink.

"And for that very reason, you are deeply appreciated. I don't know what I would have done without you and Little Jimmy."

"That road goes both ways, Camille," he said with a big grin. Then his brows pinched as if in serious thought. "Haven't seen that young fellow of yours around lately. Country life prove to be too much for him?" he asked with one brow higher than the other.

"Oh no. Nothing like that at all. Kendall had to fly back to DC. He planned on being gone for a week or so. Had to take care of some unexpected legal matters. But you never know about these things. No telling how many legal enterprises his law firm had in store for him once he got there. Maybe much more than he had anticipated," I added. Thankfully, a text from him late last night informed me that he should be pulling in about midnight. I must confess, I had been counting the days until his return. However, I had no intentions of sharing that information with Brian.

"One of those city lawyers, huh? Don't know too many city slickers that end up conforming to country living, so don't get your hopes up. He may never come back."

"Oh, he'll be back. I can guarantee that."

"Look Camille, I don't usually stick my nose where it don't belong, but for your sake and out of respect for your father, I'm going to give you some good advice," he said with both his brown eyes as wide as lily pads. "I've been around long enough to know those city boys can promise you the moon, but can't even deliver space debris. All talk and no do," he confirmed, shaking his head.

"Don't worry Brian. Kendall's not like that at all. If push came to shove, I think he would choose living here in this valley over his concrete jungle any day of the week. Trust me, he's not that kind of a guy."

"Yeah right. I've heard that story before. Just keep your guard up. That's all I'm asking. Give it some time. Most people reveal themselves given a little time."

"I'll keep that in mind. I promise." I felt a tinge of guilt having made that pledge because I knew I was already in over my head with this relationship.

"That's good enough for me."

"And for the record. You can feel free to advise me any time you want. My father trusted you and that's reason enough for me to trust your judgment," I said which immediately put a broad smile on his face.

"Well, I had better get back to work while the gettins' good." With that, Brian disappeared beyond the south corner of the house.

I shook my head. Good man with old fashioned ways. A lot of my father had rubbed off on him for sure.

I turned my focus back on the natural beauty of the landscape surrounding me. The oak trees on Indian Head Mountain had shifted into their autumn glory. The cold, crisp nights recreated the ancient passage of the green transforming into wide swaths of yellow, orange and gold. The brilliant colors marked the ridges and knobs on the mountain and their changing reminded me of the age old wise man who watched over us. I pondered if the Great Spirit was truly with us and shepherded the passing of the seasons, year after year. I found myself thinking of this Great Spirit, or Heavenly Father as He is more affectionately known, and wondered if I sought Him, would I truly find Him and how would I know? Quiet mountain mornings and peaceful evenings lend themselves to deep thinking. I never get tired of this peaceful lifestyle.

CHAPTER 14

Having put a sizeable dent in the barn project my thoughts returned to Carolyn Young and the promise I had made this summer to visit her again. With the slight chill of fall in the morning air and the kisses of color in the oak leaves, I felt enough time had passed and I needed to honor my word to her.

Recalling our last two visits the day of my father's funeral and our pleasant luncheon, I was unsure of how I would approach her. Her faith was strong indeed, but unfortunately, she was waiting to unwrap a gift that I knew would never arrive. I have never been a good liar, which is a positive character trait, but it did not serve me well in social settings where a veneer of untruth would make the situation easier to manage. I was uncertain how to visit with someone who had a tenuous grasp on reality.

The discovery Kendall and I had made in the barn two weeks ago was still fresh in my mind and I did not anticipate sharing it with Carolyn. I expected that I would follow my father's lead and keep my silence about the bent and twisted bike, still resting in the dark corner of the barn, held in the bed of the old truck. There really was no reason to share it with her. Why reopen an old and deep wound in a mother's heart? Especially since I had no factual explanation for the presence of the bike in the barn? In the interest of kindness, I would simply refrain from telling her of the discovery and in that moment, I felt a small flicker of understanding for my father. Maybe there were some secrets better left untold. I highly suspected that this one fit into that category.

So on this bright, but crisp Tuesday morning, I called Carolyn on the phone and arranged for a nice visit at her house. With only two knocks, she opened the front door of her home. She was all smiles and sunshine. Enveloping me in a hug that was surprisingly strong despite her thin and frail appearance she said, "Camille, it is so wonderful to see you again! We have so much to catch up on. Come on in," she graciously invited me. Closing the door behind me, she asked, "Coffee or tea?"

"Tea sounds good," I offered.

She chattered brightly as she preceded me into the kitchen. She turned and smiled at me again, as she filled a kettle with water, her thin hand quavering slightly as she held it under the tap. Setting the kettle on the stove, she turned on the gas and then lifted two decorative teacups from the shelf above the stove. Dressed in a pair of warm pants with a red cardigan, she tugged the sweater around her thin shoulder for warmth and I again marveled at the bird like appearance of her tiny body.

I was becoming familiar with the feeling of disorientation as I revisited childhood memories as an adult. I recalled Eli and me sitting at this same table, eating a sandwich and cookies for lunch on weekends. Why is it that kids find every other mothers' food better than their own? I wondered idly. My own mother was a great cook, but I loved to eat here in Carolyn's kitchen. The entire dining area had been repainted at some point, but the room was for the most part the same as my memories, with the red industrial clock still ticking on the wall and the view of Indian Head through the window. Carolyn had decorated her kitchen with generous splashes of red and I recalled how cheerful it was to me as a young girl. The curtains were different, but still in red and white. The teapot was red and the salt and pepper shaker on the back of the stove were bright pops of color against the white wall.

I blinked my eyes and realized that Carolyn had been chatting the whole time I was lost in thought.

"You are so grown up and so beautiful, Camille. Your college years have served you well. I always told your mother you would be beautiful! It is so great to see you."

I fleetingly wondered if she was wishing me well or if she was really wishing it were Eli sitting here visiting her instead of me. My survivor's guilt gnawed at my insides. Of course, she would want her son here, sitting at her kitchen table, but I would have to suffice. And I renewed my promise of silence to myself. This sweet and kind woman did not deserve to know the ugly secret lurking in the back corner of the barn.

I had worn jeans with a hoodie sweatshirt this morning to ward off the early chill. I fingered the turquoise stone that I wore on a silver chain, nervously. "It is good to be home," I told her. "Greenville will always be my home, no matter what."

"I'd have to agree with that. I think that most folks don't realize how attached they are to the feeling of home until they have to leave. When they come back to live, they feel differently about their home town. They are here because they choose to be, not because they have to be or because they never left and think they are trapped. It makes a big difference in how you feel about your hometown and I am glad that you left for a while. It makes you miss the small town values. Although it was under very sad circumstances, I'm also very glad you have returned!"

I nodded, seeing the wisdom in her words. I knew I would always feel the call, the tug on my heart for my home town. The clear mountain air scented with the pine and the cold rushing waters of Wolf Creek. It doesn't get any better than that.

As she made tea and served it in floral, vintage tea cups, with honey and lemon, she continued to chat about fellow friends and extended family. I found myself sinking into a thoughtful daze, the tenor of her voice washing over me and filling me with content.

Rousing myself, I realized she had posed a question. "What'" I asked, feeling foolish.

"I baked some cookies this morning. Would you like a couple? They are your favorites," she assured me.

"You didn't?" I said, but hoping that she had.

"Chocolate chip, just like you loved as a little girl," she replied. "I remembered because they were also Eli's favorite." She settled her head back on her neck and garnished a generous smile. "You two were so much alike. Same interests, same taste in food and so inseparable," she remarked, accentuating her last word.

Feeling awkward that she had introduced the subject of Eli, I just gave her a slight grin of agreement. Right about now I could use a good strong ale, because I knew where this conversation was going. It's a painful sensation to experience when you are stirred to sympathy by another's great loss. I tried to ward off the intensity of her stare, so I quickly bit into the cookie. A flood of memories washed over me. I tried to focus on the moist, flaky texture with hints of vanilla and brown sugar with the crunch of walnuts and the softness of the chocolate chips which was still all too familiar to me. Closing my eyes, I hummed with delight, feeling myself smile as I tasted the sweetness of childhood. I was hopeful that our visit would go well with no references to unrealistic expectations of Elis' return.

"There is a scrapbook I put together of you and Eli," she said, breaking my spell of normal. "Would you like to see it?" she asked with hopeful anticipation lighting her face.

Ah yes, the ever present camera. I had forgotten how she always had a camera in her hands, strap dangling between her long fingers and the cry of "Wait, let me get that shot!" causing groans of annoyance from Eli. "Sure. I'd love to see some shots of the old days." A sadness gripped my heart as I dreaded to dig up the past, but I had to do this for her sake since it seemed to put such a delightful smile on her face.

Pushing aside our tea cups, she gently set a large, dark blue volume on the table. As I flipped through the pages of the scrapbook, I marveled at her artistic ability. Not just in her photography, but how she arranged the photos in the book with a sense of balance and color. "Did you take one of those scrapbooking classes? This looks so professional."

"Oh heavens no. It's much like sewing a quilt. Coordinate your colors and designs and it just falls in place. Easy as that."

"It is so beautiful. But believe me, if I tried this, well let's just say I wouldn't dare put my artistic talents to the test."

"You never know till you try."

"Oh, believe me I have tried. So let's not go there," I advised feeling the blood warm my cheeks.

We both giggled at that comment and went on to share more comments of memories and stories, finding some that made us smile and others brought us to laughter. I was filled with a feeling of childhood joy tinged with sadness as I followed Eli and me from the toddler years to elementary school. Dressed up for Halloween, on our bikes, proudly holding up a fish or a special quartz crystal, Carolyn had captured far more memories on film than I remembered. It made me realize that my memories were those of a child and that the adults in my life may have had completely different recall of my childhood. I knew that I had received the gift of childhood friendship and despite it ending in loss, the memories of that gift would be with me forever.

Carolyn smiled fondly at a photo of Eli and I, flanked by her and my mother dressed in our Easter Sunday best, complete with baskets of eggs that we held proudly. "I knew you would enjoy looking at these pictures," she said. "I have other photos of Eli that make me feel that he's not really gone. I look at them and I feel as if he is just at school or work. Maybe on a vacation somewhere." She smiled faintly again, her eyes misty. Looking back at me, she said, "Would you like to see them?"

"Gone on a vacation?" I mimicked her words beneath a gated breath. Oh dear, here we go, I thought. Be kind, Camille, I admonished myself. Besides, it's not like I have a buffet of options here. Either I run for the nearest door like a scalded dog or simply humor the poor woman. I resolved to settle for the latter.

"Would you like to see the pictures of Eli?" she asked again.

I considered briefly she had lost her mind, like her husband, the dance between sanity and unreality just a few steps apart. I nodded my head and forced a fake, weak smile. "Sure," I agreed. I briefly gazed down into my teacup with a short sigh. How would I gracefully extricate myself from this one, I wondered? My head moved slowly back up and caught her staring at me. "So you have more pictures like this album?" I asked her.

With a soft laugh, she replied, "Oh no, dear. I have progression enhanced drawings of how Eli would look today. Right here. Right now. They are so lifelike," she added as if he had been here the day before posing for a photo shoot.

Words failed me. I did not know how to answer a woman who put too much faith and hope in a miracle that is too far-fetched for me to believe. Be kind, Camille, I reminded myself again. I nodded at her and said, "Sure." What else could I say?

She smiled at me gently as if I made her day and taking my hand, said, "I have a friend, Mr. Shepherd, who does contract work for the FBI. He is an age progression artist and a very good one, I think. He was authorized to do age progression on Eli and over the years and we have become very good friends. He gives me a new one every year. His kindness has helped me through some of my loneliest times. Looking at these drawings has made me feel in a small way, Eli is still here. Somewhere close by. I would love to share them with you." She looked deeply into my eyes, "But only if you feel you can handle seeing them, dear. He will look like a grown man," she explained.

I was stunned. How did I not know about her friendship with this Mr. Shepherd? Why was I unaware of these pictures of Eli? I was beginning to wonder about my own grip on reality in the face of her confidence and her concern for me.

"Sure," I repeated again. Only this time with a tinge more interest.

I watched her as she stepped down the hall, her thin shoulders held straight. I then looked out into the dining room and saw the large family photo hanging over the buffet table. Framed in dark wood, the three of them, taken on their last Christmas together. The pose showed a family that loved one another, youthful joy mirrored on the faces of both parents and Eli himself.

Carolyn returned with another scrapbook, bound in denim. She placed it on the table before me and turned to heat the kettle again. I opened the book and began to watch Eli grow from 12 years old to manhood. His hair was wavy and longer in some photos and short in a few more. His freckles lightened and faded. His muscles grew and maturity lines appeared around his mouth. The texture of his skin aged slightly and thickened, and one photo featured a scruffy beard. As I peered down at him with that three day beard, I felt a prickling in my stomach. I slowly turned the page on the 24 year old Eli and felt the prickling grow stronger, heat rushing through my body. The last five photos took my breath away and I gazed upon each one, flipping back and forth. I was stunned at the man with the bright green eyes, who changed subtly from year to year, but still remained the same.

Looking up, I saw Carolyn smiling at me over her tea cup. "That book is for you, Camille. I have the original copies. I thought maybe it would be of some comfort to you to know how he'd look today."

Lurching to my feet, a deep groan escaped through my lips. "Thank you Carolyn for the tea and cookies," I managed to mumble. I took in a quick breath. "And yes, I will treasure these pictures. Thank you for thinking of me. But I have to run now and I promise

I'll be back again," I said, before I bent over and heaved out the cookies setting like a hard lump in the pit of my stomach.

"Soon, I hope," she said.

"I promise, I won't stay away so long next time. Thanks again," I repeated as I clutched the scrapbook to my chest and made my way to the front door. I fled down the steps and into my car, where I laid the book on the passenger seat. Driving North Valley Road back into Greenville, I felt a creeping panic crawl up my spine. What now? I wondered what my next move would be. Do I drive back to my house and hide under the covers and pretend I didn't see what my eyes are telling me I saw? Or do I stand on shaky legs, and confront a ghost from the past?

CHAPTER
15

I pulled into Greenville, resting for a moment at the stop sign, then crossed Highway 89 and eased into a parking space in front of the Sterling Sage. The little gift shop was filled with the beautiful and the odd; vintage jewelry and serving utensils with deer antler handles. I stepped inside and inhaled the fragrance of scented candles and expensive paper.

"Good morning Camille. You're out bright and early," Craig Huddleston cheerfully greeted me.

Craig and I go way back from kindergarten to graduation night. "Hi Craig. I thought you went off to college," I said. "Last I heard you were never coming back to this little rat hole."

"Big talk from a kid who thought he knew everything. I found out real quick that city life is not all it's cracked up to be. I'll take this small town atmosphere any day of the week. I'm actually the proprietor here. Bought this little joint about five years ago. Best decision I ever made," Craig confirmed with an easy shake of his head. Then he waved his hand through thin air. "But don't let me stop you. Take your time and browse around."

"Thanks," I said, thankful he didn't want me to stand and chat for another ten minutes. I wasn't in a very sociable mood. I politely nodded with a weak smile and wandered aimlessly through the artful displays. I was unable to think clearly, so I tried to focus on something insignificant. I picked up a couple of leather bound journals, riffling through the handmade paper pages idly. A large lead crystal vase with silk peonies in a soft pink rested atop a little piecrust table and I found myself smelling the flowers, seeking their fragrance. Wincing at my idiocy, I moved to a display of copper cookware. In the background I could hear Craig chatting on his cell phone oblivious to my current state of mind. He continued to chat easily as I browsed mindlessly along the counter. I stopped to admire some small beaded pill bottles.

"I can order those in different colors if you'd like," he said out of the blue.

"Oh, okay." He didn't seem to mind my mumbled reply and I was grateful for his calm acceptance of me in his lovely little shop. I felt as though my brain was in a thick and gelatinous mold, not unlike the aspic I remembered from potlucks in my childhood. Retail therapy is a genuine treatment, I had discovered. I didn't need to purchase anything, just the act of looking at and sometimes holding an object of beauty or creativity, allowed me to process extreme emotion. I found myself clutching a jar of gourmet, gluten free salted caramel sauce and felt the tears flood my eyes. Setting the jar of sauce gently back on its shelf, I quickly excused myself. "Thanks Craig. See you later," I said in a flat, monotone voice. I wiped my cheek bones with the back of my hand and moved out of the shop onto the sidewalk, the bell on the door tinkled behind me.

I sat down on the sidewalk, my feet resting in the street and closed my eyes. I inhaled deeply, the country town scent of pine trees and asphalt, clearing the fragrance of the clary sage candle I had sniffed inside the shop. Then the tears began again and I rested my head on my knees as the grief overwhelmed me. An unpayable amount of loneliness crawled up beside me. Sobbing shook my body and I wailed silently in my loss. I could not comprehend the events of my past and I was unable to understand current events in my life, either. As my weeping calmed, I felt a hand on my shoulder which immediately arched my head upward. Craig stood towering over me with a sympathetic, but comforting expression on his face that didn't make the moment feel awkward or embarrassing. Without a word, he carefully tucked a delicate lace trimmed hanky into my hand, and then just as quietly, stepped back into his shop. I felt fresh tears as his little act of kindness made me cry again.

My mind gradually stilled and I found myself, somewhat out of character, asking the Great Spirit for his help in my life. A prayer for consolation and guidance. The confusion and emotions of the new facts in my life had completely undermined me and I was at a loss how to proceed. Blowing my nose on the little hanky, I found myself with the tiniest of smiles on my face as I contemplated the utter uselessness of the beautifully embroidered confection. I silently thanked the Great Spirit for the kindness of friends and asked again for guidance. My next move would require courage and resolve; not exactly heroic actions, but at least put more of my energy into seeking the truth.

I pulled out my cell phone and found the contact for Kendall and sent him a text requesting a meeting. Rereading the text, I realized it sounded terse, but I was beyond caring. Pressing the send button, I sighed and slid the phone back into my pocket.

Lifting myself from the sidewalk, I shook out the little hanky, folding it into a neat square. I pulled open the door of the Sterling Sage and caught Craig's eye. Holding the hanky aloft, I said, "Hey, thanks. I'm not sure what happened. I feel so foolish, but thanks." I sighed and grasp the door handle as if it was my security blanket. Now I felt childish.

Craig was folding tissue paper with the unflappable air of a man who has seen everything. "You know, Camille, losing a parent is a tough thing and sometimes it hits you out of nowhere. And then you cry. And then you go on with life and then cry again," he assured me with a gentle smile.

"And it brings a lot of other stuff with it," I choked out a little laugh. "But thanks for the hanky. I'll wash it and bring it back. It's really pretty, I almost hated to use it."

"Ah no, no. You keep it. It is pretty and useless except as a shawl for a little girls' Barbie doll and I am tired of looking at it. You needed it and it's yours now. Thank you for taking it," he said wistfully.

We shared a faint smile and as I stepped back out to the sidewalk, I heard the chime of a text coming in on my phone.

Kendall's text let me know he was at his rental at the Lake and would be in Greenville in just under twenty minutes. I gave him my location, but didn't bother to end my message with the little smiley face as I normally did. There was nothing to smile about, especially since one more anguished question had just been added to my list of many.

Kendall arrived in what seemed like no time at all and pulled up next to my car, his jeep grumbling into place. As he stepped out, his tousled sandy hair was lifted in the early afternoon breeze. He smiled over at me, his green eyes squinting against the sunshine. "You have no idea just how good it feels to be back here breathing the pure mountain air. I could get used to living here," he declared with a warm smile directed at me.

Wearing a dark blue t-shirt emblazoned with the label of Kokanee beer, jeans and boots, he pulled on his Guinness sweatshirt as he moved onto the sidewalk.

Suddenly worn out by my bout of weeping, I sat down again on the sidewalk and he easily sat next to me, his long legs stretched out into the street.

He gave me a quick grin and said, "So, did you miss me?" he asked with a silly grin.

"Sure. I missed you. It's good to see you again," I answered in a tone less than enthusiastic and a glum expression on my face. I just couldn't fake my feelings right now.

"Ah, should I drive around the block and come back again? This isn't exactly the welcome back party I had expected. So am I missing something here?" he asked doubtfully with narrowed eyes.

Tilting my head back and contemplating the puffy gray and white clouds scudding through the clear sky, I asked coldly, "Who are you?" I waited silently, my eyes on the cloudbank to the north.

He shifted slightly and remained silent.

"I mean it." I could hear my voice rising with my anger. I was intent on the sky over Indian Head. "Who are you and why are you here? And better yet, why are you asking me about cemeteries?"

He let out a long sigh and drew in a deep breath. "Honestly Camille, I don't know who I am."

"Really? Are you kidding me right now? I mean it, Kendall. I need to know who you are and what you are looking for here in Indian Valley!" I was insistent, "So what is your story? And I want the truth this time! The whole truth!"

"I'm telling you the truth. I don't know who I am," he repeated slowly. "For thirty years I thought I was Kendall Danielson, son of Owen and Alice Danielson. Now I'm not so sure about that. I do know I was born here in Greenville, but other than that, my existence seems to be cloaked in a bit of a mystery. I have learned some things here lately that make me question everything I thought was true about myself."

I turned to stare at him, our eyes meeting. The green of his eyes was deepened by a pain I had not seen before. Briefly, I wondered if I was so wrapped up in my own misery that I had failed to see the suffering of a fellow human being. I was overtaken by the possibility that the world did not revolve around me alone. Maybe it isn't always about me? But I've come too far to stop now, so I asserted my right to know the truth about this man. "I want it all Kendall. Tell me what you do know."

He gazed at me silently for a moment, then shrugged again. Shifting slightly, he readjusted his legs, crossing one booted foot over the other. "When my mom died early this spring, I was really torn up and I started spending more time with my dad. He has severe dementia and has been in assisted living for a while now. I think it was caring for him that made my mom's heart give out. She was so exhausted from being his sole caregiver for so long that I truly believe she just couldn't recover her strength. Then she had a massive heart attack about 8 months after we had to put him in a home."

I sat there for a moment longer pondering over what he had said. I finally spoke to him in a gentle tone. "I am sorry about your parents. I really am," I said. But my inner compulsion to press on with my questions was irresistible. I needed to get to the bottom of this new set of circumstances before another sun slipped behind the mountain.

I stood up and moved over to my car. My words trailed behind me. "I need to show you something," I said. I turned my head away from his wide curious eyes and leaned into the open window. I pulled out the album that Carolyn Young had given me. Flipping through the glossy pages, I removed the last two photos and held them inches from his face. "Who is this?"

Reaching up, Kendall took the pictures from me and smoothed them over his lap. Peering at them closely, he held up the last one and shook his head. "Man, this is crazy," he muttered. "Crazy." He held his intense glare on the drawing as if it was speaking to him. I noticed his hand was trembling slightly, causing the paper to wiggle. Running his other hand through his hair, he whispered again, "Crazy."

Finally, he looked up at me and asked, "Where did you get these?"

Dropping back down to the sidewalk, I mumbled my response. "They were given to me this morning by Carolyn Young."

"Really! Where did she get them?"

"She has a friend who has been doing age progression sketches and computer generated aging on Eli's last school photo every year since he disappeared. This is how Eli would look today," I confirmed. "There is no denying these sketches are the spitting image of you. So now you see why I asked you who you are and why you are here," I said.

Again his head moved slowly from side to side, his eyes remained glued to the green eyes staring back at him. His confusion was apparent on his pinched face and I reconsidered that he might not have any more answers than I had. But he was obviously the man in the photo. That fact weighed heavy on my mind and made me that much more determined to get some answers. I deserved an answer from him. He knew he was searching for something, so the least he could do was to reveal exactly what it was he was seeking. Frustrated, I built up my courage and opened my mouth, but before I could speak, he stood up.

"Let's go for a ride," he said. "This sidewalk is hella uncomfortable and we have a lot to talk about."

CHAPTER 16

Glancing across the street, he said, "How about if I just follow you down the highway to Crescent Mills? I discovered that Crescent Country does brew a great cup of coffee and we can just sit and talk," he said with his eyes full of some emotion I didn't fully understand.

Anxious and on edge, I nodded in agreement and without another word, got in my car. Starting the engine, I puffed out a breath of relief and worry at the same time. Was I going to get answers or just a cup of coffee and more of the same evasive conversation he had given so far?

Winding along Highway 89, up the grade, through the shade of the tall pine trees with brilliant splashes of oaks interspersed, I passed the cemetery on the south side of the road. The old cannon, a relic from World War 11, situated at the bottom of the hill caught my eye as I zoomed by. I briefly wondered what secrets that artifact had recorded within its' marred surface which was a constant reminder of some of our country's darker days. Most likely stories much more unpleasant than the ones Kendall and I are dealing with today. With a parched face and narrowed eyes, I continued my drive down into Crescent Mills, the highway paralleling the railroad tracks. I pulled into the graveled parking area in front of Crescent Country. Kendall's jeep rumbled in behind me and parked a short distance away.

Crossing over to join me, his long legs covering the distance quickly, he stepped ahead to open the door for me. "Ladies first," he said in gentle tone. He gave me a tentative smile as I nodded my thanks.

The owner of Crescent Country Store, Lisa Forcino, waved at me from behind the counter as we entered the store. She was a lovely lady, a good friend of my father and now in her older years. She was a bit on the frail side, but her inner spirit of kindness gave her face a glow and an energetic spark of enthusiasm. A sweet smile lit her face as she maneuvered out from behind the counter at a surprisingly quick pace. I knew a big bear hug was waiting for me.

"Nice to see you again Lisa."

"So good to see you too, sweetie," she responded as she wrapped her arms around me with a tight squeeze. "Once a beauty always a beauty."

"Okay, enough of that stuff," I confirmed. We both released our embrace at the same time. "Lisa, this is my friend, Kendall Danielson."

Lisa nodded and gave Kendall a generous smile. "Nice to meet you Kendall."

"The pleasure is all mine, Lisa," he eagerly returned reaching for her hand.

"We were hoping to have a cup of your killer latte," I interjected.

Her face blossomed into a full blown smile. "Two hot lattes coming right up. Best in the West if I say so myself," she bragged. Gesturing to a little table in the graveled back yard, surrounded by a grape arbor, the leaves brilliant red in the autumn sunshine, she added. "Take a seat out there and I'll be right back with your drinks."

We turned and ventured out into the open air. Kendall had lagged behind long enough looking at some of the unusual trinkets and gift items Lisa's store had to offer. I reached the table first and immediately pulled out my own chair and took a seat. Once

Kendall slid into his seat, I spoke firmly and to the point. "You first," I suggested, my pulse quickening as I intuitively realized that maybe, just maybe, he was finally going to give me the truth in his own words.

He met my stare. His long frame dwarfing the little metal table. Readjusting his chair, he bumped the table with his knees, rocking the small bouquet of fake flowers stuffed tightly into a clear glass vase. "I feel like I am in Lilliput," he attempted to joke but grew serious again as he saw my sober expression.

"Don't be afraid. Just start at the beginning. That's always the easiest way," I urged.

Lisa appeared in the door and made her way to the arbor. Smiling at both of us, she placed our drinks on the small table. "Enjoy," she said, turning with a little wave as she disappeared back indoors.

Sighing, Kendall took a sip of his drink and then carefully set his cup back down on the table. He let his eyes drift over my head and gazed at the hillside behind as if gathering his thoughts into words. He took another deep breath and began.

"As strange as this might sound, sometimes even the atmosphere around us can be a forewarning to what is yet to come, may it be good or bad. For me, even the humid heat of summer in DC held an air of apprehension. The oppressive warm air and the incessant traffic and hustle seemed to hum and buzz with a menacing energy. Don't get me wrong," he said, catching my eyes with his intense stare. "I love my home city, but this summer presented me with challenges that turned my whole world upside down."

I just stared back at him giving him the time he seemed to need to unload his troublesome story. However, I could in some ways understand what he was trying to say about big city life. It can be depressing. Even when you are surrounded by hordes of people you can still feel alone. To me, DC represented nothing more than a big playground for the rich and famous who made big decisions for the rest of us peons. I have always been one to read and keep up with what was going on in the political arena whether it was here in California or where the elite mover and shakers reside. I knew DC had been besieged by protesters enraged by various pieces of legislation and movements. Activists considered leaders in their respective arenas had moved in on the little city to create an atmosphere of continuous discontent, anger and division. It was a different kind of heat that had steamed around business on the hill; politicians and their eager toadies seeking to generate more income to satiate their unending greed. As far back as I could remember it had always been that way. The battle for power led many to the compromise of personal integrity and to destroy opposition in an uneasy atmosphere of war against one's fellow citizens. The quest for political influence creeps through the layers of society and leaves an acid smell of manipulation behind. The continual quest for power and money that has threaded through the generations stitching the decaying social fabric into a semblance of reality. All in all, according to CNN it seemed to be a typical summer in Washington DC. So why would any of those normal occurrences bother him now?

"As I told you before," he went on to say, "my mother passed away just this spring and my father has been in assisted living since last fall. His dementia is a painful and disturbing process to observe. Alzheimer's is like a hungry leech, chewing away at what little is left of his former brilliant mind. One of my last visits with my dad gave me a glimpse into the mind of a man many years younger with a love for his wife, a powerful passion in his life. To me, it seemed for a few moments, I had my father back, unspoiled by the ravages of time. However, in retrospect, I knew my father had just visited a place in his mind that to him, he was having a conversation with a longtime friend and not his son. A friend I'm sure he felt would never betray his trust."

147

I continued to listen, clinging to his every word because I felt all the truth he had been hiding was finally going to be revealed.

"I tried to keep the conversation going by asking him for names, hoping to trigger more memories from his decaying mind. No need for names, he told me. He said all he cared about was keeping his wife safe and bringing his son home. His tone of voice had such a bitter bite. He looked at me as if I had said something that had offended him, but I hadn't said a thing. Then he looked me straight in the eyes and barked out some confusing words. He said I don't dwell on it. Never have, never will. Then his eyes seemed to glaze over and he began to stare out into empty space and repeated the same words over and over. It was evil. Evil, evil, evil.

"What was evil," I asked before I could stop myself.

"Unfortunately, the switch that had been flipped on in his head quickly flipped off. All I know is he talked about my birth and how he had carried a grave burden on his shoulders since the day I was born. He admitted I was not his biological son, but he loved me as if I were. He was surprised at how much he loved me. He said my mother didn't know about his awful deed and he would never tell her, because he loved her so much. Then he began to talk about someone he called Little Miss and how she had given him a gift the night I was born. That's it. He just stopped talking. I tried many times to bring up the subject again, but that brief moment of remembrance had been swallowed and pushed back down in the dark hole of nothingness," Kendall explained, his emerald eyes troubled and confused.

As I waited for him to continue his story, Kendall paused to take in a long breath. He slumped back against his chair and rubbed his weary eyes. I held my gaze to his face and watched the color go pale as if the sun had suddenly disappeared behind a cloud. I wondered what dark thought had enveloped his very soul, piercing him with despair.

"Just like that, it was over and his mind was gone again," Kendall picked up where he had left off. "During my next three visits, I tried again to get more information out of him, but it was no use. I realized that he would never re-visit that subject again no matter how much I prodded him. But I couldn't get it out of my head. His strange ramblings drove me crazy and I couldn't stop thinking about it. I had always known that I was born in Greenville. My parents were vacationing up at Lake Almanor and my mother went into labor two weeks early. As far as I knew, I was born here and then we all went back to DC and the rest is history."

His eyes sought mine as he talked and I began to sense the extent of his confusion. In the short time I had known him, I had always had a sense of his strength and this confusion was unfamiliar in him. I thought over his words carefully. My mind shifted like a kaleidoscope, the different hues and shapes of my thoughts creating a pattern that made no sense, but was colorful and yes, confusing. I considered carefully my father's possible involvement in Eli's disappearance, the resemblance between Kendall and the age progressed photo of Eli. Could things get any more complicated than this? But then I remembered his tedious search of various cemeteries in the area. "So why are you searching cemeteries?" I finally queried.

"I'm looking for someone who went by the name, Little Miss," he replied. "I couldn't locate her myself on any searches I did, so I am guessing she has passed on by now. I thought if I could find her, maybe I would be able to locate a family member who might know something. Or maybe not," he finished gloomily. "This has been a frustrating hunt. I searched online for weeks and I even considered hiring a local private investigator, but then I decided this was something I really needed to do myself." He shifted on the little metal chair, "I just want to find my birth parents," he finished, frowning down into his coffee.

I blew out a wispy sigh and said, "And I thought I had the market on mysteries. Aren't we a fine pair," I added in frustration.

His green eyes darkened as he looked up at me, his expression pained. "Now you understand why I say I don't know anything. Frankly, I feel like my life has been one big lie. Ironic huh? All my expensive schooling in research and fact-finding and I'm not even close to finding out more of the truth that my dad hid from me. And my mother, as well," he added. "Poor woman. She lived and died believing I was her flesh and blood."

"Look Kendall, maybe that's not such a bad thing. I think there is some truth in the old cliché'; 'what you don't know can't hurt you,'" I pointed out. But he acted as if he didn't hear one word I said.

Then he squared his shoulders and his eyes grabbed mine again. "How did he pull this off? What happened to the baby my mother was supposedly carrying? Or was my father just rambling like a senile old man?"

I gazed at him, getting a sense of his angst. "I imagine you are wondering what else about your life your father withheld from you? What other details he left out of your childhood?" I offered, with no proof of what I was suggesting.

He again snatched my eyes and spoke with determination. "Somehow, I am going to find out everything about my birth. Every life leaves behind a paper trail. All I need is to find one set of eyes or one pair of ears that heard or saw something that could lead me to the identity of my biological parents and the secrets my father kept. It's not like I'm going to hold a grudge against them if they put me up for adoption or left me on some doorstep. There are usually good reasons why people are forced to take such drastic measures. All I know is that I won't give up until I know what happened back then."

Considering all he had said, I carefully weighed my words. "Well, maybe if we put our heads together, we can figure this out. But I can tell you this much. At this moment I believe you are in some way connected to Eli. I am sure of it. The photos prove it. And someone, somewhere knows about your birth." I smiled wearily at him. "We'll have to do some sleuthing, and that is hard to do with all of the HPPA laws, but a small town always talks, so we might be able to find out something in the gossip circles. But I am not sure where to start," I admitted.

His long fingers wrapped around his mug, he lifted it and saluted me. "We will do a discovery. We lay out all of the facts and see what leads to what," he confirmed, taking a sip, swallowing deep and then he set his cup back down on the table.

"This is what we have so far. There is a boy who went missing eighteen years ago with no clues left behind. We also have his bike in the back of your dad's old pickup truck. There is paint evidence on the front passenger side that leads us to believe that the truck hit the bike, but we have nothing that leads us to who was driving the truck or riding the bike. We just know who owned each one. We also know that my father lied about my birth. We don't know exactly what his lies comprise, but by his own admission, I am not his biological son. We have the missing boys' age progressed photos that look like me. The fact that Eli Young's photos resemble me may be just a coincidental happening. But I don't trust coincidence." He stopped and frowned as if his summary was incomplete.

I thought this over and wondered aloud, "Who are you and how do you fit into all of this?"

He nodded, "Yeah. I know. And I don't know. The answer, that is." He sipped on his coffee again and remained silent with a pensive look on his face.

The more I thought, the more I felt. My emotions were winding up inside of me and I felt tension building. I decided to lay out my thoughts. "Well, here is my take on the situation. And you can laugh at it, this is kind of a woman's intuition thing. Maybe, somehow Eli survived the incident between the truck and the bike. Maybe he had amnesia or something, who knows. But I do know this, you don't just have a resemblance to how Eli would look now, you have a lot of his dominant characteristics. You talk like him, you have some of the same mannerisms and in my heart I feel like I have known you forever. Well," I said and then hesitated dropping my eyes to my fingers fidgeting with the handle of my coffee mug. I moved my head back up and met his curious stare. "I must confess that I did carry mace the first few times we met. A woman can't be too careful these days and I'm not stupid. But any reservations I had about you quickly faded away because you have this way about you that makes me remember him. I am going to find out who you are. First, I am going to find out how Eli's bike ended up in my father's truck. And hey, we can do DNA testing! That is pretty easy and we can get Carolyn to help, I am sure she will." Eagerly, I collected my thoughts and began a mental checklist.

Kendall looked at me as if I had taken the last drink of water before the well went dry. With sad eyes he stayed silent for a moment and then finally asked me a question that was obviously bothering him. "What if none of this works out the way you want it to? What if I turn out to be Kendall Danielson, whose parents gave him up for adoption to a vacationing couple with no kids from DC?" He leaned forward, his face close to mine. "What if I am not who you want me to be? What happens between us then?"

"I never said I wanted you to be Eli. I never said that at all!" I denied.

"Not in so many words, but I see it in your eyes. You have a longing to bring back someone whom you loved deeply and his loss is unresolved. These similarities between Eli and me, are they real or are they supported by a need you can't control? An unresolved need to get back what you lost at such a young age?"

I turned away from his intense gaze and looked down at my hands, twisting my napkin into pieces. His ominous words hung in the air between us. I felt their sting and I was embarrassed because part of what he said was true. I was unwilling to admit to myself that Kendall could see the truth in me that I wanted to find my childhood friend. I was also finding Kendall himself to be a wonderful and unexpected presence in my life. Fleetingly, I wondered if this is how 'normal' people fall in love. I was still staring down at my napkin when he spoke again.

"Let me tell you what I think. I think that no matter how this plays out, it was our destiny to meet. I agree with you about feeling like we've known each other forever. I felt that way the first time I met you and the first time I looked into your beautiful brown eyes. I want to see more of you and every time I do, I want to see you again and again."

Looking up at him, into those intense green eyes that caused a million goosebumps to blanket my skin, I felt a tremor in my stomach and I shivered unexpectedly. He smiled a slow smile and continued to gaze into my eyes. I felt exposed and was unsure of the emotion. How do normal people fall in love? I had a fleeting wish for an instruction manual on the art of love and/or relationships, but I knew from my education no such thing existed and I was on my own. I had to follow my own heart and my personal integrity.

He lifted his eyes from me to the mountain behind us, the dark verdure of the evergreens and the colorful displays of the fall oaks interspersed, creating a crazy quilt that only Mother Nature could design. "I just want to know you better, Camille. I am willing to wait until you are ready to consider the idea that maybe all of this has happened for a good reason. Maybe none of our suspicions are true. Maybe this was just destiny's hand at work, a simple way of bringing two hearts together who otherwise would have never met. I'm a simple man with a simple deduction," he said with the cutest smile I have ever seen. He placed one of his large hands over mine and let it rest for a moment. The warmth and strength of his touch calmed me and I was able to return his smile.

"Maybe you're right," I gulped. "We can just let the chips fall where they may. I'm not one to fight destiny anyway. And while we're testing the waters of affection, we can continue to work together trying to solve the mystery of your birth and everything else crazy and nuts that has landed in our laps," I said, trying to keep my smile in place. "We can do it together and see what we find?" My eyes narrowed as I put my other hand over his. "Who knows, maybe this will be my opportunity to understand how to love and live life to its fullest."

"I'm with you on that one," he eagerly agreed with a tempting grin that warmed my heart.

CHAPTER
17

The following day was hectic for me. I spent most of it reviewing cemetery records and organizing them into a semblance of order. It took everything I had to finish the tedious chore because anything over two hours of paperwork felt more like spending two hours of watching paint dry. However, I also face-timed one of my college roommates about creating a website for the cemetery, developing a user friendly site for genealogists and family to use. He was enthusiastic about helping me with the project. He now worked for a large commercial web design firm in San Diego and all employees were encouraged to find pro bono projects to pursue in conjunction with their paid contract work. I was excited for the collaboration and we sketched a rough plan of action and a time-line to pursue. I was completely immersed in the process and was startled by the lateness of the afternoon when I finally finished.

My phone chimed and Kendall texted to invite me to dinner in Greenville. My stomach growled and I remembered that Kendall and I had a sleuthing project to pursue as well. We agreed that he would pick me up and we would head to the Way Station.

The sun was slipping behind the mountains, the distant pines silhouetted against the softening sky, the coral glow reflected in the streams of clouds to the west. Dusk's chilly air carried by the evening breeze, brushed my cheeks as I stepped out of Kendall's jeep. Fresh with the scent of the pines, the mountain vista of my hometown has offered this breathtaking view so many times, I have to remind myself to stop and breathe a thought of gratitude. Taking a deep breath, I watched as the clouds spread and shifted before my eyes. The lovely apricot and lavender colors of sunset blurring and softening, a dance of unending beauty. I felt the mist arise in my eyes at the sight of the perfect and exquisite close of the day.

"Hey, you okay?" Kendall's voice came thru my thoughts.

"Oh yeah, just loving the sunset. I never get tired of that sight," I told him as I moved toward the cracked sidewalk. At this moment I felt such a sensory overload.

"I'd have to agree with you. I think looking at those rich colors is like a tiny glimpse of what heaven must look like," he surmised.

"Postcard perfect," I confirmed.

"Couldn't have used a better analogy myself," he said, his contented expression completely readable.

Stepping up on the hard cement, I stopped and turned around to face him. "This is the town's official dive bar," I continued. "Be prepared. Lots of beer mirrors and mounted wildlife on the walls. But they can serve a great burger, so here we are." I let out a little chuckle.

I saw Kendall give a double glance at the sign stating the premises are for Ages 21 and Over Only, and a second sign attached that specified no pooping on the sidewalk.

"Long way from DC, huh?" I teased him.

He shrugged his shoulders and shook his head. "In DC, the only public pooping occurs when a politician with his padded pockets starts talking. Good to know Greenville has standards." Smiling he opened the door and stood back for me to enter.

As we stepped inside, the warm ambience of the pine ceiling and walls enveloped us. Built in the 1930s, the Way Station is a long time Greenville fixture. A weigh station, in Greenville's logging history, was a place where timber was measured and graded, so the play on words in the name was completely appropriate. A bar that served food when requested, the walls are covered with murals of the logging industry and the local Indian history of the valley. A disco ball shimmered in the dim lighting and raddled wildlife mounts stared glassily with disinterest from the all sides. Luke Bryan had kicked up some dust from the jukebox and the low chatter of the regulars filled the air. Vinyl barstools against the long bar top for the regulars who were pretty serious about their adult beverages and a few little tables for the amateurs and tourists lined the walls.

We made our way to a small table in the back; self-designated amateurs. The look on Kendall's face as he inspected a stuffed badger with a vicious growl made me laugh. I saw appreciation for the low key atmosphere and the warmth of a small town pub in his eyes, as he turned to me and said, "This place is great! Back home, a building like this would be on the historic register and the pub-lican would have to get a permit to change a light bulb. But then, he can charge 18 bucks for a draft beer, so I guess it all works out ok." With an easy laugh, he pulled out a chair for me and then set-tled in his own seat directly across from me. Simultaneously, we both picked up a vinyl clad menu placed in the center of a huge red napkin and the eating utensils that were as old as the hills.

Our server, a hard bitten but somewhat attractive blonde woman I didn't recognize, stepped up to the table. "Cocktails for this eve-ning, Studmuffin?" she asked, with eyes only for Kendall. She ges-tured to the small drinks menu tucked between the salt and pepper shakers and a bottle of Tabasco sauce.

Smiling past her at me, Kendall asked, "Do you like champagne?"

"'Sure. That sounds good," I told him.

"Bring us a bottle of your finest champagne, please," he said, with a formal air.

"All we got is cold duck, Hon, but it's cold. That's all I can say about it. But we got lots of different beer on tap if you change your mind." She seemed somewhat scornful of our drink choice, but she smiled widely at him anyway, still ignoring my presence. "I'll get it right out to you. Let me know when you are ready to order some eats." She turned to the kitchen and left us, shouting to another patron waving for her. "Hold your horses Daryl, I'll get your beer in a minute. You ain't going to die of thirst," she snorted without a moment's hesitation.

With a sly grin, I couldn't resist the temptation to tease him. "Well now, Mr. Studmuffin, do we have an admirer?"

"Been rode hard and put away wet," Kendall observed. "Poor dear." With a pinched brow, he grabbed my eyes. "What the hell is cold duck, anyway? If she thinks it is lousy, it must be pretty bad," he scoffed, his expression guarded.

"What is the celebration that requires champagne from a sketchy source, such as this?" I asked him in a teasing tone.

His eyes still on me; I found the intensity of his gaze unsettling. A look of adoration in his eyes that was knocking on the door of my heart and beamed with appeal. A slow smile curled over his face as he softly answered me. "Because you are beautiful to me and such beauty deserves the best."

Shaken, I frowned, not with displeasure, but trying to bluff my way thru this unfamiliar intimacy. "Did you read that on a poster somewhere? Or was it a meme on face book?" I let out a nervous giggle.

His intense look remained, but he took a deep breath and said, his voice still soft but definitely more confident, "People waste too much precious time beating around the bush. I think the greatest respect I can show someone I care for is to be direct with them about my intentions and feelings. Like I said yesterday, I find myself thinking about you all the time. I want to spend more time with you. I see purpose and future and meaning in my life now, and you created that feeling in me. I feel so alive when I am with you. The sunrise, and like outside just now, sunsets too, take on a new meaning when I share them with you. You make me laugh, you make me think, you make me feel and you make me want to be more like the man I should be. And the more time we spend together, the more you leave me wondering if you are the one I have been waiting for and praying for all my life."

"Kendall," I said. "That's…" I couldn't finish my words because I really didn't know what to say. So I just sat there like a big dummy staring into his beautiful eyes that were staring back at me. I held his gaze for a moment before closing my eyes and dropping my head. My fear of emotional entanglements holds a strong grip on me. Also, I wonder if this is what that elusive element of life, true love, really looks like. I have always considered true love to be like hunting for Lewis Carroll's snark. Hard to find because no one knows what it actually looks like and it is open to any one of many interpretations. Is it possible that true love can show it's soft glow in the murky light of a dive bar with a disco ball over-head and a badger glaring at us from the wall? And to add to the romance, Mark Chestnut's signature song, Bubba shot the jukebox, was blaring in our ears at that moment. I shook my head and began to laugh quietly. "Ahh." I smiled sheepishly as paranoia swept over me. I lifted my head and gazed again at his handsome face which was such a distraction. "I really don't know what to say. Don't get me wrong, I'm flattered and moved by your words, but at a loss for words myself," I confessed. But deep in my heart, I found myself wanting this all to unfold into a relationship where the newness never ended.

Kendall continued down the same path without breaking his eye contact with me, "I don't expect anything from you but a chance to prove myself worthy of your affection. I hope that you will give me the time it takes to show you that what we have is something special and well worth trying hard to keep. I'm not saying I deserve it, because I am kind of self-absorbed and selfish and you have opened my eyes to that. But without a doubt, from the first moment I saw you, I thought you were the most beautiful woman I have ever met. And in the last few weeks, I have fallen even more in love with your inner beauty. You have opened my eyes to the simplicities and loveliness in life and that makes me want to be a man you could be proud of."

I chastised myself to be kind, and I smiled faintly at him. "Kendall, you are describing Mother Theresa, and Mother Theresa, I am not. I am Camille and I have my own collection of quirks and foibles. I don't want you to develop a false sense of who I am and then be deeply disappointed when you get to know the real me. You have been processing a lot of information about yourself, your childhood, your parents and even your existence, and I do not want to discourage you in any way." What I really needed at this moment was some of the swill that Blondie had promised. Some cold duck, yeah, that was what I needed. A little quaff of liquid bravery.

Kendall continued to paint a picture of me that was literally impossible to live up to. "I feel like you are the missing link that makes me whole. Don't ask me how I know, but there has always been somewhat of a void inside of me like something was missing. Sometimes I felt even though I was successful in life, I was like a bird flying with only one wing. And yet even while I was missing it, I always knew I would find my missing wing. And here you are." He dropped his head and with a low chuckle finished, "Who knew I would find it in a town so small, it is a census designated place, actually."

My mouth fell open but no words came out. His revelation was amazing, but fear paralyzed me, my breathing seemed to have ceased. Yes, I found him very attractive, the keenness of his intentions darkening his green eyes to a shade that fleetingly reminded me of the dark emerald of the midsummer oak leaves. But one big question muddled my mind. Did I really want to fall in love at a time when my life is like a shuffled deck of cards? Each day I never knew what card I would pull; a new heart ache, a new disappointment or a new unsolvable mystery which left such a deep emptiness within my soul. Do I want to pursue this friendship deeper into the unknown territory of commitment? I am so terrified of loss, am I capable of sustaining an intimate relationship? The many questions caused me to reflect that every man I dated had many of Eli's qualities of friendship, Kendall included. Every relationship I have had has been marked with the piercing loss of my best friend as an undercurrent of doubt. In my enlightened and educated mind, that was a serious obstacle to a flourishing and sustainable love affair.

"Kendall, I am so touched by your thoughts," I finally said cautiously, feeling the need to warn this good and decent man of my internal struggle, but wanting to be as kind as possible. "I really am touched, but I am pretty pitiful, emotionally. I don't want to mislead you in any way. You must understand that tearing down the barriers I have built around my heart and letting love in seems so unobtainable for me right now. I have lived with unpredictability in my life for so long that I don't know how to respond in a way that should come as natural as breathing. I'm a disaster waiting to happen," I admitted, even though in the back of my mind I was still toying with the idea that having some stability in my life was a refreshing concept. Even though I was stumbling with my reasoning process, I finally managed to form some direct words. "May we agree to take this slow and really get to know one another better?" I was certain that when he eventually discovered the authentic and broken me, he would extricate himself.

"Don't you see that none of that matters?" Reaching for my hand, he continued, "Love is accepting someone for who they are and also for who they aren't. All I ask is that you give me a chance," he pleaded in a tone so touching that it literally moved my heart.

I feel the strength and warmth of his hand and I sense I am being pulled to him as if by an unseen force. How can I refuse to water a garden so radiant in growth and color that it stirred my soul with such positive energy and absolute contentment?

Blondie thumped a bottle of cold duck and glasses on the table between us, breaking the romantic enchantment that held our eyes mesmerized. Having already popped the cap, she filled our glasses. I watched as a half a dozen little bubbles rose to the top and burst. She bestowed another wide smile on Kendall, "There you are. Are you ready to order, handsome?" she asked.

Not taking his eyes off of me, he said, "Give us a few more minutes, please."

"Well, let me tell you the specials for today," she announced as if she hadn't heard a word he said.

"The only special today is sitting across the table from me." He tore his gaze from me and gave her a quick smile and a nod. "We haven't decided yet, thank you."

I assumed she got the message this time, because without another word, she turned and walked toward another table with a pouty look on her face.

Kendall shrugged and smiled at me again. I found myself touched by his courtesy. Kindness to those who are irritating is an admirable quality and I realized in that moment, that I was finding the company of this man to be extremely satisfying and had already acquired a vital interest in everything he had to say. I extricated my hand and took a large sip of the wine. It was terrible and I reactively grimaced. And then laughed. "Not sure this is the best place to find a good, quality glass of wine," I tell Kendall. "But I need some liquid courage! Your compliments are, well, flattering for the lack of a better word, but I am not sure how to process all of this," I admitted.

He gave me his crooked grin, but uncertainty seemed to linger in his green eyes. "I guess my romantic speech was unexpected and probably a bit over the top." He paused dramatically. "I hope

I didn't scare you off?" he quizzed. I could tell he was trying to keep his voice casual.

With a coy smile, I reassured him that I wasn't the type of person that spooked at the first sign of a rough surf. "A bit unexpected, but it won't scare me off. I may drink more wine to process it, but I do enjoy your company. And, I'm not too proud to admit I want to see more of you, too," I said in a playful tone.

His confidant look reappeared and he smiled at me. "Thank goodness. Two more of your strong virtues I appreciate; patients and understanding," he offered. "Cool," he said smiling wider. "Well, let's have dinner and you can rest easy that I am not a crazy, deranged stalker."

We both busted out laughing and the comfortable ease of the day descended upon us again. Heidi Newfield sang to us about Johnny and June from the jukebox and the badger snarled his displeasure from the wall. Waving to Blondie, he signaled that we were ready to order. As soon as she breached our table, he spoke before she could. "A couple of beers please, maybe something from the Lockdown Brewery, if it is available," he asked.

She gave him a weak nod and walked away with a forced wiggle in her sagging behind. Within minutes she returned and plunked the beers down on the table. I was relieved I didn't have to finish any of the cold duck.

"I've done my research," Kendall pointed out. "There's this brewery located near Sacramento in Folsom that makes a beer to brag home about. I found the play on Johnny Cash's words especially amusing; the brewery was known as the 'home of the Folsom Prison Brews'."

Suddenly, loud voices from the far end of the bar interrupted our conversation. I whipped my head around to see what the commotion was all about. A man wove his way unsteadily toward our table. With the restrooms in the rear, it is always a gamble to choose to sit here.

Kendall and I must have been on the same wave length. "Hope he makes it," he observed.

Lurching to a halt beside us, the drunk set a trembling hand on my shoulder, causing a look of concern to cross Kendall's face. His guarded eyes widened and the muscles in his neck stiffened. I turned and saw a face that was almost unrecognizable. I was shocked at his appearance. Clad in soiled work pants and a sweat stained t shirt, his face puffy and eyes bloodshot with unkempt greasy hair, he had aged almost beyond recognition. "Butch?" I asked in disbelief.

Butch Jackson was a bully, a sneak, a thief and the bane of my elementary school years. His petty misdemeanors, small crimes and abuse of other children were relentless, and his final expulsion from school was a relief to me and many of my classmates.

"Ahh! Umm, it was my fault, you know," he said, with the slow slur of the intoxicated. With a tipsy stagger, he moved to and fro from one foot to the other. Then he gripped my shoulder with a clutch of desperation as if I could hold him upright.

I sat without moving, leery that he was going to land in my lap at any moment. "I'm sorry, Butch, but what are you talking about?" I asked in a confused tone.

His bleary eyes held a weariness which seemed to represent some kind of torturous scars from his past. "It's all my fault. Thass what I'm saying," he repeated. His expression creased into a mask of sadness.

A brunette, in a pair of Dickies work pants tucked into Doc Martens, appeared out of nowhere and stepped just inches from Butch. Her plaid flannel shirt was worn, but clean, and she had an air of gentle resignation about her. Tugging his arm, she said softly in his ear, "Come on, Butch. This isn't the time or place," she pleaded.

Pulling away from her with a sudden jerk, he thrust his hand into the front pocket of his filthy jeans. He pulled out a quartz crystal, lovely, in the rosy, creamy pink of the local stone. Shaped with the perfection formed in the quiet places of nature, the soft glow of the crystal shimmered against the grime on his quavering palm.

"Umm. I know he wanted you to have this. Yeah, he wanted you to have this alright. It's yours." He dropped the crystal on the table before me.

Still confused, I picked up the crystal, smoothing its surfaces with my fingers. Looking back up at Butch, I queried him again. "What are you talking about?"

Swaying against the brunette, he glared at me with the intense effort of an inebriate attempting to focus. "I took this from Eli. I knocked him ass over teakettle and took it from him. Thasss why he went out the next day to find you another one. And then he disappeared. Just disappeared." His thin shoulders began to shake, as he begins a blubbering wail, and tears came down in waves, dropping off his puffy cheeks.

The brunette, sliding an arm around him, began to beg again. "Come on baby, it's ok. You've told her. You got it all out, now let's go," she said in a soft tone, obviously trying to keep her calm.

Butch shrugged her off and shouted at me, as if frustrated with my incomprehension. "Don't you see, it's all my fault? I took this from Eli. It was your birthday present. He was all sorts of proud of his gift for you when he showed it off. But I took it from him and thass why he went out to find another one for you. I as much as killed him myself!" he admitted. "I killed ummm," he repeated in exaggerated slowness. "I killed ummm!"

Stunned, I stared up at his bleary face. As I thought over his words, I could feel understanding tugging at my heart. I reached up and took his trembling hand, "Butch, don't be so hard on yourself. You were just a kid. Teasing was a part of your makeup," I lied, because throwing the truth in his face that he was a pestering bully would not serve a good purpose this many years after the fact. "There were other kids who teased as much as you. Besides, we don't know that Eli is dead, we just don't know where he is."

"Don't talk down to me, Camille! I'm not stupid. I've carried thass stone around with me for 18 years as a reminder of what a piece of crap human being I am. Nothin' you can say will wipe out my guilt." He shook with silent sobs and swayed against the brunette, who put a steadying hand on his arm. "If I hadn't roughed up Eli that day and stolen thisss damn crystal, then he'd be sitting here with you today instead of this dude." Giving Kendall a brief but hostile glance, he shook his head and swallowed hard.

I was torn, I wanted to strike out at him for his childhood transgressions, but I also felt somewhat sorry for his pitiful state in the present. He was trapped in a reality that was years in the past. "Listen to me Butch. You can't be sure of anything you are saying. You don't know for a fact that Eli went out to look for another crystal. He may have just gone out to fish Wolf Creek. You know he loved to wet a line first thing in the morning. For all we know, he may have been on his way to Round Valley Lake to catch some bass. No one can be sure of what he was doing or where he was headed. He just disappeared." I tried to keep my voice even, but the pain of that summer so long ago was just beneath the surface of my emotions.

Butch sought to find his precarious balance and gripped the edge of the table, and shook his head, "You're so predictable, Camille. Such a Pollyanna, always looking on the bright side of everything. But at the end of the day when I try to sleep, I know it is my fault he is gone and nothin' you or anyone else can say will change that." His voice held the hurt and pain he had nurtured over the past eighteen years.

"Butch, listen to me," I pleaded again. "Eli would not want you to carry this guilt on your shoulders. Even if what you say is true, you can't give up hope. Or give up on yourself."

"You're a thousand times wrong, Camille Cameron. Eli's dead and I am going to rot in hell." His voice broke and he swayed again.

"Please, Butch, let it go. I'm telling you that this is not what Eli would have wanted. You know he didn't have a vindictive bone in his body. He carried no grudges against anyone for any reason. This is enough just to give me this crystal," I said, still concerned for his state of mind. The brunette tugged gently at his arm and he turned and looked at her as if seeing her for the first time.

"Butch," I say his name again which brought his hazy glare back down on me. "You must forgive yourself. That's all part of the recipe of moving on," I declared, but he stared right straight through me as if I wasn't there.

"Yeah, yeah, you're probably right. Good old Eli would want me to let it go. But there's just one big problem with that grand idea. Every night, every damned night," he repeated, his voice rising with a quivery wail. "Every damned night, I can't sleep. I see his face. I see his mother's pitiful face and I can't forgive myself." Raising his hand as if to ward off any more conversation, he turns away. "I'm going back over to that bar," he gestures drunkenly. "And I'm gonna drink Eli out of my head like I do every night."

The brunette dropped her arm and with a look of despair on her countenance, she shook her head and mouthed, "Sorry," to me. Her pretty face held the pained expression of a woman who knows she has lost the battle for her man to the demons in his head and the rum he uses as a tranquilizer. Obviously something that is played out often and publicly.

Both Kendall and I watched them silently as they returned to the bar and were again safely seated. His eyes sought mine and then stared down at the crystal in my hand. The glow of the pink quartz was a rosy shimmer in my palm. Raising his eyes to mine again, he spoke almost in a whisper. "Not sure if I should be irritated at the poor man or simply pity him," he admitted. He sounded ashamed, as if he should have intervened and put a halt to the conversation before it got out of hand. "But I couldn't read your expression to know what your reaction would be if I stuck my nose into your business. All I could see in your eyes was compassion for his suffering so I kept quiet. Honestly, I don't usually take the coward's way out, so I do apologize if I have disappointed you."

"Don't be silly. It's not the first time I've tried to reason with someone who has over-indulged and it won't be the last," I assured him with a one sided grin.

His eyes were surprisingly tender and caring, but still agonized. "Are you sure you are okay?"

I can hardly contain my excitement as I gazed down at the crystal in my hand. Raising my head once again to look into his marvelous green eyes, emotion making my voice husky, I say, "Better than okay. I think I now know where Eli was going that day."

CHAPTER
18

I awoke early and showered with some haste. I dressed in jeans with a t-shirt and pulled on my Keen's without socks. I surveyed my face in the mirror for a moment. My dark hair, damp from the shower, hung past my shoulder. I had neglected regular haircuts over the busy summer and I fingered it with some dismay. I had a darker tan than usual, the result of all of the outdoor chores and my brown eyes looked back at me critically. I smoothed on some sunscreen, swiped on a little waterproof mascara and hooked in my earrings. I tugged on the silver and turquoise pendant that hung from my throat, the stone warm in my fingers. Giving myself a last glance in the mirror, I pulled on a pink hoodie and went into the kitchen.

Kendall arrived just as the sun's glow peeked over the mountains in the east and fingered luminous trails over Indian Head. I heard his jeep rumble up the slope and he parked in front of the deck. I watched him through the kitchen windows as he stepped out and stretched while looking down over the cemetery. Then he turned and climbed up to the kitchen door, his long legs taking the steps two at a time. He rapped on the door and poked his head inside.

"Oh man, I'm going to let my nose follow the aroma of that coffee," he said as his face exploded with excitement.

"Come on in. I've just finished grinding the beans and I'll start a fresh pot of coffee. How does AK-47 sound this morning?" I laughed quietly to myself over the name of the coffee blend.

"I'm game for anything new and different," he replied as he opened the door all the way and stepped inside. Despite the slight chill in the morning air, he was wearing cargo shorts and running shoes. Giving me a quick grin, he stepped further into the room and in the warmth, unzipped his sweatshirt. I scented the faint woodsy spicy scent that he wore and I smiled at his t-shirt. 'Buy Beer Right Here' lettered in white inside the outline of the state of Montana. The dark brown of the t-shirt made his green eyes glow in the tan of his face. "Nice shirt," I told him as I pulled a couple of mugs from the cupboard and then placed my eyes back on him.

Glancing down at it, he frowned and said, "Yeah. I think I won it on a bet one night. I don't really remember. College days," he said ruefully with a laugh.

"Been there and done that, too," I told him as I gave him his coffee. "Great times and good people, but I'm glad I am done. Now it's onto other adventures, like discovering who you are and what happened to my childhood friend. The mystery continues for us!" I made light of our plans, but I was somewhat nervous about the day ahead and the possibilities of what we might find.

"Positive thinking Camille. At least we have something to go on which is a whole lot more than we had two days ago," he confirmed.

"I suppose you're right. I need to focus on the positive," I agreed. "I promise. No more pessimistic perspectives out of me for the rest of the day."

"Fair enough," he said.

Our plan for the day was to search the three crystal beds south of Crescent Mills. Given the scant information we had and the very few facts in our possession, we had decided to start with retracing what we hoped were Eli's footsteps his last day.

I poured coffee in a thermos and tucked it into my backpack with sunscreen and some granola bars. I added two apples and four bottles of water. Hesitating a moment, I noticed my mace canister. I could have never imagined in a million years the rapid change in direction my feelings for this man has taken me. Smiling to myself, I turned to face Kendall and asked, "Are you ready for this?"

"I was born ready," he stated confidently and held the door open for me.

We sprinted down the stairs and climbed into the jeep. Our tires crunched down the drive onto the smoother pavement. Turning right on Highway 89, we drove south the short distance to Crescent Mills. Passing through the small town, I silently marveled at my fellow citizens of Indian Valley. A little bedroom community for the timber industry, Crescent Mills had seen some hard times. It was nestled between Indian Creek and the railroad tracks to the south and a mountain set at an angle to the north. Thirty years ago, Crescent Mills was a bustling and prosperous little town. A large Louisiana Pacific lumber mill rested along the railroad and employed many of the local residents in the lumber production. Logging trucks rumbled through town to the mill and the train stopped regularly for lumber shipments. I remembered the sound of a mournful train whistle and the rumbling thunder of train sections jerking together as the train left town towing flat cars loaded with lumber. The Crescent Hotel had a happy hour for loggers and locals. Despite good timber stewardship practices, there was a decline of the logging industry in California; less timber was harvested from the large tracts of woodlands, the mill closed and the town sank into a depressed somnolence. Businesses shuttered and many residents left to make a living elsewhere. The strong and sturdy souls who now resided in Crescent Mills had recreated the little town as their home and as an attraction for tourists and sightseers who traversed the Feather River Canyon for its wild beauty. We passed the little gas station and my favorite place for a latte, the Crescent

Country Store, on the right. The small market on the left and the closed hotel, with a cluster of small houses made up the south side of the highway. The tiny post office with 95934 in large lettering over the door and a few more homes and then we were out of town and on the highway southwest again.

Our destination was a crystal bed just south of town on the Feather River. I felt a lurch in my stomach as I knew I would be retracing my lost friends' last footsteps. He had climbed on his bike and ridden off into the early morning sunshine, leaving a space behind that time and life had not filled in my heart. I was somewhat nervous to be sharing this experience with Kendall, unaccustomed to opening myself up to others. I recalled one of my mother's sayings, drifting along to me on a silvery thread of childhood memory. 'A joy shared is a joy doubled and a sorrow shared is a sorrow halved.' With the immaturity of youth, I had not understood the meaning, but now it was becoming more comprehensible to me. I was also nervous about the possibility, given the condition of my father's old pickup and Elis' bike, that this was where time had ended for Eli, and I swallowed hard to hold back my emotions.

"Right over there, Kendall," I said. Motioning with my pointed forefinger I instructed him some more. "Pull off the highway onto the narrow graveled shoulder and turn around and park on the south side of the road overlooking the river."

He deftly maneuvered the jeep around and into place, pulling the parking brake sharply. With a little frown, he surveyed the river over my shoulder through the jeep's open window. "Looks fairly calm," he said. "With all those rocks, I bet it's great for fly fishing?"

"Looks can be deceiving, so don't let those calm waters over there fool you," I advised, as I pointed to the far north just before the large rocks separated the water into bubbling ripples. There are some treacherous undercurrents lying just beneath the serenity of that deep water. There has been more than one drowning in that exact spot," I added.

I wasn't certain about the fishing in this particular spot, but I remembered it as a great place to find quartz crystals. I never revisited it after Eli disappeared, but I had good memories of the two of us on the warm rocks in the hot sun during the summer, our bare legs dangling in the liquid coolness of the river.

Kendall and I climbed down the bank, stepping carefully from rock to rock, slipping occasionally on the red dirt gravel.

The Feather River is a deeply tempestuous river; narrow in some places and widening out over gravel beds in others. It can range from a sleepy flow, safe for wading in the shallows during the summer to a rising and wild crest during spring thaws. The water flows and crashes over the many granite boulders and burbles over the gravel in the shallows. The power and speed of the river is contained in places by hydroelectric dams and is a source of electricity. It is not a river that is to be trifled with as many have found to their dismay. Its' beauty is incomparable and its' temperamental flows make it a breathtaking sight as it chases itself down the curves and twists of the picturesque Feather River Canyon.

This section of the river split and we stood on the bank of a narrower gravel shallows, the crystal bed in the center, edged by willows and reeds. A wider, deeper and wilder arm of the river ran just to the south. The water flowed and rippled below us, the quartz and granite rocks glinting in the light glow of the early sun. The water was a clear amber gold in the depths between the rocks, as it reflected the clean sand. It splashed over the rocks, and lightened to a pale green gold as it swept over and swirled back down to the tawny colored sand beneath. A light mist was rising off of the calmer pools and threading its' way through the willows on the far shore. Wisps of the mist hung over the willows, giving the scene an ethereal appearance. The fresh scent of the water and the sharp tang of the willows and wormwood bushes filled my nose and aroused hints of memories held dear and close to my heart. I inhaled deeply. The fragrances of my home valley in all of its' hidden and special places was something I could not describe, but I felt gratitude in my heart for the beauty before me.

Kendall reached the bank and turned to hold a hand out to me. "Careful," he said. "That rock there is not very stable."

I stepped out onto the rock next to it and then over to the one with him. We both looked down into the foamy water as it splashed from stone to stone. Glancing back and forth along the river, Kendall asked rhetorically, "Well, where do we start?"

I motioned to the crystal bed along the far bank of the river. "There is a path to get over there. We just have to find the right rocks to hop thru the water and I sure hope you don't mind getting a little wet. Sorry to say, but that water isn't exactly lukewarm. Bear in mind, the last time I did this, I was in grammar school so I might not be the best guide on the river and the river can change every year depending on weather and water flows," I warned.

"Lead the way," he said as if he had all the confidence in the world in me.

"I'm not sure how or what happened, but since this is the bed that is closest to the highway, it makes sense that he would have been here or coming here when his bike was hit by my father's truck." I paused a moment, wondering what on earth I was trying to do with this eighteen year old mystery, piecing together a history out of a few thready facts. "I know it's a long shot, but the other crystal beds are not close enough to the highway and the damage to his bike indicates that it must have been hit pretty hard, so the truck was moving fast." I gestured up the slope to the highway. "The curve of the highway is pretty gentle, so a vehicle could move along at a pretty good clip so I am thinking that this is where the impact happened," I explained as my eyes met his.

Kendall blinked several times. His brows lifted and I could see the questions swarming like bees in his eyes.

My shoulders slumped in frustration. "I don't know what we are looking for here," I admitted. "Just any indication that Eli was here, I guess."

He smiled at me and said gently, "Camille, we'll look as long as you want. This is important to both of us, so even if we don't know what we are doing, we'll do it together. Agreed?"

"Agreed," I answered with a renewed sense of anticipation.

Kendall took my hand and we both waded through the splashing waters to the next rock. We spent the next several hours climbing over the rocks and moving stones. Splashing in the shallows, the cold water numbing my toes, we stepped in between some of the larger boulders and peered into crevices between the smaller rocks. The granite and quartz glistened thru the water in the sunshine and the water burbled around us. I showed Kendall the crystal bed and we dug for a while, but found none worth keeping. We tramped along the bank for a few hundred yards on both sides of the crystal bed. Swishing through the tall grasses and in between the many willow trees, alternately swatting at a mosquito and holding branches back for one another. Neither of us knew what we were searching for, but I was determined to cover every inch of ground. The sun rose and the day warmed, casting off the autumn chill.

Exhausted, I finally stopped and turned to him and asked, "How about a granola bar and an apple?"

"Sounds good to me," he returned.

I lead the way to the bank on the south side of the river and sat down on a fairly flat boulder. Kendall followed close behind and took a seat on the same rock just inches below me. Then he stood back up and pulled off his sweatshirt. I admired his lean muscled form under his t-shirt with the goofy Buy Beer Right Here as he settled back down. His unruly hair waved in the little afternoon breeze and he impatiently brushed it back off of his forehead.

Trailing his hand in the swirling eddy at his side, he commented on the possibility of fly fishing again. "I think there could be some great fishing along this river. The water is the right temperature and these rocks can have lots of hidey holes for fish."

"I'm not exactly into fishing. Never did seem to catch my interest," I admitted.

"It's not everyone's cup of tea. Kinda messy with worms and fish guts," he offered with a sense of understanding into a woman's perspective on the matter.

"It's not that. Bugs, worms and hellgrammites don't bother me. Trout are such a beauty of nature. They are like a rainbow beneath the water. I just can't bring myself to, you know? Smack it in the head once I catch it," I enlightened him with a pinch of embarrassment warming my cheeks.

"Oh. Gotcha. That tender heart of yours getting in the way of a good fish feed," he said with a cute grin.

I just shrugged my shoulders and didn't bother to deny it. Instead, I ran my eyes around the circumference of his cute little dimples. That was much more pleasant than thinking about dead fish. I continued to listen as he talked about different fishing flies for different times of year and even different times of day.

"I must personally own at least five fly fishing rods. A man can never have too much fishing tackle," he told me. "And believe me, it's important to know the local insects and when they hatch and how it affects the feeding habits of the fish." He stopped for a second and studied my face. "Go ahead and tell me to zip it. I'm sure by now you are bored stiff," he said with a slight huff.

"No, not at all. Never know when all this information might come in handy," I lied.

He contemplated for a moment with squinted eyes and then went on talking.

As I sat there patiently listening to him going on about every aspect of fishing, I found myself impressed with the depth of his knowledge. It was interesting to watch his face as he warmed to his subject. He explained how water temperatures affect the spawning and development of fingerlings and was passionate about teaching younger kids to fish.

Eventually, even though he was well-informed on the subject, I finally lost interest in fly fishing and decided enough was enough. I cupped my hand, filling it with water and threw it at him.

"Enough already," I whined. Then quickly I tossed more at him.

Surprised, he laughed and rallied quickly, tossing water back at me. His hands being larger, he drenched me with just two large splashes and I shrieked and jumped up the bank.

"Maybe I'll just throw you in," he threatened.

"You wouldn't dare."

"Don't tempt me," he warned as he grabbed my shoulders and we wrestled a bit.

"Laughing at him, I pulled away and struggled to climb a little higher on the boulder behind me. Slipping as I scrambled, I felt him grab my foot and I slid over the back of the rock, kicking free as I slid. He climbed up behind me, miscalculating his speed and tumbled over the back and down into a quiet, shallow space, with just a few reeds and dislodged a fairly large sized rock with one booted foot. Standing up, he stood there dripping, and as I laughed at him, he smiled back at me and my heart seized as I fell into the green pools of his eyes.

He tried to step back up onto the rock with me, but his left boot-lace was caught by the stone he had loosened. Struggling to free it, he tugged at the rock and rolled it over. Frowning, he reached down and fumbled around in the silty depth beneath. Pulling his boot free, he continued to dig and then triumphantly held up a waterlogged and muddy object.

"Tada!" he crowed." I found the buried treasure!"

"What is it?" I asked him.

"Whatever it is, it is slimy and gross," he responded with his nostrils pinched.

Stepping back to the river's edge, he stooped and washed the object in the waters, turning it over and over in the flow to rinse it clean. I peered over his shoulder as he rubbed it gently to remove more mud and sand.

Standing up again, he lifted it high enough for me to get a clear view. Toying in the palm of his hand was a small leather bag, half rotted with a dangling drawstring. Opening it gently with two fingers, he pulled out a perfectly shaped quartz crystal.

I felt the waters of the river begin to swirl higher and higher, chilling my legs and compressing my heart, reaching my eyes until I closed them to stop the dizziness. Stunned, I found myself forced into clutching at his strong back for support.

"Camille, what's the matter?" He turned and wrapped both arms around me. Standing on the river bank, I felt the waters recede and the warmth of his arms filled me. I just stood there shell-shocked and shook my head. I allowed him to hold me until the panting subsided and I could catch my breath. It took me another moment to answer him.

"This bag belonged to Eli," I told him. "He carried it everywhere. He made it in 4-H as a leatherworking project and he kept it with him all the time. If it wasn't hanging from his neck, it was tied to his belt," I elaborated. I swallowed the lump in my throat and pulled back, reaching for Kendall's hand that held the sodden relic. "See here, on the side? He burned his initials on it and you can just make out a Y. Even though it is falling apart, that is recognizable. And this crystal, I'm willing to bet that this is the replacement for the one Butch stole from him? And I'm pretty sure he wouldn't have left this bag here by choice. In fact, I don't think for one minute that he mistakenly left it behind or accidently dropped it. What I'm saying is, whatever happened to him, it was tossed here in the process," I concluded. My voice was stern, more abrupt than I had intended. But when I looked at him, I saw a peculiar expression on his face I couldn't quite read, causing my sudden anger to subside and my tone to soften. "So what are your thoughts?" I challenged.

Kendall's eyes were fierce, staring down at the leather pouch. His jaw twitched when he grit his teeth. Then his face seemed to relax as if resigned to my idea. He spoke to me cautiously and composed. "I can see how it was protected from the current, tucked in behind those rocks. I think somehow it was partially buried under that rock and that prevented it from complete destruction over the years. I'm not sure what else it means, but there may be a great deal of truth in what you say. At least we have to consider that your friend may have been here the day he disappeared," he admitted. After a few more seconds of staring down at the pouch, possibly trying to absorb this crazy concept, his eyes suddenly widened and demanded my attention. "Was the river ever searched or dragged after he disappeared?"

A long silence hung between us as I fought against the pain that threatened to overpower me. After all, thinking Eli was gone for good hurt bad enough, but to find evidence that could quite possibly prove that fact felt like a sucker punch to the side of my head. I tried to commit my mind to a past memory. "I think the river area was searched, but I was a kid, so I'm not sure exactly where the search took place. I do remember my dad saying that no one really knew where to look because no one really knew where he was going. But people talk and they talk in front of their kids. It was big news around the school grounds that divers were brought in to search the river," I said and then dropped my eyes to the crystal he held in his hands. I reached out and touched this small creation of nature and marveled at its beauty, glowing in the early afternoon sunlight. The pale opalescence of the stone shone with slight veins of gold in its depths.

Looking up into the early fall sky, clear blue with just a few puffy clouds, creamy white against the cerulean, I wondered if this was perhaps the last view of our world that Eli had seen. Surrounded by the burble of the clear water splashing over the rocks and the scent of willow in his nostrils. Did he lie here in the river and watch the clouds tumble and roll by as his vision darkened? And was he alone? I stifled a sob as I considered that my dearest childhood friend had departed this world by himself, walking into eternity with no one beside him.

Kendall wrapped his arms around me again and I inhaled his spicy woodsy scent and found myself returning. Rubbing my face into his t-shirt, my voice muffled, I said, "I just can't bear the thought of him being all alone. The wondering about what really happened that day still torments me. I hate hearing the questions roll off my tongue. Every time I say anything about that day, just seems to open the raw wound encompassing my heart. But there's no easy way of getting around it. There's no way to step back from the edge of the ugliness of reality, because the proof is in your hands. And as hard as this is to say, I now believe this is where it all ended for him. Something horrible happened to him right here, and now I wonder, did he suffer in his last moments? Would he have even come out here in the first place if it hadn't been for trying to please me with the perfect birthday gift?" I asked not really wanting to know the answer to that particular question.

"You can't blame yourself, Camille," Kendall spoke firmly. "You were just a kid, even you admit that. He was doing something that he loved if this is where he was, and he was doing it for someone he loved." He tightened his arms around me and bent his head over mine and gave me a little kiss on the top of my head. "If I could figure all of this out for you, I would, but there's too much we don't know yet. But I promise you, we'll work on it together. Okay?"

"Okay," I said and forced a slight grin to raise the corners of my lips.

He lifted my chin with his finger and smiled down at me. His intense green gaze bored into my eyes and I felt hope trickling back into my heart and I could feel his strength in his arms and could see it in his eyes. He kissed my forehead just above my brows and I felt my heart warm.

Releasing me, he took the precious quartz and pushed it back down into the pouch. Then he took my hand and placed the little bag in my palm. He wrapped my fingers around it and held it in his hand. "Keep this in a safe place," he instructed, his velvety voice so gentle and compelling. "We have a lot of work to do, so let's look around this area a bit more. Are you okay with that?" he asked.

"Yes."

Our obsession with finding anything else began to grow as we explored another fifty foot area around where Kendall had found the pouch. But an hour later with no new articles found, we were both exhausted.

"What you say we call it quits for the day. We have the pouch which proves he was here at some point on the day in question. Let's just get out of here and make some sort of a plan."

I tried to focus on what he had said instead of the agonizing brokenness inside of my heart. Allowing myself to be overwhelmed by the magnitude of our find would only limit my brain's ability to think clearly. I needed to comprehend the significance of finding Eli's pouch and grasp it with gratitude because we were one step closer to possibly solving this mystery. But still I had to admit that to process something this important was far more painful than I could have imagined. "I'm good with that," I agreed.

Kendall took me by the other hand and led our way up the rocky bank, skirting boulders and crunching over the red gravel up to jeep.

His unconditional commitment to me sent flutters through my stomach. Everything about him uttered the promise of a better tomorrow. I clutched the damp leather in my hand and I could feel the angular presence of the crystal against my palm, the only tangible object I possessed of Eli Young on the day he disappeared.

CHAPTER
19

Back at my home, I changed into some dry clothes. I sorted through one box of my father's clothing that I just couldn't part with and found a pair of shorts and a T-shirt suitable for Kendall to wear. I made ham and cheese sandwiches on sourdough bread. Kendall made himself at home, opening cupboards and searching my pantry, finding some chips which he put on the table along with a jar of pickles he found in the refrigerator. While we ate our late lunch, he began to organize his ideas and sketch out a plan of action for us to follow.

Having pulled out a yellow legal pad I kept on the counter for telephone messages, he turned to a new page and began writing quickly. I admired his long fingers sliding over the paper, writing neat and concise notes. He caught my glare which pinked my cheeks, but he didn't seem to notice that I was now examining his exquisite face that raised goosebumps on my skin every time I indulged in that pleasure.

"First we need to get the case records for Eli's disappearance," he pointed out. "We need to learn about any and all searches, witnesses and all information that was used," he said, choosing his words carefully.

I could tell his scratches on the paper outlined exactly what he had said in detail. Then he turned to a fresh sheet and began jotting down other tasks. "Do you know of any hospital staff from approximately 30 years ago that may still live here?" he asked, thinking outside the box like a true mastermind.

I let out a throaty giggle. "Kendall, that was before I was born. But I will make some inquires around town," I said. "There's bound to be someone who knows something."

He ignored the obvious sarcasm in my voice and went right on hatching his plan. His ideas seemed to be limitless. "I haven't had much luck in finding hospital personnel myself, but I thought with your hometown connections, you could find out more than I could and do it quicker," he explained. Then he gave me that all knowing confident look. Frankly, I think we might accomplish more if each of us worked on the others' case. As an attorney, I would be more adept at researching police records, contacting witnesses and finding case files. On the flip side, you would be able to talk to the locals that you knew had worked at the hospital or in the medical profession at the time of my birth," he told me, holding my eyes on his.

"Makes perfect sense to me," I eagerly agreed, trying hard to follow his train of thought. I felt calmed by his capability to organize our muddled thoughts into some sort of concise plan; a blueprint of sorts to follow. The shock of finding that Eli's age progressed photos were identical to Kendall was replaced with the realization that somehow the two incidences might be connected. Working together would make it easier to progress and easier to process the new knowledge.

Kendall finally finished his notes and read them back to me. It seemed a good summary to me, given that we knew very little, but I felt hopeful that we might be able to make some progress now that we had a plan. He would look for records and legal files and I would find someone to ask about birth records. Sounded simple enough, but I knew there would be undetected snags along the way. Resurfacing faded memories due to the passage of so many years would definitely be my biggest obstacle, but I was more than willing to tackle the challenge.

Finishing his sandwich, Kendall blotted his mouth with a Christmas napkin I had dug out of a drawer. "Thanks for lunch. And next time, I'll bring the beer," he promised. "I'm going to get on this search record this afternoon. By the way, where is the local police station located?" he asked. "I could ask Ramona, but I might as well ask you," he added. "You're prettier and a thousand times more enjoyable to talk to," he said giving me one of his big dimpled grins.

I rolled my eyes and sank my head toward my left shoulder. "Well, it's such a relief to know you think my brains work as good, if not better than your mechanical girlfriend," I joked.

"Way smarter and way prettier."

"Yeah! Whatever you say," I sighed, shaking my head. I let a few seconds pass as my eyes enjoyed looking deep into his cute little dimples. I couldn't help but wonder how on earth any man could be so smart and so unbelievably handsome and wrapped in one sweet little package and delivered to my front door step? I cleared my throat trying to comprehend the wonderment of it all which gave me a whole new level of delight.

"Okay then, you turn left and go over the bridge into Greenville proper. It's about halfway thru town, but it's located on the left hand side just behind the Plumas Bank. So look for the bank and then you'll see the cop shop. It's an off white, stucco building, with a south of the border trim work. You can't miss it," I said with a grin lifting the corners of my mouth.

"See, I told you," he said. "Ramona would never have said cop shop. She doesn't have a very extensive vocabulary," he said ruefully. Then suddenly his eyes got serious and his expression became grave.

I knew he wanted to say something important. My heart skipped a beat.

He reached out and placed his hand on my cheek. I could feel the softness of his palm, the warmth and the strength of him felt comforting. His anguished eyes looked deep into my mine, his green gaze intent and urgent. "Camille, we'll work on this together. I know it was a shock to find what we did this morning. I don't know where it will lead us and I can't make any promises about the outcome, but I can promise you this much. I'll be with you. By your side all the way. And I don't break my promises, no matter what," he confirmed in a tone low and confident.

I placed my hand over his and murmured, soft and whispery. "Thank you. I'm thankful I'm not alone in this. I really am," I said. I didn't know what else to say, but I found his touch reassuring. There was so much to think about, so much I still didn't know about this beautiful man who had waltzed into my life out of nowhere. All I could think was that it would be so easy to let down my guard and fall in love with him. I let out a short gasp. Too late, my heart told me. I'm pretty sure what I was feeling right now with the warmth of his touch, was indeed love. And with that welcomed thought, simultaneously our lips met. We shared our first kiss. If ever I had to remind myself to breathe, it was now as his lips softly explored mine and then moved slowly up to my forehead.

"I love you Camille," he said as his words caressed my skin along with his soft lips.

I concentrated on breathing normal as his lips once again found mine. I knew at this moment that there was no turning back. He had found the key and unlocked the door to my heart. My mind was whipping around trying to think of the right thing to say at a moment like this, but thankfully, he did the talking for me.

"Don't say anything," he said as two of his fingers covered the rounds of my lips. "I'm sorry if I'm being much too brazen. I just can't seem to hold my emotions in check when I'm around you." His voice burned with regret.

"You didn't upset me." I forced my words through his fingertips.

"Good. It's not my intentions to overstep my boundaries."

"You didn't," I replied, my voice composed. I smiled wide, a smile of encouragement.

Kendall gave me a pleasant smile in return and then suddenly backed away. He looked at the clock over the sink and then dropped his face to my eye level. He spoke to me matter-of-factly as if nothing out of the ordinary had just taken place. "I'll meet you back here tomorrow and we can compare notes. Until then, pretty girl, keep a smile on your beautiful face and think positive. We are finally making some headway. That's reason enough for both of us to dream big tonight."

He pecked me on the cheek and let his hands drop away from my shoulders. And with that, he turned around, stepped outside the door and bounded down the stairs to his jeep. I followed him to the edge of the railing and found myself admiring his athletic build and grace in motion. I had to shake my head to clear my thoughts and focus on the task at hand. Sighing, I walked back into the house and picked up the phone to make the call I hoped I would not regret.

CHAPTER
20

T he phone must have been the old fashioned wall mount. It was fumbled and then dropped with a loud clunk. I held the receiver and waited patiently. I heard mumbling in a male voice and then a woman's voice asking questions in an indistinct murmur. The phone was picked up from whatever hard surface it had landed on, the cording creating a scuffling sound in my ear. The woman spoke cheerfully, "Hello."

"Mrs. Batson?" I asked politely. "This is Camille Cameron. I hope I haven't caught you at a bad time?"

"Oh honey, any time can be a bad time, but it can be a good time too," she replied.

I could almost see her welcoming smile in the depths of her gentle tone.

"You know once a doctor always a doctor and this old doc still thinks every phone call is for him. Every time it rings it represents some sort of emergency at the hospital or a quick house call. Wilbur just hasn't quite gotten used to the meaning of retirement," she said, her tone taking on somewhat of a serious quality. She paused to take in a breath and let out a long sigh. "And unfortunately, with his dementia, he's not quite sure how the phone works any more either. My apologies for the confusion. But enough of that. How are you?" Her warm voice was reassuring.

"I am doing well, under the circumstances," I told her. "I try to keep busy. The cemetery is a never ending task and I can't seem to get ahead of all the chores. I certainly have a new appreciation for all of my father's hard work. You never really know what it is like until you walk in another man's shoes. Sometimes I wonder how he managed to get it all done," I explained, talking too freely and suddenly embarrassed for monopolizing the conversation. I quickly put the ball back in her court. "How are you and the doctor?" I asked with true concern as a million memories about this beloved couple flooded my mind.

Mrs. Bertha Batson, wife of Greenville's long time doctor was a sweet lady in her late 70's. I remembered her well. Not only did she assist her husband with a few of his many duties, she also was a substitute teacher in my elementary school. Her cheerful demeanor made her well liked in our little community. Sadly, her husband, Dr. Batson, was in the gluttonous grips of dementia and at the age of 84 was struggling mentally and physically. She cared for him, with the assistance of a daily caregiver, in their longtime home, a white clapboard with green shingles on a quiet side street just off Highway 89. They had been a busy and socially active couple in Greenville before the doctors health took a turn for the worse. My father had admired Mrs. Batson for her kind heart and enjoyed her company socially. They were pillars of the community, but more like royalty in the eyes of the locals. However, they chose not to live a lavish lifestyle, raising their three children to be well-mannered and well-grounded. They lived like the rest of us around here, cut from the same common cloth.

"Oh you know how it goes. Some days are good and some not so good," she declared with a sheet of sadness cloaking her voice.

For another five minutes or so we chatted about inconsequential issues like local politics and the price of gasoline. Finally I found the nerve to get to the real reason I called. Taking in a deep breath, I cut to the chase. "I was wondering if I could ask you some questions about births here in Indian Valley. Specifically, I was hoping you could give me some information about babies that were born here in Greenville around thirty years ago and then put up for adoption," I said, immediately feeling the muscles tense up in my back.

"Oh dear, I don't know about all of that"' her voice was untroubled. "Back then, I was so busy with other things, I never really paid attention to that part of hospital business. Over the years, many babies found better homes when the birth mother was not able to care for them properly, but I can't remember many details. But I tell you what, you should get in contact with Marilyn Crouch. She owns the little beauty shop on Main St. called, Curl Up and Dye. Silliest name I have ever heard, but then I was never a big fan of puns. She works all hours and I think most days of the week. A hard worker, that girl is. But, fortunate for you, she's a history buff and keeps track of births, deaths and every detail in-between. Her grandmother kept local records too and Marilyn has continued the practice. She might be able to answer some of your questions."

I did remember Marilyn. She was older than me, but had always been nice. I had never been to her shop as I left for college before she opened for business.

"Thank you so much, Mrs. Batson," I said.

"Anytime dear. Now you come by in person sometime for a visit. Doc may not recognize a face, but he hasn't forgotten names. He could tell you what the weather was like the day you were born," she reassured me.

"I promise. I'll come visit you both real soon."

"The caregiver is here from 9 in the morning until 4:30," she told me. "It's best if you come when she is here. Then we can have a proper visit without being interrupted too often. The Doctor may want to perform surgery or something," she told me with a laugh. "And when he's tired and in a confused state, he can get a little cantankerous at times." Her breezy laugh came over the line and I could picture her face, merry blue eyes and sweet smile.

"I'll keep that in mind. You take care now."

"You too dear," she said before I heard the phone click dead.

As I stood there with my phone still in hand, I thought how some people never change. They are just who they are and they remain the same. Mrs. Batson was that kind of person. I marveled at her grace and charm under what must be difficult circumstances. I remembered that she always wore a dress or a skirt and pinned her hair up neatly. Her necklace and earrings matched. She had a lovely smile and she accented it with a range of lipstick colors. She knew many people in town and had a kind greeting and warm word for everyone she encountered. I truly hoped I would be like her when I was her age.

I stepped into my bathroom and ran a brush through my hair. Crinkling my nose at myself in the mirror, I then rummaged through the basket on the counter. I found what I was looking for, a neglected tube of Mary Kay lipstick in Tuscan Rose. Swiping some on my lips, I smiled at my reflection. The color suited my tanned face and I liked the look. Tucking the tube into my pocket, I decided I would become like Bertha Batson; forge ahead with determination and don't look back with any regrets. I tugged on a wool sweater against the fall chill and pulled on my boots.

Driving into Greenville, I thumped up over the little bridge and followed the highway through town to Main Street. Turning right, I spotted Marilyn's little shop on the north side of the street near the auto parts store. The window was painted with a floral design and the services offered within. Haircuts, Styles, Manicures and Pedicures, Waxing and Spray Tans. Children and Long Hair welcome as well. I pulled into a diagonal parking spot just across the street and parked. Glancing up in my view mirror, I reaffirmed my determination. "You got this." Then I rolled my eyes, scooted out of the car and crossed the street.

As I stepped inside, the warmth and the fragrances of the salon met me. The pleasant scent of shampoo and styling products, with the sharper odor of nail acrylic and polishes, a large overhead fan lazily turning the air. The shop was cheerfully decorated with a floral theme with splashes of autumn color and had a welcoming air. It was larger inside than it seemed outside and it was busy. Three stylists had clients in the chairs and the two manicure stations were in use as well.

The thing about living in a small town is that you know almost everyone. If not personally, certainly by sight. I recognized Marion Hamblin, my childhood Sunday school teacher at the Methodist Church tucked away on Pine Street. She was an elderly lady and I guessed in her eighties now. She had a head of lovely, thick white hair, was strikingly beautiful then and still was now. She had rows of blue rollers clipped into her mane of snowy hair and was under the dryer reading a copy of Home Cooking magazine. But as I looked closer, I could see her eyes were closed and she appeared to be napping in the relaxing warmth of the dryer.

Jayne Chelotti, a very pretty girl I remembered from high school was at the next station, having her hair blown dry by a heavy set stylist with bushy, brown hair. She had been a busy girl in school; active in sports and student government. She was very attractive and had worn her blonde hair long. I remembered her as being very popular with the guys. We had not been friends, but we had not been enemies either. She looked over at me with a frown, glancing at me up and down. I felt somewhat uncomfortable at her inspection, wondering if I had done something unbeknownst to me to displease her. But then she reached forward and picked up a pair of glasses, sliding them carefully over her ears as the stylist blasted her hair. She looked at me again and smiled in a friendly way, giving me a little wave. "Hi Camille. Looking good there girl," she shouted.

I moved my lips upward and improvised the widest smile I could muster and wiggled my fingers in the air. I realized her frowning look had been due to her inability to see me. I was somewhat disgusted at myself to jump to such quick negative conclusions.

To the left of the front door were the manicure tables and I saw Mary Ann Little, a shy sweet girl I had also known from school, giving a manicure to Denise Zunino, who had been the town librarian for a few years. Mary Ann gave me a wink and a weak smile, but she and Denise were discussing something very serious and she bent her head back over her work.

Glancing behind the manicure tables to a seating area, I saw a woman a few years older than me with a discontented look on her face. Clad in a severe black dress, her thin, angular body fitting it perfectly. The bones of her face were well formed, but her frowning expression marred her beauty. She wore large pearl earrings and her mouth was a slash of red lipstick. I fleetingly thought of my resolve to wear lip color and wondered about the softness of the Tuscan Rose on my lips and what this lady in black thought of it.

She caught me eyeing her and called out crossly, over the hum of the blow dryer, "You'll have to wait. Walk INS are first come, first served and I am next," she declared with a bitter bite in her voice. Her eyes smoldered with resentment.

Denise raised her head at the comment, and she looked over at me. "Hey Camille, nice to see you. And you be nice, Julie," she demanded in a tone not befitting a lady. "Don't mind her, Camille, she got out of bed on the wrong side today. You remember my older sister, Julie? The bitchy one?" she blatantly stated, still giving her sister an embittered look of disapproval. Then she tipped her head back and laughed out loud.

Julie let out a groan of indifference and gave her sister the evil eye. Then she turned her gaze to her iPad on her lap. I didn't know Julie personally; I just knew that Denise had an older sister.

Obviously age didn't seem to make a difference in who called the shots. Julie definitely held the upper hand when it came to control.

However, Julie's indignant attitude was hard to overlook and definitely set the mood to a low level, dismal grey. I was eager to escape her piercing stare so I skipped like a scalded chicken further into the salon.

I finally spotted Marilyn in the rear of the shop at the same time she saw me. She hadn't changed a bit. The same reddish blonde hair, most likely Loral over easy. Still energetic and cheerful. She was probably ten or so years older than me, but she had always been friendly, and had a smile for everyone, including the heartbroken little teen that I had been. She set her shears on the counter and gave the lady in her chair a pat on her caped shoulder. She walked away from her station and came out to greet me.

"Camille! How great to see you! You are so beautiful, just like your mama. Without a doubt, one of the prettiest girls this town has ever manufactured," she said, flowering me like a spring garden. She wrapped me in one of her well known hugs and squeezed, whirling me around in a circle.

Julie called out, "You are using the word manufactured in the wrong context. Beauty is not manufactured, it is produced," she snarled.

Marilyn just laughed her off. "Ah Julie, just because you are a big shot lawyer in a big city back east doesn't mean you have to be uppity in your home town. It is ok to be yourself when you're with friends!"

Julie shook her head and grumbled, "Gingers. You can't trust them," she piped up in a snarky tone. Then she turned back to her iPad.

"I'm going to pretend I didn't hear that," Marilyn quipped. Stepping back, she surveyed me, "Don't mind Julie. She's just being cranky today." Then she eyed my hair. "Hmmmm, yeah, you could use a trim and a little shaping. But come on over here while

I finish combing out Phyllis." Taking me by the hand she led me to the chair adjacent to hers. "Sit, sit, sit," she ordered me. "We need to catch up on about ten years or so of news here."

I smiled apologetically at Phyllis Brown, waiting patiently in the chair. "So sorry, Phyllis, I didn't mean to interrupt. And to tell you the truth, I'm really not here for a cut or a shampoo," I elaborated. "I just need to talk to Marilyn."

"No problem," she said, tilting her head to the side with raised brows. "Quite certain anything you have to say will be ten times more interesting than what happens in this sleepy little town. Besides, I'm in here every week and we had just about talked it all out, so fire away," she urged me with a friendly gleam in her brown eyes.

Marilyn agreed, "We've covered everything from the football team to who didn't sleep well last night," she said with a quick laugh. "I think Phyllis and I have pretty well solved most of Greenville's immediate problems. We'll work on Taylorsville and Crescent Mills next week," she added as she smoothed Phyllis's bangs down over her left brow.

Obviously not innocently eavesdropping from across the room, Julie called out, "Haw, that will be the day when you two are all talked out. I don't know about you Phyllis, but one can be rest assured that even after death, someone will still have to kill your mouth Marilyn." Again her tone was colored in rich sarcasm.

I felt my eyes widen as an eerie quiet asserted itself in the salon. Only the dull hum of a dryer broke into the uncomfortable silence between the two angry sisters, but after Denise cleared her throat, more insults simply started tumbling out of her mouth.

"Julie, maybe you better come back tomorrow when you find some manners," her sister piped in. "Besides, fixing your hair is like putting lipstick on a pig anyway. One ornament can't disguise the many defects in your unusual species," Denise said, drawing more blood.

"Mind your own business," Julie muttered under her breath.

I kept my eye on the two sisters for the first sign of fists flying, but to my relief, only another uncomfortable silence followed. I hoped it would stay that way at least until I got what I came for.

I watched as Marilyn expertly combed and styled Phyllis's hair into an attractive Bob with a stacked back. The warmth and friendliness of the salon finally returned and I felt somewhat relaxed. I inhaled the aroma of shampoo, conditioner and tangerine scented hairspray. Several lavender candles burning throughout the shop helped to defuse the sharp odors of nail acrylic and hair dye.

As Marilyn polished off the finishing touches on Phyllis's neckline, I surveyed the posters of hairstyles and products, neatly framed and hung on the brick walls. There must have been at least two thousand dollars' worth of retail items that lined the shelves mounted on the walls and stacked neatly in several glass enclosed cabinets. Marilyn ran a first-rate retail establishment, with not only hair care products, but skin care, jewelry, scarves and a line of purses and wallets as well. It was a common small town phenomena, a little shop that had a little bit of everything to accommodate the needs of the locals. It took a particular skill to create an atmosphere such as that and it was a skill I admired. So completely different from the cookie cutter stores and corporate culture I had experiences during my years in San Francisco.

I mulled over how best to broach the subject to Marilyn. I knew so little about my search and I didn't want to thrash and flounder around, wasting time and possibly not getting any answers. I forced a grin, hoping my apprehension didn't show on my face. "I've been talking to Bertha Batson lately, and she told me about your history project. How you've gathered quite a bit of information about the babies Dr. Batson has delivered over the years. You know, keeping track of how many sets of twins, triplets and how many babies were put up for adoption. General birth records, actually." My tension lessened once I delivered my words. It was beyond me to understand why my emotions welled up so powerfully inside me over one simple question.

"Oh sure, I have all of that in my birth journal at home. My grandma started it when she was a doula with Doc Batson years ago. I took it up when she got too sick to do it herself because it made her happy. When she passed, I just kept on. It is harder to get information nowadays, with all of the privacy laws and some folks are going to Quincy or Chico to have their babies too. But, I have a pretty accurate record, if I say so myself," she bragged, then gave me her crinkly-eyed smile.

"Oh, that's awesome," I told her. "May I see it sometime?" I asked cautiously, hoping I didn't sound too brazen with my odd request.

"Of course, you can. I have Friday off this week if you want to come by. Just give me a call to make sure I am home. I'd love to show you. It is a really neat thing, if you think about it," she claimed. Then her eyes lit up like she was reminded of something cheerful. "Aubrey Stokes, the nurse practitioner who used to assist Dr. Batson actually gave me all the new born photos they had collected over the years. They had them hanging in their break-room. When they remodeled about ten years ago, they were just going to throw them away. Luckily she asked me first if I wanted them. You know me, I jumped on it," she explained.

Phyllis smiled at me again as Marilyn removed the cape from her shoulders and shook it on the floor. "Camille, I'm so sorry about your dad. He was such a gentleman and well liked in the community."

"Thank you. I never tire of hearing kind words about my father. I miss him more every day."

"I lost my mother about a year and a half ago and there are days when I pick up the phone to call her," she said, her lips pressed together into a hard line. "Then reality slaps you upside the head to remind you that that simple pleasure you once took for granted will never happen again. It is a hard thing to get over and you may never get over it, but time does help ease the pain. Keeping busy helps too," she added as if it were an afterthought.

"Hey Phyllis, speaking of Camille's dad, have you ever told her who wrecked his truck back when we were in school?" Julie's harsh voice came over the salon interrupting our conversation. "It's about time somebody came clean on that big fat secret."

I swiveled around to look at her, surprised and horrified that someone knew about the wrecked truck in the back recess of my father's barn. I eyed her and deciphered her expression. She glared back at me with a cold, but gloating look on her face and then turned the icy glare on Phyllis.

Phyllis shuffled uncomfortably as she stood. She glanced at me, her face tight and as horrified as I felt. Then she landed a dark look back on Julie. Her face was pained and her cheeks were blood red. Marilyn stood silently between us with her jaw hardened, watching Julie with a guarded expression.

"Thanks for nothing, Julie," Phyllis said coldly into the sudden silence.

"You're welcome," Julie replied in a haughty tone. "People really should be accountable for their juvenile crimes."

"How do you sleep at nights?" Phyllis asked, her tone sharp and laced with poison.

"With my eyes closed," she retorted with a martyred expression.

Phyllis gave her one last dirty look and then drove her bronze eyes in my direction. "About the truck," Phyllis said, her low voice cracked. "It is ancient history. You were just a kid and I was in high school." She grimaced, "With Julie. Gah." Shaking her head, she asked, "Do you remember my brother, Dave?"

Dave Wilson. He was Phyllis's little brother and at least three years older than me. I remembered him well, a delinquent with a big 'D'. He stopped up the toilets in the gym with towels. Ran stark naked across the football field one year during the homecoming game against Chester. He waxed the windows of teachers' cars. Although I didn't know him on a personal basis or run with the same crowd of people in school, I had been well aware of his reputation as a rowdy brawler, most likely destined for a life of crime. I got to know the real Dave after he started doing odd jobs at the cemetery for my father. According to my father, there was always a place for Dave at our table during those troublesome years.

I contemplated, trying to choose my words carefully as not to humiliate her any more than she was already. "Well, I remember he was quite a spunky kid," I lied. Some of the folks in town placed bets that he would wind up in prison before he was twenty.

Phyllis sighed, then smiled, "Yeah, that's putting it mildly. Thankfully, he has changed a lot since those days. He is married now and has six kids, can you believe that?" She laughed and shook her head. "I think your dad had something to do with that major miracle. Dave always claimed it was Divine Intervention and Mr. Cameron who turned him around. He works at Papenhausens Gas Station now. Master mechanic; the best in his field," she explained, then her voice cracked again. "You should go talk to him about your dad's truck. It's always better to hear it from the horse's mouth."

"Horse's ass you mean," Julie called out over the hum of the dryers. "Just call a spade a spade, Phyllis. He was a little thug destined for a one way ride to San Quentin and you know it."

"Lighten up, Julie," Marilyn said crossly with a dismissive wave, shears clutched in her hand. "Just give it up. There's no call to be so downright vindictive. We're adults now, so quit living in the past," she advised, the pent-up annoyance flowing freely now.

Phyllis grimaced. "I know what a problem child he was. Our whole family had a wide range of fears of what was to become of him," she admitted. "But that was then and this is now and now he is a good husband and father. People can change you know. Fortunately, he mended his ways before it was too late," she said frostily.

I could feel the waves of infuriated disapproval rolling off of Phyllis and Marilyn. I too, was thunderstruck with Julie's vicious outbursts. But unbeknownst to the multiple personalities confined within these walls, this new information that she had revealed through her angry, biting sarcasm is actually information that I needed, but had no idea how to find. I should have come to the beauty parlor first, I thought to myself. I probably would know a lot more about everything in town, if I had. My amazement quickly turned to excitement. If there was a good explanation for the damage on my father's truck, I wanted to hear it. All thoughts of births at the Greenville hospital fled from my mind and I was eager to find Dave Wilson. A million and one questions began to formulate in my head.

Suddenly, I realized I needed to tone my excitement down a notch. I felt like a child full of anticipation and expectancy, but neither of these ladies would understand the slow smile stretching across my face, because I was struggling to understand it myself. After all, my questions for Dave would once again take me down a dark path that would be painful to follow. I quickly bit my lip so I couldn't say anything rash and reveal what had sidetracked my thoughts.

Turning my focus back to Marilyn, I spoke direct and to the point. "Look, the past is the past, so let's just leave it at that. But getting back to our meeting on Friday, you're sure you are fine with giving up some of your time to go over your records with me?" I asked, already knowing her answer.

"Actually, I'm looking forward to it," she replied with a gracious smile lifting the corners of her lips.

"Okay then. We've got a date. I'll call you closer to Friday to set up a time. Gotta run girls," I said, quickly excusing myself with multiple hugs exchanged with both women.

I left Curl Up and Dye with a sense of purpose; my only thought now was to find Dave Wilson.

As I moved quickly toward my car, I thought about how my nature had taken on a whole new level of craftiness. I was getting good at playing the question and answer game. Frankly each day seemed to present a new game of charades. I was capable of extracting information under the pretense of it being just normal conversation. Obviously, my expensive education has come into play in the most unlikely situation. It has taught me to be wickedly sneaky. I gulped. Hopefully, this is not the real me.

CHAPTER
21

I drove through Greenville in a slight daze, taking the side streets before crossing Highway 89 and pulling into Papenhausen's Gas Station. The garage, gas station and mini market were all housed in one building on the south side of the highway, overlooking Wolf Creek. To the east of the garage, across a paved parking area was the large structure that comprised the Evergreen Market with a small Laundromat on the west side. Across the highway, on the north side, setting back from the highway behind a large lawn and a gravel parking area was the high school, home of the Greenville Indians the letter board proclaimed. I felt a little surge of nostalgia for Greenville High School as my eyes lingered on the sign. I had made some good friends and good memories in that high school and I had a feeling of fondness for it. Basketball games and dances in the gym, cold nights cheering on the football team with my gaggle of girlfriends on Friday nights. Warm memories blending with a sense of relief that I had outgrown the school.

I pulled up onto the concrete apron in front of the little store and parked. I peeked into the garage first, looking into both bays but did not see Dave anywhere. He was not in the full serve gas station area either, so I moved over to the front door of the pint sized convenience store. The door swung open with the ringing of a little bell mounted on the inside. Greeted with the scent of warm hot dogs and popcorn, the usual view garish displays of snack foods, sodas and energy drinks, the t-shirts and hats and a wide magazine rack. I stood in line behind three teenage girls, giggling over photos on their phones as they paid for their jerky and bottles of hideous orange and black nail polish. I wondered briefly if I had been like that in my younger teen years, or if I was a solemn child, overcome by grief and loss.

Stepping up to the counter, I asked a simple question which I thought deserved a simple answer. "Is Dave Wilson working today?"

"Who wants to know?" The bearded man behind the counter asked in a clipped voice. He peered at me through thick glasses and waited for me to respond. Judging by his serious, angry eyes, I thought for sure if I said one wrong word he would have me arrested.

"Ahh, my name is Camille Cameron. Dave and I are old high school friends. I just got back into town a little while back and I wanted to catch up with him," I replied, hoping he would be satisfied with my answer.

"Just want to make sure you're not a bill collector or private investigator," he elaborated. "Dave's identity got stolen by some real creepster and he is having the devil of a time getting it cleared up. Lotsa people want to talk to him about lotsa things. It's gotten so bad that some idiot in Texas has him mixed up with someone else and has threatened to come out here and rearrange his face," he clarified.

"Oh my gosh, that's terrible! But I can assure you that I'm not party to that mess. I'm just an old classmate wanting to catch up on old times, that's all," I pointed out, hoping his bark was worse than his bite.

He gave me a weak smile and let out a sigh. "You can find him out back. He's on his dinner break. He works long hours to pay for all those kids and all that crap with his stolen identity." He gestured with his chin, "There's a table out back. He'll probably be out there."

"Thank you," I said and beat my own breath out the door.

The paved area spread out around the entire building. I began my nervous walk to the back portion of the station, in fear the proprietor would have second thoughts and run me off his property. Once I breached the side of the building, I could see a little space with an untidy lawn and a large picnic table placed in the center. Wolf Creek splashed cheerfully just below the embankment and I could actually see parts of an old swimming hole Eli and I frequented as kids. A gentle breeze with the bite of oncoming winter rustled through the pine trees and the privacy made the space attractive.

I felt a thrill of excitement the instant I caught sight of Dave sitting alone at the table with a book before him. He was drinking from a large water bottle and had a small cooler on the bench next to him. He was of average height, very muscular with a shock of reddish brown hair. He heard me behind him and turned to look. The bright smile he flashed me was welcoming. His burst of laughter crinkled his big hazel eyes. I smiled wide.

His smile grew more pronounced. "Camille! It's great to see you! I heard you were staying in town after your dad's funeral. I am so sorry, he was a good man."

I picked up my pace, my eagerness to talk with him growing with every step.

Reaching for me, he enveloped me in a bear hug, and whispered, "It's good to be home, near friends and family, at a time like this."

Releasing me, I could smell his cologne. It was a faint scent, but recognizable as Avon's Wild Country. I chuckled inwardly wondering if everyone who stayed behind after high school remained stuck in the dark ages when Avon products reigned supreme.

"Sit down," he invited, gesturing toward the boarded seat. "I have about 15 minutes more of break time left, so let's put it to good use, he suggested. "Wow! You look amazing. City life must be treating you well."

"Highly over-rated, I can assure you," I said shaking my head.

"Seriously, it is so good to see you. How are you really doing?"

"Thank you, Dave, and yes, it's good to be home. I'm doing as well as can be expected. Keeping busy," I finished lamely. That seemed to be my stock answer. I was unsure how to bring up the subject of a possible criminal activity in his distant past, but I needed to know. So I decided to ease into the minefield slow and careful. "Wow! Talk about your life taking an about face. I hear you're married now with six kids to your credit." There, I squeezed it in with subtle simplicity. Hopefully he blindly picks up my indirect subject matter and runs with it.

His lips stretched out into a thin line from ear to ear. A loud burst of laughter rounded them like a full moon. "Yeah, they are a handful and a houseful, but I wouldn't have it any other way. My wife and I spend most of our time at 4-H meetings, Little League games and supervising short people. I'm coaching a Pee Wee basketball team right now. My kids are my life and I can't even remember what life was like before I became a dad!" he said, dropping his head to his lap and then just as quickly lifting his serious stare at me. "Or should I say I don't want to remember the kind of life I led pre-wife and kids. The only thing good that came out of my past is that I was such a wicked little punk myself, I actually know what devilish tricks my kids are up to before they even think about trying to pull one over on me. Actually, it's pretty comical to catch them in the act of misbehaving and conniving their wicked little schemes to get what they want. Because I'm able to give them my famous old, one liner that stops them in their tracks. Hey kid, I rode them high and I rode them low. I rode this way myself." Turning serious, he stared at me, his pained expression readable. "Camille, I meant it when I said your dad was a good man. He literally saved my life when I was fifteen and your loss is a loss to this whole town," he confirmed with pressed lips and a deflated expression that slowly drained his face of color.

I sat silently for a moment, just nodding in agreement. Emotion struggled in my chest and I breathed deeply, the scent of the pine trees and the creek below bringing me calm. I pulled my sweater tighter and formed the words I had been hiding just beneath my tongue. "Thanks, Dave and I know for a fact that all the youth in this town meant a lot to my father. He truly cared about every kid in this town and hoped they would all get a fair shake in life. And if he could help in any way, he wouldn't hesitate," I explained. I took in a deep breath and continued. "And, well, that's part of the reason I am here. I found my father's old pickup in his barn and it looked like it had been in some sort of a collision. I wondered if you knew anything about it. How he did it and why didn't he just get it fixed? I'm not sure if I should have it repaired as a classic or if I should sell it as is or what to do with it, really. Phyllis told me I should talk to you about it. Maybe you could give me some advice about it or maybe I just need to let the insurance company handle it. What do you think?" I asked, hoping he would open up and come clean if indeed he knew what the rest of us didn't.

Dave sheepishly dropped his gaze down to his hands on the table. I heard the swish of a few deep breaths. A chill streaked up my spine the instant his face tightened and his jaw began to twitch.

"Yeah. Actually, your dad didn't wreck his truck. I did," he confessed. He hesitated and drew in another deep breath. Then he grabbed my eyes and continued to reveal what he had hidden from others all these years. "It was me. Me and Earl Brakeman wrecked your dad's truck."

Even though the conversation at the beauty salon had led me to believe he had something to do with it, or at least knew something about it, I was still surprised to hear the confession come out of his mouth. "You? But how?" I asked in confusion. "How on earth could two young boys manage to wreck a truck that no one else but my father was allowed to drive?" I asked, mystified.

"Well, we didn't exactly have your Dad's permission to drive it," he said in a disparaging tone, admitting one more ugly truth.

I felt my face flush hot, but I tried to hide my building enthusiasm to hear the rest of his long, hidden secret. His stare was intense and I could tell he was struggling to formulate his thoughts. I nodded at him with a slight grin, hoping that would dislodge his words that were obviously still stuck in his throat.

He took in a deep breath, then his words came gushing out. "One morning, me and Earl had this crazy idea that we would swipe ourselves a car and go joyriding for a bit. We came up on your dad's truck parked at the bottom of the cemetery. He'd left it by the side of the road, the keys were in it and nobody was around. Too tempting for two boys bent on looking for some excitement. So off we went. I was driving and you know, that truck was one hot ride. That beauty had some gitty up and go. We drove around a bit, then headed down to the Quincy Y and turned around to head back to the cemetery." He paused to take another deep breath, his eyes still focused on mine. "But you know where the highway loops real close to the river just on the outskirts of Crescent Mills?" he asked, using his hands as a visual guide.

I nodded. "Yes, I know where you are talking about," I said with a sudden sinking feeling in the pit of my stomach where my raw nerves wound a hard lump.

"Well, while we were out driving around, the fog had come in over the river and it was getting really hard to see. A big, old buck jumped out of nowhere and I hit it right on. I was driving fast, probably too fast for the conditions and couldn't stop," he admitted, shaking his head.

I was starting to feel the familiar dizziness and I could hear a faint roaring in my ears as he spoke. "Where did you say this was exactly?" I asked only to confirm what I already knew.

"Just south of Crescent Mills, where the river runs right close to the highway," he repeated. "You know where that huge quartz bed

206

is? Right in that area. It was just a freaky morning fog that lifted from the river and I could hardly see."

"Yeah. I know the spot," I said feeling faint. Then I asked him a question that I knew would rip my heart into a thousand pieces. "What about the deer? Did you kill it?" I wanted to find out if he had stopped to check.

"Nah, it must have been a tough old bruiser. But it was a buck all right. Got a quick glimpse of his antlers at the moment of impact. But like I said, it was just so foggy right in that spot we could hardly see a foot or two in front of us. We looked over the bank down to the river, but couldn't see anything."

The roar increased in my ears and I shook my head to clear my thoughts. I sat quietly, looking down at the creek through the trees. The only reasonable answer to an eighteen year old question rolled over in my mind. Could a pair of joyriding punks blinded by fog really mistake a set of bicycle handlebars for antlers? Yes, they could.

Dave interrupted my thoughts, "Your dad was righteously enraged when we got back to the cemetery," he confirmed with repentant eyes.

I looked at him and tried to force an understanding smile, but all I could manage was a sympathetic look even I wouldn't fall for.

"Your dad was standing there right where he left the truck as if he was waiting for us," Dave went on to say. "Ripped me and Earl both, big time. Had me shaking in my boots because I had already racked up more juvenile offences than most kids my age. I knew where I was headed if I messed up one more time. I was going to be in big trouble, like a stay in juvie trouble. I begged your dad to give me a break. He told me to get on home and he'd let me know. I spent the next few days sweating it out, wondering if he was going to call the cops or worse; my parents. I knew my old man would beat my butt to Quincy and back if he found out what I had done. It was a bad time for me. I knew with my juvie record, I would be locked up for quite a spell, maybe even a year or so," he said, his shame colored his face pink. Taking in another deep breath, he met my stare and just shook his head.

I kept my silence, giving him time to get it all off his chest.

"This all happened right around the time that Young boy disappeared, and there was a lot of commotion over that, too." He shook his head, remembering. "But you know your dad, all heart and pure wisdom. He called me a few days later and said he had decided to give me a break. Made me promise to keep this incident just between us, but of course I was expected to work off the damage to his truck. Believe me, that was the last break he gave me," he chuckled. "I worked my tail off for the next two years at the cemetery. Your dad also made some kind of work exchange deal with old man Peterson. He had me clearing brush, raking leaves and splitting wood up at the Peterson's Resort. Came every day to inspect my work. He flat made me hustle, but I learned so much from him during that time." Shaking his head again, he continued, "Your dad, he was a class act. He made me grow up in those couple years and I'll never forget it. He made a lady out of Lizzy, only in the male sense of the word. And oh, howdy, he didn't stop there. He made me go with my mom to church every Sunday, too. The Lord covered me through your dad and I owe him a debt of gratitude. The only way I can repay him is to be a good man myself." Heaving a sigh, he said, "I'm not sure about insurance, though, Camille. I hate to say this, but there's probably a statute of limitations for charges or claims like that. Your dad and I were square by the time I graduated high school, but if you think you and I should settle up with a few more bucks, I'll be happy to do some monkey wrenching on your car for you, if you need it," he offered.

I listened quietly, feeling the beat of my heart in my ears. The simplest of explanations, found years later, for the burden of loss that I have been carrying for so long. I did not know if I should weep at the sadness of Eli most likely having lost his life, pedaling down the road on his bike and being unexpectedly struck by a couple of joyriding, juvenile truck thieves. Or, if I should let out a sigh of relief in the knowing that my father had done the right thing, as he always did. I took courage from that thought. But for obvious reasons, my internal struggle was still churning at full speed. My emotions swirled around and it took me a moment to compose myself.

"Ah, no, Dave. Your word is good enough for me. I am sure if you were square with my dad, then everything is fine. I was just not sure. About anything," I said lamely. "Thank you so much for your kind words about my father. You're absolutely right about one thing, if a life can be changed, then my dad was just the man to do it. I really miss his strength and his courage to meet life head on. It's much harder to stay on the straight and narrow when you've lost that unbreakable guidance. I really miss my father. But I guess when you get right down to it, I don't think I could really get rid of his truck. It was so much a part of who he was; old and reliable. "I guess I'll face that issue another day," I sighed.

I looked out over Wolf Creek, thinking through everything that had been said. I swallowed hard and turned back to face the man across the table from me. I formed a faint smile. The sun glinted in his red brown hair and highlighted the gold flecks in his eyes. I could see the sincerity in his eyes and I felt a rush of gratitude for my father's wisdom and grace. I marveled at how his strength had somehow empowered Dave to change his ways, developing into a hard-working, loving husband and father. A man who is now a strong part of Greenville's social fabric. Blinking away tears, I held out my hand to Dave. Shaking his work roughened hand, I said warmly, 'It's so good to see you again and I am glad that you are doing well."

Returning the handshake with a firm grip, a slow grin grew across his face. "Don't be a stranger, Camille," he said in a polite, caring manner. "I know you have to do your grieving in your own way, but be sure to reach out to your friends. Greenville is full of good people. I found that out the hard way," he admitted. He capped his water bottle and snapped his lunch cooler closed to indicate the end of his dinner break.

Nodding, I stood up at the same time he did. "Thanks again Dave for the nice walk down memory lane," I lied. It wasn't a pleasant walk, but one I needed to take to get back my peace of mind. "I wish you well in the upcoming basketball season."

He let out a hearty laugh. "Nothing beats a team of seven year old boys on the basketball court. Kind of like herding cats."

That made me smile. "See you later," I promised as I walked back around the front of the building to my car.

My thoughts overpowered me again. I opened my car door and sank down into my seat and rested my head on the steering wheel. Then, with a sigh, I started my car and drove back home, to the land of the dearly departed. I slowly picked my way through the headstones and reached my parents grave. Kneeling down in the moist grass, I closed my eyes and rested my head on the chilly ground. In the midst of the pure air of the mountains, I felt lacking in not only the oxygen I needed to breathe, but lacking in the ability to process all I had learned about Eli's last day and the burden my poor father had carried all these years. It was unbearable. Every second that ticked away, meant I was that much further away from the last time I had spent quality time with my father. Oh what I would give to hear his nurturing voice and to be able to ask him one more question. "What do I do now Dad?" With my swirling thoughts, I felt the tears begin slipping down my face, then the sobbing began. I laid face down on my parents' last resting place and wept inconsolably.

CHAPTER
22

I was awakened by the chiming of my phone in the kitchen. I rolled over and peered at my clock. It was 5:45 am and the early light was just beginning to filter through the lace on my bedroom window. I snuggled down under my quilt and wondered why I had not shut off my phone last night. It's not like I'm on some sort of a time schedule. My father is not here with his daily wake-up call; to sing his favorite song by Frankie Lane, 'Ghost Riders' in the sky'. He was the best father ever, but that man couldn't carry a tune if his life depended on it. I wish he were here right now screeching in my ear and once he was done, I'd ask him to sing it again. You really don't know what you have until it's been taken away.

Even the pleasure of remembering wasn't as pleasant anymore, because once the good ones pass through my mind, the ugliness of the not so good ones take their place. Like right now, the events of yesterday and the new facts that had come to light had given me relief that my father was the good and decent man I had known. But, the emotion of finding of Eli's leather treasure bag knocked me back a few pegs. My bout of weeping on my parents' grave yesterday left me exhausted. I had staggered back to the house, chilled, and put on a pair of sweats and a long sleeved tee. I crawled into bed after a cursory splash in the sink that left my hair damp but my face clean and fell asleep almost immediately.

Today is a new day. I lay here wrapped in my quilt, my mind already beginning to think about all that has happened in such a short amount of time. I mull over the previous day and reconsider my findings which seems to be the flashlight at my feet guiding me through the next process of our amateur investigation. If Eli was struck by a speeding pickup, with a teenager with a lead foot and impaired vision, the impact could have caused his death? Or did it just cause amnesia so severe that he wandered off to live a whole new life? What did finding his treasure bag so close to the crystal bed, hidden from sight and protected from total destruction by rocks, mean? Had he hidden it, lost it or worse, had it dropped from his grasp and he was unable to pick it up and carry it with him? I revisited my conversation with Dave Wilson yesterday, as well. I was gratified to know that my father had extended a merciful hand to Dave despite his teenage angst and thuggish tendencies. Yet he had held the teenager accountable for stealing a truck and putting not only his own life at risk because of his reckless driving, but that of his young friend as well. Dave had certainly matured into a good person, acknowledging my father's discipline and mentoring. But I still did not have an answer to the question that concerned me the most; why was Eli's bike in the bed of my father's truck, hidden under a tarp in the back of the barn for so many years?

With a sigh, knowing I would be unable to go back to sleep, I tossed back the quilt and padded to the kitchen to start some coffee. I opted for Coffee or Die and found the beans, measuring the water and setting up the coffee pot soothed me. The familiar ritual gave me peace and as the fragrance of the freshly ground beans and the hot liquid dripping into the carafe filled the kitchen, I picked up my phone.

The screen showed I had missed a call from Kendall and that he had left a voicemail a few moments earlier. My, he was up and about with the chickens, I thought sourly. I would have liked to have slept at least another thirty minutes.

I dialed my voicemail and tapped the speaker icon on the screen. Kendall's voice came through with a suppressed excitement. "Camille, I've talked to the police, read the reports and had had a conversation with a dive company in Quincy. I'm on way to give you all of the facts."

"Dang, you don't mess around when you set your mind on something," I whispered under my breath.

I looked out the window and saw Indian Head, the vibrant splashes of color of the autumn oaks had spread over the old mountain and wisps of mist rose from the irrigation ditches in the fields below. The sere colors of the autumn grasses were somber in contrast to the cheerful riot of colors on the mountainside. I felt weary. I was so anxious to discover the truths I was seeking, that I had not considered what the answers may be or how I would feel once I knew them. I found myself calling upon the Great Spirit, creator of our universe and asking for His guidance and strength for this day. I opened the window and breathed in the cold, fresh mountain air of the morning. Closing my eyes, I felt a calm and peace come over me and I wondered if that unaccustomed serenity was a gift from the Great Spirit in answer to my prayer. I wasn't sure if He worked that quickly, but breathed a soft sigh of gratitude. The oak trees along the road rustled with a breath of morning breeze and I watched as a pair of gray squirrels scurried across the lawn, tumbling back and forth in their haste and then skittered up one of the trees, one behind the other. As I stood there in my sweats and rumpled hair, breathing in the cool and peace of the morning, I heard Kendall's jeep; a throaty rumble drifting to me on the morning air, and a moment later I spied him turning from the highway and crunching up the gravel drive.

Wearing his Guinness sweatshirt against the morning chill, his long legs in jeans with running shoes, he bounded up the steps of the deck and rapped quickly on the kitchen door.

The thought crossed my mind that I wasn't exactly going to be easy on his eyes this early, but it was too late to do anything about it now. Maybe when he got a good look at the real me without makeup and designer jeans, then possibly he would turn tail and run the other way. But then I call em as I see em. Kendall was the kind of man who didn't care if I had been washed out to sea and hung up to dry. He looked beyond the outer shell and appreciated a woman for her inner beauty. My kind of man.

"Come on in," I called out as I poured our coffee. I plunked two mugs on the little kitchen table and sat down as he stepped over the threshold along with a burst of fresh air.

He moseyed on in like he owned the place and stepped up close to me and pecked me on the forehead.

"Make yourself at home," I said, gesturing to an empty chair situated right next to me.

His eyes widened when he spied the coffee. He smiled widely and took his mug, pulling out a chair and turning it around backwards, straddling the seat.

Why do guys do that? I wondered idly. Sit on chairs backward. It was sort of like wearing their ball caps backward, a heinous offense in my father's eyes. Apparently I had inherited the dislike of it as well.

Kendall appeared not to notice my raddled appearance, rumpled hair, sweat pants and annoyed attitude. He gulped some coffee and then set the mug back on the table. He looked at me clearly for the first time.

"Good morning, sunshine," he smiled. "How are you? Or is this too early for you?" He asked with way too much perkiness in his voice.

Seconds ticked by as I sat there like a big dummy staring at him and wondering what he was really thinking about my frowsy appearance.

"Well, if it is too early, I guess it is a little late to apologize. But I am sorry about that," he rattled on, holding my gaze.

How could I be irritated with someone who looked like a Greek God carved out of granite with a smile as bright as a full moon? But how could anyone be this cheery so early in the morning? Sheepishly, I shook my head. "No, early doesn't bother me too much. I am just still tired from yesterday. And I look like an old hag right now and you show up looking like a GQ model and I am a little embarrassed, if you want to know the truth," I said wryly.

"It's important to know how a woman looks first thing in the morning," he answered. "Seriously," he added, taking another sip of coffee. "It just tells a guy a lot about her. By the way, you look great." He shrugged and smiled at me over his cup. "That's my opinion; you can take it or leave it, but you are beautiful."

I had to laugh, he was so simple and disarming. "So tell me what's got you so excited that you had to be here before 6:30 in the morning?" I asked.

He gave me another wide smile that reached his eyes and caused me to flush. What was it about his perfect mouth with his perfect set of white teeth that made me feel fuzzy inside? I asked myself, still staring at his perfect face.

He finished his coffee, stood up and inched toward the counter to pour himself another cup. He gestured towards me with the coffee carafe. "Want some more?" he asked, which I easily accepted a refill. Even the way he poured coffee into my cup was done in a graceful manner. Everything he does, it seems to come as easy as breathing to him.

He returned to his seat, backwards of course. "So I went to the cop shop and sweet talked the secretary there. She's been there for decades and remembered when Eli disappeared. She seems to know everything about everyone, and she even has a police scanner on her dining room table at home and another one by her bed," he told me.

He was incredulous, but I just nodded. Home police scanners were a common entertainment in our rural communities.

After a huge swig of his coffee, he quickly picked up his pace. "To be quite frank, I was impressed; google has nothing on this gal. Actually, the code for google was probably written with this gal in mind as a model. Crazy how much she knows and it took me awhile to get out of there because she tells good stories. Good stories with a little pizazz, I might add," he admitted after a slight pause. "At any rate, she provided me with all of the reports and records pertaining to Eli's disappearance. I read thru them all last night and I was able to see there wasn't much in the way of forensics or evidence, because no one knew where he was when he disappeared. A general idea of the locations he frequented, yeah, but beyond that, there was very little. And apparently, the river was running really high and fast that year and it was treacherous in most places. A dive team from Quincy did some diving, but there again, they did not have any exact location pinpointed. It was risky to have the divers in the river because of the height of the river flows especially since it was somewhat exploratory." His half empty coffee cup touched down on the table with a loud thud. He looked at me full in the face, "But here's the thing Camille. Your dad contacted some of the divers while they were on the river and asked them to check out another location," he said, his voice trailed off dropping an octave and his expression saddened.

I waited, but he stayed silent, staring at me. "Go on," I prodded.

He acted hesitant to get back into his story, but finally began again with words that caught me off guard. "Your father wanted them to check out the area around the crystal bed where we were yesterday." His tone made it sound like he was confessing something he feared would rock my world.

I sat up in my chair, my blood racing through my body at the speed of light. "What?" I asked, disbelieving. "How could this be?" I screeched in a high pitched tone. All the while my thoughts were spinning in circles. I had already absolved my father of any wrong doing during my conversation with Dave Wilson. "But why? Did he say why?" I asked, drilling the question in deeper.

Kendall nodded, his curly hair springing with the movement. "Yeah, he wanted them to see if they could find anything in that approximate area. He told them that he knew the young boy frequented that particular place. Did you ever hear anything about that when you were a kid?" he asked with an expression on his face I couldn't quite read, but his body language made it clear that he was as uncomfortable with this subject matter as much as I was.

A swell of nausea washed over me as I sat there stunned. Shaking my head, I exhaled a long sigh, "Nooooo, no, I didn't." My eyes toyed around my coffee cup. I lifted my head and grabbed his eyes more intently with mine. "But yesterday, I did find out that a local boy by the name of Dave Wilson, claims that he and another kid stole my dad's truck and took it on a joyride along the Feather River as far as the Quincy Y. He said on the trip back the fog had rolled over the road from the river and he hit a buck. Both boys swore they saw the antlers. He and his friend stopped and looked around, but couldn't really see anything because of the fog. They figured the deer survived the impact and ran off." I huffed out a breath. "And he for sure didn't see a bike. Dad must have suspected what really happened when he saw the paint on the front fender," I concluded. "This must have been so hard on my father to live with the strong suspicions of what really happened," I determined, feeling his emotional stress gnaw at my nerves.

Kendall didn't respond to my last comment. We just sat and stared at each other for a long moment. Then his eyes drifted over to the window above the sink as if someone outside had called his name. He burrowed his brows, contemplating something in his head. "Do you suppose your dad knew? Really had it all figured out and maybe suspected that Eli had been hit with his truck?" He asked after a pause.

I shook my head, uncertainty resting heavy on my mind. "I don't know. Maybe that's something we will never know for sure. The way I feel right now, I don't think I know anything," I mumbled beneath a frustrated breath with my shaking hands wrapped around my coffee cup.

He reached over and gently placed his hands over mine. The strength and warmth of his touch gave me the courage to look up into his eyes. His smile crinkled his green eyes and he held my hands a moment longer. "'I'm so sorry, Camille. I just dumped all of this on you. To me it is an interesting mystery, but to you, it's your past, your history, your family and friend. I am so sorry I just blundered in here all excited about what I discovered." He winced in regret.

I appreciated his kind words and as I thought them over with careful consideration, I knew that if we continued to pursue the answers to the questions we both had, he would have his uncomfortable moments, too. I smiled at him briefly. "This is the way it has to be. It may not be pleasant news, but we must continue no matter how much it hurts," I said, trying to absorb all the new questions that had been raised.

"There's more, if you want to hear more," he admitted as if he was giving out too much information. As if he feared my emotions were already approaching the breaking point.

I nodded. I wanted to hear it all no matter how much it hurt. "Yes. I want you to tell me everything," I said, feeling the raw edge of a razor scraping inside my stomach.

"I spoke by phone with the owner of the dive shop in Quincy. He was part of the dive team that searched for Eli. He remembered it very clearly; it was one of his first search and rescue missions. He owns his own shop now and teaches scuba and rescue diving as well. When I asked him to tell me all he could remember, he didn't hesitate. He said the river was so high and running so fast, it was very risky to do the searching they did. He remembered that there was no clear location to search, and most of the searching was done on guesswork. Your dad asked him specifically to check out the area near the crystal bed. They did find a couple of old bikes and car parts just along the river. He said it looked like trash that had been thrown down the embankment from the highway, but landed in water that was just shallow enough it didn't get washed away. He also said that your dad was adamant that neither of the bikes belonged to Eli, so the team was back to square one as far as a search location."

Kendall stopped short, presumably to check to see if I was okay. "Go on," I coaxed.

Gripping his coffee mug, he said, "So I went out on a limb here and asked if he would consider searching the area again, given that we had found one of Eli's personal belongings." Again he studied my eyes for approval to continue.

"And?" I asked, getting a little impatient with his stalling.

"He was planning a field day for some search and rescue trainees and Boy Scouts. He agreed to check with his insurance and the Sheriff's department, but he thought he'd be able to do that for us. It will take a couple days for him to get everything organized, but he was happy for the opportunity to maybe finally bring some clo-sure for the family."

Kendall stared at me, his eyes surprisingly fearful, as if I would be angry that he made a command decision to make that request.

"Wow, Kendall, that was a great idea and I am not sure I would have thought of it," I reassured him. Immediately the flakes of apprehension fell from his eyes, exposing a tenderness I had come to understand and appreciate.

"It'll be a few days before he gets out on the river?"

"Will he let you know when he does?" I asked with a sense of urgency.

Kendall nodded vigorously, his hair flopping over his forehead. He swiped it back and said, "Yeah, he's going to shoot me a text when they get operational. It might be short notice, but if you are up for it, why don't we go along and watch them as they search. And train," he amended.

"The threat of a natural disaster couldn't keep me away. If they do find something, I want to be there when they do," I said, making my intentions known.

Standing up, I stepped over and set my coffee cup in the sink. With slumped shoulders, I pondered over all that had been uncovered so far. We were getting closer to answering many questions that had plagued my life since I was a kid. So why was I standing here feeling so disappointed? I should be overwhelmed with excitement instead of acting as if my last dollar had just been spent. With that good scolding, I finally felt a twinge of enthusiasm that suddenly brightened my discontented frame of mind.

I turned around to face him. "Tell you what. I've got a good idea of my own. How about if you make some breakfast with whatever you can find in the fridge?" I suggested more than asked. "I'll jump in the shower and then we can figure out a plan of action for the day." I gave him my best coy little grin and then pointed toward the counter. "The yellow pad is right there where you left it. So go ahead and do what you do best," I prodded.

"And, what is that, pray tell?" he asked with a silly grin playing around with his lips.

"Cook like Martha Stewart and mastermind like Einstein," I said with a short giggle.

As I turned to leave the kitchen, he quickly stood up just behind me. I felt his arms go around me and he tug me back around to face him. His green eyes, intense with emotion, were on me. I felt my heart begin to dance a little and I dropped my gaze, burying my face in his chest. He held me tightly for a moment and then released me, chucking me under the chin and kissing the top of my rumpled hair lightly. Although he said nothing, his actions spoke louder than any words of concern and kindness. His physical expressions of love came through a smile that spread all the way across his face as I broke free of his embrace and walked toward my bedroom. I sure hoped that love could make some scrambled eggs and toast.

I showered quickly, pulling my still damp hair into a messy bun. Dressing in jeans, a t-shirt and a warm green plaid flannel shirt, I returned to the bathroom and swiped on some mascara. A smudge of lipstick and I was ready for the food I could smell and for whatever the day held.

Over a simple and delicious breakfast of warmed mashed potatoes, scrambled eggs and toasted Irish soda bread, I felt that maybe I was falling in love with this generous, tender hearted man. Food prepared with love and care always tastes better. It nourishes the heart and soul as well as the body, doesn't it?

Finishing my toast, dunking the crust into my second cup of coffee, I reviewed quickly what I had learned so far and walked Kendall through what new discoveries were made yesterday. "Okay, this is what we have to work with on my end. My visit to the beauty salon eventually led me to find Dave Wilson which in turn gave me some insight into what really happened the day Eli disappeared. Evidently, Dave and another kid did swipe my dad's truck and take it for a joyride. They claimed to have hit a deer before returning the truck to my father. My father in turn made an agreement with the boys to work off the damage to the truck and he wouldn't report the incident to the officials. I can kinda see where my father's thought process was taking him. My conversation with Dave has given me back much more than just simple respect for my father," I explained.

"That certainly ties in with the information given to me yesterday about your father's request for a search around the crystal bed," Kendall offered.

"Well anyway, my original intent was to see Marilyn and ask about her historical birth book. She is more than eager to share her information with me. Actually, I have an appointment with her on

Friday. Would you like to accompany me?" I asked, expecting him to jump on board immediately. His eyes flashed up to mine, then just as quickly darted away. I wondered what that was all about.

Kendall contemplated for a moment, then nodded in agreement. He seemed somewhat reluctant, so my next question I asked with deep concern. "Are you okay with this? I mean I can go this part alone if you'd rather bow out."

"'It's just hard. And personal. And it has really bothered me over the last few months," he finally admitted. "I had a life that was just so normal, so mundane and then, all of a sudden, it's not. It's so unfathomable to wake up one day and realize you don't know anything about yourself. I don't know who I am, nor do I know who my parents are. Or should I say biological parents? I do know this much, my mother knew nothing about any of this. I do believe my father loved and protected her to the extent that he kept all this from her, which is a mystery in itself. How does a man keep a secret like that from his wife for so many years?"

The flush on his cheeks grew to a deeper rose as I watched him shake his head slowly. I began to see the fragility of the young boy beneath the visage of the man.

"We'll do it together," I said to him, taking his hand in mine. I marveled at the long fingers, with clean cut nails, the small golden hairs on his knuckles. I could feel the latent strength in the bones of his hand. Turning his hand over, I traced on the palm a crisscross pattern, the roughened palm catching the skin of my finger. He closed his fingers over my hand and squeezed them gently and smiled at me.

"Yeah, ok. We'll do it together," he said.

CHAPTER 23

It was two days later when Bill Hanson, the owner of the Quincy Dive Shop was able to bring his search and rescue trainees to the quartz bed along the Feather River, where it gamboled close to Highway 89. The same area where we presumed he had found Eli's bike eighteen years ago. The day was sunny, but chilly and breezy with a cloudless blue sky.

"A great day to be on the river!" Bill called up to Kendall and me as we approached the riverbank, sliding down the rocky slope to join him and his team.

I felt my jaw drop in a staggered expression. I glanced at Kendall and understood completely why his lips were pressed tightly together in a thin line. A brief awkward silence ensued. For Kendall and I, there was nothing great about it. Productive, yielding maybe, but not adventurous like he made it sound.

Bill was a stocky man with a sturdy build. Short cropped, salt and pepper hair and dark blue eyes. He had a calm demeanor and a frank gaze. "The river is relatively calm for this time of year, so that's a plus for sure," he pointed out. A couple more guys stepped up beside Bill, taking the focus off the river and placing their eyes on us.

Kendall quickly took charge. "Bill this is my friend, Camille Cameron. Camille, this is Bill Hanson."

"Nice to meet you young lady," he said extending his hand out in my direction. His eyes seemed to be assessing me, but his warm smile was welcoming.

"Nice to meet you. We appreciate you putting this all together on such short notice. Thank you for that," I said with a weak, pathetic smile.

"I can't promise you anything, but we'll give it our best shot. Rex and Broderick here are a couple of the best students I've had the opportunity to work with, so I have high expectations," he said pointing to a short guy and a tall guy both dressed in complete dive suit and equipment. "We will follow search and rescue techniques and keep our eyes open for anything out of the ordinary. This cooler weather is perfect and this is a good training exercise for my class. Hopefully we can find something that can put this age old mystery to rest," he said and then turned toward his students and began his instructions with words I couldn't make heads or tails out of.

Kendall and I stood at the water's edge watching the team finish securing a large pin that would hold a cable. Bill continued to give lengthy instructions to the dive trainees. We watched in awe as he explained and showed with gestures what he wanted them to do and how to do it. It didn't take us long to realize that our best contribution to the operation would be to stay out of the way. We found a large granite boulder, warmed by the sun that gave us a good vantage point and had the added benefit of keeping us from interfering in any way.

Ten minutes later the divers entered the water at various points and crossed back and forth in a systematic search. California had suffered from a four year drought and the waters of the Feather River were at an all-time low, but the flow was still powerful and the divers needed to use strength and caution in addition to their appropriate equipment. Bill had explained that due to the passage of time, various years of spring runoff, the results of the drought and other factors, the river was configured a little differently than it had been eighteen years ago. Even taking that into account, he would make no promises of any kind of new discovery.

The day progressed, the hours passing with no apparent find, and the sun became warmer. I shifted uncomfortably on the big boulder, but I was unwilling to leave the river while the search continued to chew the morning away. I found Bill's instructions and methods to be fascinating and despite their grim task, I was beginning to enjoy watching the skilled divers work. The search and rescue community in the Greenville was a small and tightly knit group of brave and resourceful individuals and I assumed the same would be true of the Quincy group as well. It was a pleasure to see the precision of their work and to see the care they took with each task. Kendall spoke very little, keeping his eyes glued to the river the whole time.

I shifted again on the hard rock which tugged Kendall's focus in my direction.

"Not exactly the best seat in the house," he commented with raised brows. "Are you alright?" he asked, staring at me, measuring with his intense green eyes.

"Oh, I'm alright. This boulder isn't very comfy. It's speaking to my behind in a language it doesn't like," I complained. "But I don't dare move in case they do find something."

He gave me a sweet grin and nudged my shoulder. "Hard as a rock huh?" he joked and then chuckled at his own humor.

I raised my brow and rolled my eyes. "I'll survive." My tone bitingly sarcastic.

"I've got a cushion in the jeep if you want me to go get it," he offered.

"No, I'm fine. Really, I'm fine now that I've scooched over a bit."

"You're sure?"

"Sure," I said.

He smiled with half his mouth and turned his attention back to the team still searching in grid pattern on the river.

The tallest of the divers was in the center now, anchored by the cable stretched across the river. He appeared to be focused on an area between two large boulders that crouched in the middle, splitting the flow of the river between them. I watched as Bill shouted and gestured to him, relaying instructions and information that was lost to me in the breeze and the chatter of the rushing water. They searched along the banks for over an hour and then searched it all over again.

Kendall turned to me again. "Are you thirsty?" he asked.

"Yeah, I could use a drink."

"I'm a little parched myself, so I think I'll head up to the jeep and get us both some water," he said. "Do you want your sunglasses too?"

I nodded my assent and watched as he began his scramble up the sloping bank to the highway. His form was pretty darn good which made me think how fortunate I was to have this unbelievably handsome man come into my life just at the perfect time. Coincidental or a master plan from a Higher Power? I really wanted to believe in the master plan, a preferred working theory at the moment. I liked the idea that maybe The Great Spirit was looking out for me even if I was a neglectful, undeserving part time believer.

Turning back to the scene in the river, I watched as the tallest diver was joined by a shorter man. They then ventured out into the deeper water and I knew this would be where the searching would be tricky and the risk to the divers higher. Both were trim and in good shape, but the force of the water as it crashed around the boulders struck them with some force and they both clutched the cable and held steadying hands on the boulder itself. Taking turns, they gingerly searched the area between the boulders. Reaching deep and rising up again, an ungainly dance dedicated to inspecting every part of hidden places. I marveled at their strength and tenacity and breathed a sigh of relief each time their heads popped up above the rough surface of the water.

Lifting my eyes to the steep hillside beyond them, I gazed at the pines, the fir trees and the gaudy splashes of fall oaks sweeping down to the river. The willows draping themselves in autumn gold, trailing their tresses into the water along the edge, completed an artist's dream of a perfect collage of colors.

Allowing my mind to drift, I wondered about my increasing need to call upon the Great Spirit. I was unaccustomed to seeking help outside of myself and I wondered if it was possibly a small sign of my emotional healing. I wondered if God was watching over this search, surely small in comparison to the universe, and if it was truly worth His attention. And then an uncomfortable question crossed my mind. Was this Eli's final resting place? If it was, then I would have to accept that this garden of splendor was in some way painted by the hand of God in Eli's honor. Another one of my working theories.

The divers continued their patterns of search, and even though there had been a four year drought, the river was still swift and somewhat dangerous. The divers dipped below the surface, returning again and again in a cadence that was almost hypnotic. But then, the pattern was broken by one of the divers gesturing to another. They both disappeared for a few moments and then reappeared, one of them clutching an item to his chest. I stood for a better look, squinting in the bright sunlight to see. As they struggled, single file, along the cable to reach Bill on the shore, I could see the shorter diver held what looked like a boot in his hand. I covered my mouth with my hand feeling the pounding in my chest and the rushing in my ears. Removing my hand, I turned to the bank and screamed loudly, "Kendall! Come back! I think they've found something!"

By the time the divers had reached Bill, speaking in low tones together, Kendall was by my side. He placed the water bottles on a flattened edge of the rock along with my glasses. Then he held out his hand and helped me down from the boulder and we both slid down the rest of the bank to join the men. Bill turned and looked at me, his brown eyes seemed tortured and torn.

"What did you find?" I asked, sounding more demanding than I meant. "What do you have?"

"I'm not sure you want to see this," Bill said slowly in a tone wrapped in sadness.

"I have to," I said. "I really have to know what you have found. Please show me," I practically begged.

With an uneasy look at his divers, then at Kendall, he held out the object that had us all quivering in fearful anticipation.

My eyes beheld the dread of eighteen years of awfulness. It felt like a grenade exploding inside my head. My stomach twisted into a tight knot. I tried to hold on to the fragile link between consciousness and passing out as the waves of pain washed over me. After all these years, my biggest question answered. The dreaded truth lay here right in front of me in the form of a sodden boot. Bill held the awful truth in his hand. I couldn't deny it. I couldn't make it all go away. The realization that this was Eli's boot was painful enough, but the stub of whitened bone protruding from the top of the boot successfully drained the blood from my face and sucked the air from my lungs. I felt my legs weaken and wobble. Kendall immediate wrapped his arm around me in order to keep me upright.

Bill said quietly, "I'm pretty sure it is safe to say that whoever was wearing this boot did not survive." He sighed deeply and looked at Kendall. "And by the look on Miss Cameron's face, she most likely knows who this boot belongs to. This changes things," he said. "I have to notify the Sheriff and we need to make this a certified search and this is now considered a sensitive area or even possibly a crime scene. I'll have to ask you folks to leave. I am so sorry, but it is necessary and I will try to keep you updated," he explained.

Then Bill handed the boot to the diver standing closest to him and then turned back to us. He shook Kendall's hand and held out his work roughened hand to me. Blindly, I took it and gave it a squeeze. Kendall snaked his arm around me again and turned me back towards the bank and the ascent to the highway.

As we climbed, my thoughts darkened. This is all there is left of such a beautiful life; a bone in a boot. He's really gone. As this horrible, terrible truth sunk into my brain, everything inside of me collapsed like a wilted flower in a winter's first snow. My sobs echoed across the river of death, because now I knew this is all where it happened. This is where his spirit soared like an eagle through heaven's gate. I hated the fact that I didn't get to say good-bye.

CHAPTER 24

As I scrambled up the bank to the highway, grasping at bushes as I clambered, my heart pounded with more than the exertion of the climb. I felt a lump in my throat and the familiar tightness in my chest and my mind churned with a myriad of troubling questions. Was this all that was left of Eli's remains? Would it be possible to find more of him buried in the rocks further down the river? How will poor Carolyn handle this? What on earth would I tell her about this discovery and would she despise me for my meddling? I had to go see her as soon as possible. I felt a panicked sense of urgency to find her and tell her before someone else broke the horrifying news.

We stepped up onto the verge of Highway 89 near Kendall's Jeep. I turned to him and just blurted out my intentions. "I have to go see Carolyn and tell her what has been found." I could hear the quaver in my voice and I swallowed hard to speak clearly and calmly. I closed my eyes and breathed deeply. I felt Kendall's warm hand on my shoulder.

He remonstrated with me, "But Camille, what exactly will you tell her? Yes, a boot and part of a bone was found, the scene is now closed except to law enforcement and scene techs and other than that, you will be giving her no solid proof that that is indeed Eli's remains. Are you prepared for how this would affect her? You said yourself she has lived all these years in the hope that Eli would once again come walking through her front door. She might go into cardiac arrest, and deservedly so, if these are the only remains of her son."

"She's a courageous woman. I don't think she will buckle under the pressure. No matter how heartbroken Caroline is, she manages to look at life and death through hopeful eyes. I think she is someone who believes heaven is full of white, puffy clouds with angels sitting around playing harps. She will accept the fact that Eli is in a better place. But I can't allow this kind of news to come from some stranger. I have to do this, Kendall," I confirmed.

"Don't you think you should wait for the results of the DNA test?" he asked with a flash of fear in his eyes.

"I don't need a DNA test to tell me what I already know," I protested in a much firmer tone than I had intended.

"Then I'll go with you," he offered with wide eyes and a clenched jaw.

"You can't go waltzing into her house looking like Eli reincarnated. I told you that you are a dead ringer for Eli in those age progressed photos. Seeing you would put her in an early grave," I confirmed. Then I felt a tightness in my throat and my eyes began to water.

"Camille, I don't mean to undermine your decision, but you should wait for the DNA testing to be certain that is Eli's bone," he demanded in a cautious tone. "And to be quite frank, you need to let law enforcement handle the legal aspect of the investigation as to how and when Eli ended up in the river, if indeed that is his boot. And it might be a good idea to proceed with caution or a lot of people could suffer some pretty serious consequences," he pointed out with a somber expression.

"I told you, I don't need a DNA test to tell me it is part of him," I wept. "That's his boot. That's all I need to tell me how this all played out. She can't hear about this bad news from law enforcement or on the news; she needs to hear it from a friend, someone who cares as much as she does. I need to tell her myself."

"At least let me drive you there," he insisted. "You are so upset. Come on, Camille, you're strong, but you're not that strong. It's ok to have some help in a time like this. And you really shouldn't be driving," he suggested. His eyes were tight.

"I'll be ok," I sniffed. "Just take me back to my house. I need to do this and I need to do it alone," I repeated. "But thank you for your concern. I do appreciate everything you have done for me. I really do."

Kendall wrapped his arms around me and held me under his chin and let me weep. Standing along the side of Highway 89, safe in his arms, I gathered courage for what would be a difficult, but I felt, a necessary task.

The drive back to the cemetery was silent and stoic. It would take us five minutes to get there and another few minutes to say our good-byes. I ran into the house to the bathroom first and then freshened up my tear stained face. Staring at my flushed reflection in the mirror, I gave myself a pep talk. "Keep it together, Camille. You have to do this for Caroline. You must do this for Eli."

I hurried through my kitchen and zipped down the stairs. My mind was a blur as I got into my car and drove to Carolyn's house. Sitting in her driveway, trying to compose myself for the moments ahead of me, I was horrified to see Agnes Morrow step out of Carolyn's house holding a hanky over her nose. She met me halfway down the cracked cement walk, her eyes glistening with unshed tears.

"What's wrong?" I asked fearfully. "Is Carolyn all right?"

"Oh honey," she said, her face drooping with sorrow. "Haven't you heard? They found some of little Eli's remains in the river today." She clutched at my shoulders in a possessive way.

"No, no, please Agnes, you didn't tell her that, did you?" I asked, my voice cold and hard.

"Now honey, you know it's always better to hear bad news from someone who cares rather than some stranger. Don't you agree?" Her tone purred like a kitten.

Frustrated, I shuttered with instant regret, for those were the exact same words I uttered to Kendall not thirty minutes ago. I stood for another few seconds shaking my head in stunned silence.

"Don't worry my dear. Carolyn is a strong woman and definitely not foreign to devastating news," she pointed out. Her voice was almost a whisper.

"Yeah, but what if you are wrong?" I asked frostily. "And how did you hear about this, anyway?" I was still appalled that I was hearing my own words coming from Agnes' mouth and I now understood the caution that Kendall had spoken to me.

"Oh my grandson works for Bill Hanson. He is the diver who found Eli's bones in the river. He always keeps me up to date. Then the police scanner was all full of chatter about it right after he called me. He's so good at keeping me posted on things that are happening in all of Plumas County."

Shouldering my way past her as I shook my head in dismay, I attempted to reach the porch, but to my utter shock, she grasped my wrists in her hands. She was surprisingly quick and strong for a woman of her bulk. "No, listen, Camille. Carolyn needs some time alone to think and to let this all settle in."

Wrenching my hands free, I hissed at her. "How could you know what she needs? You've never been through something like this," I snapped in a harsh tone. I was becoming more agitated and angry with her. I just wanted to slip past her on the sidewalk and get to Carolyn's door. But I also knew I needed to kill my hostility toward this woman. After all, she was Carolyn's dear friend and she had just as much right to share the truth with her as I did. This type of hostility has become a pattern for me. I hope these new character traits don't transfer into my life like moss growing over rocks.

Agnes grasped my hand again, but more gently this time. "Ah honey, sweet Camille. You are so mistaken. I have been through troubling times with her before. Many times. And I do know her well and I know what I am talking about. I was with her when she miscarried her first baby girl and I was with her when Eli's twin baby brother died. Nor did I leave her side when the Mr. took his own life."

I involuntarily sucked in a gasp of air. "What did you say?" I stopped in my tracks and lessened the tension between her hand and mine.

I helped her clean up after he shot himself. Such a sadness to leave behind for those who loved you." She shook her head slowly. "Such a terrible sight for your loved ones to see. I guess when a mind is in such a muddled state, they just don't think about the folks they'll be leaving behind," she said.

"No!" I shrieked, unable to contain myself. "What did you say about a twin brother? What twin brother?" I reached up and shook her shoulder, despite myself. "What brother are you talking about?" My tone was much more demanding than I had intended.

"Such a sad thing. Carolyn had twin boys, but the second one died about six hours after birth. So unexpected because he really was the picture of health up to that point. It grieved Carolyn so much, she had him cremated. Didn't even put a notice in the paper; she just couldn't bear to talk about her loss. She said it would be easier if Eli didn't know he had a brother. She named him Jeremiah and his ashes are in the lovely vase she has on the mantle. He's been there in that pretty blue and gold vase all these years," she explained.

I swallowed hard and inhaled deeply, marshalling my thoughts. "Agnes, please do me a favor? Don't tell anyone you told me about Jeremiah, please? Not even Carolyn?" I pleaded.

"Oh honey, Carolyn wouldn't mind you knowing. She considers you family, almost like the daughter she never had. Well now, I take that back, she did have a daughter, her firstborn. But she lost her to Placenta Previa. Only nineteen weeks, she was, but perfectly shaped and formed." She shook her ponderous head, heavy with the thoughts of grief long past.

"Please, Agnes, promise me you won't tell anyone what you've told me," I gasped desperately. "And certainly don't tell Carolyn. It is her place to tell me. Promise me?" I said pleadingly as I stared into her dark, birdlike eyes, alive with inquisitiveness and energy.

"Sure, honey, I promise," she said solemnly. "Cross my heart and hope to die," she stated formally, crossing her voluminous bosom with a plump hand.

"Okay then," I almost groaned with relief. "Thank you Agnes. Thank you. You have no idea what this means to me." I attempted to hug her, my arms stretched, but unable to reach all the way around her bulk.

"So glad we could talk and let's meet up again later," she chirped, her cheerfulness somehow agonizing in this sad moment.

"Soon," I agreed with a quick nod.

I was not looking forward to another heart to heart with Agnes, but I at least owed her that much. I squared my shoulders and stepped up onto the porch, steeling myself for another difficult conversation. For now, I would step outside my comfort zone and do my best to help Carolyn navigate through this very difficult time.

And yet while it may seem like a noble effort on my part, I still felt like everything was suffocating me. But beyond drowning in news of sadness, there was also the news of hope and joy. Today had been a weird mixture of both. Sad in that Eli was for sure never coming back, but hope in the thoughts that maybe Kendall was in some way linked to this whole tragic set of circumstances. Hope is all I had to hold onto now.

First I would try to console Carolyn. I shuddered at the thought of rehashing the dreadful truth with her. For behind closed eyes, his presence was still indelibly etched into her mind. How do you help a mother to say her final goodbye to her young boy she had tried so hard to keep alive for all these years? How could I prepare to let the tide of dismay roll over me once again? But I know that we both need our internal sense of calm restored because that is the healthy language of day to day living. I have to see this through the lens of my Father's eyes. For deep down I know He is the great comforter. I'll pray that He fills my mouth with all the right words.

Second, I would find Kendall. This is a call for unity, because I knew we were searching for something unequivocally impossible to understand in its' immense mystical form. Thankfully, Kendall has chosen to roll up his sleeves and embrace the seemingly impossible with unbreakable fortitude. Me on the other hand, have days when I feel like I'm flying high, completely unlimited without boundaries. But in the next moment, like now, I'm flapping around like a tiny bird with broken wings which tends to spoil everything and muddle my mind. I needed to get into the weeds with this one, so I'm determined not to let that little cramp in my brain stop me.

CHAPTER
25

My visit with Carolyn had been more of a soul to soul talk than a heart to heart talk. She helped me to realize that there is no finish line in our race in life. Life does not stop with death. Death is merely a short detour onto a road we will all have to travel someday, but a road that will bring sunshine and fulfillment back into our hearts. We all need to be ready for departure day. She explained that all children were born ready and that Eli truly was in a better place. We needed to cherish what time we had with him and not focus on what we had prematurely lost. I had to admit that when I walked out of her house, I felt emotionally and spiritually calmer than I had in a very long time. I wish I could bottle her emotional strength and courage and drink from that cup every day.

I drove slowly up Highway 89 out of Greenville, following the twists and turns of the road. Flanked by stately pines and banks of Manzanita bushes, the highway snaked north. I reached the little town of Canyon Dam and turned right, the highway hugging the shores of Lake Almanor. Following the directions Kendall had given me earlier in the week, I drove slowly, reading each numbered address in order to find his house.

His rental cabin, an older but well-kept and cozy lakefront home was tucked back under the pines. A sandy sweep of beach made up the front yard and the lake lapped at the shore. A chilly breeze lifted off the water and blew through the pines. I shivered and zipped my jacket, wishing I had thought to throw on a cap as well.

I shuffled through the sandy yard and stepping up onto the tiny porch, I hesitated a moment, searching for a doorbell. Finding nothing, I balled my fist and knocked sharply on the paneled wood. After a moment, I heard a rustling, a thud and movement within. Kendall opened the door and peered tiredly out at me. He gave me a generous smile. "Come on in," his voice invited.

"I'm sorry I didn't call first," I apologized.

His brows pinched and his neck stiffened. Then his lips stretched out in a straight line. "Camille, don't be ridiculous. I believe we are beyond the stage of strict propriety in our relationship. So quit being so formal and come on in. Me casa es tu casa," he replied with a chuckle.

I gave him a weak smile and walked past him. "Awe, the joys of youth. That line came straight out of a ninth grade Spanish class," I commented.

"Yes. And after all these years that's the only quote I remember," he joked with a wide smile showing his perfect white teeth.

"Same here," I admitted as my eyes took a giant sweep around the room.

The interior was dim and the décor was 1950's cowboy. Pine paneled walls with wide planked floors, the draperies and curtains in western print bark cloth. The lampshades were fringed and the chairs and a small couch were upholstered in brown leather. I felt as if I could channel Dale Evans. There were several empty beer bottles on the table in the dining area. Picking one up, I saw it was a locally crafted microbrew from Lassen Ale Works. Turning to Kendall, I held it up as in a toast and I smiled at him.

"Research," he said. Dropping onto the couch, he gestured for me to take a seat. "How did it go with Carolyn?" he asked, trying to hide his concern by focusing on a pillow he quickly tossed to the other end of the sofa.

So Kendall; cut to the chase and come right to the point, I thought to myself. Part of what I admired about this man who has absolutely captured my heart. Now he was staring right at me so he could read my reaction to his question. I tried to remain calm by keeping a straight face, but I could feel a storm brewing in my eyes. I severed the intense stare we shared and settled down on an ottoman in front of the couch. Taking in a deep breath, I leaned forward and laid my hand on his arm.

"Kendall, I did talk to Carolyn this afternoon," I said, my voice was faint. I hesitated, trying to prolong the moment and gather the right words.

He nodded and took another sip of his beer, his eyes never leaving mine. "I know," he said gently. "Remember, I tried to talk you out of it?" he reminded me patiently. He smiled ruefully, "And, how did it go with her?" he asked again, only more intent on getting an answer this time.

"Oh, it was okay. Hard, but okay," I said. "However, Agnes Morrow beat me there, so I didn't have to tell her anything she didn't already know so that made it somewhat easier."

"Greenville's notorious town crier, Agnes Morrow?" he questioned with a pinched face.

"One in the same," I answered.

"How on earth did she find out so quickly?" he asked with tight eyes and a definite frown.

"Like many of the other locals, she has a police scanner. And her grandson is one of Bill Hansen's divers. No secrets in Greenville, I'll tell ya for sure."

Kendall shook his head, his expression amused.

My heart rate quickened. "Agnes told me something else."

Kendall nodded and rolled his beer bottle over his forehead. He took another drink and swallowed deep. "Continue," is all he said. His eyes still examining my face as if it had a story to tell as well.

I was beginning to think maybe he already knew what I was going to say, but that was literally impossible. "This might be a bit uncomfortable for you," I warned.

"Nothing you can say can make this whole situation any worse than it already is, so fire away Camille. I'm a big boy and I'm not going to run away and hide," he confirmed, his eyes boring into mine.

What it is about men that they fill it is a cardinal sin or a sign of weakness to cry or feel even a little bit vulnerable to emotional pain. Obviously, Kendall was taught from infancy to hold his torn emotions behind his quiet, unrevealing eyes.

Grasping his hand tight, I could tell he was trembling just slightly. Maybe he couldn't hold up under the pressure. Maybe the decades, old unwritten rule to hold your stuff together didn't apply to him after all.

I forced the next unavoidable words out of my mouth. "Agnes and Carolyn have been friends for years and have helped each other through some pretty tough times. A lot of shared history that happened before you and I were even born. But, listen to this," I said, my voice nearly caught in my throat. I clutched his hand tighter. "Agnes told me that Carolyn actually birthed twins; Eli was a twin. A twin, Kendall," I repeated. I looked searchingly into his eyes for the shock to rise, but he seemed to take in all in with channeled intrigue, rather than staggering shock.

"And," is all he said.

"The twin brother supposedly died a few hours after birth. Carolyn was so grieved, she didn't tell anyone anything. She just had the baby cremated and kept the secret about his birth and death to herself. So painfully private; it floors me that she kept that all to herself all these years. I wonder if she even told my mom. They were such good friends."

Kendall set his bottle down softly on the table and gazed through the window. A long silence descended between us and he continued to stare, unseeing, a small frown wrinkling his forehead as he processed these incredible facts. Finally, he shrugged and turning back to me, he said, "supposedly! It all makes sense, don't you think?" He stood up allowing my hand to slide back down to my lap. His head began to shake as if to clear his thoughts. Looking down at me, he grabbed my eyes with his. "I'm not sure how to process this news," his voice, nearly a whisper now, trailed off as he turned his attention back on the window again.

I wondered what craziness was filling his mind now, the possibility that he is indeed tied to this unbelievable story in some way, or still brewing over his father's decades, old lie and deceit. I waited patiently.

"Maybe I need some time to think. It's been a long day. Do you mind?" Looking pointedly at the door, he raised his eyebrows at me. His expression was pained.

I felt the sting of rejection prick my heart. I didn't understand his cold response. But then, I reminded myself that at this moment, it wasn't about me, it was all about who he was and what was to become of him now.

I dropped my head, inhaled deeply and stood up. I stepped in front of him and gave him my best, gentle, understanding smile. Looking up, deep into his green eyes, I could sense a weariness and grief that I had not felt before. I touched his face gently, feeling the bristly stubble on his cheek. He closed his eyes and swayed a little, his hands grasping my shoulders. He lowered his head and rested his cheek next to mine. I breathed in his unique fragrance of spice and the scent of beer. I knew I needed to think about him and not my tinge of disappointment that he didn't want to lean on me now in his time of need. But again, I whispered beneath a quiet breath, this was about him and his feelings right now, not mine.

He spoke softly in my ear. "Maybe I'm not as tough as I thought I was," he concluded, letting out a sigh. "They say time heals all wounds, so I guess in time I'll find out just how true that is. But I think I had better take that advice."

"I understand. Really I do. We both need a little quiet time to process everything that has taken place over the past few weeks. Normal people would buckle beneath this kind of pressure, you know," I reminded him, hoping it would cushion his pain and turmoil.

"I guess that makes both of us a little on the odd side."

"I like odd," I confirmed. Then he put his hand lightly on the small of my back and leaned over, giving me a soft kiss. "One of your amazing characteristics. You don't conform to the norm."

He didn't say anymore, just slid his arm around my shoulder and led me to the door. We stood there for the longest time with our bodies pressed together, my head buried in his chest. All I could think about was how our casual friendship had ripened into so much more. I felt more alive than I had in a very long time, and that was because of him. I was beginning to see the first glimpses of the healing and the strengthening power of love. I wanted to be strong for him during this emotionally stormy period of his life. That to me was a clear picture of how love works.

"I'm not going to be good company for a while," he sighed.

I could feel my heart beginning to pound in my ears and I wrapped my arms around him tighter, holding him close and feeling the warmth of his body against mine. With my head still buried in his chest, I mumbled the first thing that came to mind. "Keep in touch, okay? Let me know how you are? You know I'm just a phone call away."

Having said that, he gave me another gentle peck on the lips and released his grip on my back. As my hands dropped free, he stepped over and opened the door. He gave me a little smile as I stepped through.

"I promise. I'll be in touch. Thank you for coming all the way up here to tell me this in person. I do appreciate your kindness," he said in a formal manner which took me back a bit. He nodded and gave me a half-hearted wave as I departed.

Driving slowly down the highway back to Greenville, my thoughts and emotions clamoring for equal attention in my head, I realized that I was somewhat worried about his emotional stability. I couldn't escape the depth of so much normalcy now taken from him. It worried me that he suddenly seemed so distant from even me. But then maybe that's the only way he could handle all the craziness and chaos in his life right now. I knew I cared deeply for Kendall. I wanted to help him in any way I could. I wanted to find out about his birth and his history. Not as a curious mystery, but to find out more about him. To know him. Whether or not he was Eli's twin brother didn't change the fact that I was in love with him and I hurt because he was hurting.

As I wound down the highway, the tall pine trees swayed gently in the evening breeze, the retreating sun casting long shadows over the road. A lone deer picked its way through a small stand of brushy growth, its' head swinging sharply to look at my car as I approached, ears aloft in alarm. Was it possible for me to actually love another human being and is this how it felt? With a small chuckle to myself, I ruefully wished there was an instruction manual available to novices of love. The possibility that life wasn't just about me and my personal pain, and that I was concerned for Kendall opened a new horizon of thought for me. Despite my wealth of book knowledge and advanced degrees in human psychology, I was very ignorant of the next steps and even more discerning, I was very afraid of what was yet to come.

The dark blue of the evening sky was laced with a soft pink glow in the shredded clouds in the west. I flicked on my headlights in the dimming light and drove south into town, not knowing what tomorrow would bring. But one thing for sure, I did know this much. I wanted the whole world to know what my wonderful news was. I want the world to know that this amazing man had come into my broken little world, healed my wounded soul and gave my life purpose.

CHAPTER
26

K endall and I met in Greenville on Friday morning at Anna's Café on the corner of Main St and Highway 89. He was waiting for me in a booth, wolfing a breakfast burrito and washing it down with hot coffee. A man with a good appetite is definitely a man who is in good spirits. I was relieved to see that he appeared to be so chipper. Even his voice on the phone last night sounded as if he had finally come to terms with the fact that his world was more like a war zone and that he was going to handle the next crisis with unwavering strength.

He stood and gestured at me to sit which I immediately eased down in the seat across from him. Sitting back down himself, he finished his bite and then stuffed one more into his mouth as if he hadn't eaten in a month.

"Ah, don't forget to come up for some air," I teased with one raised brow.

"Sorry, I couldn't wait. I was so hungry. No dinner last night," he responded in mock defense.

"Coffee for you Camille?" Anna, the waitress offered before I could respond to Kendall's comment. "House blend on the dark side if my memory hasn't escaped me," she added.

"No thanks Anna. I've had my fill for the day," I answered with a wiggle of my hand in the air.

She grinned wide and stood at our table for a moment longer chatting about the chill of the fall weather and the gorgeous autumn colors on Indian Head.

"Great burrito," Kendall complimented her. "Can't remember when I've tasted a breakfast burrito this good." His face was all smiles.

"We aim to please," she boasted with a grin stretching her lips wide across her thin face. Then she quickly cleared his plate and left us to plan our day.

I was still exhausted by our day on the river and the emotions of the find. My visit with Carolyn had been draining as well even though she already knew the news and I was spared the hard duty of sharing that with her. She had been her usual kindly self and sent me away with a hug and a promise of prayers. She wore the skin of a motivational speaker and wore it well. But today was a new day with a new vision. Last night on the phone, we both recommit to search for more conclusive information about Kendall's true identity. Our plan was to see Marilyn and look through her birth records.

As I sat across from this beautiful man staring into his gorgeous green eyes, I noticed that although cheerful, he had a weariness about him that was unusual. At least unusual for the short time I had known him. He had dark smudges under his eyes and a tiredness in his gaze. And as I critiqued his abnormal appearance, I shivered, imaging only too clearly all the unstoppable pain he was experiencing.

Kendall unzipped his sweatshirt, exposing another beer t-shirt, this one emblazoned with Mad Bomber Brewing Company. At my raised eyebrows, he shrugged and grew a coy little grin. "It's a little hole in the wall brewery in North Idaho. It was started by a buddy's little brother who spent time in Afghanistan. It's my way of showing support for the military," he concluded on an honorable note.

That comment made me smile, because I knew the truth. He might be supporting his friend's business, but his love for a good brew definitely fed his addiction to collecting beer T-shirts.

"Are you sure you don't want a bite to eat before we go?" he asked with his head cocked slightly toward his right shoulder.

"No," I answered. I cringed at the thought of food. My stomach felt like a minefield of emotion. "Don't have much of an appetite today for some reason," I explained.

"That's understandable. We've both been through a lot in a short amount of time. Depression's the best diet out there you know, but it's a killer," he added. "So don't fall prey to its deadly tentacles."

I agreed with a nod of my head. I quickly changed the subject of bad days and depression, because I wanted to put all that bad stuff behind me. "Well, are we ready to go?"

"As ready as ready can be," he asserted with that goofy little grin I had come to adore. "Shall we go in my jeep? No sense in taking two vehicles."

"Sounds like a good idea to me," I said, allowing my eyes the pleasure of roaming over his beautiful face.

Once in the jeep, I directed Kendall to Marilyn's house. Ramona wasn't needed since I had been there many times myself.

Driving out of town, the road snaking the base of Indian Head Mountain, we rode in silence, appreciating the riotous autumn colors of the oaks trees. The sere yellows of the pastures stretched out to our right and I rolled down my window to inhale the crisp morning air and the scents of crushed, dry grass.

Pulling into Marilyn's yard, Kendall parked next to her red Bronco in the driveway. We could see her round freckled cheeks surrounded by wild, red hair behind the lace curtains. She stepped out the heavy wooden front door and waved excitedly to us.

Kendall looked through the windshield at her for a long moment and turning to me, he said solemnly. "You didn't tell me she was a ginger." Again that sly grin curled up his lips.

Surprised, I just stared at him. "She's a strawberry blonde," I corrected him confusedly. "What does her hair color have to do with anything?" I didn't have a clue where he was going with that odd comment.

He shook his head with a stern expression on his face. Then he shrugged and exhaled heavily. "Don't you know? Gingers have no soul."

I stared at him, dissecting his expression. "Are you serious? That's the most ridiculous thing I have ever heard you say," I said with a creased forehead.

His half smile faded. "Are you sure we can trust her?" His tone was low and froggy.

I continued to stare at him. I was baffled by this conversation, especially since his fair hair had the same reddish cast as Marilyn's. "That's the most ridiculous, old, unwise tale I have ever heard. In fact, it's just plain nonsense," I scolded him with the best evil eye I could muster. His words, though delivered in earnest, stung like a hornet because Marilyn didn't have a mean bone in her body.

"What do you call a ginger with an attitude?" he asked. "Normal," he started to smile. "What's the difference between a ginger and a shoe? A shoe has a sole." He began to laugh out loud.

A faint smile touched my lips. I rolled my eyes and shook my head. Belatedly, I realized he was joking. My seriousness about our searches was overwhelming and his levity brought a relief that made me laugh along with him.

"Sorry about that," he chuckled. "I've heard all the jokes. And they were all on me." Continuing to laugh, he stepped out of the jeep and waved to Marilyn on the porch.

"Yeah! You missed your calling alright. Don't want to burst your bubble, but you really need to stick to law," I said, playfully, but my tone was laced with sarcasm.

He flashed me a wide wicked smile over the hood of the jeep and then winked at me. Thankfully, our attention was now drawn to

Marilyn holding a small grey kitten under one arm and beckoning for us to come on in with the other hand.

As I closed the distance between us, I took a good sweeping glance around the place. It was an older white house east of Greenville on North Valley Road. It was a home familiar to me. An auntie on my father's side of the family had lived here when I was a child. Upon her death, the house was sold and passed through several owners until Marilyn and her husband, Russell, purchased it a few years ago. While keeping the character of the venerable home, built in the old farmhouse style, Marilyn had imposed her own cheerful decorating style on it. I remembered it well from one of my previous visits during Christmas vacation one year. The white-washed walls were hung with framed floral prints and houseplants gave the entry a cheerful outdoorsy atmosphere. Today, the autumn sun glowed warmly through the big windows, leaving squares of brightness on the wide planked floor.

Throwing one arm around me, squeezing me into a bear hug, she was quivering with excitement. "Come on in. I've been on pins and needles all week waiting for today," she said. "Now this here is Josey. Not a pretty cat with her drab grey color, but she's lovable." Then she quickly ushered us into the front room. Two more cats paraded before us in a dignified saunter, as we moved further into a room crowded with antique furniture. She gave us a speedy history of the house and waxed enthusiastically how she and Russ had come to purchase and remodel it. As she wound down, her curiosity about Kendall became palpable. "And where did you find this handsome man?"

"He's just a friend. A history buff of sorts and is residing in a cabin at the lake to do some exploring around our beautiful countryside," I explained.

"Is that so," she said, easily warming up to him. "I've known Camille since I was a flat chested, bony little girl which you can see is a very long time by the looks of these two dangling torpedoes now," she expressed with a giggle at her own humor. "And so solemn, this one is. Even I have to work hard to get a smile out of her," she commented as she reached over and tickled me under my chin. "As a longtime family friend, I've watched her grow up, developing into a lovely young lady. And I'd give anything to have some of her skinniness now!" She patted her tummy, smiling and slapped her generous behind.

Kendall listened, nodded and smiled in the appropriate spaces in her conversation and I marveled at his courtesy. But judging by the flush in his cheeks, he was a tad bit embarrassed with her explicit description of her voluptuous body parts.

We chatted inconsequentially a few more moments before she clapped her hands in pure joy, exclaiming, "I can't wait to show you these journals! They are amazing." She turned around and with a wave of her hand, instructed us to follow.

Seating herself on the plump white couch, and pulling a small table closer to her, she picked up a large notebook from a basket at her feet and opened it with some ceremony, smoothing the old paper with gentle fingers. She slipped on a pair of orange framed reading glasses, and Kendall looked at me behind her back, nodded and mouthed 'Ginger,' with a knowing expression on his face.

"Come here. Sit right here," she said patting the sofa with her hand.

I motioned with a slight movement of my head for Kendall to follow suit. I sank down on the couch beside Marilyn and Kendall filled in the seat right next to me. I looked over Marilyn's shoulder at the opened journal.

"Did you know that we actually had a set of triplets born here in Greenville in the 1930s?" she asked. "Natural birth and all lived," she went on to say. "Amazing really, given the state of health care at the time. Even more remarkable is the fact that those babies were born at home. The story goes, that they were so tiny that they were placed in separate dresser drawers for the first few weeks of their life."

Marilyn turned back to the journal as if eager to get started again. She continued to turn the pages slowly and then suddenly stopped to look over at me and grabbed my eyes. "So what exactly are you interested in? Is there a specific time frame or situation that you wanted to know about?" she asked, her expression a trifle puzzled.

I threw a quick glance at Kendall, turned my eyes back on the pages of her journal and then gave her my idea as a starting point. "Actually, we would like to know about twin births in the last, say, thirty five years and any possible adoptions during that time frame," I told her.

"Hmmm, well that will be in a different journal, then," she said, peering at me over her orange framed glasses. "Let me find those books, but I'll tell you, I don't think there will be any adoption information. That was usually of a private matter back in those days, if you know what I mean," she elaborated.

"I see," I said, although I didn't really understand.

She adjusted her orange glasses and sighed. "Adoption was usually an arrangement between families or friends of the family. Back then, a surprise pregnancy was not generally celebrated. It was very common for an unwed mother to quietly give birth and then she or her parents would adopt the baby out to willing families. Unlike today's privacy issues, it was more of a secrecy issue.

Rummaging through the basket, she selected two more of the notebooks and pulled them onto her lap. Opening the one on top, she set it on the little table and sifted through some loose papers inside the front cover. "Let's see here, several sets of twins in the last few decades. Hmmmm," her voice whispered through partially closed lips. "It looks like there were the Johnson, Morehead, Carter and the Young twins."

My breath caught in my throat, but I managed to push out a few words. "Tell me about the Young twins," I blurted in a more demanding tone than I had intended.

Again, she flipped gently through the pages and obviously found them. "Let's see now. Yes, here we have it. Young Twins; Elisha and Jeremiah. Born to father, Cadence Young and Carolyn Young, maiden name Lowry. Oh my goodness! This is one of my grandma's last few entries and I had no idea Carolyn Young had twin boys." She shook her head at the discovery.

"What is the birth date?" I asked her, raising my head to catch Kendall's eye.

"Can we trust her?" he mouthed at me silently.

I shook my head and sternly tightened my eyes. Then I turned back to Marilyn. "Does your grandma have any details about their birth or anything else relating to the Young boys?" I asked her more curious than ever.

"July 17th, 1982," she said. "Let's see, 4:33 in the afternoon. But it says here that Jeremiah died later that night. No cause of death that I can see here." She shook her head sadly which was no surprise to me. I knew Marilyn had a very soft heart and the loss of a baby decades previously would still grieve her. "How very sad," she repeated. "I didn't know Carolyn lost a baby. And then to lose Eli as well. That's a cryin' shame. Makes you wonder just how much one woman can handle." She sighed, shaking her head in sympathy.

Glancing back at Kendall, I wanted to make sure he was keeping up with the flow of the information. His eyes were narrow and his face was pinched tight in a frown. It's not easy to learn about the death of any child, but this death held a special meaning for him. I knew if I were in his position, I would want more details.

"Kendall, do you have any questions?" I asked.

His eyes widened, but he hesitated, obviously in deep thought. "Marilyn, did your grandmother record any other births around that same time? I know you said these are some of her last journal entries, but what else does she have written down there?" he asked in a low tone. His expression was serious.

"Well, let's see," she said, slowly running her finger down the page. "Oh yes, here is another birth later that same night. Baby boy Danielson. Kendall Danielson," she clarified further. Then her head flew up in that all too familiar, 'Aha' moment. She looked over at Kendall, then at me, her eyebrows pulling together. I guessed, she was looking for answers in my squinted eyes which weren't there, because it was up to Kendall to satisfy her curiosity.

"Is that what you wanted to know? Where you were born? But didn't your parents tell you?"

Kendall nodded, "Oh yeah, I always knew I was born here in Greenville, but I didn't know much about the circumstances of my birth and we never visited here after I was born. My mom is gone now and my dad is in very poor health, so I am just finding a few things out for myself."

Marilyn nodded kindly at him with saddened eyes, as if to acknowledge Kendall's pain over his mother's loss and his father's circumstances. Her capacity for empathy and kindness was generous and one of the reasons I liked her so much. "Is there anything else I can help you out with? I have all of these journals here if there is anything else you are curious about," she said. Hesitating, her smile faded. Then she stared down at the books that recorded the birth and death of every infant born in this town for the past sixty years or so. "I don't loan these out, but you are welcome to read through them now or anytime in the future, if you'd like," she went on to say.

I looked at the journals thoughtfully for a moment, wondering how to address my next question without arousing her suspicions about the real reason we were here. "Say, Marilyn, do you know of anyone who may have worked at the hospital during that time? Maybe someone who might be able to answer some questions Kendall may have?" I asked trying to keep a subdued expression on my face.

She tipped her head back and squinted her eyes as she thought, her face tilted towards the ceiling. "Hmmmm, I do know that Jimmy Doyle's sister, Lois, worked there for years. But she passed away about five years ago, give or take. Meryl Strickland was a nurse there for many years and she assisted at a lot of births. She's gone now, too." Then she grinned widely, showing all of her teeth and a good portion of gum. "You might be able to talk to Brenda Jones. I am not sure if she was there at the time of your arrival, Kendall, but she was on staff for a long time. She's in the assisted living wing of the hospital now. Her arthritis is pretty bad, but her mind is still sharp and I'm sure she'd have some good stories for you. I do know for a fact that she loves company and the opportunity to visit about old times."

As soon as she mentioned little Jimmy Doyle, I felt a flutter of excitement in my chest. Little Jimmy's sister was a sweet faced woman who had cared for him after their parents died. She was a great deal older than him, maybe fifteen years or so, and although I did not know her personally, Jimmy spoke of her with great affection. Maybe she had talked of her work to Jimmy over the years. Of course, Brenda Jones would be our best lead, and for that very reason I couldn't wait to find her and have a lengthy conversation. I knew her only in passing much like many of the older folks when I was young. I could attach a name to a face and that was about it. I couldn't even recall the last time our paths had crossed.

I looked into Marilyn's eyes, filled with nothing but true concern for Kendall and his precarious situation. I gave her a generous smile, hoping to convince her I was satisfied with what information we had uncovered so far. "Marilyn, I can't thank you enough for your help," I said, my mind still concentrating on our next plan of action. I stood as I spoke. "I know this is your day off and I don't want to take up any more of your time."

Marilyn smiled brightly, her eyes flashing between Kendall and me as she jumped to her feet. She chattered as we made our way, following the arrogant parade of cats again, to the front door. "I sure hope you will visit again soon. And Kendall, I know you will enjoy your stay in northern California. Can't beat these fall colors. This entire valley is so gorgeous this time of year."

At the door I gave her a generous hug. "Thank you again," I said with a smile that backed up my appreciation. We walked out to the jeep and slid into our seats. Marilyn stood on her front porch with her hand waving like a flag in the wind as we rumbled out of her driveway.

Kendall blew a sigh and shook his head. "She has the ginger energy, for sure," he said with a long pause. "But I'm not sure we have much to go on though, given that two of the witnesses she proposed to us are dead and a third is as old as the hills." He navigated the rocky driveway skillfully and turned onto the pavement back into town.

I formed each word carefully, considering it was his life, his history we were sifting through. "Energetic she is, but has a big heart as well. And I can guarantee you that right now she is looking through those journals to see if there is any more information that will be of help to you," I confirmed.

He let out a long sigh. "I don't doubt that one bit," he said in a low, subdued tone. "So what do we do now?"

I slouched back in my seat and gazed through the windshield with unseeing eyes, the brilliant fall colors lost to me as I considered our options. "We go talk to Brenda Jones. There's no time like the present." But no sooner had those words left my mouth, I felt the familiar anxiety clutch at my chest. Unanswered questions raced through my mind. Where would this journey lead us and where would it end? And what do these new facts mean to Kendall? But I knew all the wondering in the world wouldn't change the fact that we couldn't stop now no matter how much it hurt. Every door that closed so far seem to open a new one. I could only imagine what waited for us behind the walls of a home for the aged. But one thing I did know for sure; I wasn't sorry we had taken on this incredible journey together. I believe everything that has taken place so far is exactly as it should be.

We rode in silence as the tide of uncertainty rolled over me once again.

CHAPTER 27

The silence between us was deafening on our short jaunt to the Indian Valley Hospital. I glanced once at his face, but his expression was one of pained concentration, so I looked away and watched the trees and rows of houses whiz by in a blur.

The hospital was located on Hot Springs Road, a half a block from the high school. A short paved road, with homes on both sides, ended in the hospital parking lot with a rough softball field in the distance beyond. Over the years, the hospital has adapted to the changing face of Indian Valley. It was a clinic in the early days and due to the hard work of Dr. Batson and his staff, had been designated a hospital for many years. With the fluctuations in population, changes in the timber industry and health care, an assisted living wing was added and housed local residents who were unable to live on their own, but wanted to remain close to their mountain homes and families.

Kendall pulled into the small lot and parked. We sat quietly, listening to the engine tick under the hood for a few moments. I knew he was trying to assemble his thoughts. I watched the muscles in his jawbone twitch and jump as he grit his teeth. Running his hand through his hair and rumpling it wildly, he blew out a breath. "Well, I suppose we had better go chat with our only living witness. Hopefully she's got enough grey matter between her ears to pick."

I smiled at him and as I gazed into his green eyes. I sensed a weariness and nervousness in him that I felt as well. We were both trying to hold on to some sense of sanity. But were the circumstances of his birth creating a concern in him that maybe he wasn't ready to deal with? I wondered, but was not sure what to say, so I touched his face, feeling the roughness of his unshaven cheek and the warmth of his skin on my open palm. He rested his hand over mine and looked down into my eyes. I could see the apprehension in his eyes and I smiled at him again, trying to give him some unspoken assurance that we were doing the right thing.

"Remember Kendall, we're in this together," I told him again. He nodded, answering my gaze through weary eyes.

I let out a short sigh and turned away to place my hand on the handle. I opened my door and stepped out into the chilly autumn sunshine. He met me at the back of the jeep. My heart jumped frantically as he took my hand in his and we walked in silence toward the front entrance of the hospital.

The small foyer was clean and smelled faintly of alcohol. I wrinkled my nose at the odor. Hospitals all smell the same and the last time I had been here was when I held my father's hand as he passed from the suffering of this world into the endless journey into the next. With a small shudder and taking a deep breath, I moved further into the designated waiting area. There was a dated maple side table, littered with magazines. Good Housekeeping, Guns & Ammo, Highlights for Children. There were four upholstered chairs, worn but clean. The front desk was to our left and appeared to be empty behind the sliding glass partition. The nurse's station was just ahead and I could see the top of someone's head behind the counter.

Kendall and I stepped forward and the woman raised her head and smiled at us. She was dressed in white scrubs and her name badge read, 'Heather RN.' "May I help you?" she asked in a pleasant voice.

I stepped up closer to the counter and spoke to her in a low tone as not to wake any of the patients who might be sleeping. "I'm Camille Cameron and this is Kendall Danielson. We are hoping to visit with Brenda Jones, if possible."

"Are you family?" she inquired as she placed some paperwork in a wire basket to her left.

"No, just friends stopping by to say hello," I offered.

"Ah that's nice. When you reach 88, you outlive most of your friends, so it's nice when young people like yourself take the time to stop in and see her. She is down the hall," she gestured to her left. "Room thirty. She naps every afternoon, but she should be up and about by now. Let me walk you down there." Coming out from behind the nurses' station, she gestured for us to follow, her soft soled shoes squeaking on the polished floor. Knocking gently on the partially closed door to room thirty, she called out in a low whisper. "Brenda? Are you up? You have some company," she informed her.

From inside, a quavery voice called out, "Come on in."

Nurse Heather, RN, smiled at us and pushed the door wide open. "Have a good visit," she said. She turned and headed back down the hall, the echoes of her shoes squeaking on the floor growing fainter.

Kendall and I entered the room to find a tiny little woman, wizened with age and arthritis in a wheelchair near the window. Her gray hair was neatly pinned in a bun on the top of her head and her bright eyes peered at us from a wrinkled face. Fleetingly, I thought of the old fashioned dried apple dolls and how her visage reminded me of one. She wore a soft pink dress with a bright sweater the color of bubblegum over her shoulders and she had a faded quilt draped over her legs. A Bible lay on her lap and she rested an age spotted and frail hand on it lovingly.

"Come on in, you two. Don't you look like a fine young couple!" she proclaimed. Holding out her other hand, she reached for me as I stepped closer. "Ah Camille, you have grown into a beautiful young lady. Just like your mother, God rest her soul." She tugged at my hand and as I leaned towards her she kissed my face and smiled up at me.

"I wasn't sure you would remember me, Brenda," I said. "It is good to see you, it's been a while. How are you?" I asked. The years had not been kind to her, but her sweet face was wreathed in a big smile that I remembered about her.

"I thank the Good Lord above for every bonus day I am given. At my age, every day is something you can't take for granted. I also appreciate that my mind is still intact and my memory is in pretty good working order," she laughed. "It's my body that is shot. I have been retired about thirteen years now and it was only because of my arthritis." She paused to take in a deep breath and graze her eyes over my face. "Of course I remember you, dear girl. How could I forget the girl with a face that mirrors her mother's? Besides, like I explained, my mind is sharp. My granddaughter tells me that my brain is like an Intel processor." She nodded sagely. "Plenty of RAM, too." She smiled at our expressions, "Ha. You young folks always underestimate the older generation's capacity for learning new technology." Shaking her head, she gestured for us to sit in the little armchairs by the wall. "Please sit down and make yourself comfortable."

As we sat, I marveled at her new age verbiage and her ability to conform to modern day technology. "That is so cool, you are so computer literate. Did you take some classes or teach yourself?" I asked with curiosity, appraising her expression.

"Ah no," she replied. "My children got me a desktop," she said, with a furrowed brow and a pinched nose drawing out her next word as if trying to get her time frame exact. "Ohhh, probably about twenty years ago or so. And yes, I did take some classes. Thankfully, it came easy to me so eventually I ended up teaching computer usage classes to a group of senior citizens for a few years too." She gave a ladylike snort of disgust. "Some of those old farts couldn't tell the difference between email, g-mail or female and they didn't seem to care, either."

Kendall met my glance with a wide smile. A sudden burst of laughter from all three of us filled the room. I heard Brenda clear her throat which brought our eyes back in her direction.

Shaking her head, she continued to speak her mind, picking up where she left off. "How on earth are you going to stay in touch with grandkids if you don't learn the technology? Communication is important. It is also important for the human mind to continue learning. I don't care how old you are!" she finished with a firm nod of her head.

I looked at Kendall. He had an admiring look on his face. He appeared to respect smart, elderly females.

Suddenly, I recalled the fact that I hadn't even properly introduced the young to the old. "I must have left my manners at the front door. Sorry about that," I said as my eyes landed on the sweet little old lady now searching my eyes for an explanation for my expression of regret. "Brenda, this is my good friend, Kendall Danielson. Kendall, this is Brenda Jones."

"Ah yes, Kendall Danielson. Baby Boy Danielson, to be exact, born to Owen and Alice Danielson. Let's see, 1982, am I right?" Her bright eyes peered at us inquiringly.

Kendall cleared his throat, staring at her intently. "Yes, as a matter of fact you are accurate. But how on earth could you possibly recall that? Thousands of babies born in this hospital and you remember my name and my birth date? How is that humanly possible?" he asked, his eyes more serious than I had ever seen before.

I sat in silence wondering the same thing myself. I drug my eyes away from Kendall and landed them back on Brenda.

Her eyes crinkled as she smiled, and I again fleetingly thought of the apple dolls, "Well, should we say a special gift bestowed upon me? I have what's called a photographic memory. Not eidetic, mind you, but close to photographic. It is a God given gift, a blessing and sometimes a curse. And, of course, I cared very deeply about my work and everyone I came in contact with," she elaborated.

"You must admit that is pretty amazing to have recalled something that trivial," I pointed out. "As Kendall said, there must have been thousands of babies born at this hospital over the years. I could feel the shock parch my face.

"Oh yes, there were. But the same night this young man was born, we lost one of our babies, so that impresses my memory even more," she explained.

That remark caused my heart to take a dive. "Do you remember that baby's name?" I asked, feeling a sudden surge of nausea washing over me.

"Oh honey, I am not at liberty to say. That is confidential information, you see. There are new privacy laws in force now that would put even an old relic like me in jail without a moment's hesitation. Confidentiality is the golden rule now. You do understand that don't you?" She peered over at me, her eyes full of concern.

"Of course, I understand and I don't want to put you in a compromising situation," I reassured her. "But could you at least tell us if you were on duty the night that baby boy died?"

"I didn't say the baby was a boy," she said guardedly. "How did you come by that information?" she inquired with an intense stare.

"Well, Kendall and I did a little bit of research before we came to see you and found out it was a baby boy." I hoped she wouldn't close up on us.

"I see," she said with more suspicion in her eyes than I was comfortable with. "No, I worked that day, but wasn't supposed to be on shift that night. However, the entire town of Greenville was under a mandatory evacuation due to a raging wild fire approaching our little community at a very rapid speed. There was a great deal of confusion and chaos trying to move all the patients to the Seneca Hospital in Chester. Sometime during that process the little one passed away. I was so surprised because although he was born a bit premature, he seemed to be holding his own very well. The hospital had just invested in a little better equipped delivery room and a new incubator for our babies," she said as her frown deepened.

Then her eyes suddenly fell on Kendall. Her frown faded and her entire face grew into a saddened expression. "If I expected anyone to pass, it would have been you. Your mother also came to our facility in preterm labor. We all thought your immature lungs were just not developed enough to sustain your life. You were very weak and on oxygen. This especially rings true with baby boys. We've found that baby girls' are much stronger than boys when it comes to undeveloped lungs, but you fooled us all. It had been a very long night, but sometime in the early morning, they were able to get a line around the fire. So we woke to the good news that our town had been spared. As soon as the evacuation order had been lifted, we started moving our patients back home. You had improved overnight, which surprised even Dr. Batson. We were grateful and happy for your parents that you had survived the night. You see, it was hard to keep premature babies alive until we could get them to Chico back then. Now, it is just a quick helicopter ride, but then, it could be a touch and go situation," she added.

Kendall turned his head to look at me. Catching his eyes, I was again caught up in the intense green and the weariness in his gaze. At this moment we were also of one mind and one conclusion.

Turning back to Brenda, I asked, "Just one last question. Can you tell me who was on duty the night the baby died?" My heart jolted inside my chest. I tried to brace myself for the truth that I felt I already knew.

A vivid disapproving look came over her face and she tightened her lips, shaking her head slightly. The silence lengthened between us and her eyes were troubled. "It won't really help you. Little Miss, as we called her, passed away a few years ago. I don't think she would answer any questions even if she were here to do so. Believe me, I tried, but she was so evasive when I asked her anything about what had happened that night," she elaborated with a mixture of emotion parching her face.

Kendall's eyes widened at the mention of the name, Little Miss. I thought for sure he was going to fall over because he had leaned forward so far that I instinctively grabbed his arm pulling him back. But he remained silent, listening to Brenda and I exchange words back and forth.

"You had questions?" I asked. "What kind of questions?" Anticipation gripped my heart and squeezed much too tight.

Brenda looked down at her Bible, stroking the cover with her gnarled fingers, as if deliberating.

There was something behind her sad eyes that told me there was much more to this story than she was letting on. She sighed, seeming reluctant to answer my question.

"What kind of questions, Brenda?" I asked again, in a softer tone.

She looked back up at me, her eyes now filled with tears. "Questions that went unanswered," she said disapprovingly. "Answers that Little Miss took to the grave with her. I had my suspicions, but speculations without facts would do more harm than good if I pursued the matter legally. She never spoke of the baby and I never asked again. But whatever happened, it took a toll on her. She aged visibly and always seemed strained, somehow," she explained.

I felt the wheels of anxiety churning in my head. I couldn't let this lie. As difficult as this was for Kendall to hear, I had to press her further for my own peace of mind. "You referred to the nurse that night as Little Miss. I don't remember a Little Miss, was she new to the valley?"

Brenda waved a frail hand in front of her face, "Oh, heavens to Betsy no. Her name was Lois Doyle. I believe you know her little brother, Jimmy. He's worked for your father for years helping at the cemetery. I assume he is still part of the fixtures around there?" Her face crinkled as she smiled with fondness.

Hearing her name made my heart jump so fast, I could hardly catch my breath. "Oh yeah, Jimmy is still with us. I think he is under the impression the place would crumble if he weren't there to oversee the works." I smiled back at her, trying to appear as calm as I could. "There is a lot that goes on behind the scenes in a cemetery and he and Brian both help enormously. I couldn't have done it without them. I handle the paperwork and they take care of the manual labor. They have been wonderful since my father passed away," I said, keeping our conversation going with small talk.

"Ah your father, Camille. I offer you my condolences. I was so sorry to hear of his passing. He was a wonderful man." She shook her head gently. "A wonderful man, indeed."

"Yes, it seems most of the town shares your sentiments," I agreed. "It is a great comfort on days when thoughts of him are heavy on my mind."

Brenda let out another slight sigh and met my gaze. "I am truly sorry I couldn't help you out more. I can only say what I know to be the truth. I hope you understand," she said with kindness in her eyes.

"On the contrary. You have been more help than you know. But enough about all of that. Let's talk about you. Tell us about your family and what you've been up to all these years," I suggested with a sense of calm coming over me.

The sadness in her voice was gone and her face lit up with joy. "Hope you have some time," she said.

"We have all the time in the world," I confirmed, looking over at Kendall. He nodded, with a distant look in his eyes.

CHAPTER 28

The next day, after a busy morning of paperwork and more cleaning most of the afternoon, I walked down the graveled path with my arms folded across my chest. The sun was beginning to empty its' pot of golden light as it ventured into the declining moments of the day. It glowed on the stones and gave a golden and timeless ambience to the cemetery. As I stepped off of the path, the grass brushed against my boots. I strolled south, past my mother and father's graves, hesitating long enough to read their names. Feeling the prick of tears, I moved past.

I shifted my head slightly to the left to watch a grey squirrel run across the manicured lawn in front of me and scurried up a tall pine. Its' bushy tail twitch as it stopped halfway up the tree to stare down at me. Beady eyes alert, as if it was thinking which way to go next if I tried to climb the tree as well. He chittered at me and continued his ascent.

I turned my attention down the slope of the sepia green landscape in front of me and again I began my slow walk. Two more rows and ten stones to the right was my destination. Within moments I was there, staring down at the grave that held all the answers to the questions I couldn't ask. I squatted by her gravestone and read the words printed on the upright granite slab below an engraved picture of an angel holding a young boy in her arms. I've always heard that a picture is worth a thousand words. I could feel the warmth of tears beginning to brew in my eyes as I traced the outline of the angel with my forefinger. It does seem to appear that she must have loved children and children must have loved her in return.

Lois Mae Doyle, Gone but not Forgotten. A keeper of children. A flower taken long before her time. Born January 21, 1948, Died May 3, 1998.

I leaned in closer and moved a small vase filled with silk flowers from the base of the stone. There were the words that Kendall had been seeking. Little Miss. Engraved into the hard granite and partially hidden by a patchy growth of dark green moss.

Maybe she was like a beautiful flower. Maybe she was a woman who loved children. Maybe her gentle heart led in her actions. But was she a woman who took destiny into her hands and altered history? Had she taken one child away from one woman to give to another like I suspected? How could such a loving woman do such a despicable thing? What could prompt a woman of her high integrity to cause such pain to one family in order to meet the needs of another? All the answers lay beneath the depths of this stone, buried forever in time. The questions continued to tumble in an endless chant in my mind. How could she do it? How could she do it and live out her life as if nothing out of the ordinary had happened. How could a flower child become such a cold-hearted, callous woman ignorant of the pain she had caused? Now she lay six feet under still guarding her secret for eternity. I didn't know whether to despise her or feel sorry for her.

"She used to sing me a song every night before I went to sleep when I was a young boy," a voice said behind me, causing me to jerk around.

"Jimmy!" I screeched louder than I had intended, feeling the pounding pulse in my ears. I slapped my hand on my chest. "Let me jump start my heart," I gasped as I used every effort to keep from falling backward. I quickly stood up to meet his glare.

"Sorry. I didn't mean to startle you," he said in his reedy voice.

"Not a problem. I was just daydreaming. Thinking about happier times I guess," I commented as I glanced back down at the gravestone.

Jimmy laughed, a sound more like a cackle. That was the first time I noticed his front teeth were crooked, one crossed slightly over the other. Was I so self-absorbed that I didn't even notice details about other people?

"Did you know my sister?" he asked with blunt curiosity. He winced slightly as if her loss were still a deep physical pain.

"No Jimmy. I'm afraid I didn't have that privilege. I've heard a lot of nice things about her," I answered him.

"You would have liked her. They didn't come any nicer than my Little Miss," he said, his love for her surfaced so easily and openly.

"Little Miss," I repeated. "How did she come by that nickname?" I asked out of curiosity, a sense of déjà vu tickling at my mind.

"I have to take the credit for that one. When I was a little guy," he said, then let out a short huff and added, "still not much bigger. I couldn't pronounce Lois, so I guess I would just say Iss. Somewhere along the line I tagged on an M. For as far back as I can remember people called me Little Jimmy, so eventually I called her Little Miss. Made sense to me at the time. But who knows how and why a little kid's brain works?" he explained.

"Makes perfect sense to me too," I said. I could tell he was pleased with my comment by the way his face glowed with a prideful grin.

"Not necessarily common knowledge, but our mom was bipolar and sometimes just couldn't handle a rambunctious kid like me, so my sister stepped into the parenting shoes .She was fifteen years older than me and I kept her on her toes for sure. But she did it. She did it all. Played kick the can, hide-n-seek, red light-green light and she played a mean game of baseball. Took me to my scout meetings, the movies and treated me to a coke at the Dew-Drop-Inn. In those days that was a big deal you know. Only the high school kids hung out there, but she didn't care. She'd waltz me in there and sit us at the bar like we were ordering cocktails. She was the one who helped me when I got sick. You know, when I was a teenager and my kidneys went bad. She actually donated one of hers to me. It must have been a good one, because it is still inside working away and doing its' thing. She was such an angel to me." He shook his head, his mind in the mists of the past; his eyes with a far-away look remembering his beloved and much missed older sister. "I remember how hard she worked to save money for that operation. It was hella expensive and she saved up for a couple years to make it happen. She did garage sales and worked extra shifts at the hospital. She even wrote a book of poetry and sold it at all the touristy places in Quincy and up at Lake Almanor," he said. He looked down at her stone as if it were speaking to him. Then his tortured eyes grabbed mine. "She was a saint for sure."

I felt the flickering in the back of my mind again. I wasn't sure what kind of realization, but I knew we were on to something here. "She saved for a couple of years? How much did an operation like that cost?" I asked, knowing it really wasn't any of my business.

He shrugged his shoulders and pursed his lips. "Well, we didn't have any insurance, so the price tag was pretty high. What with follow up and medications and what not, the numbers just kept adding up. Probably well over $100 grand." He offhandedly shrugged again, smiled and said, "She was just so happy that I was feeling better and could finish school. She said every sacrifice she made was worth it. She really was my angel and I miss her every day." He quickly crossed himself, whispered, "God rest her soul."

"So she wrote poetry. Interesting, since I'm a bit of a poetry addict myself. I'd love to read some of her work sometime, if it's still available that is?" I fished. Which boiled down to asking and hinting at the same time.

He shook his head, "Noooo," he said sadly. "She left strict instructions that all of her papers had to be burned after she died. I kept a little notebook of hers that I found, but I felt bad, like I was disrespecting her by not burning it as well. But it was something so important to her. She seemed to work in that small journal more than others. So me and Brian buried it with her. We just dug down one day and laid it on top of her coffin. Brian was real helpful and it made me feel better for sure."

He crossed himself again and adjusted his cap. He struggled to compose himself. "She was my angel, no doubt about that," he confirmed. "She saved my life. I could never repay the sacrifices she made for me." He nodded to me and quietly ambled back toward the upper road with a slow gait.

As I stood in stunned silence, everything suddenly fell into place. The unexpected death of one healthy baby and the sudden recovery of another one not expected to survive. Money needed for a life-saving surgery. Money paid to keep a desperate woman's silence. A despicable crime. A secret hidden and taken to the grave. So many lives affected. So much pain. This was a no win situation because in the end, other than Little Jimmy, everyone suffered in one way or the other.

I now had a very clear motive for Little Miss to seek the money. And it was out of desperation and love for her brother that she had altered families and lives that were not her own.

I was not smiling as I walked back toward my house. Even though I knew I had all the answers, there was no cause to celebrate.

CHAPTER
29

The following morning, I was lighting a fire in the wood stove when my phone rang, but my hands were sooty from emptying the ash pan and cleaning the stove, so I let it go to voicemail. The fire began to glow and crackle behind the glass in the door and I stood back to enjoy the sound and the warmth. A wood heated home is so cozy and it was one of the small things I had missed while living in the city. My various apartments had never had the warmth a wood stove can bring to the chilly dampness of the Bay Area during the autumn and winter seasons. Switching on the fan behind the stove, I stepped into the kitchen to wash my hands and get my coffee started.

Mindlessly looking through the window as I ground the fragrant beans, I admired the shimmer of the frost coating the trees. The crystals caught some of the morning sun and sparkled like twinkling gems in the soft rays. Most of the fall leaves were lying on the ground in untidy heaps, like cast off clothing the morning after a late party. Their bright colors were softer and muted, the sepia shades of late fall creeping into the world. As I gazed up at Indian Head, the old man serene in his drab autumn garb, I felt a flutter of gratitude for all that I could see through the window. The roll of one season into another, life moving forward despite what we humans think or feel. My thoughts lingered on the Creator of time, of life and how the seasons mirrored the growth He intends for each of us. I was surprised at myself. I cannot remember the last time I allowed such thoughts to linger in my mind. But here in my mountain home, surrounded by the results of nature's inexorable march forward, where the natural world more than lived up to any country girl's expectations, I was lingering.

Shaking my head, as if trying to free myself from the spell of woolgathering, I remembered the chirp of my voicemail and reached for my phone. Ah, a voicemail from Kendall. I listened to the music of his voice, but his tone sounded submerged under a river of depression. He also sounded tired, but he tried hard to cover up his blue mood as he asked if we could meet at Anna's Café again for coffee.

I looked at my full coffeepot and quickly texted him an invite to help me drink it. While waiting for his reply, I made my bed and started a load of laundry. I heard his jeep rumble up the driveway and I stepped out the door and waved to him. Ducking back inside, out of the chill, I rummaged in the fridge for some eggs and cheese for a breakfast sandwich and I was pulling the toaster from the cupboard when he came through the door into the kitchen.

Turning to him, I gave him a quick smile and gathered up the coffee mugs. "Hey you," I said, gesturing at him to sit at the table. I turned back to the coffee pot and filled the cups and then quickly joined him at the table.

Pulling out a chair, he sat, properly, facing the table. Dressed in jeans and a dark blue hoodie, his spicy scent was fresh in my nose. He took the mug from me and wrapped his long fingers around it, cradling the cup in his grasp. He still looked so tired, but he no longer had the haunted look of last night.

He stared at me for a long moment and then finally loosened his tongue. "Sorry I wasn't good company the other night. I had a lot to think about and I had a lot of beer to drink while doing it," he admitted. "Not a good decision," he added with guilt coating his flushed face. He shrugged, sipped at his coffee, his eyes crawled back to me. "Strange isn't it. I want answers, but as soon as I get them, I almost regret asking them. They say be careful what you ask for. I'm beginning to feel the painful truth of that old saying deep in my tattered heart."

"I can't argue that point," I agreed, feeling his pain.

Kendall paused again to take another big slurp of his coffee. "Well, enough of that," he said, somewhat plaintively. "How about I put my productive energy into making us some breakfast?"

"No argument there," I declared, thrusting my hands in the air. "Make yourself at home."

He quickly went to work and I marveled over his efficiency in a kitchen. I watched as he skillfully managed to scramble eggs and toast some croissants he found in the freezer. I was awestruck at his deft movements and how gracefully he maneuvered around in such a small area as he cooked and talked at the same time. He was certainly right at home in a kitchen.

"So, if I recap everything, starting with you," he said, looking over his shoulder for possibly my approval, I guessed. "I know this is as difficult for you as it is for me," he added.

Spoken like a typical attorney with all his ducks in order, I quietly thought. I nodded with a smile to encourage him to go on and yet maintain my calm. I knew this was the path we needed to take despite the fact that every time we mulled it over, the pain just seemed to intensify.

"When you were ten, your friend, Eli, who was twelve at the time, disappeared. He has never been found, but his bike was wrecked and we found it in your dad's truck. That led us to dig into his disappearance more deeply. Dave What--sis-name admits to stealing your dad's truck, which he inadvertently took on an unauthorized joy drive. He also admits to hitting a deer, only because he thinks he saw antlers through a thick fog. But divers have found a boot with some bone remaining close to the scene which leads us to believe it was actually Eli's handle bars the boys saw and not a set of antlers.

I winced as he spoke of the boot and the bone that protruded from it. He noticed and gave me a gentle pat on the shoulder as he served me a plate of eggs with cheese sprinkled over the top and a toasted croissant.

He moved over to the fridge and began to probe around. He found a jar of salsa and with a proud, 'Aha!' and placed it on the table with his own breakfast. Spooning salsa over his eggs, he frowned a little and continued.

"So, I was born here in Greenville. That much I do know. Although my parents both seemed to have good memories of this area, they never returned here after my birth. That's a red flag right there," he noted, raising one brow. His tone was matter-of-fact, but I detected a slight quiver in his lips as he stared down at his eggs.

I gave him a moment to digest what he had just said.

He lifted his head to look me straight in the face, his eyes grabbed mine like a magnet. "Apparently, there had been a set of twins born to your friend, Carolyn. One being Eli, and Jeremiah, the other twin, unfortunately didn't make it. However, Brenda, the good nurse has let us know in no uncertain terms that both babies were doing quite well when her shift ended that night. Now this is where it gets sketchy. I make my grand appearance at some point during that same day. And, Brenda also made it known that Baby Boy Danielson was not in good shape when she left," he said, picking through everything we had learned so far.

His face grew serious and I could detect that familiar helpless look in his eyes. The color seemed to drain from his face. "This is beginning to smell pretty fishy," he said, point blank. "And I'm beginning to believe the babies were switched. And having made that bold statement, I'll go you one further. It's much too coincidental to think that this nurse, Little Miss didn't have something to do with this. I'm just wondering now, if she carried out this despicable crime on her own or if she had help," he declared, his intense glare boring into me.

"That's most likely something we will never know for sure, but I don't believe she needed any help. How hard is it, to take one baby from its cubicle and replace it with another? It would take thirty seconds at the most," I guessed.

He just nodded his head in agreement. Then he turned his gaze out of the window at Indian Head as if the old Indian with his infinite wisdom had spoken to him. Quietly, almost in a whisper, he said, "I just don't know anything for sure anymore. It's all so overwhelming."

Turning back to me, he continued in a low voice. "After hearing what my father said, I was so, I don't know, angry or something. I felt like I had been lied to my whole life and I really had to get to the bottom of my birth issues in order to feel better. But after thinking it over last night, I realized that I was just really upset about life in general and blaming it on my dad. My mom is gone, now my dad's health is failing and my whole life is going to be so different from now on. I'm taking all of this much harder than I figured I would. I have been so consumed with finding answers that I lost sight of what I have always done before under stressful circumstances," he recalled. He hesitated long enough to take in a few deep breaths.

I listened quietly and gave him the time he seemed to need to finish putting his thoughts into words.

He shook his head and continued as if speaking to himself with his eyes fixed on his uneaten eggs. "I had completely forgotten that I have a Father in heaven who watches over me and He will guide and lead me. I know that you don't really think the same way, but faith in the Lord really is a firm foundation in my life. I just had to, you know, think it through and process it all." Lifting his head back up, he smiled weakly at me. "I know you think differently and I didn't mean to go all churchy on you, but the fact is, I live my life with faith," he confirmed with conviction. "Maybe at this time in my life, I need to take a step back and let things follow its' natural course. Maybe I have to accept the fact that all the people involved in this crazy mess are either dead or like my dad, brain dead. Maybe it's not meant for me to know the truth, or at least the whole truth."

I stared into his gentle green eyes, still torn with pain and tried to process his train of thought. I wanted to understand what he was saying. But I had to admit that all this religious stuff was still such a cloudy area for me. How does one just shrug off happenings and be peaceful within about the pain of those happenings? How do I go about letting this amazing man I do care about him and I want more than ever to share in all aspects of his life whether happy or sad and yes maybe even his religious convictions. Maybe it was time for me to come clean. But how do I do that when I'm still so unsure of myself? Should I confess my recurring thoughts of the Great Spirit and how I have felt lately that He possibly might be watching over me as well and guiding me through this extremely difficult time in my life?

I took his hand in mine and gave it a little squeeze. "I'm beginning to understand more than you think. I know I don't want to live my life without you in it. I know it is important to deal with troubling issues before any couple can begin to think of developing a long lasting relationship. This whole birth thing; who you really are and who's hand played the ugly card that has turned your life upside down, has to be settled before we can even think about how we feel about each other. And this may surprise you. I have felt the tug of a higher power giving me strength to make it through this, horribly confusing mess," I admitted.

I noticed a sense of peace wash over his face.

"There's something more I need to tell you," I went on to say, which instantly put a look of unease in his emerald eyes.

"Go on," he coaxed.

With uncertainty still pulsing in my veins, I said, "I think I may have found another piece of the puzzle. But we may have to do something sort of unethical to finally answer all our questions and lay this whole matter to rest."

With his eyes wide with curiosity, he repeated my words, "unethical? Just how unethical are we talking here?"

With a sheepish grin I formed some pretty outrageous words in my mouth. "Well, as unethical as it can get," I said and then paused to press my lips together. With raised brows, I added, "Maybe a little on the morbid side as well."

CHAPTER
30

Frowning, Kendall leaned back in his chair, his arms intertwined across his chest. "Are you sure about this?" he asked with absolute disbelief evident on his face.

"Yes, I'm sure," I answered as quickly as I could so he couldn't detect any reservations on my part. And brother there were plenty. Risks too many to count on one hand. But my need for answers masks my fear of any potential consequences. I lack self-control which I know is a serious chink in my armor. But then again, how else will we be able to gain understanding and be able to gently close this door to the past?

"Tonight?" he asked. I could tell he was still struggling with the idea.

"Of course, there's no better time!" I exclaimed. "We wait on this, then maybe we will both back out. Then we will never know for sure if Little Miss did the unthinkable. If she is responsible for what we believe to have taken place, then maybe she recorded her feelings in her poetry. That's what poet's do, they write what they feel and experience. We need to just get it now, check it out and then we can put it back right away. No one will ever know about it, but you and me," I tried to convince him. My voice definitely not sounding as strong and sure as I wanted.

He shook his head again and let out an exasperated sigh. "I can think of at least a half dozen legal statutes that we will violate," he pointed out. "I know you own this cemetery Camille, but that doesn't give you, well, give us the right to go digging around for our own personal reasons."

"This isn't just personal. It's the right thing to do," I argued. This time my passion for the truth made my voice hoarse.

I waited for his response, but he didn't speak. He slumped down in his chair and stared out the window again.

"You know Kendall, we always want to move mountains. But this one I can't move for you. It's your call. Either you want to know the truth or you don't. So make up your mind." I could see that guarded look in his eye. One that told me he was leaning in a direction I knew would not give him peace of mind. "Look Kendall, you will not be defined by this one supposedly despicable act, but by your honest intentions. You are not here to desecrate the dead. You are here to get back what is rightfully yours; your identity. Little Miss wronged you. It's not the other way around," I sternly pointed out, trying to prod him along.

His eyes widened and his lips pressed into a thin line. "The absurdity of all of this is almost too much to handle."

"Then don't think about what you are doing. Think only about why you are doing it. We'll never have a better time than now," I coaxed him again. "Brian and Little Jimmy are gone for the week hunting and it's just me here. Me, you, and the secrets Little Miss took to her grave," I said. Then my voice came out in a whisper. "But it's your decision to make, not mine," I reminded him again.

His eyes narrowed into slits. I could tell he was still struggling to come to terms with the enormity of the offense we were contemplating. Finally, he nodded and met my stare. "This is a whole new level of human nature at its worst," he proclaimed.

We sat in a moment of silence just staring at each other. Then his face softened and he rose to his feet and moved toward me. His long arms grasped my shoulders pulling me up to within inches of his chest. He held me tightly, the warmth of his breath on my head was soothing.

"I know you're right about this. I will never be able to move on if I don't put all this craziness to rest."

I felt a prickle of tears in my eyes. Anything I could say right now would be inadequate, so I just stayed quiet and let my mind ponder over all the possibilities of our actions. Were we finally closer to the secrets Little Miss took to her grave? Was this really the right thing to do? Yes, I told myself. That answer gave me the courage to speak to him from my heart. "This is the only way we can put all our questions to rest. This is the only way that we as a couple can move on in life. The other option would be to remain in limbo. But believe me, you have chosen the healthier path," I explained.

"I sure wish there was another way. One that's not quite so repulsive," he said, his voice raw and still sounding appalled at the idea.

"Unless you can communicate with the dead, there is no other way," I said with a firm press of my lips.

"I suppose you're right," he agreed, nodding his head.

"This is the right thing to do Kendall. You have to trust me on this one," I said as I moved in closer and slid my arms around his midsection and cuddled the small of his back.

I enjoyed our closeness only for a few seconds. He suddenly stepped back and looked down at me with a serious gaze. "But here's the deal, Camille. If we are going to do this, we will do this in the daylight. I am not going to skulk around a cemetery in the middle of the night like a criminal. Besides, unless you can see in the dark like a cat or something, you'll need a flashlight and that will attract unwanted attention. We sure don't need law enforcement to come poking around as we are digging up a grave under the cover of night. I can see the front page of the paper now. 'Grave robbers nabbed and taken into custody. Local cemetery owner and

wayward attorney caught robbing the dead of their personal items,'"
he said, with a sly grin.

I laughed, despite myself. My plan did sound somewhat juvenile. My familiar sense of drama was beginning to lose its' attractiveness when illuminated by his pragmatism and his sense of
humor. "Okay then," I agreed. "Follow me. We set out to the barn
to find some shovels.

I retraced my steps from yesterday in the weak sunshine of the
morning; leading him to the headstone of Little Miss. Standing
over her grave, we held hands and looked down at the image of
the angel with the little boy in her embrace. The love of a big sister
for her little brother was palpable to me as I shivered in my pea-
coat. I knew in my heart that she wasn't a bad person as it would
appear by her actions. It's just that her love for her younger brother
was more powerful than the sting of what was unethical and cruel.

Kendall let my hand slip from his. He grabbed my eyes with
his and shook his head. "Well, I guess it's now or never," he said,
his expression pained.

"I guess so," I responded, but my voice cracked. My tears
betrayed me, letting him know I wasn't as brave as I once appeared
to be. But in my defense, the moisture in my eyes were out of fear
of what effect the possible truth would have on him.

He turned his anguished eyes toward the thick grass below
our feet and with a firm grip of his shovel, he carefully and neatly
outlined an area to dig, punching through the sod and into the rich
brown earth below. He dug quickly, the muscles of his shoulders
bunching through his sweatshirt. I began to dig in a slower fashion,
closer to the headstone, because we weren't certain exactly where
Little Jimmy had placed the journal. We scraped and dug in silence,
until my shovel hit something with a dull thud.

"I think I found something," I practically screeched. I immediately dropped to my knees and loosened the dirt a little more with
my hands. Feeling around the dirt, the scent of the rich loam and

the earthy smell of the fall leaves strong in my nostrils, I felt a box. It was buried fairly shallow so it was easy to maneuver around. I found a corner and wiggled it back and forth. With a final tug, I freed it and pulled it up onto my lap. Kendall knelt beside me and brushed some of the dirt from the top. The box was a wooden cedar chest, with a set of tiny hinges and a little brass hasp over a peg that held the lid closed.

Looking at one another, I knew we were both of one thought; all the questions spinning in our heads had all come down to this very moment. I shuddered at the sudden bleakness of what we were doing, but there was no other way to uncover the truth.

With raised brows, Kendall spoke in a calm tone. "Well, here goes." He gently lifted the hasp and we looked down at a cloth wrapped bundle.

Reaching in, I loosened the folds, exposing a leather bound journal. Slowly, I removed the journal and opening it, found it full of writings and snatches of poetry, the penmanship well-formed and lovely. There were pencil drawings, and pastel sketches fading but marvelous. Kendall looked over my shoulder as I leafed through the journal. I assumed he was scouting for any unwanted foot traffic in and around the cemetery.

My eyes skimmed over bits of the writing. I marveled at the sketches of birds, squirrels, and the face of a child, indistinct yet instantly recognizable as Little Jimmy. The final page held a few lines, brief yet poignant and nearly stopped my heart as I read the words out loud.

"She had two, the other had none

At the end of the day, each had one.

God forgive me for what I have done."

Kendall," I gasped and then took in a deep breath. "Look at the date. It is the day after Eli's birthday." I could hear and feel my heart pounding in my ears.

"It's the day after my birth as well," he reminded me in the saddest tone that literally crushed my heart. He inhaled sharply and looked up at the sky, blinking rapidly. He stood abruptly and walked a few paces away, his back to me. Standing, with his hands in the pockets of his hoodie, he remained silent.

With my eyes on him and bewildered by the poem, I pondered his words. My heart continued to pound in my chest as I felt the pieces of the puzzle begin click in my mind; the final mystery in the cemetery secrets. Eli was the surviving twin, yet Kendall looked almost identical to Eli's age progressed pictures. Little Miss seemingly raised the large amount of money needed for Little Jimmy's kidney transplant. But with the information disclosed by Kendall's father, wracked by dementia, we now know where in all likelihood she got her hands on that much money. Kendall had been born in Greenville the same day as Eli and his twin, to a mother who went into early labor. As the puzzle pieces shimmered and slipped into their proper places, full realization dawned on me without an ounce of doubt. Kendall was actually Eli's twin, the one Carolyn believed had died shortly after birth. The twin that Little Miss had given to Owen Danielson after the death of his own preterm son. And motivated by love and concern for her gravely ill little brother, Little Miss accepted recompense for her actions that day. I felt a wave of nausea and sorrow wash over me, yet what could Kendall be feeling? He was the most integral part of the mystery.

I replaced the journal in the box and smoothed the old fabric over it. Gently, I nestled the box back into its' former resting place. Remaining on my knees, I simply watched Kendall.

Turning back to me, he shrugged, his green eyes intense but glazed over with a distant glare. "Let's get this cleaned up," he stated quickly in a formal, business like tone.

Quietly, we smoothed the soil into its place and replaced the sod. Tugging the last bit into place, I looked up at him. His face inscrutable, he picked up both shovels and without another word, simply turned around and led the way back to the house.

I found my breath and finally spoke. "You know what all of this means, don't you?" I wanted to talk things over, but he seemed so remote, and I found myself wanting to respect his personal space.

Kendall just nodded his head and continued to walk three paces ahead of me. When we reached the barn, he replaced the shovels, closing the door with a slam. Then he turned to face me. "Yes, Camille, I do know." He sighed and shook his head. Reaching down, he took both of my hands into his. "Camille, thank you so much for all you have done for me. You are a very special lady and I appreciate you more than you know." He leaned in and gently kissed my cheek. Giving my hands a squeeze, he continued, "But strange as this may sound, I know I should take the adult approach, but right now wisdom seems like a stranger to me. I'm happy, but afraid as well. I should beat it over to Carolyn's house," he said, "I guess I should have said my mother's house. But how do you show love to someone you don't even know?"

"Remember to take baby steps. One day at a time Kendall," I reminded him.

"I know, but how do I start. How do I even approach that poor woman? The more I learn, the less I seem to know about what to do," he said. Then he stiffened his back with his face void of a smile. "I guess what I really need is some time to process all this craziness. I need to get some things wrapped up. Will you be patient with me?"

"Of course I will. Kendall take as much time as you need. This isn't about me right now. It's you I'm concerned about."

"Okay then. I'll be in touch, but I am going to be busy for a while. So you take care, okay?" Looking at me with concern in his green eyes, he smiled and kissed my cheek again. There was an undercurrent to his words that I didn't quite fully understand.

I clutched my arms and watched him walk the short distance to his jeep and climb in. I stood in the gravel listening to the now familiar rumble of his jeep fade off out of my sight. The wind kicked up and a flurry of fallen leaves whirled around my legs.

"What just happened?" I asked myself. My mind was thrust into a whirlwind of disillusion. I know he's a bit overwhelmed, but shouldn't we both be jumping for joy? I had hoped for a few special moments with him to share in our jubilant find. Instead I am standing here alone in a garden planted with the dead and literally scratching my head in confusion. I heard his words again in my mind. "I'll be in touch." What does that mean? Had he been playing games with my heart? Had he been using me merely to help him unravel his identity mystery? Those questions stung like a hornet. Or was he just so overwhelmed with all we have uncovered that he can't deal with anything right now, especially me? Negative thoughts swarmed my head and drove my heart into my stomach. My mind delved deeper into a terrifying minefield of negativity. But then my sensitive side finally kicked in and I convinced myself that all he needed right now was some time and space. "Quit being so selfish," I spoke to myself sternly. I needed to be adult enough to grant him what he needed; time and space.

At this moment, I had no idea what that tremble in his voice meant, but as time ticked away, I soon found out what that distant look in his eyes really meant.

CHAPTER 31

"Today is like a Norman Rockwell painting. Smoke rising from a few chimneys. A beautiful blue sky with white, puffy clouds. Autumn leaves blanket the ground, their magnificent colors reflecting the sun. It doesn't get much better than that," Agnes said as she turned and walked back over to the kitchen table where Carolyn was sipping on a hot cup of sweet tea.

"Yes, it is a picture perfect scene suitable for framing except there is something missing," she proclaimed with a strange far-away look in her eyes.

"Really! And what would that be?" Agnes asked.

Caroline just gave her another peculiar look, empty and void of pleasure but brimming in pain. She slowly stood up and walked over to the picture window and stared out into the yard. "I wonder what this day would look like if Eli were standing on the lawn throwing a few pitches to his father. You remember how baseball practice had been a year around tradition at this house. The bond between father and son had put more than a twinkle in my eye," she confirmed.

"Yes, I remember those days very well."

"I miss those days. I miss the companionship of my husband. But most of all, I miss my Eli," she said.

"I know you do. A mother's heart will always cry out for her child no matter how long the separation," Agnes replied.

"If I close my eyes and concentrate real hard, I can almost picture his deep green eyes and those cute little dimples that all the ladies at church couldn't resist to pinch."

"I haven't heard you talk like this in a very long time."

"I know. I feel something strange today. Something tugging on my heart. I feel so close to Ely that I feel like I could almost reach out and touch him."

"He will always be right here in your heart," Agnes said, tapping four fingers to her robust chest.

Carolyn exhaled and nodded her head in acknowledgment. A gentle smile crossed her face as though she had thought about something meaningful that brought her a moment of peace. She seemed to be emotionally and spiritually calmer. "You know, the other day I was standing right here in this very spot looking out over the school grounds and I saw a young boy flying his kite. I was overwhelmed by my curiosity because he looked so much like my Ely from the back. I actually walked across the street to get a closer peak at him. They say the sense of smell carries the oldest memories. The instant I got close enough, I knew it wasn't him. He smelled of stale cigarettes. Eli always smelled like his father's cologne. He would get into his dad's cabinet and use his Old Spice," she said, letting out a slight huff. "We finally got him his own bottle one year for Christmas. But you know, for a few brief moments I felt that joyous twitter in my heart when a mother gazes upon her child and feels she is the luckiest woman on earth," Carolyn explained. Then she sucked in a deep breath and caught Agnes eye. "Don't get me wrong. I am a blessed woman. There are many women out there such as yourself who were not, and will never be fortunate enough to experience the true joy of giving birth and the amazing bond between mother and child. I know the joy of carrying an infant within me. I know the utter miracle of birth and have experienced that moment when you look into your child's eyes and they look back at you with an expression of unconditional love. Yes, I am fortunate. Very fortunate," she confirmed.

"Well, thankfully for people like me, there are people like you who allow people like me to become an important part of their family life and participate fully in the care of their child," she graciously pointed out.

"I couldn't have done it without you. Have I even told you lately how much I appreciate your loyal friendship?" Carolyn asked.

"All the time. And believe me, that road goes both ways," she declared with a smile that puffed her cheeks like a blowfish.

A light tap on the door brought Carolyn's attention back to the window. She arched her neck, but even though the tree beside her porch had released its' leaves, the spindly branches obscured her view. "That's strange. I didn't see anyone walk up the sidewalk," she pointed out as she turned and moseyed slowly toward the door. She removed her hands from her apron pockets as she approached the door. She grasped the knob and opened it. With bulging eyes and her gaze squarely on the face of a handsome young man staring back at her, her right hand flew to her breastbone and she let out a loud gasp. Finally, her mouth began to move and the silence between them came to an end. A little sound came out. It was low at first, like a soft breeze seeping through the leaves in the front yard. Then with a forceful swish she finally spoke. "I knew you would one day come home."

Kendall's eyes grew bright and he nodded his head as a smile blossomed across his face. "I'm not exactly who you think I am, but I'm as close as you can get to a modern day miracle."

"I'm a big believer in miracles," Caroline said. This was one of those times when no more words were needed at the moment. Instead, she melted into his welcoming arms as if mother and son had never been apart.

CHAPTER
32

Fall deepened over the next month or so. Rain and winds washed the color from the leaves and whipped the oak trees bare. Leafless branches twisted in the wind and the sighing of the evergreens was a constant refrain in the autumnal chorus in my mountain hometown. The ground was sodden beneath my booted feet and the leaden skies brought no promise of sunshine. Falling temperatures indicated the annual march of the season into winter and time inexorably rolled forward. The rain ceased for a few days, only to be replaced with the slow, steady drift of snow falling. Great mounds of white covering all, the trees groaned and bent with the weight of it. The air was crisp, cold and clean. The mountains slept beneath their snowy mantles and the old Indian perched on the highest peak remained still and reserved as if waiting for the suns liberation from the oppressive elements of winter. Even the most stubborn person surrenders to something.

And as for me, I felt more empty and alone than I had ever been before in my life. I woke each day only to allow myself fully available to my pain. Not only was I tortured by the old pain of loss, but to my deepest disappointment, had been thrust into the long gray days of loneliness. For I willingly gave Kendall the space he needed to choose his own timing to let love grow. Instead, we seemed to have grown further apart. It's not like he had completely shut me out of his life, but a few text here and there and one lengthy phone call certainly does not keep love alive with forever in mind. Punctured pride and alienation had produced a lot of pain and plenty of self-pity. Although Kendall insists he will return at any time, I have come to realize that his promises now seem hollow and possibly meaningless.

But life goes on, I try to convince myself. And despite my misgivings about new love's cold and sterile paralysis, I am determined not to allow my emotions to well up so powerfully inside of me that I will shut the door to any future love to enter my life. For I don't want to look at Kendall and our short term relationship as anything other than a positive experience. For as the saying goes. "Love is life...and if you miss love, you miss life." I truly believe God had a hand in placing me right where He intended me to be; in the center of true love given and true love received. No one can ever take those amazing memories away from me.

The prospect of celebrating my first Christmas without my father is a difficult thought to entertain. But December has descended on this sleepy little town very quickly and I know I need to push aside this giant helping of hopelessness I have carried within my heart as if it were my prized possession.

I called Carolyn a couple of times, but never seemed to catch her at home. I later found out through the grapevine that she had taken a trip to Washington DC. I thought it a bit strange that neither Kendall nor Carolyn had informed me about their intentions to take the trip together. Didn't they know it would be even more exciting when shared by others? But then, who am I, but an outsider looking in.

Agnes had invited me to an evening potluck service at the little white church in town. I can't say I was head over heels crazy about the idea, but I didn't go kicking and screaming either. I joined her and several other long time family friends for a few hours of small talk and tasty treats. The lovely choir and the candle lit service touched my heart and I found myself thinking of the Great Spirit as an infant, having come to this earth to save us all.

Two weeks before Christmas, I awoke to a window rimed with frost and I shivered as I pulled on my jeans and a warm hoodie. My breath was visible as I stepped out onto the deck and listened to the early morning silence, that isn't really silent in the mountains. The shrill of a squirrel, the soughing of a short wind through the pines, the thump of falling snow. I watched a doe and her yearling fawn pick their way between the headstones, pausing occasionally, ears and eyes alert. Leaving a delicate trail of hoof prints in the snow, they meandered into the tree line beyond the road and disappeared from sight. Taking a deep breath of the cold air, I wondered if life was composed of a series of vignettes, not unlike the sight of deer, who daintily step into view, delight the eye, then disappear.

I wondered if I would ever see Kendall again. He had stepped into my life, declared feelings for me; spending time together as we untangled the web of secrets and then had raced out of my life like a speeding car on the interstate. I found I missed his green eyes and his uncanny sense of humor. I missed the spicy fragrance that was unique to him. I wanted to be wrapped in his arms and pressed against his strong chest, feeling and hearing his heartbeat beneath my cheek. With so little contact, I had glumly concluded that chapter of my life was probably over.

I thought of Carolyn, and how her frail body held the spirit of a strong and courageous woman. She had been delighted at the return of one of her sons, yet the heartbreak of Eli's definite loss was intense. The results of DNA tests on the bone in the boot found in the river proved conclusively to be Eli. She chose to grieve and recover in privacy. I'm certain the time she is spending with Kendall will help to heal that newest wound.

Brian and Little Jimmy helped me push my father's pickup out from the back corner of the barn and parked it out front. Of course once we removed the tarp, their eyes fell on the wrinkled fender.

"She's still a little gem, no doubt about it," Brian said.

Little Jimmy puffed out his cheeks and let out a chuckle. "Um, yeah," he said. "As long as you keep a giant bandage on this owie here, she looks as fit at a fiddle."

"Wonder what happened," Brian asked.

I just shrugged my shoulders and played it off as a big surprise to me too.

"Well, whatever happened, I'm guessing the other guy didn't get off scot free either," Little Jimmy surmised.

"I could pound that out and have her looking as good as new if you want me to," Brian offered.

"No. If dad wanted that done, he would have taken care of it years ago. I think I'll just leave it as it is," I said, hoping they would both just drop the subject. The less said, the less lies I have to tell. Thankfully, they both went about their business without another word about it.

The next day, I called Dave Wilson to see if he wanted to take it. A lot of pain was now attached to that truck. The old rusted piece of metal wasn't the mastermind behind the fateful act, but it was the unintentional weapon used to end a young boy's life, and for that very reason I couldn't bear to look at it.

Dave and I had arranged to meet early in the morning around nine o'clock. I couldn't shake loose of the notion that this was most likely going to be more painful than I had bargained for. At least my senses were still in good working order, because the instant I saw his lowbed pull up the hill and snake around the road, I felt like I had been stung by a bee right in the center of my heart. Despite my reservations, I forced a smile and gave him a generous wave as he pulled up in front of the barn where I was waiting. "Hold your stuff together Camille," I scolded myself. "You're not going to go back and forth on this issue." I knew beneath the shiny surface of my smile, my emotional resources were being put to the test. But somewhere, deep in the depths of my conscious mind, I managed to refuse to fall prey to these petty mood swings.

Dave literally leaped from his truck, I'm sure driven by a surge of adrenaline. "I can't believe this old relic is actually mine," he said in a tone of utter excitement. Then he cast me a cautious glance. "You're sure about this?" he asked, his eyes glued to mine.

"I'm sure Dave. I know my father would have been pleased with this decision as well," I said, with a lump in my throat.

"I'll take good care of it," he promised. "This is going to be a summer project for me and my boys."

"Dad would have approved of that idea wholeheartedly. You know how he felt about nurturing young minds," I reminded him.

"Up close and personal," Dave agreed. "Like I told you before, mine is a success story only because your father intervened and changed the course of my imminent fate."

I just gave him a wide smile and nodded my head.

"Well, I guess I had better get this baby loaded up," he said as he turned on his heels and jumped back up into his truck.

I watched as he carefully maneuvered his truck back and forth until it was directly in front of my father's little gem. In no time at all he had it loaded, strapped securely and driving back down toward the highway.

"I hope that makes you happy, dad," I whispered with my eyes on the vast celestial expanse above my head. I knew in my heart that if he were standing here right now, he'd slap the old bumper and say, "Well Betsy, you're on your way to a good home."

I turned around and eyed the vacant spot where the truck had been stored for so many years. My shoulders slumped and my face stiffened as my thoughts drifted to my father and the last words he spoke to me. I wondered if he had known how his secret, kept under a dusty tarp in his old pickup would become entangled with Kendall's search for the facts around the beginning of his life here on earth. After turning it over in my mind, tugging on the corners of the thought to unravel it further, I mused, "Of course not." There was no way he could.

"Hey," came a familiar voice behind me which immediately turned my head around.

"Hey," I returned. "How's it going?" I asked.

"As good as good can be," Little Jimmy said. "I hope you don't regret getting rid of the old truck."

"Nah. No sense in letting it sit in the barn just rusting away with the years. Giving it to Dave Wilson was the right thing to do. I'm sure my dad would have been pleased to see it go to someone who will appreciate it as much as he did."

"Can't argue that point," he agreed.

Then a moment of silence ensued which took me off-guard because Little Jimmy was never at a loss for words.

"Ah, I noticed some snow flowers planted on my sister's grave and ah, I wondered if you planted them there?" he asked.

"I'm sorry. I guess I should have gotten your permission first. I took a walk out through the picnic grounds the other day and spotted a whole patch of them and thought they would look so nice next to her stone," I explained.

"On the contrary. I think that was a sweet gesture. But you do know they most likely won't survive the transplant?" he informed me with a slight weariness in his eyes.

"I know. Just a temporary fix. I noticed they are already beginning to lose their red flare."

"Odd thing is, they were my sister's favorite flower. She always compared them to me and my kidney transplant. Two peas in a pod, she would say. A snow flower braves the cold of winter and I braved the medical miracle of the transplant," he said with the pain of his loss coating his sad eyes. "She was the best big sister a kid could ever wish for. Took care of me my whole life and handled everything with my surgery. She was such a great nurse," he enthused.

"I'm sure that God had a hand in placing you in her care. Miracles like that just don't happen. They are planned by a Higher Power," I said which surprised me. I didn't know I had it in me to start putting credit where credit was do. I had to admit it felt good.

"She took care of everything with my treatment and recovery. Told me not to worry about anything except getting well." His smile faltered a little. "I sure miss her, Camille. She was a wonderful, wonderful person."

I felt my heart soften for the motherless boy he had been. His sister wasn't a terrible person. She was motivated by love for him. That didn't justify her actions, but at least I now knew why she was prompted to commit such a horrible act of injustice. She was human and subject to human frailties. I found myself wondering if life was shaded, not unlike the colors of the sunset, an impossibly deep purple sky close to the western mountain and lightening to a periwinkle as the color stretched back to the zenith. The brilliant apricot hue of the sinking sun, reflected in ever softening waves as it pierced the purple and lavender heavens. All beautiful and all mixed up, sometimes terrible and all amazing and wonderful at the same time.

"She was a good woman," I confirmed with an easy smile. "Your memories of her are yours to keep forever. Our memories are what help us to appreciate all the blessings we have been given," I said. Wow! I thought silently. I'm getting good at giving inspirational advice.

"I'll hold that thought for the day. Well, guess I had better get to work before my boss fires my little butt."

We both busted out laughing.

"Oh, and by the way. I want to thank you for helping my friend, Christine."

"Christine?" I asked, not having a clue as to who he was referring to.

"Christine Huber. I really believe the kind words you shared with her completely altered the course she was on, which was a one way road to destruction."

I had to think for a second. The name Huber sounded familiar, but I couldn't place it in my memory bank.

"I got to know Christine during the times she came to visit her husband's grave. Such a nice young lady."

"Oh yes, I remember her. How is she doing?"

"Doing real good. She's busy taking care of her little boy. What a chunky cheeked critter he is. Full of piss and vinegar that one is."

"I'm glad to hear she is doing well."

Little Jimmy smiled wide and I watched him as he ambled off toward the tool shed. I in turn closed the barn door and walked slowly back to my empty house.

Later in the day, I stood on the deck, drinking in the view of Indian Head, resplendent in his snowy glory, the sun broke through the clouds in the east, lighting up the old man with a golden cast. Kissed with the glow, I could see the outline of his nose and chin, the color softening to pink in the recesses of the hillside, the evergreen trees piercing the snow. I breathed deeply as I slowly thought over the many secrets held in this cemetery and my father's last words to me. What a whirlwind of amazement this whole adventure had been. The pursuit of the secret had held me fast as Kendall and I had unraveled the mystery before us. This was all a part of God's great handy work. I lifted my eyes and my heart to the Great Spirit and whispered a prayer of gratitude to Him, for the activity that kept me from falling into the abyss of grief. I thanked Him for Kendall's friendship, short lived as it was, to keep me company on my journey through the meadow of mourning. I prayed for Little Jimmy, for his health and healing. I asked for peace for Carolyn and that she and Kendall could fall into the secure embrace of the final chapter of their life and learn to love one another as if they had never been apart. I asked the Great Spirit to watch over my home town and all those who lived in the valley, blessing them with His presence and wisdom. With blurry eyes now, I whispered a prayer of thanks for my father's life and his unending love for me and the positive effect he had on this entire community.

I truly wanted to grow in gratitude and peace on this cold, clear day, breathing in the piercing mountain air. Still looking toward Indian Head glimmering in the pink and golden chill, with the holiday season before me, I raised my arms and inhaled life and love and the opening of my heart to grace and growth.

CHAPTER 33

Winter crept forward; the days were getting chillier and darker. Wolf Creek crashed along below the cemetery, swollen with several good rainy weeks. Despite two fairly good snow storms, we were able to take care of the basic needs of the community, although there had been more funerals than normal, due to respiratory infections and a nasty influenza that seemed to accompany the winter months. I reminded myself that while my father had always said people were just dying to get into the cemetery, I was grateful that this winter hadn't been as bad as one particular winter I had seen back when I was young. A bad flu bug swept through our small community like a black plague leaving many of our elderly citizens completely defenseless against its' deadly grip.

I had busied myself with a seemingly endless list of chores and housekeeping. I had completed all of the paperwork surrounding my father's estate and with the kind assistance of his financial advisor, Jim Moll, now had a financial plan with savings and investments to tide me through the near future. I had done more painting inside the house and had sorted through seemingly endless boxes from the attic. The leftovers of busy lives, well lived, and I was able to donate most of the items to the American Legion thrift store in Greenville. I was ready for most of the winter tasks that the cemetery would present and was keeping a running project sheet on the table.

I made several trips in the past weeks to Chico for various errands and had treated myself to an Expresso coffee-maker for my morning ritual of at least two heaping bold cups. The sight of the bright red appliance on the kitchen counter made me smile in the morning and I enjoyed crafting lattes for friends who dropped by for visits, as well. I was learning to appreciate the small things in life and to live in a state of gratitude.

This morning had dawned, clear, crisp and bright. The blue of the sky was intense, with streamers of high clouds shimmering in the distant heavens. Although the day was not yet warm, the sun was shining gloriously, spreading golden light over the cemetery and pouring in through the big windows in the kitchen. I gazed out at Indian Head as I ground beans for my coffee. I was expecting Brian and Jimmy for a project planning session and I quickly shoved some cinnamon rolls into the oven for them to enjoy with their coffee.

Pulling open the kitchen door, I stepped out onto the deck and inhaled deeply and exhaled slowly, appreciating the richness of the forest surrounding my home. The scent of earth was in the air and the fresh blanket of snow had nearly melted away. Turning my head, I sniffed the sleeve of my hoodie, the fragrance of coffee and cinnamon permeating my sweatshirt had followed me outside. Homey fragrances that evoked my childhood and made me long, for just a moment, to rush back inside and find my parents sitting at the table having their coffee and rolls together, planning their day. I could picture them, turning to look at me, smiles of love on their faces. I breathed deeply again, past the lump in my throat, and focused on the gigantic Indian Head, the old man freshening in the clear morning sunshine with a white beard of snow from two days prior. Closing my eyes and turning my face up to the sun, I silently thanked the Great Spirit for this day and for my life. It may not be the life I had envisioned for myself, but I was determined that I would make it a good life. I had come to the understanding that

I would honor and respect not only the Great Spirit, but also my parents by my choices and actions in my future. I knew I needed to be grateful for what I do have, and not focus on what I have lost. The ability to mend my brokenness I have within me.

Giving myself a shake and a mental slap on the back, I realized that Brian would be coming up the driveway soon and I turned to the kitchen door. Hearing a vehicle from the highway slow and turn onto the cemetery road, I peered through the trees to see if Brian and Little Jimmy had arrived. Frowning a little, I was unable to make out the vehicle as it shifted down and turned to the left to take the lower road along Wolf Creek, parallel to the lower part of the cemetery. Shrugging, I realized it was just an early morning visitor, come to honor or remember a loved one. Then Brian's truck turned into the drive and chugged up the incline to the house. Waving at me, he parked below the deck.

Climbing out of his truck, he shouted up to me, "Hey Camille! Good morning. Jim'll be here soon. I had him stop for gas and oil for the mowers," he explained with a big, old goofy grin on his face. He bounded up the stairs and greeted me with a hefty hug.

"Come on in," I said as he followed me into the warm kitchen. "Coffee's hot and the cinnamon rolls are ready to take out of the oven," I said as I pointed to a chair at the table. "Have a seat."

His eyes brightened at the mention of cinnamon rolls and he handed me his travel mug for his coffee. "Is that the real stuff?" he asked with a cautious eye. "I don't want to wait for half an hour while you grind and steam and fluff and whatever else it is you do to make your fancy drinks," he complained. "All this old boy needs is a simple cup of black coffee and none of that artsy fartsy, fancy dancy stuff." He pressed his lips together, staring at the cinnamon rolls through narrowed eyes. "But man, oh man, do those rolls ever smell good."

"Help yourself," I said as I removed them from the oven and slid the pan of hot rolls onto a heating pad in the middle of the table. I had to laugh at him because he hid his good heart behind his gruffness.

"Don't mind if I do," he said, digging in faster than a mole looking down the barrel of a shotgun.

I laughed and handed him the carton of half and half from the refrigerator and set a small saucer with a fork in front of him. I set about creating a quick Americano for him as well. While I crafted my own latte, he read over the project list out loud and commented on each one. I listened with half an ear, hearing things about early mowing, thatching, oil changes, fertilizing and pruning. His wisdom and experience would shrink my project list into manageable tasks and I was appreciative of his help.

I set his coffee down by his plate and took a seat beside him at the table.

He looked up at me and smiled with a mouthful of food that made his cheeks look like a blowfish. "This is delicious. Thanks for taking such good care of us," he mumbled through his food.

"It's the least I can do for you guys. You are both always doing extra work and not asking for one penny more. Frankly, I don't know what I would have done with this place if it hadn't been for you guys being here with me every step of the way," I explained.

"That road goes both ways Camille. You kept us on here after your dad passed and we appreciate your kindness. This is a good paying job and we both want to stay as long as you'll have us."

I gave him a generous smile. "I guess it's a good arrangement for all of us," I admitted. Then I broke eye contact and took a sip of my latte.

"So, have you seen Carolyn and that boy of hers yet?" he asked out of nowhere.

Feeling a quick thump of my heart, I shook my head no and raised my eyebrows quizzically. Why would that particular thought pop out of his head like a strike of lightning midst a clear blue sky? Once again, I felt a sense of despair to descend on me?

Taking another slurp of coffee, he continued on the same subject. "Well, I saw Carolyn the other day and she said that boy from back east, you know the one you were spending time with last summer?" he asked and hesitated for a second and then like a drum roll finished what he was going to say. "He's back in town and apparently, get this. That young fellow is her son. Man, the secrets in this town. Sure surprised me." He shook his head. "Women and their secrets. Give me a fishing pole any day," he said and went on chewing.

Stunned, I carefully placed my cup on the table, because by now my hands were visibly shaking. Feeling my heart continue to pound in my chest, I breathed deep and shook my head. "No, I haven't seen them," I answered, still trying to unscramble my brain. It was ridiculous, after all this time, just the mention of Kendall sent flutters through my stomach. My thoughts continued to tumble and roll around in my head which was making me dizzy. I shook my head again, trying to clear my mind.

"Actually, I think that's his rig down there on the lower road. I saw him and Carolyn in it yesterday. That's when she told me about him being her son. Not sure what they are doing here," he continued, looking over his shoulder out the window. "And I wonder what's keeping Jimmy? He probably had to stop to dig an oil well and build a refinery," he rambled on. "Don't know about that kid sometimes. I told him I wanted to get a jump on the early thatching so we could get that chore done today," he enlightened me. He frowned, and his eyes were mere slits as he drank the remainder of his coffee.

With my head still swirling, I tried to calm myself. I thought for sure I was going to lose what little I had in my stomach. I swallowed deep as all his words slowly sank in.

"Camille, you sure make a mean cup of coffee," he complimented. "Any chance of getting one for the road?" He held his mug out toward me and smiled real big.

I fought back a shiver before it could expose my raw emotions. "Oh sure, no problem," I managed to say. My voice crackled.

I grabbed his cup and moved slowly over to the counter. I made another Americano for him, smiling distractedly at his grumbling about Little Jimmy not showing up on time.

By the time I turned around, he was on his feet. "Thanks again for the coffee and rolls," he said as he made his way out the door. Shouting back over his shoulder as he thumped down the stairs, "You tell that Jim not to be lollygagging around here drinking coffee and eating rolls. I need his help. The sooner we get started the sooner we get done!" he quipped.

Normally, I would have laughed at his words, but right now I wasn't in a humorous mood. His conversation was about a subject of interest, but also one that inflicted great pain. Brian had unlocked the door to things I didn't want to think about anymore. And now he has pushed out the deep seeded question that lay burning a hole in my heart; why did Kendall abandon me? But then, maybe my preconceived notion that we had something special between us was just stupidity on my part. An illusion of my own making. Maybe I was seeing an incomplete picture of reality. Sometimes a heart can be foolish and untrustworthy and sees only what it wants to see. Ignorance is its own punishment. Once again my tiny boat was rocked and I was anchored in a sea of sadness.

I closed the door quietly, walked back over to the table and sank down into my chair. My mind was a muddled blur. I didn't know which warbled thought to concentrate on first. I had no idea that Kendall was back in town. I hadn't tried to reach him for the past week or so. I tried hard to think of him as little as possible. Why churn up more pain from the milk of my memories?

Again, I could hear a rushing in my ears and I felt a stirring of hope in my chest. I breathed deeply and pondered the possibility of seeing Kendall again and how I would react. Fear gripped my heart. What if I couldn't contain my emotions? Closing my eyes, I breathed deeply again and found myself not only thinking out loud but in the middle of a desperate prayer as well. I heard myself ask for His guidance. "Please, Heavenly Father, help me to be a good woman in whatever circumstance I find myself."

But then it was like a grenade exploded inside my head. Had he been misleading me the full time? Acknowledging his possible deception hit me like a wrecking ball. The sweet talk, the warmth of his arms, and the promises for a future together, those emerald eyes that pretended to look upon me with absolute love and adoration. All of it, for what reason? Just to use me to get answers to his questions. Suddenly, all my anger intensified. I came to a quick decision. I couldn't stand this back and forth question and answer exchange trying to decide if our relationship had been something real and tangible. It was devouring me from the inside out. I was going to put this crazy mess to rest once and for all.

Feeling the combination of anger, anguish and hurt, even though I had just prayed for peace, I rose to my feet and moved quickly toward the door. I pulled my jacket free from the hooks on the wall and thrust my arms into it. Determination spurred me on. I would walk down and see for myself if Carolyn and Kendall were on the lower road. I took the steps down off the deck two at a time and strode down the driveway to the lower road. I would confront this head on and settle matters. If only to give myself peace of mind, I would see things settled between Kendall, Carolyn and I. As I crunched down the drive, I reflected on my experiences through autumn and well into winter's first breath of snow. I thought about my personal growth through it all, and I agreed with the committee in my head that Kendall had been rude in his disappearance and the lack of daily contact. In my agitation, though, I knew it was better that the mystery of Eli's disappearance was solved and I did not regret any of my actions leading to that resolution.

Arriving at the lower road, I moved purposefully along the graveled surface avoiding the few deeper patches of snow that hadn't melted yet. I slowly approached the vehicle I had seen earlier through the trees. It was a late model Rubicon, almost identical to the one Kendall drove while he was here his first visit, except it was dark blue and had a Washington DC license plate. Standing beside the jeep, I gazed up the slope, sighting two figures kneeling by a small stone under a large oak tree. Rays of sunlight filtered through the trees, giving the scene a dreamy appearance. Feeling somewhat shaky, and taking a deep breath, I climbed up, arriving just as Kendall stood and held out his hand to help Carolyn rise from a kneeling position.

As agitated as I was, I had to admit, he looked good. His reddish blond hair was longer, curling down past his ears and he had a short stubble on his cheeks. He looked rested and healthy. Wearing jeans, a dark green hoodie and his hiking boots, he moved with the lithe grace that I so admired.

Silently, I watched them as Carolyn carefully brushed some earth from her knees. They both turned at the same time and together, they smiled at me. Carolyn's ivory face glowed with peace and happiness and Kendall had a big grin, the crinkle around his eyes deepening the green. I was surprised to be greeted with such openness and joy and I found myself giving them a tentative smile in return. The air around us almost crackled with the energy of their shared joy and happiness and I could feel its warmth. Kendall stepped forward and embraced me, wrapping his arms around my back and lowering his head over mine. Closing my eyes, I inhaled his spicy scent and felt my heart calm as if I had reached a safe place. I relaxed into his hug and felt tears prickle my eyes.

After a long moment, he released me, but kept his hands on my arms as he turned back to Carolyn. "You're right, she is as beautiful as ever." She smiled back at him, the two of them sharing some secret that I was not privy to, as yet. He reached for her hand and holding onto both of us, he looked down at us and just smiled. A breeze tousled his fair hair and again, I could scent the spicy fragrance that was uniquely him. He smiled back at me and turned to Carolyn, raising his eyebrows with an unspoken question.

Carolyn then pulled me into her arms and gave me a long hug. I could feel her physical frailty with that surprising strength beneath. "Ah Camille, you dear girl. I am afraid we have been inconsiderate of you. Kendall had a great deal of business to attend to back in Georgetown and when we returned a couple of days ago, we selfishly spent our time together without telling anyone. We felt we needed that time alone. So many emotions to deal with. So many important decisions to make. We had a lot of catching up to do, you see, and I apologize that we didn't include you sooner."

Wide eyed, I managed to mumble a few words. "I understand. Really, I do," I assured her with a low whisper. I considered her feelings, trying to put myself in her place.

Then she turned back to the large oak and gestured toward the small stone at its' base. It was engraved 'JEREMIAH' with July 1982 below. "It was so long ago, but I was so heartbroken at his loss that I didn't want the pity or sympathy of others. I just wanted to hold my Eli and grieve for my Jeremiah." She smiled up at Kendall, "And here you are."

Turning back to me, she continued. "Your parents were so kind to me back then; true friends. Your mother sewed a gown for his precious, beautiful little body. Your dad made a tiny coffin, perfect size for a baby. But in the end, I couldn't bear to part with him, so I had him cremated and kept him close to me. I knew one day that I would be able to place his urn here, maybe after I was older and wiser and mentally stronger. I made your parents promise not to talk about it to anyone and they respected my wishes. Your dad insisted on this little stone though after he buried the empty coffin with nothing but the beautiful gown and a picture of Jeremiah inside. He said a child is a blessing no matter how long his life on this earth and he deserved to be remembered. He told me that someday I would be comforted by this place. I just didn't believe him. Now, thanks to you and Kendall, I know this won't be the final resting place of my Jeremiah, but of the real Kendall who departed this earth so soon after his birth. My son here has told me everything the two of you discovered and I was so shocked and upset, I just had to have some quiet time to think it all through. You both have given me so much peace of heart that I cannot thank you enough," she explained in detail.

"I think it will take many more tomorrows to absorb all that has come to pass. I feel just as at peace as you do now that all the questions have been answered," I said, with the seal of finality in my tone.

Carolyn smiled, but it quickly faded from her face. "We have a favor to ask. We are here today, because this little boy here," she said, lifting the urn, "deserves to be remembered and loved. I can do that for him now especially since his birth mama is gone. Is it okay with you if we place him inside the coffin?"

"Absolutely. I'll get Brian and Little Jimmy right on it today," I assured her, trying to make my voice sound enthusiastic. "That's the least I can do."

"Thank you, Camille," she returned.

Kendall wrapped one arm around her thin shoulders protectively and kissed the top of her head. "This is a day to remember. A day of closure and a day of new beginnings," he said, looking directly at me which sent flutters through my stomach.

She smiled up at him and moved a half of foot away, allowing his arm to drop back down. I wondered if she was just pretending to be drawn to the small grave, in order to give us some breathing room.

He immediately reached for my hand. "I owe you an apology too, Camille," he said in a different tone, serious, but hesitant. "I was just so, I don't know, mixed up when I learned the facts of my birth, I needed to be alone for a while too. I was totally rude about it. I admit I should have responded more often. To tell you the truth, I wasn't sure if I was what you needed in the midst of all your pain and loss. Then my father passed away and I was thrust into a whirl-wind of legal matters to take care of. I'm so sorry and I hope you can understand?" he pleaded in a voice so soft and gentle. "I hope you can forgive my inexcusable neglect to your needs," he added.

I just shook my head in disbelief. I felt my face flush with frustration with this new revelation. Hadn't I made my feelings known and perfectly clear that I was in love with him? I would have waited for as long as he wanted if he had just kept in contact with me. Confusion still tumbled around in my head.

He gazed at me hopefully, his eyes intent and his face serious. "And I really felt that I needed to connect to my birth mother," he said, casting his focus on her for a mere second and then back on me. "I wanted to do that first, out of respect for her and for my own mother, Alice. I think my mother would have been horrified at what my father did, switching babies and paying a nurse for her silence. She would have returned me and just lived with her broken heart had she known. She was as honest and thoughtful as they come." He shook his head vigorously. "And that is exactly why my father never let her know," he admitted, his eyes dropping once again to the beautiful vase that held the real Kendall Danielson. Then he grabbed my eyes with his again and continued to explain his actions. "I had to think about all of this and I didn't want to dump on you or be unkind to you during my process. So, I just went on radio silence and I hope you can forgive me for that. I know now that you didn't deserve to be treated that way whether I was drowning in a storm of emotion or not. My mother taught me better than that." He fell silent and gazed at me, his green eyes boring deeply into mine, the silence heavy between us.

My thoughts swirled through my head. I had stormed down the driveway feeling anger in my heart, charging up to this oak tree, intent on confronting Kendall and settling things, and instead, I was greeted with love, warmth and an honest request for forgiveness. Feeling slightly ashamed, I knew I wanted to be part of what these two people had. The strength and love that was glowing from within both of them. The capacity for kindness even in the face of great sorrow and uncertainty. What gave them that grace?

I squeezed Kendall's strong hand and smiled up at him. "Thank you for sharing that with me," I said. "I'm ashamed to admit that I had given up on you. In the face of no facts, I tend to make stuff up. I know I felt so comfortable around you and I now know it is because you are a part of Eli and he is a part of you. I admit that I did feel in some little sense of the way that I had my best friend back in my life. Sounds crazy I know, but I'm just laying it all out there for whatever it's worth."

I felt the circle of life gently wrapping around us and closing the loop with a soft twist. It was perfect that Carolyn was here with us, her son standing before me and a precious little child, loved and wanted by another woman and much grieved in his loss, resting in the quiet strength of the big oak tree. I also felt the love of my parents shimmering thru the tears in my eyes. They were here with me, as Carolyn shared with deep affection, their long ago kindness. In one small glimpse, I was able to see that the loose weaving of the warp and woof of my life had led to this crystalline moment, in the morning sunshine with a slight winter breeze blowing in my ears. I felt enriched and surrounded with love and peace.

Carolyn smiled and nodded. Tears slipped down her face as she glanced from me to Kendall and she then whispered out of love and consideration. "This is more than a dream come true. This is a miracle. God has answered my prayers beyond any way I could have ever imagined."

I looked deep into her tear filled eyes and said the words I knew she wanted to hear. "Yes Carolyn, this is truly a miracle from God."

Turning back to Kendall, I said, "I hope we can be friends. I so enjoyed our adventures together and I am so glad you are back and doing well. And no apologies needed, you had to process through everything and you are the only one who can do that for you. I am just glad you are here and I have my new best friend back!" I confirmed. However, those words tore at my heart. Because the last thing I wanted was to be just his friend, but I also didn't want to make this awkward situation any harder for him than it already was.

Kendall let out a loud gasp. "What? Just friends?" His eyes narrowed, nearly pinching his brows together. "Camille," he said my name like it came from the heart. "I meant what I said when I told you before that you are the piece that was missing in my life. I want to be more than just your friend," he said in a determined tone.

Carolyn quickly spoke up. "Ok, I think you two need some time to yourself, so I'll see you both tonight at six sharp for dinner. Okay by you?" she asked with determination in her glare that wouldn't allow either of us to refuse her request.

"Sounds like a plan," Kendall responded not taking his eyes off of me. "Here's the keys," he offered, digging them out of his pocket and thrusting them in her direction with his eyes still boring a hole into mine.

I heard the keys rustle and knew she must have grabbed them. I couldn't stand the intensity of his stare for another second, so I broke free of his glare and watched her cross the manicured lawn and slip into Kendall's rented car. I kept my eyes on her as she drove down the paved path that severed the cemetery in half.

"Camille," he picked up where he had left off, placing his forefinger under my chin, bring my focus back on him. "I want more between us than just friendship. I want to be your partner for life. I want to be the father to your children. Your husband forever. I want us to be lovers and grow old together. Please tell me you share these same feelings," he said as a tender smile graced his lips.

I sucked in a deep breath, totally taken back by the commitment he was offering me. I felt weak in the knees, but scolded them silently to keep my body upright. This wasn't the time or place to lose my self-control. "Honestly, I thought that maybe you had changed your mind about me," I responded with squinted eyes.

"With not much of a response to my text or phone calls, I really thought you had moved on. A move that didn't include me."

I could see my words, although delivered kindly and in earnest, stung like a scorpion. His eyes widened and his gentle smile fell from his face.

"I'm so sorry I gave you that false impression. My sadness and torn emotions only masked my true feelings for you. I'm so sorry I hurt you. I promise, that will never happen again."

A brief silence followed as our eyes met in another intense stare, but this one was expressing his powerful hidden desires.

"Please understand what I was going through. I needed to be alone in my thoughts. Unfortunately, the only drawback is, that I tend to gravitate toward the negative when I think too much. I'm what you'd call a critical thinker, a steward of the worst of all the 'what if's' could possibly happen." His voice became a soft murmur. "But then as lost and confused as I was, I came to understand that no matter how doubtful I was about our relationship, all those puzzling roads still led back here to you. No matter how fierce my mental battle, I still knew I loved you. But of course my most pressing question was, did you really love me or do you love what I represent?"

"You care to spell that out a bit more clear?" I asked before I could calm my tone.

"Don't you see Camille? I represent what you hold dear and close to your heart; Eli.

"Is that what you think? Is that the real reason you put me on hold for so long?"

His eyes told me yes, but he remained silent.

"Yes Kendall, I hold every memory I have of Eli right here," I said tapping my hand over my heart. "And yes, my love for Eli runs deep, but not in the same way as I love you. Eli and I had a childhood friendship so close it felt like we were bound together like Siamese twins. Both loves run deep, but are entirely different.

Grant you, had Eli and I been given more time together, maybe our bond would have blossomed and grown into what you and I have now. But that is a question that will never be answered," I confirmed with conviction.

I could see a little excitement wash over his parched face, filling his cheeks with color.

"Don't you see, our love is so different? Our love for one another is defined by compassion and generosity. Our love breathes in the fresh air of completeness. I know my own heart, but it is up to you to decide if you are willing to taste the flavor of commitment despite your reservations about Eli and me. In fact, are you sure about anything? I mean, you've been through a treacherous storm of emotions over the past few months. How can you be sure of any-thing right now?" I asked, fearing he was just talking with a tongue of appreciation instead of a heart full of love.

"I know the difference between love and feeling obligated to someone who has been overly kind and generous. I know my own heart. And yes, I admit my thoughts were tangled for a while, but believe me, I'm standing on solid ground now. I know the real person behind your pretty face. I like what I see and I love what we have together. It is so easy to talk to you. You understand me more than I understand myself. We have managed to crawl out of our pain. That says a lot about your character. I love your stamina and determination. I admire your natural beauty, but I love the ten-derness in your heart even more. I know this is a much overused cliché', but I have come to realize you are my soul mate. We were destined to meet and meant to be together. All of this and much more I know in my heart. And if you'll have me, I'm asking you to be my wife. My soul mate through this life and beyond. Believe me Camille, you have filled an emptiness inside of me that I thought for sure would stay that way. You are my world. You mean everything to me. Everything I could ever want or need. Will you make me the happiest man on this planet and marry me?" he asked with sincerity.

I couldn't believe what I was hearing. I woke up this morning feeling like an abandoned puppy in a blizzard. And now, all my hopes and dreams have been fulfilled with one simple question; will you marry me? "Yes," I whispered. "Oh, yes."

First I saw his smile shine and then I saw the shimmer of a beautiful ring held before my eyes. I raised my hand and he slipped it on my finger.

"Forever," he said.

"Forever," I repeated.

CPSIA information can be obtained
at www.ICGtesting.com
Printed in the USA
LVHW020609271119
638505LV00002B/131/P

9 781545 662458